#murdertrending

Gretchen McNeil

For John, my heart, who won't find this creepy

First Hardcover Edition, August 2018
First Paperback Edition, July 2019
10 9 8 7 6 5 4 3 2 1
FAC-025438-19144
Printed in the United States of America

Library of Congress Control Number for Hardcover: 2017034201
ISBN 978-1-368-01370-3
Visit www.freeform.com/books

"Capital punishment should be capital."

—THE POSTMAN

ONE

THE INSTANT DEE GUERRERA PEELED OPEN HER EYELIDS AND gazed around the dimly lit warehouse, she knew she was screwed.

Fifty million people are about to watch me die.

She lay on the concrete floor, its chill permeating her clothes, and recalled the insanity that had landed her here. Three weeks ago, the most important things in her life had been college applications and securing a date to the prom. Then the body, the trial. She'd hardly had time to process what had happened before she'd found herself sitting in a courtroom, listening to a jury find her guilty of first-degree murder.

Was that this morning? Yesterday? Dee tried to remember how much time had passed since the verdict, but her mind was fuzzy, her breathing labored as if she'd been drugged. . . .

The bailiff. As the judge read her sentence, she'd heard the bailiff come up behind her. She'd expected to be escorted back to her cell, but instead felt a hand on her wrist, a pinch on her arm. It must have been a needle. She'd been rendered unconscious before they hauled her off to Alcatraz 2.0.

Alcatraz 2.0. She'd heard the judge say it, but she still could hardly believe it. That sentence was usually reserved for the most infamous of convicted killers: mobsters, mass murderers, terrorists, assassins. They were notorious. They were dangerous. They got good ratings. Dee was just a seventeen-year-old nobody who couldn't even throw a punch, let alone stay alive long enough on Alcatraz 2.0 to gain a cult following.

Yet here she was, about to be the star attraction on the number-one live-streaming show in the country.

Yay?

Alcatraz 2.0, the suburban island in the San Francisco Bay where convicted murderers were hunted down by government-sanctioned serial killers for America's amusement, had been the brainchild of an anonymous television mogul known only as The Postman. When a former reality "star" was elected president of the United States, The Postman had used his clout to sell the federal government on the idea of capital punishment as entertainment. Broadcasting the over-the-top theatrics of The Postman's psychotic killers—each with their own thematic brand of murder—not only reminded citizens of what awaited them if they broke the law, but kept them glued to their screens, where they were less likely to break said laws in the first place.

The Postman app had been a runaway success. Fans could watch 24/7, cycling through a range of live camera feeds from all over the island: inmates at "home" in their apartments, at "work" on Alcatraz 2.0's Main Street, and, of course, the murders. A double-doorbell notification alerted users of a kill in progress, which they could watch live or in a variety of replays on the app. Users "spiked" videos to show their appreciation, and before long, all The Postman's killers had their own fandoms, forums, merch, video games, and RPGs, plus the lucrative betting markets, all controlled by Postman Enterprises, Inc.

The Postman's killers were media-driven celebrities, just like the president, though they were faceless, masked. There were even conspiracy-theory web series devoted to speculation about the killers' secret identities. Were the Hardy Girls actually minivan-driving soccer moms? Didn't Gassy Al's voice sound like the announcer on *The Price Is Right*?

The whole thing was fucking nuts.

But while all of Dee's friends and even her stepsister, Monica, had been obsessed with The Postman, Dee had refused to watch. In fact, just hearing the telltale *Ding-dong! Ding-dong!* notification triggered a full-on PTSD panic attack as Dee internalized the inmate's fear and instantly relived the six days she'd spent trapped in a white windowless room by a deranged kidnapper when she was eleven years old.

So yeah, Dee loathed everything about The Postman, even if technically it was justice served.

That had been the main selling point of The Postman—justice. But was it really delivered? Dee's trial for Monica's murder had been a complete joke, from dubious DNA evidence to a psychiatrist who'd only interviewed Dee once, then testified that she suffered from a deep-seated jealousy of and hatred for her stepsister. Total bullshit.

But the jury didn't think so, which had landed Dee in one of The Postman's kill rooms.

Dee had thought she'd get at least a few weeks to settle into her life on the island. Didn't most inmates hang around for a while until the audience became invested in their stories, personas, jobs, and intra-island relationships? Crap. Dee should have paid more attention to The Postman app when she'd had the chance. At least then she'd have some knowledge of what she was in for. Now she'd have to rely on what she'd learned from Monica, or picked up during her trial, when she'd been forced to watch a nonstop Alcatraz 2.0 feed in her prison cell.

Well, she knew one thing for sure: one of The Postman's psychos was about to shed her blood. Who would it be?

Would she end up as the main ingredient in one of Hannah Ball's cannibalistic casseroles? Or starring in a Cecil B. DeViolent splatterporn re-creation of *Gone with the Wind*? Was Gucci Hangman at that very moment constructing a designer noose for her neck, expertly crafted to match her complexion and outfit *and* the latest trends from New York Fashion Week while it slowly strangled the life out of her? Or was Molly Mauler about to flood the room with water and piranhas and make her choose death by suffocation or mastication?

No, wait. She'd seen Molly kill with piranhas just last week. A bank robber who'd knocked off a security guard or something. So no piranhas. Jellyfish, maybe? Or sea snakes? Was that even a thing?

With a heavy sigh, Dee pushed herself to her feet and took stock of her situation. She glanced down at her clothes and realized that her orange prison jumpsuit had been replaced by a floor-length ball gown of iridescent pale blue tulle and satin, with a pair of clear Lucite kitten heels on her feet. An outfit fit for a princess, which meant . . .

"Crap." She was about to be Prince Slycer's next victim.

Slycer was *the worst.* Not only did he chase his victims through booby-trap-riddled mazes, but he made them dress up like cartoon princesses while he hunted them down and skewered them with an arsenal of increasingly large and bizarre cake knives. Dee spun around, looking for the mirror—Slycer always left one for his victims—to see what twisted fairy tale she was about to relive. The cracked pane was ten feet away, hanging from a rusty nail on the wall. Blue dress, black choker, elbow-length gloves, matching sparkly headband. And her dark brown hair had been twisted up into a bun.

"Cinderella?" A blond housemaid. Seriously? He couldn't even pick a brunette?

This sucks on so many levels.

Slycer's last victim had been done up as Rapunzel, complete with an elaborately long wig that the poor girl kept tripping over as Slycer came in for the kill. Monica had been obsessed with her death, watching it over and over again as Rapunzel crawled away, pathetically begging for mercy. Immediately #SlowCrawl trended on The Postman feed as millions of people critiqued Rapunzel's performance. What would Dee's death include? #ExplodingPumpkins? #KillerMice? So freaking humiliating. Bad enough she was seconds away from getting a twelve-inch blade through the sternum, but she had to trend as well?

Still, Dee knew better than to fight back. There would be no escape, no appeal. There never was after an Alcatraz 2.0 sentence. And Dee didn't stand a chance against The Postman's killers. Even badass MMA fighter Nancy Wu had only lasted four months. No, the most Dee could hope for was to put on a good show in her final moments, maybe sell some merchandise from The Postman's e-store to help her dad and stepmom with the legal bills.

So, best-case scenario: T-shirts depicting her mangled corpse, a smartphone case sporting her skewered Cinderella silhouette and the hashtag #ADeathIsAWishYourHeartMakes, a shot glass shaped like a cracked glass slipper.

The world was so messed up.

Footsteps broke the silence of the warehouse, jarring Dee back to reality.

It's starting.

Glancing around, Dee saw that she was in a small chamber, walls on all four sides, lit by a single spare bulb suspended above her head. In each shadowy corner, a red dot of light indicated a live camera filming her every move, and to either side dark, narrow corridors snaked off in opposite directions. Slycer's footsteps were coming from her right, which meant she was supposed to run the other way. Like a good convicted killer.

Because maybe you really are *one.*

"Stop it!" Dee said out loud, clenching her fists by her side. "You didn't kill Monica."

It wasn't the first time that doubt about her innocence had nagged at her. Doctors had warned Dee's dad that she might have been more scarred from her childhood-abduction trauma than anyone realized, and then, after hearing Dr. Farooq's testimony . . .

Dee's eyes welled up, and she bit her lip hard enough to draw blood as she tried to fight back the tears. *You didn't kill her,* she repeated silently. *No matter what they say.*

And then something snapped. Why should Dee be the victim here? The country wanted to see blood, but why did it have to be hers? Prince Slycer had brutally murdered dozens of people, which in Dee's mind made him more deserving of justice served. Besides, if she died, there would be no one left to find Monica's actual killer. That was something worth fighting for, wasn't it?

Dee didn't run. She didn't flee blindly down the pitch-black hallway, stumbling toward whatever sadistic traps Slycer had laid for her. Instead, Dee grabbed the only thing she could use as a weapon—the mirror. She ripped it off the wall, the decrepit nail on which it had hung clanking to the concrete floor, and waited beneath the single suspended lightbulb.

A figure emerged from the corridor. Prince Slycer was dressed all in white: crisp straight-leg pants, shiny patent-leather shoes, and a wide-shouldered coat bedecked with gold buttons and matching epaulets. He was Cinderella's prince, just like the cartoon character Dee had loved growing up. But instead of a glass slipper, he gripped a nasty serrated knife in his hand, and his face was obscured by an enormous pair of night-vision goggles.

Oh, so he'll *be able to see in the pitch-black maze, but I won't. Coward.*

It seemed so cheap, so ridiculously lopsided. A kitten versus a cheetah. Except that Dee had seen enough Hollywood blockbusters to know that this cheetah had a weakness.

Prince Slycer stared at Dee from the shadows, head cocked to the side, as if he was confused by her lack of abject panic. She wondered if he was worried about the ranking of this video. Prince Slycer was pretty popular, but even he wanted to make sure each and every kill got a high number of spikes to up his profit-sharing potential. So Dee's refusal to play along had to be worrisome.

Good. Fuck this guy. I'm not a toy.

He flicked his head toward the opposite corridor, prompting Dee to run, but there was no way in hell she would plunge recklessly into the darkness. She shook her head defiantly from side to side.

Prince Slycer sighed, epaulets sagging as his shoulders drooped. The body language reeked of irritation, though he never said a word. This time he pointed the blade at the hallway, like a parent punishing a child. *Go to your room. Now.*

"Screw you," Dee said.

That did it. Prince Slycer lowered his chin, his goggled eyes boring a hole right through her, and marched across the room.

Dee barely had time to react. She took two steps back until the mirror was directly under the light; then she angled it to reflect the overhead bulb and aimed the concentrated beam at Prince Slycer's night-vision goggles.

"Shit!" she heard him say, although it sounded more like "shite," as if he spoke with an accent.

No one had ever heard Prince Slycer's voice, and Dee imagined that

#SlycerSpeaks would be trending within seconds. But she didn't have time to ponder the newest megahit hashtag: Slycer shielded his eyes with his arm and charged.

Dee dodged just as he slashed at her face with the menacing blade, missing her by inches. She darted out of the way and kicked at the pristine white legs of his costume. He stumbled, and as Dee swung around, she cracked the mirror against the back of his head.

Prince Slycer sprawled onto the floor, momentarily flailing his arms and legs, and then all was deathly still.

Except for the blood pooling beneath his body.

Well, shit.

TWO

DEE STOOD FROZEN, MIRROR IN HAND, STARING DOWN AT THE body of Prince Slycer.

What the hell had she just done? Every single one of The Postman's killers would be after her now, not just for sport, but for revenge. Maybe two or three of them would capture her at once—she'd be skewered by one of Robin's Hood's arrows while Gassy Al asphyxiated her with hydrogen cyanide.

She heard a noise, the soft patter of footsteps, as if someone was moving through one of the corridors. What if the rest of The Postman's killers were in the warehouse with her right now?

As if in answer, the power suddenly switched on, flooding the dingy space with an aggressive amount of artificial light. Dee blinked and spun around, searching for an escape route as she expected a half dozen maniacs to assault her all at once.

Instead, a lanky guy about her age with carefully tousled blond hair and more teeth than one person's mouth should be able to accommodate entered the room the same way Slycer had come. "Well, I'd say you just became the most notorious girl in the entire bloody world," he said in a crisp British accent.

"Stay away from me!" Dee cried, holding the mirror in front of her like a shield. "Or—or I'll kill you, too."

The Brit paused, and his unnaturally blue eyes scanned her from head to toe. Then he gestured to one corner of the room. "Don't worry. They've stopped filming."

Dee's eyes drifted up to the cameras. The red lights had all gone dark. "Oh." Was that a good thing? Not a good thing? Damn it, why hadn't she paid more attention to this stupid app?

"And you didn't exactly kill him, now, did you?" he continued, as if scolding her. "I mean, he fell on his own sword, so to speak."

Dee's grip on the mirror tightened. He'd been watching. Holy shit, was this The Postman himself?

The Brit nodded at Slycer's body. "I'm not one of *them*, if that's what you're worried about."

He smiled, inviting her trust, but Dee hesitated.

Point in his favor: there was no way this guy was old enough to be a successful Hollywood producer like The Postman was rumored to be.

Point against: dude was literally hanging around, waiting to watch Dee get murdered. And since she'd survived, maybe he was there to finish the job?

Either way, his appearance in the warehouse wasn't exactly trust-inducing. She needed to stay on her guard. "Who are you?"

Instead of answering, Blondy McBrit crouched beside Prince Slycer's body, surveying the corpse. "Brilliant. I haven't seen anything like this since Nancy Wu round-kicked the Caped Capuchin into a broken neck." He whistled low. "When The Postman finds out, it'll do his nut."

"Is that good?" His carefree attitude was disarming.

He smiled knowingly. "All the Painiacs will be after you."

"Shit."

He arched an eyebrow. "What do you think?"

About him? About the fact that, by some bizarre turn of fate, she was still alive? About the ten other serial killers who were about to be unleashed on her?

He pushed himself to his feet and stepped closer, skillfully maneuvering around Slycer's coagulating blood. "'Painiacs,'" he repeated. "It's a portmanteau of my own invention. 'Pain' plus 'maniacs.' Do you think it'll catch on, or should I get more of a Postman reference in there, like 'Postmaniacs'? Except I'm using 'Postmantics' for the fans, so that might be confusing."

"Umm . . ."

His face dropped, disappointed at Dee's lack of approval. "It's a work in progress."

Was he for real? "There's a dead guy in a pool of his own blood two feet away and you're worried about your hashtag?"

Blondy McBrit sighed. "Sorry. I forgot. This is all new for you. Personally, I abhor violence, but after a while you get callous."

A while? "How long have you been here?"

"Seven months, one week, three days," he said without hesitating.

Dee's eyes grew wide. She'd never heard of anyone surviving that long on Alcatraz 2.0.

"Don't be impressed," he said, reading her reaction. "My case is in appeal, so I'm off-limits for the moment. That miscarriage of justice you Americans call a trial was over so quickly they didn't get a chance to find out to whom I'm related."

Dee arched an eyebrow. "The Queen?"

Blondy McBrit snorted. "Look at you! 'The Queen?'" he mocked in falsetto. "Certainly not. But my mother's cousin's first husband *is* the second assistant to the foreign minister. He's filed an appeal on my behalf due to diplomatic immunity."

"Oh." It was a plausible story, but he could also be full of shit and this was just another trap on Alcatraz 2.0.

I'm not taking any chances.

"Actually," Blondy McBrit continued, "I'm surprised he's helping me at all, based on my conviction."

Dee took a step away, eyeing Slycer's body. If this guy lunged at her, maybe she could flip it over, pull the knife out of Slycer's gut, and use it to defend herself. "What did you do?"

His face was unreadable. "I was convicted of murdering my parents."

See? Don't trust anyone on this island. It was a good mantra. Dee was in a maximum-security prison, so in addition to The Postman's government-sanctioned killers, all her fellow inmates had committed heinous crimes. She was literally surrounded by murderers.

"I loved my parents." His blue eyes narrowed; his affable manner vanished. "As much as you loved your . . . sister, was it?"

"Stepsister," Dee snapped. Then she paused. "How did you know that?"

Blondy McBrit stepped between Dee and Slycer's body and reached into his pocket. Dee stiffened, her eyes darting toward the far corridor. Was he going to pull out a weapon? She couldn't reach Slycer's knife now, but maybe if she chucked the mirror at Blondy's face, she'd have time to run for her life?

But instead of the murderous glint of a recently sharpened blade, Dee saw a folded piece of paper in his hand.

"'Dee Guerrera,'" he said, reading from the page. "'Convicted of premeditated murder in the first degree. Victim: Monica Patterson, seventeen. Stepsister.'"

The image of Monica's strangled face, purple and swollen, flashed before Dee's eyes. She'd been the one to find the body, the one to call 911 as she desperately tried to administer first aid, even though she knew by the stiffness of her limbs that Monica was beyond help. "I didn't kill her."

She had no idea why she felt the need to proclaim her innocence to this stranger, but the words just came flying out of her mouth before she could stop them.

"Of course you didn't. We're *all* innocent on Alcatraz two-point-oh."

Sarcasm dripped from every word. He didn't believe her for a hot second.

But instead of saying he thought she was full of shit, he shoved his hands into the pockets of his black corduroy jacket. "Shall we go?"

Dee glanced from the Brit to Slycer's body. Was this a trap? "I'm not going anywhere with you."

He tilted his head to the side, just as Slycer had when Dee had refused to run into the maze. "Whyever not?"

His earnestness threw Dee off. "I . . ." *I think you might be a psychotic killer? I don't trust you no matter how cute your accent is?* "I don't even know who you are."

"Oh!" He smiled, his eyes warm and crinkly. "Sorry. I'm Nyles." He paused, as if that was enough explanation.

It wasn't. "And you're here right now because . . . ?"

"Because my Alcatraz-mandated job is to introduce new inmates to life on the island. I get a note like this one," he said, dangling the refolded paper in the air, "shoved under my door in the morning, telling me where to meet the newbies. Though it's usually just at the gate to the guard station. This is the first time I was instructed to go to a Painiac's kill room.

Must have been an administrative mistake or something. I mean, why would you need an orientation if you weren't going to survive your first hour on the island? Anyway, I almost didn't show. Can you believe it?" He chuckled as if he'd made a hilarious joke.

"Yeah," she said, her voice flat. "Funny."

"I would have missed the death of Prince Slycer," Nyles continued, either not picking up on her sarcasm or ignoring it. "*That* would have been a tragedy, Dee. By the by, is that short for Dorothy? Deirdre?"

What were they, best friends? "No."

"Ah, I see." Nyles gazed at her for a moment, then shrugged. "Come along, then."

Dee still didn't trust him. If she followed, would she round a corner and run directly into a Cinderella-themed booby trap of sentient rodents, pumpkin time bombs, and projectile glass shards?

Then again, her other options were to find her own way out of the murderous maze, or stay with Slycer's body until someone else got to her. Neither was particularly tempting. "Where are we going?"

Nyles's smile widened, flashing his oversize teeth. "Fancy an ice cream?"

7m

Regina Showalter @ChoppinChopin2017

Are you kidding me with this bullshit? There is no way @PrinceSlycer's dead. He's going to stand up and stab her through her solar plexus, right? He can't let that sister-killing skank get away. I CAN'T EVEN WITH THIS.

← | : 2,440 ₪: 87

7m

Benny Nda Jetts @EltonJohnForevzz

I knew Slycer's refusal to use restraints would eventually backfire on him. He's consistently underestimated his female victims.#MisogynyKills

← | : 34 ₪: 11

6m

Regina Showalter @ChoppinChopin2017

Did you just take credit for his death?#DouchePatrol #ICANTEVENWITHTHIS

7m

> **Benny Nda Jetts** @EltonJohnForevzz
>
> I knew Slycer's refusal to use restraints would eventually backfire on him. He's consistently underestimated his female victims.#MisogynyKills

← | : 2,001 ₪: 62

6m

ArMeLiO rInCoN @rinCON_notRINcon

HA HA @EltonJohnForevzz. You know more about helpless tied-up chicks than anyone. Only way you can get them to date you.

← | : 336 ₪: 20

6m

Benny Nda Jetts @EltonJohnForevzz

@rinCON_notRINcon Check your heteroprivilege, friend.

← | : 890 ₪: 3

6m

Regina Showalter @ChoppinChopin2017

We should be more concerned with the fact that a CONVICTED KILLER just got away with murder. Again. #JusticeWillBeServed

← | : 727 ₪: 43

5m

The Griff @awakewideopen

You people are blind. Slycer vs. a mirror? This is a CONSPIRACY. IT'S ALL FAKE! #SlycerLives #FakeNews #EyesOpen #DontTrustTheFeed

← | : 5,332 ₪: 4,250

5m

ArMeLiO rInCoN @rinCON_notRINcon

@awakewideopen Maybe ur blind? And dum?

← | : 67 ₪: 8

4m

ArMeLiO rInCoN @rinCON_notRINcon

@awakewideopen Or maybe that chick in the Cinderella dress is.

← | : 50 ₪: 8

1m

Benny Nda Jetts @EltonJohnForevzz

Your bickering is amusing, but you miss the point: @PrinceSlycer is dead, and Cinderella? She's a survivor. #CinderellaSurvivor

← | : 89,211 ₪: 50,734

THREE

SAN FRANCISCO'S SUNSHINE WAS UNDERWHELMING.

Though the sky was vivid blue, dotted with puffy wisps of clouds that stretched like chubby fingers from the west, the sun gave off zero warmth, and Dee's skin prickled beneath the thin fabric of her Cinderella gown. It was the total opposite of November in Los Angeles, where it was probably seventy-five and sunny, and Dee's crappy costume would have been adequate protection from the elements.

Did I seriously just compare the benefits of a penal colony versus my hometown in terms of a princess costume? As if this day could get weirder.

Except it had. Though Dee had watched the endless live stream from her holding cell, she hadn't fully appreciated the creepiness of Alcatraz 2.0 until she stepped outside the warehouse.

The prison had been established on a man-made island in the middle of the San Francisco Bay, connected to a natural outcropping of rock that had served as the midway point for the old Bay Bridge. Once known as Treasure Island, it had been built for a world's fair almost a century earlier, then transformed first into a military installation and then into a series of Hollywood soundstages, before finally being redeveloped for housing. But once the tunnel was built to connect San Francisco to the East Bay, and the Bay Bridge was demolished, the island had been abandoned.

Until The Postman purchased it.

The heavy creep factor came from the island's infrastructure, which had been retained when it was transformed into a prison. Duplexes, storefronts, library, warehouses—all the remnants of its former glory had been shined up and repurposed. Now convicted murderers like Dee worked pedestrian jobs, lived in traditional homes, and did everyday crap like cooking meals, navigating neighbors, and, oh, trying to stay alive as long as possible before they were ambushed, kidnapped, and brutally executed while the entire world watched.

It was fucking surreal.

Nyles had fallen quiet. He'd seemed edgy since they'd stepped outside the decrepit warehouse, moving quickly down the wide, deserted street as his eyes continually darted from side to side. This part of the island was packed with enormous structures of corrugated metal and waterlogged wood, mostly ruined. Some were missing roofs; others had entire chunks of siding stripped away. Even the air smelled musty and rotten.

And though the neighborhood looked vaguely familiar, as Dee hurried to keep up with Nyles's long strides, she noticed that there were no cameras around. Based on what she'd seen of The Postman app, she had half expected there to be cameras everywhere: attached to fences, mounted on streetlamps, lining the tops of buildings. Instead, the only ornaments in this dilapidated industrial wasteland were the dozens of black crows perched atop the warehouse roofs, stoic and unmoving.

Nyles sped onward, past an abandoned gas station with a hand-painted sign on one boarded-up window reading DON'T FEED THE BIRDS.

So there were rules on Alcatraz 2.0 after all? Good to know.

"I'll introduce you to your job first," Nyles said, breaking the silence as they rounded a corner onto Main Street. A row of brightly painted shops stretched down both sides. "So you can meet your coworkers."

Dee cringed. "Coworkers?" *Translation: The convicted killers I'll have to hang out with every day.*

"Everyone has a job on Alcatraz," Nyles said. He cast a sly glance at her. "Even a princess."

"Ha-ha," Dee replied without an ounce of humor in her voice.

"It won't be anything complicated, I can assure you," he said cheerfully, as if he were giving her the rundown on her new after-school job at the mall. "Normal hours, ten to five and all that."

Nothing about this place was normal. "And if I don't show up?"

"That's your choice." Nyles shrugged. "But no work means no money on your island debit card. Which means you can't buy food."

"Good reason to show up."

Nyles smiled. "Isn't it?" He shot another clandestine look at her, eyes sweeping down from her sparkly headband to her dress, and just for a second, the happy-go-lucky façade slipped away, revealing a significantly more somber expression. Then he turned, and it was gone.

"Anyway," he continued, his tone light and airy, "we'll have to get to the Barracks before dark. We do *not* want to be out after the sun goes down. That's usually when the Painiacs . . ." He paused, musing over the word, then shook his head. "That's usually when the killers strike. Unless it's a foggy day. Or rainy. Or an eclipse, I suppose." He stopped and faced her. "Basically, only be outside with the sun."

"Noted."

Nyles pointed to a quaint structure across the street that looked like a converted cottage. "So we've got the stationery store there, library next door. Farther down there's the bodega—that's where you'll buy groceries and whatnot—the hair salon, and the gym."

"So I can look good and get in shape for my murder?"

Nyles smiled, his blue eyes bright with amusement. "Quite." He shifted his gaze to a spot above Dee's head. "Here we are, then."

They stood in front of an old-timey ice-cream parlor complete with pink-striped awning and hand-painted lettering on the window.

"'I Scream'?" Dee said, reading the name of the shop. "You've *got* to be kidding me."

"You'll find an abundance of dark humor on the island." Nyles pushed open the glass door. Above, a silver bell tinkled an announcement of their arrival.

Dee followed him inside and felt as if she'd stepped back in time. The black-and-white-checkered floor was dotted with ornate wrought-iron tables, painted white, with matching chairs. The walls, like the awning outside, were bubble-gum pink, and crammed with sepia-toned photographs of ice-cream parlors from ages past. Pink stools lined the front of a counter that held jars of neon candy, lollipops, and jelly beans, plus a refrigerated display of ice-cream flavors. It was neat and cheerful and totally fucked up. Because, just like in Slycer's maze, Dee quickly noted the cameras affixed to the ceiling in each corner of the shop: rounded black mounds, surveying the entire room. A chill ran down her spine. Four red lights, one in each camera dome, were all pointed directly at her.

"I'm back!" Nyles called out to no one in particular.

A door on the far wall, camouflaged by pink toile wallpaper, swung open, and an attractive, heavily made-up girl appeared in the doorway. Dee recognized her immediately: Griselda Sinclair.

Griselda had a huge fan base, and every time the feed switched to her apartment or to a shot of her working out in the gym, the fan comments that ran up the side of the screen would explode. She even had her own hashtags—#ConjugalVisitsForGriselda and

#GriseldaIWantYouInMyPants—because the fans were super classy like that.

But Griselda seemed happy to play the role of Alcatraz 2.0 hottie. She wore a plaid miniskirt paired with combat boots that laced to the knee, plus an off-the-shoulder midriff shirt that exposed a black lace bra strap on her right shoulder, and her long dishwater-blond hair had been flat-ironed stick straight. She paused in the doorway while she smoothed down her hair and tucked it behind both ears. Then she pulled on the right sleeve of her shirt, shifting it so far off her shoulder that it practically exposed side boob, ran her tongue over her teeth to check for stray lipstick, and stepped into the shop.

It was like watching an actress backstage before she made her entrance, and as Dee saw the red dots of the cameras swivel in Griselda's direction, she realized that was exactly what she had witnessed.

"You're the only person on this island stupid enough to be wandering around the warehouse district this close to nightfall," Griselda said.

"It's touching to know you care, Gris." Nyles tossed a white plastic card onto the counter, then reached into a large glass jar and snagged a piece of red licorice.

She picked up the card and swiped it through some kind of electronic reader, then slid it back to Nyles. "I see you've brought the newbie."

"Ah yes." Nyles bowed low with a flourish of his licorice. "Griselda Sinclair, may I present your new coworker, Dee Guerrera."

"H-hey," Dee stuttered, trying to sound casual. She didn't want any of these people to see her fear.

But Griselda made no attempt at friendliness. She folded her arms across her chest and examined Dee from head to toe. "So we're stuck with Cinderella Survivor, huh?"

"Who?" Dee asked.

Nyles's eyes grew wide with excitement. "Is *that* what they're calling her?"

Griselda nodded toward the front of the shop. "See for yourself."

Mounted on the wall above the door was a large, flat monitor. One half of the screen showed several small boxes, rotating slowly through a variety of camera feeds. The other half showed strangely familiar night-vision footage of a girl in a long dress holding a mirror, and in the upper right-hand corner of the screen she saw a symbol that she immediately recognized: *PEI* in red block letters, the bottom of the *P* extending into the spine of the *E* and tail of the *I*. The logo for Postman Enterprises, Inc.

It took Dee several seconds to realize that she was watching a replay of her first moments in Slycer's maze.

Beside the video, the comments feed scrolled at a breakneck pace, but even at that speed, Dee caught the same hashtag used over and over again: #CinderellaSurvivor.

"Our little princess has twenty million spikes," Griselda said flatly.

Nyles whistled low as if impressed, but Dee was pretty sure it wasn't a good thing. "What does that mean?"

Griselda smiled sweetly, exposing a perfect dimple in her right cheek. "It means, Princess, that you won't last a week."

FOUR

THE POSTMAN GLARED AT THE MONITOR, TEETH CLENCHED SO hard they ached, while the one they were calling Cinderella Survivor slowly lowered herself into a wrought-iron chair at I Scream.

She killed Slycer.

At first The Postman didn't believe it—much like the fans, who peppered the comments feed with incredulity and intricate conspiracy theories. It seemed too bizarre. A teenager with a mirror just took out The Postman's number-one killer? Impossible.

But it wasn't. The Postman had seen Slycer's corpse, felt the pulseless body already stiff and cold before the guards arrived to haul it away. The blood had stopped pouring from the wound by then; the pool was sticky and thick. And while all of that could have been attributed to the special effects frequently employed by The Postman's killers to fake out their victims, this time the blood and the corpse and the death were real.

"And now I have her all to myself," The Postman said out loud, though there was no one to hear. "Voice command!" The voice-recognition control panel beeped twice to acknowledge activation. "Engage autodetect on camera banks thirty-two through thirty-seven." Cinderella Survivor would be leaving for the Barracks soon, and The Postman wanted to make sure that every single moment of her time on Alcatraz 2.0 was covered.

"You won't be out of my sight for a moment."

She was the only priority.

So many months of planning, all destroyed in an instant. No one's time on Alcatraz 2.0 was particularly pleasant, but the moment Slycer's body hit the floor, Dee's fate was sealed. She'd be broken, tortured, begging for the end.

And she'd watch anyone she cared about die.

FIVE

NYLES LAUGHED NERVOUSLY. "GRIS, DON'T SCARE THE NEW girl."

"You want to give her false hope?" Griselda said, arching an eyebrow. "Make her feel like she can win?" Her eyes shifted to Dee. "News flash—you can't."

Dee expected Griselda's bravado to mask an underlying fear, but her eyes were hard, her lips firmly set, and all Dee detected was a no-nonsense *This is how it is, Princess* attitude that matched the businesslike primping Griselda had done before entering the camera shot. Between Nyles's cheerfulness and Griselda's casual indifference, Dee was relatively sure they were both nuts.

Nyles pulled out a chair, and the metal legs scraped against the tile floor with a nails-on-a-chalkboard screech. "She did manage to kill the Slycer."

Griselda stiffened, clearly irritated. "Beginner's luck."

You try it.

A new voice chimed in from behind the counter. "If that's beginner's luck, I want some."

Dee turned, instantly on guard even though the female voice sounded friendly, and neither Nyles nor Griselda appeared alarmed by her presence.

A short Asian woman with freckled cheeks carried two large boxes from the back room, both marked POSTMAN ENTERPRISES, INC. She wore an abundance of light blue eyeshadow and matching blue lipstick, and as she passed beneath an overhead light, Dee noticed that her black shoulder-length hair was streaked with blue as well.

Nyles jumped to his feet, ever the gentleman, and seemed about to offer his assistance, when she shook her head. "I'm good." She slid the boxes onto the counter beside the ice-cream freezer, pushing aside a napkin dispenser and a framed sign that read HAVE YOU *I SCREAM*ED TODAY? "First rule of Alcatraz: Don't offer to help anyone."

Nyles sank back into his chair. "I've never been good with rules."

"Then you're lucky you have immunity," the newcomer replied curtly. She thrust her hand over the counter. "I'm Blair, your boss."

Dee started, realizing the introduction was meant for her. She stood up and took tentative steps toward Blair's outstretched hand. Was this a test? A rule she had yet to learn? Was she supposed to take the offer of a handshake, or stay away?

"I'm not going to slit your throat," Blair said, the bluntness in her tone matching the sharp angle of her bobbed hair.

"Sorry." Dee clasped hands with Blair, who gave her a fierce squeeze before letting go. "Dee."

"Short for Daphne? Dulcinea?" Nyles asked, still trying.

Dee grimaced. "No." Her name wasn't short for anything. Not anymore.

Blair hoisted herself up on the counter, knocking the HAVE YOU *I SCREAM*ED TODAY? sign flat. "Well, Dee-not-short-for-Daphne-or-Dulcinea, welcome to Alcatraz two-point-oh."

"Thanks?"

"Princess needs to learn about sarcasm," Griselda said, rolling her eyes.

And you need to learn about manners.

"You'll get used to Gris," Blair said. "Her bark is worse than her bite."

Dee seriously doubted that.

Blair straddled the counter, one leg on each side. She wore black leggings that hugged her stout calves and disappeared into a pair of gray Uggs, and a heather zip-front tunic with a drawstring waist. "I'll give you the same lecture I give everyone when they arrive."

Griselda pulled out the chair opposite Nyles and sank into it, crossing one long leg over the other. "I need a drink."

"There are two sets of rules," Blair began. "Theirs . . . and ours. *Theirs* are simple: work, get paid, eat."

"So I've heard," Dee muttered.

"You have to show up to your job every day, and funds are added to your island debit card accordingly."

Nyles fished a key ring out of the pocket of his jeans and handed it to her. It contained a single shiny silver house key and a plastic card, branded with Postman Enterprises, Inc.'s signature logo. She flipped it over and saw her name and photo printed on the back. It was her mug shot from when she was arrested. *Wonderful.*

"It works at all the businesses on Main Street," Nyles explained, "and you can use it as a library card."

So I can catch up on some light reading while running for my life. Classy.

"Do *not* lose it," Blair said emphatically. "You won't get another one."

Good to know.

"And you have to stay alone in your own house each night," Blair continued, "or they'll zero out your account."

That rule was pretty much unnecessary for Dee. No way in hell would she be inviting a convicted killer over for a late-night coffee.

"Oh, and you can't kill other inmates," Nyles added, chuckling to himself. "No matter how much you want to."

"Why not?" Not that Dee was contemplating murder, but who cared how they died? They were all condemned anyway.

"The Postman doesn't want any carnage he can't control," Blair said with a shrug.

Griselda pulled out a tube of lip gloss and reapplied. "Bad for ratings."

Dee had a hard time buying that. "I've seen those prison documentaries on TV. Inmates try to kill each other all the freaking time."

"Not on Alcatraz two-point-oh," Nyles said grimly.

Blair laughed. "You sound like you've never watched the app or something."

"Oh, I totally watch it all the time," Dee lied. People who didn't enjoy The Postman were considered anti-American or plain crazy, so it was easier to play along.

"Hold up." Blair slid off the counter, her eyes locked on Dee's. "You've never seen it."

"No, I have." It wasn't a lie—she'd been forced to watch it in her prison cell after her arrest. They didn't need to know that she'd avoided the app like her life depended on it before that. How could she explain it? *I spent six days trapped with a psychopath; I don't need to relive that through an app on my phone, thanks?*

Dee had only voluntarily shared her past with one other person, and that had ended badly. Besides, opening up to a bunch of convicted felons—coworkers or not—wasn't high on her list of things to do her first day on Alcatraz 2.0. These were *not* people she should trust.

Blair and Nyles exchanged a glance, and for a moment Dee thought they were going to press her for more information. She thrust her chin forward in defiance, preparing for the onslaught of questions, but they never came.

"Oh," Blair said, leaning back against the counter. "Okay. Well, killing another inmate will earn you a fate worse than death."

Dee thought of the murders she'd seen from her holding cell, and tried hard to imagine how much worse it could be. "Worse than getting nuked in Hannah Ball's microwave?" she asked. "Worse than a full-body straight-razor shave from Barbaric Barista?"

"If you care about the people you love," Blair said, swallowing hard, "then yes."

It took a moment for the full horror of this statement to take effect. She pictured her dad trapped in one of Gassy Al's torture chambers, and had to bite her lip to keep the tears from welling up.

Blair took a deep breath. "Right. And remember: The cameras are always watching."

"Always watching," Dee repeated. This place got better by the minute.

Then Blair smiled and her entire demeanor changed. "*Our* rules," she continued, "are more complicated, but they might just keep you alive, so pay attention."

Staying alive was a good reason to pay attention.

"Rule number one," Blair said, holding up her right index finger, "you already—"

"Wait . . ." Dee cast a sidelong glance at the nearest camera. Blair had literally just said that someone was always watching. Should she really be sharing vital survival tactics in full view of the cameras?

"Don't worry about them," Blair said, waving her hands at the red light. "Watch this." She cleared her throat, then spoke up loud and clear. "I'm going to tell the new girl how to stay alive for as long as possible. Do you want to have that on a live channel?"

Dee stared at the camera in amazement. Before Blair had gotten the first few words out, the red light had blipped off. She spun around and found that all four of the surveillance devices in the shop had gone dark. *What the hell?*

"They don't want to humanize us," Nyles explained. "If the fans internalize our struggle to stay alive, the ratings might go down."

"Seriously?"

Blair nodded in agreement. "Read the comments feed sometime. The fans love to justify their bloodlust by reminding themselves that we're all heinous murderers and deserve what we get. Starting a conversation about day-to-day survival is a surefire way to get a channel feed shut down."

"Wouldn't The Postman want to know what we're up to?"

"Trust me, he's still watching," Blair said with a grimace. "But it's nothing he hasn't heard before."

"Oh." Suddenly, Dee's enthusiasm for survival tactics seemed foolish. What was the point if The Postman and his killers already knew?

"Back to rule number one," Blair said, unperturbed by the seeming futility of it all. "Don't offer to help anyone. Half the time it's a trap, and the other half, it's a trap."

So staying alive means you have to be an asshole? Griselda made more sense.

"Rule number two: Don't be out after sundown."

"Already covered that one!" Nyles cried, excited like a child who got the correct answer on a pop quiz. "See? I can learn rules."

"Good boy." Blair reached over and pulled a red licorice rope from the jar, then tossed it to him. "This one's on me."

"Can you lie down and roll over, too?" Griselda sneered.

"Three: Don't sleep at night. Viewership goes up between eight p.m. and two a.m., so that's when most of the executions happen." Blair held up her index finger again and wagged it back and forth. "And just because you're locked in your house doesn't mean you're safe."

Dee doubted anyplace was safe on the island.

"Four, five, and six." Blair seemed to be enjoying herself, her voice buoyant as if she were reciting a nursery rhyme. "Make sure the seals on your food haven't been tampered with. If you feel like someone's watching you, they are. And this one's important: When chased, run outside."

"Outside?" Dee asked. It sounded counterintuitive. There was no place to hide outdoors, and didn't the wide-open streets and storefronts leave more places for other executioners to pop out and grab her?

"Outdoor murders get fewer spikes," Nyles said. "If you manage to get outside, there's a sixtyish-percent chance that the killer will give up and try again another time."

Dee arched an eyebrow. "Sixty*ish*?" Not exactly foolproof.

"There's a ninety-percent chance," Griselda chimed in, "that Nyles makes up his statistics."

He pursed his lips. "It's not as if we have the scientific apparatus around here to make an actual controlled study of survival rates based on interior and exterior—"

"I was joking, Nyles," Griselda said. Then she added, in an excellent fake British accent, "Don't get your knickers in a twist." Well, at least her snark wasn't *solely* focused on Dee.

"Ah yes," he said, clearly not appreciating the joke. "Hilarious."

"And last," Blair said, redirecting the conversation back to the rules, "don't draw attention to yourself in a negative light. The more the fans hate you, the more desperately The Postman's killers will want to up their spikes by taking you out."

"Too late," Griselda said.

"Oh." Blair's eyes drifted up to the screen on the wall. "Right. Well, don't worry too much about that."

Dee exhaled slowly. Blair was trying to be nice, which Dee appreciated, but she could see the truth written all over her new boss's face. Griselda was right: Dee wasn't going to last a week on Alcatraz 2.0.

Suddenly, Dee was exhausted. Her arms and legs were heavy, and her eyes burned. She knew she wasn't supposed to sleep at night, but there was no way she'd be able to keep her eyes open for much longer.

Whatever. At this point, who cared? Maybe it would be better if she was taken out quickly in her sleep. Life on Alcatraz 2.0 sounded like a nightmare, and with twenty million spikes and a Cinderella Survivor hashtag, she practically had a sign around her neck that said HEY! KILL ME NEXT! Why prolong the agony? It wasn't as if she'd be able to escape, and she doubted her dad and stepmom were actively fighting for an appeal, even if it was possible to get one without diplomatic connections. Her parents thought she was guilty like everyone else did, and they were probably just trying to wipe her from their memories.

So much for Dee's crazy idea that she could stay alive long enough to find Monica's real killer. What had she been thinking? If former inmates like a trained martial artist, a mob assassin, and a professional bodyguard couldn't survive on Alcatraz 2.0, how the hell could a seventeen-year-old whose greatest achievements in life thus far included publishing a poem in her local newspaper and managing to not get recognized as "that girl who got kidnapped" for the last six years?

Dee's face must have reflected her growing sense of despair, because Blair's carefully penciled eyebrows drew sharply together. "Look, it's not that bad, okay?"

Griselda snorted. "Who doesn't enjoy living in constant fear for your life?"

"Ignore her," Blair said, waving her off.

Griselda rocketed to her feet. "Here's my advice, Princess. Get used to the fact that you're going to die soon. It's going to be violent and painful and terrifying. No one is going to help you and no one is going to remember you when you're gone." Then she spun on her heel and marched into the back room.

"I'll check on her," Nyles said, hurrying after Griselda. "She shouldn't be alone." He looked anxious, and Dee wondered if they had a thing going on.

Stop it! Why was she even speculating about Nyles's love life? That was a distraction she couldn't afford. She needed to stay alive, and in order to do that, the only person she could give a shit about was herself.

"Follow the rules and you'll be okay," Blair said. Then she dropped her voice to just above a whisper. "There are people who've been surviving here longer than you realize."

SIX

FOR THE FIRST TIME THAT DAY, DEE FELT A GLIMMER OF HOPE spark to life deep inside her. "Yeah?"

Blair opened her mouth to elaborate, but something in the corner of the shop caught her eye. Dee followed Blair's gaze and saw that the red lights inside the cameras had come to life again.

"Keep your head down for a few days," Blair said; her voice was no longer a whisper, but full and loud. "The fans have the attention span of a goldfish—by the time they've swum around the bowl, they've already forgotten the other side."

"Right," Dee said, pulling her eyes away from the camera. "Thanks." She realized that Blair was just being kind, but had there been something else? Some other insight Blair had been about to share before she had seen that the cameras were back on? *There are people who've been surviving here longer than you realize.* Was there a trick to Alcatraz 2.0 that Blair had figured out? Dee made a mental note to bring it up again, maybe when she and Blair were alone. Maybe when they were away from the cameras.

Or was that even *possible* on Alcatraz 2.0?

"Shall we head home?" Nyles asked as he reemerged from the back room. He had a small backpack slung over his shoulder. "It's getting rather dark outside."

"Did you tell Princess that she'll have to take the opening shift?" Griselda zipped up a brown suede jacket as she followed him. "I don't wake up before noon."

"You'll be here at ten as usual," Blair said. "*Both* of you."

Griselda clicked her tongue. "You're making *me* train her?"

It's an ice-cream parlor. What is there to train? How to scoop a perfect ball of gelato while avoiding a maniac's booby trap?

Before Blair could answer Griselda, the door to I Scream flew open and a buff black guy with a shaved head burst into the shop. He practically had to turn sideways to fit his bulked-up arms through the frame, and despite the chill in the air, he wore only knee-length athletic shorts and a sleeveless Lycra shirt that hugged the outline of his well-developed chest muscles.

"Dudes, let's motor," he said. "I bet the douche patrol's gonna be out in full force tonight after Slycer got done by a—" He froze, eyes locked on Dee. "You killed the Slycer!"

"Ethan, meet Dee," Blair said. "She's your girlfriend's new coworker."

"I am *not* his girlfriend," Griselda said through clenched teeth.

Ethan pulled back his chin. "You're not?" He seemed 100 percent sure that he and Griselda were a couple.

Griselda brushed past him into the street. "No."

But instead of appearing crestfallen, Ethan just smiled and stuck his hand out toward Dee. "*Hasta la vista,* baby."

Dee awkwardly took it. "Um, that means 'see you later.'"

Ethan's smile grew while he pumped her hand. "I know."

"Ethan likes to quote lines from action movies," Nyles explained, eyeing Ethan's lingering handshake. "I believe that one is from *Predator*."

Ethan shook his head. "Don't you have action movies in Australia?"

"No," Nyles said, totally deadpan as he ushered them toward the door. "Shall we?"

Dee waited outside as Blair cut the lights and locked up; then together they began the trek up Main Street. Ethan walked at Griselda's side, occasionally attempting to slip a beefy arm around her waist, which Griselda discouraged by punching him in the chest.

"The Postman likes to arrange relationships," Nyles explained. "He also controls our wardrobes, our jobs, where we live. Scripted. Which makes perfect sense, since we're the ultimate reality show."

"Except it's not like *Survivor*," Dee said. "There's no way to win this game."

Nyles pursed his lips as he pondered her words. "No, I suppose not."

"Dude, you're doing better than most," Ethan said, bouncing around to face Dee. He walked backward, keeping step. "It's been a while since someone got one for our team."

"She is *not* on our team," Griselda said.

We get it. You don't like me.

"Anyone who takes out the Slycer is someone I want on my side," Ethan said, undeterred by his fake girlfriend's dissent. "That's why I keep myself in peak physical condition." He held up his fists and jabbed at the air while he danced around Griselda like a boxer in training. "Gotta be ready to kick some ass with extreme prejudice."

"Ethan," Blair explained, "was studying to be a personal trainer."

"That's something you *study*?" Nyles asked.

"Fuck yeah, dude!" Ethan smacked Nyles in the stomach with his flattened palm. "These are your abs. They support your spine and shit. See? Study."

"Yes," Nyles sputtered, bending slightly at the waist as he attempted to regain his breath. "You're a veritable Hippocrates."

They turned from Bizarro Main Street, USA, onto a tree-lined boulevard heading west toward the end of the island, hugging the dotted yellow line as they walked straight down the middle of the street. On either side, large open parks spanned the length of the block: one was set up with soccer goals at either end, the other with a softball diamond.

"The parks," Nyles mused softy, "are lovely."

"Can we hide out in them?" Dee asked.

Nyles cocked his head. "Why would you want to do that?"

"Rule six," Dee recited. "When chased, run outside. I don't see any cameras in the park."

"Oh, really?" He stopped and pointed to the batting cage around home plate. "Do you see that bird?"

Daylight was rapidly departing, but against the darkening blue sky, Dee could see the black outline of a crow, perched contentedly atop the metal structure, just like the ones she'd seen outside Slycer's warehouse.

"I see it," Dee said. *Bird on the island, whoop-de-doo.*

"Watch it as we pass by."

Dee kept her eye on the crow as they crossed by the park. It took her a while to realize that its body seemed to follow them. She gasped. "It's a camera!"

"Yep," Nyles said. "Now tell me how many of them you see."

Dee's eyes swept both sides of the street. Ethan, Griselda, and Blair were halfway down the block already, and everywhere Dee looked, she caught sight of a crow camera turning to follow them: on top of streetlights, fences, power lines. Even mounted on the side of a ruined concrete building. That one was pointed right at her. Dee could actually see the red light in the recess of its eye socket, signifying that they were being filmed.

There were literally cameras everywhere, covering every inch of Alcatraz 2.0.

She pictured the motionless crows perched on the roofs outside Slycer's warehouse. Those cameras had definitely been dark. Did The Postman not want the public to see her leaving after she killed Slycer?

"Just remember," Nyles said, gazing out over the soccer field, "nothing bad ever happens on Alcatraz two-point-oh without a camera close by."

Postman Forum * Camera Feeds * Alcatraz 2.0 Exterior

Thread: Alcatraz 2.0 Exterior

Nov-7, 4:42 p.m. **#7560**
DarknessFalls (Moderator) Join Date: April 2017
Darkness falls across the land Posts: 27,822

I have an update from Central Command:

<<Direct Message from **PostmanCentralCommand**>>
The temporary outage of channel feeds 13, 14, and 15 has been resolved. Full coverage restored. We apologize for the inconvenience.

Nov-7, 4:42 p.m. **#7561**
Ohioan_1989 Join Date: December 2018
Question Everything Posts: 3,442

Inconvenience? More like how *convenient* that the channel feeds outside the warehouses went dead right after #CinderellaSurvivor killed Slycer. Seems more likely that someone didn't want us to see what was going on after she killed him. Sorry, dude, but that reeks of conspiracy.

Nov-7, 4:43 p.m. **#7562**
DarknessFalls (Moderator) Join Date: April 2017
Darkness falls across the land Posts: 27,823

Ohioan, it is standard practice for The Postman to cut off feeds outside the execution zone to prevent inmates from determining the exact location of such events. The fact that Central Command issued an official statement about an outage seems to point to an actual event rather than a conspiracy, since dark feeds after an execution aren't unusual.

Nov-7, 4:44 p.m. **#7563**
Ohioan_1989 Join Date: December 2018
Question Everything Posts: 3,443

But killing an executioner IS unusual!!! Whatever. Believe what you want, dude.

Nov-7, 4:44 p.m. **#7564**
321Podcast Join Date: January 2018
This is where I write something funny, right? Posts: 18,339

#CinderellaSurvivor AND #GriseldaIWantYouInMyPants both working at I Scream? I fucking LOVE what The Postman is doing grouping the hotties together.

Nov-7, 4:45 p.m. **#7565**
The Griff Join Date: July 2017
Wide Awake Eyes Open Posts: 37,105

Yeah, 321, but that's just ANOTHER CONSPIRACY. Don't you think it's WEIRD that Alcatraz 2.0 suddenly has all these young attractive convicted killers around in the last six months? Don't you think it's WEIRD that they tend to live longer than the revolving door of old dudes we've been subjected to for the last year? THESE PEOPLE ARE ACTORS!!! Slycer isn't dead. #CinderellaSurvivor isn't actually some dumb teenager convicted of killing her stepsister. It's FAKE. All of it. FOLLOW THE RATINGS!!!!!

Nov-7, 4:45 p.m. **#7566**
321Podcast Join Date: January 2018
This is where I write something funny, right? Posts: 18,340

Griff, you might want to lay off the caffeine. And the weed.

Nov-7, 4:47 p.m. **#7567**
BabyEditrix Join Date: April 2018
Final Cut Pro over Magix Movie Posts: 272

Can someone swing by channel 43? Am I on crack or is there someone climbing over the rock wall?

Nov-7, 4:47 p.m. **#7568**
DarknessFalls (Moderator) Join Date: April 2017
Darkness falls across the land Posts: 27,824

BabyE, not on crack. It looks like some action. Sending out a view alert on the feed now. Thanks for the heads-up!

SEVEN

DEE FROZE IN HER TRACKS. *NOTHING BAD EVER HAPPENS ON Alcatraz without a camera close by*? Was he fucking with her? There wasn't a single square inch of the island that wasn't covered by one of those crow-shaped monstrosities.

"Don't fall behind," Blair called out from down the street. "Safety in numbers."

Dee seriously doubted that. "Sorry." She hitched up her dress and jogged to rejoin Nyles, who had quickened his pace. She had more questions that needed answering.

"I thought you said we have a sixtyish-percent chance of surviving outside?"

"You do," he said absently. "Because the cameras are farther away, not because they don't exist."

"Oh." Whatever hope of survival Dee had been able to muster in the last hour slowly drained away.

Blair fell into step beside her. "Remember, fans don't spike outdoor kills as much. It's harder for the cameras to track you, and the zoom isn't as good. The Postman's executioners want high-resolution close-ups for their kill videos."

"The Postmantics," Nyles began, trying out his term for The Postman's fans, "want to see as much of our fear as possible."

Blair nodded appreciatively. "Postmantics. I dig."

"I'm so glad you approve."

"But wouldn't it be better to stay inside?" Dee pressed. She was desperate for all the survival details she could get. "Find a spot without cameras and just hide?"

Instead of answering, Nyles continued his conversation with Blair, speaking even louder than before. "And how about this one—Painiacs. For the executioners."

Executioners. Though Dee supposed it was factually accurate, every time Nyles or Blair used that term, it pissed her off. She preferred the ridiculous "Painiacs" to a word that legitimized The Postman's killers in any way.

"I like it," Blair said. "I mean, not as much as Postmantics, but it has a great ring to it."

Dee sighed, exasperated. They were ignoring her questions.

As if sensing her mounting frustration, Blair slipped her arm through Dee's and gave her a friendly squeeze. "Check out the view."

Dee had been so fixated on the cameras that she hadn't noticed they had reached the end of the street. A row of palm trees lined a rock-wall shoreline, and waves lapped at the rocks, occasionally colliding in a spout of briny spray that shot over the barricade. A wooden sign had been hammered into a crevice: NO SWIMMING. DANGEROUS WATER.

Nyles, Ethan, and Griselda wandered down the path that hugged the beach, but Dee stood at the edge of the rocky break, gazing out over the bay. A cargo ship powered through the channel, so close that she could count the rectangular containers stacked like Lego bricks on its deck, and beyond, the skyline of San Francisco itself glittering in the fading daylight as a thick blanket of fog spread around it from the west.

The fog came quickly, tumbling across the city like an avalanche racing downhill. Every second that passed seemed to show less and less of the skyline as it was swallowed by the gray clouds. Wetness permeated the air. It clung to Dee's skin and clothes, chilling her to the bone. The weather changed so quickly, it almost felt as if she'd slipped through a portal into another dimension.

Except San Francisco was still there beyond the veil. Dee could see glimpses of light through the ever-shifting billows of fog, and was it her imagination or could she hear the sound of distant car horns blaring from rush-hour traffic, the chattering of laughter and conversation as people walked along the pier? It was as if the mist conducted the sounds of the city, carrying them across the water. Millions of people were powering through their daily lives while she was trapped in this hellhole. How many of them might be watching her on The Postman app at that very moment, tracking #CinderellaSurvivor's first night on Alcatraz 2.0?

It seemed so close: the ship, the city. Tantalizing. And there was no fence around the island. What prevented someone from trying to swim for it? A stupid NO SWIMMING sign? Dee wasn't much of an athlete, but maybe if she worked out at the gym a little, she'd get strong enough to try.

"It's beautiful, isn't it?" Blair's voice was low.

"I guess," Dee lied.

"Home, sweet home."

"You're from San Francisco?"

Blair nodded absently. "Born and raised. My whole life is right across the bay: wife, house, cat. It's weird. When the president first announced that they were turning the old Treasure Island into a televised prison camp, I was like, 'Yeah, right.' I figured someone would put a stop to it, you know? Congress . . . Supreme Court." She sighed. "But no one did."

Though it was just a couple of years ago, Dee only vaguely remembered the early politics of Alcatraz 2.0. Her dad and stepmom had just gotten married, and though it had been four years since her abduction, Dee's dad was still protecting her from potential triggers. The news was never on in their house, so the only knowledge Dee had of The Postman was what she picked up at school.

"My wife hated the app," Blair continued, her voice dreamy while she stared at the city across the bay. "But I checked it out at first. Kinda like watching a train wreck: you can't look away. And the horror seemed fair. When you considered what heinous things those people had done."

Those people. I'm one of those people now. "I guess."

"When I first got to Alcatraz two-point-oh, I used to imagine that I'd go back home one day. I'd dream that my conviction would be overturned, a new piece of evidence discovered, proving that I didn't kill the old lady next door." She glanced at Dee. "I didn't. I know we all say that, but it's true." Blair paused. Was she waiting for Dee to acknowledge her innocence? It felt that way, the charged air between them. But what was Dee supposed to say?

"I was framed," Dee blurted out. She hadn't planned on sharing this info with anyone, but even though she wasn't sure she trusted Blair or Nyles or any of these people, she felt the need to explain her own innocence.

"You too, huh? Some shrink testified that I was a paranoid schizophrenic who believed eighty-five-year-old Mrs. Pacini next door had been stealing from us for years. As if."

So Dee wasn't the only one? "The jury *bought* that?"

Blair shrugged. "They did what they were told to—"

Before Blair could finish talking, a siren tore through the air.

Like Pavlov's dogs with a whistle, Nyles, Ethan, and Griselda rushed back up the path to the edge of the rock wall and scanned the water. Dee tentatively followed, and it only took her a few seconds to find what they were looking for: in the midst of the choppy early-evening waves of San Francisco Bay, she saw a solitary figure splashing through the surf.

"Who is it?" Blair asked.

Griselda shook her head. "Can't tell."

"Shit," Ethan said, his eyes wide. "That's Jeremy."

Blair sucked in a sharp breath and broke from Dee's side. "Oh no."

Another glimmer of hope sparked to life inside Dee. "He's trying to escape," she said, realizing that her fantasy of swimming for freedom might not be so fantastical after all.

Nyles cupped his hands around his mouth. "Jeremy, you'll never make it!"

Ethan joined him. "Come back! It's not too late!"

"Why would he come back?" Dee asked, confused. "It might work!"

Nyles turned to her, his face ashen. "There's a reason no one tries to escape through the water."

Something about his tone made the hair stand up on Dee's bare arms.

The wake of the tanker rippled toward Alcatraz 2.0, and every few seconds a deep trough would momentarily obscure Jeremy from sight. Each time, Dee was sure he'd been pulled under, and each time, Jeremy's head bobbed up again as he swam for freedom.

Despite the layer of fog, it seemed like the worst possible time of day to attempt an escape—it was still light out, the water was at peak choppiness, and though San Francisco was tantalizingly close, she knew that the trek would be a challenge for even the most experienced open-water swimmer. "Why not try in the middle of the night?"

"The current is too dangerous at night, so he's using the tanker as cover," Nyles said, his eyes darting back and forth between the departing ship and the guy in the water. "He's been waiting for a chance like this."

"Fucking dumbass," Ethan said. "I warned him not to try and swim for it."

Lights flared to life from a monumental concrete structure at the south end of the island. The building appeared to be hewn directly from the rock like some kind of Bond villain's lair. Concrete crow's nests peppered the balustrade on the top floor, offering a panoramic view of the island and its surrounding waters while the searchlights panned the waves, searching for the escapee, and Dee realized that this must be the guard station Nyles had mentioned earlier.

Figures appeared on the balustrade, black-clad and swarming like ants out of their nest, and within moments, dozens of guards lined the railings, weapons in hand pointed down toward the water.

Shots rang out. Around Jeremy, the water looked electrified as small spouts erupted, the bullets striking with lethal force. But either these were the worst-trained snipers in the history of US law enforcement, or they were intentionally missing their target. Dozens of bullets peppered the water in a wide circle around the swimmer, none coming closer than five or six feet.

Jeremy seemed undeterred. He continued to swim west, heading straight for the mainland, pumping his arms with all his strength as he fought the rough waves.

Then the bullets stopped.

"They're letting him go?" Dee asked. She'd never seen this on the live feed from her prison cell. Maybe The Postman didn't want the public to know that his inescapable island prison wasn't all it was cracked up to be? Maybe there *was* a chance she'd be able to escape and find Monica's real killer?

"Princess," Griselda said, quashing Dee's hope with icy dread in her voice, "they'll never let us go."

The whir of a motor sounded from behind, growing louder each second, and Dee turned in time to see two drones racing across the island. They flew straight for Jeremy, then slowed and hovered above him. Cameras. What had Nyles just said? Nothing bad ever happened if there wasn't a camera close by. Now that the cameras had arrived, would Jeremy's doom soon follow?

Jeremy either didn't hear the drones or chose to ignore them. He seemed to be standing still, his strokes making almost no headway against the current, and as Dee and her companions watched in tense silence, she could have sworn that something red was spreading out across the water.

"That's blood!" she cried, pointing. "The guards hit him."

Nyles let out a long, slow breath. "It's blood. But not Jeremy's."

Huh? "Then whose—"

The rest of the sentence choked off in Dee's throat as she saw new movement in the water. The blue-gray dorsal fins—a dozen or more—made Dee's blood run cold.

Jeremy was surrounded by sharks.

He noticed them too. He stopped stroking and treaded water, desperately spinning around as he looked for a means of escape. Then his body jerked, and his head and shoulders disappeared beneath the waves. He popped up a split second later, arms thrashing as he gasped for breath. Then he went under again. The sharks were toying with him.

This time when Jeremy resurfaced, he let out a blood-chilling scream, and even though Dee was pretty sure the sharks couldn't actually hear him, his cry seemed to spur them into action.

There was a frenzy of splashing fins, and a churning of water around Jeremy as the sharks fought one another for a piece of his body. The foaming water was tinged with pink.

And then Jeremy was gone.

🕒 5m

Tom Ecklestein @TommyEcksInDaHouse
PWNing this one: #SharkTanked #NoEscape

← :12 ₪: 1

🕒 5m

Bradley Fornow @ForeverForFourYears
Literally the stupidest thing ever. You realize that's been used like FOUR BILLION TIMES ALREADY, RIGHT? #OriginalityIsDead #BuyAThesaurus #Sharks74Inmates0

🕒 5m

> **Tom Ecklestein** @TommyEcksInDaHouse
> PWNing this one: #SharkTanked #NoEscape

← : 122 ₪: 28

🕒 4m

Professor Xtant @TheMollyMauler4Prez46
I know I say this every time, but I wonder if #MollyMauler gets pissed off that the Alcatraz 2.0 security system basically impedes on her territory? Couldn't they think of something else? #NoEscape #MollysSpikeCampaign

← : 418 ₪: 42

🕒 4m

The Griff @awakewideopen
I've seen better special effects from my nephew's 4th grade science project. Where's the body? Jeremy clearly SCUBA'd out to that tanker. NONE OF THIS IS REAL, PEOPLE! #FakeNews #EyesOpen #DontTrustTheFeed

← : 370 ₪: 284

🕒 4m

MrsGhostHuntress @MrsGhostHuntress
This never gets old. #Sharks74Inmates0

← : 22 ₪: 8

3m

Stef Hoff @StepOffStefHoff_15

@TheMollyMauler4Prez46 I refuse to spike #NoEscape attempts. Feels cheap. I mean, I'm glad he's dead. Can't avoid justice, Jeremy. But I still feel cheated.

← | : 3 ₪: 1

2m

Tom Ecklestein @TommyEcksInDaHouse

PWNing this one: #NiceTryJeremy

← | : 31 ₪: 11

2m

Bradley Fornow @ForeverForFourYears

Better, grasshopper. But not great.

2m

> **Tom Ecklestein** @TommyEcksInDaHouse
> PWNing this one: #NiceTryJeremy

← | : 14 ₪: 9

EIGHT

THE SPOTLIGHTS REMAINED ON THE AREA WHERE JEREMY HAD been pulled under, and the drones continued to hover overhead until the frenzy of dorsal fins died down and the water calmed. The lights switched off, the drones retreated, and the island fell silent as the fog pushed stealthily forward.

But though the chaos was gone, Dee's heart still thundered in her chest. "What the hell just happened?"

"That's our security system," Blair said.

"Why not just shoot him?"

"That's not dramatic enough, now, is it?" Nyles said. His breezy manner had returned, and Dee wondered if that was how he dealt with the harshness of Alcatraz 2.0 without completely losing his mind.

"Jeremy." Ethan couldn't peel his eyes away from the water, even though the fog mostly obscured it from view. "Dude, why? I *told* you there was no way you could outswim those goddamn sharks."

"They populate the bay with shortfin makos," Blair said, turning Dee away from the shoreline, "then shoot gel capsules full of pig's blood into the water. It's only a matter of time before they show up for a free lunch."

"Conveniently, just long enough for the drones to arrive and get it all on camera," Nyles added.

"See?" Griselda said. "No escape."

"That's horrible." Ratings, spikes, fandoms. A guy had just been eaten alive by sharks, and within moments millions of people would be cheering it on. Dee swore if she ever met The Postman, she'd kick him in the nuts.

"Come on," Blair said, dragging Dee back to the asphalt street. "We need to get home."

The Barracks of Alcatraz 2.0 looked exactly the same as what Dee had seen from her prison cell. A neighborhood of duplexes clustered around the north end of the island with bland two-story buildings painted alternating versions of blue, beige, and gray, which was their only distinguishing factor. Each had a roofed carport—empty, of course, since there was no way The Postman would give each inmate a weapon, er, vehicle—and concrete walkway leading to the front door. The two sides of the duplex were mirror images of each other, with the same brown tiled roofs, the same overgrown patch of green-beige lawn, the same streetlamps casting a feeble glow across the sidewalk, and the same crow cameras perched above, staring down at them.

Ethan and Griselda peeled off about five houses down the street. Dee watched as Ethan attempted to follow Griselda into her apartment. She strong-armed him.

"I just wanted to do a sweep to make sure no one's hiding in there," he whined.

"No one's hiding in my panties," Griselda said. "I'll be fine." Then she slammed the door in his face.

Dee had to appreciate the way Griselda took no shit. She may have been a raging bitch in every conceivable way, but at least she was consistent.

"The Postman likes to create drama," Nyles said. "Housing Ethan and Griselda next to each other is good for ratings, I imagine."

"Do people, you know . . ." Dee stumbled over the words.

"Hook up?" Blair asked, finishing her thought.

Dee felt a blush creeping up her cheeks. "Yeah."

"Most of what you see on the app is fake," Blair explained, guiding her up the walkway of one of the duplexes. "I mean, not the murdery parts, but everything else. The shipping, the petty arguments, the drama. Fans get really into creating their own storylines for us."

"The app has a dedicated channel for each of the inmates." Nyles smiled mischievously and lifted an eyebrow. "Which you already know, of course, since you followed it *so* closely before you got here."

He was teasing her, Dee realized, and in order to avoid an explanation of why she'd never really watched the app, she decided to play along. "Of course."

"Fans have to pay extra for the live dedicated channels," Blair explained, "where they can tune in to see what you're doing at any point in the day, even when you're not on the main feed. Having a lot of subscribers can maximize your survival time on the island."

Dee pictured Griselda, prepping herself for the cameras before she entered I Scream. She was playing to her fans, the ones who paid extra to have access to her 24/7. Would Dee be able to do the same? She cringed, every molecule in her being crying out in resistance. *I'm not sure I could do it.*

"You have your key?" Blair asked, pausing at the door.

Dee pulled the ring with the key and ID card from the front of her dress. "Don't lose it, because you won't get another one," she recited dutifully.

Blair smiled. "Good learner. You should give Nyles lessons."

Nyles pursed his lips as he swung his backpack off his shoulder, unzipped the main compartment, and removed a plastic shopping bag. "I picked up some food for myself, but you're welcome to it." He paused, looking sheepish. "I, uh, didn't think . . ."

"Didn't think I'd need any?" Dee said.

"Yes, rather. Sorry."

Dee peeked in the bag. It contained a prepackaged single serving of microwavable lasagna, a lunch-box apple, and a bottle of filtered water. Kind of like the lunches her stepmom used to pack her for school.

"Thanks," she said, forcing a smile.

"Your neighbor is named Mara," Blair said. "Redhead. Quiet. Kinda standoffish. She used to work at the bodega, but I haven't seen her around in a couple of weeks."

Dee glanced at the house next door. "Do you think she—"

"Was killed?" Nyles suggested. "No. We would have seen it."

"Right." Because every death was public on Alcatraz 2.0.

"Unless she offed herself," Nyles mused. "It happens."

The only thing worse than living next to a killer would be living next to a corpse. Or maybe it was the other way around.

"I'm sure Mara's fine," Blair said, more loudly than before. As if she wanted Dee's neighbor to hear. Then she turned to Nyles. "At least we all hope she is."

"Yes," Nyles said, dropping his eyes, suitably chastised. "Of course."

"The first thing you want to do is search the house," Blair said, back to her bossily friendly manner. "There's a utility closet in the kitchen.

Check that first. Then the bathroom at the top of the stairs, and both bedrooms. The closets are on the far side of each room. That's the most stressful part."

Dee's stomach flipped. The dead bolts seemed like cruel irony if someone could be lurking upstairs every time she came home.

"There should be clothes up there too," Blair continued, "which will give you a better idea of what kind of role The Postman wants you to play."

"Role?"

"Yeah," Blair said. "I'm the mouthy tomboy. Nyles is the Euro geek. Ethan, the jock. Griselda, the edgy slut. Remember, he's selling a brand, and he wants us to fit into his scripts."

"Ten quid says he sticks with the princess theme," Nyles said.

Dee arched a brow. "You have ten quid?"

Nyles's face fell. "No. But if I did, that's what I'd bet on."

She didn't think she could handle a closet full of princess dresses. Maybe she should pray that someone would jump out from behind her princess-inspired wardrobe and eviscerate her on the spot?

Dee stared at the bolted front door. The knocker was rusting, and the light on the old-fashioned doorbell flickered off and on erratically. She was half hoping Blair and Nyles would offer to come inside with her, help her check the place for intruders. But that seemed weak. And she knew better than to show weakness.

Blair must have sensed that Dee was hesitant to go inside. "Between Slycer and Jeremy," she said, trying to sound encouraging, "I think the Postmantics have had enough entertainment for one day. The Painiacs should leave you alone for tonight."

Dee wasn't entirely sure she believed her, but she appreciated that Blair was trying to ease her fears. "Thanks."

"And tomorrow," Blair said, giving Dee's shoulders a friendly squeeze, "we can talk about the future, okay? Tonight, rest."

"But no sleeping until after two o'clock," Dee said, suppressing a yawn. She had no idea how she was going to be able to stay awake that long.

"You catch on quick," Blair said with a smile. "See you in the morning, Princess. Things will look brighter when the sun is shining again."

Dee thought of Jeremy and the bloody froth of water that had erupted as he was eaten alive.

I seriously doubt it.

TRAZBET.COM

(an affiliate of Postman Enterprises, Inc.)

INMATE: Dee Guerrera (#CinderellaSurvivor)
DAYS ALIVE: >1
PERIOD: 7 November 12:00 a.m. – 7 November 11:59 p.m.
CONDITIONS: Low Visibility with Fog

EXECUTIONER	**ML**	**ODDS**	**$2 PAYOUT**
Barbaric Barista	3-2	8-5	$5.20
Cecil B. DeViolent	4-1	7-2	$9.00
DIYnona	9-2	6-5	$4.40
Gassy Al	1-1	1-1	$4.00
Gucci Hangman	1-2	3-5	$3.20
Hannah Ball	6-1	7-1	$16.00
Hardy Girls	7-5	4-5	$3.60
Molly Mauler	9-2	9-1	$20.00
Prince Slycer	SUSPENDED		
Robin's Hood	7-2	3-1	$8.00

NINE

NYLES AND BLAIR HAD DISAPPEARED DOWN THE STREET, BUT Dee still stood in front of her new home. *Temporary home. One way or another, I probably won't be here long.*

Maybe Griselda was right: she just needed to embrace the fact that she was going to die on this island.

Dee shivered. The fog had pushed across the water and was now pouring over the flat expanse of Alcatraz 2.0. It seeped through the gaps between duplexes, and the houses at either end of the street had already disappeared behind the thick, damp veil. The air smelled like the sea, a dank mix of nature and decay, as if the fog brought a piece of the Pacific Ocean with it as it invaded the San Francisco Bay. Dee wasn't sure if the sun had officially set or not, but Nyles's initial warning hammered into her brain: *Only be outside with the sun.*

And yet, as she stood in front of the locked door, key gripped in her shaking hand, she couldn't bring herself to go inside.

Was she afraid that someone would be waiting for her? Maybe. But Nyles and Blair were pretty confident that any killings were done for the day, the bloodthirsty Painiacs satiated.

Painiacs. Huh. Maybe that was more trendable than Nyles thought.

Yeah, so if it wasn't that, what was Dee so afraid of?

Normalization. She had a house, with a key. Inside there was a closet full of clothes. A kitchen where she could make food. Tomorrow she had a job to work. A commute. Coworkers.

It was a life, just like people had back in the real world, and it would be so easy to succumb to that longing to feel normal again. She could embrace this role that The Postman had chosen for her, play it out until the end, try to pretend that her world was ordinary right up to the point when she was strung up by Gucci Hangman, or trapped in a game of human archery with Robin's Hood. If she bought into the illusion, would her life on Alcatraz 2.0 be easier?

Dee clenched her jaw at the idea of playing along with The Postman's plan.

"Oh, hell no," she said out loud.

Movement to Dee's left startled her. A curtain in the window next door fluttered as it was pulled aside. In the encroaching darkness, Dee could just make out a face in the window. Large green eyes, translucent white skin, and long auburn hair. The girl made eye contact with Dee for a split second; then the curtain dropped back into place, and she was gone.

Hello, Mara. At least she knew her neighbor still existed. Dee wondered how long she'd been watching. Long enough to hear Blair and Nyles's conversation about her? Probably.

Whatever. Not her problem. Dee took a deep breath, thrust the key into the lock, and swung open the door to her temporary new home.

The room was dark, lit only by a bluish glow. Dee slid her hand up the smooth surface of the wall until her fingers grazed a switch. She was half expecting the lights not to work, yet another trick in The Postman's arsenal, but the moment she flicked the lever, a soft yellow glow erupted from sconces along the wall, illuminating a small living room. The space was compact but clean, and despite the single window beside the door, it wasn't as depressing a room as Dee had expected. It was generically furnished—couch, armchair, coffee table, all made from sturdy oak. The upholstery was brown with burgundy stripes, which matched the warm oak grain wood, and the whole thing reminded Dee of a business hotel she and her parents had stayed at a few years ago when her stepmom had been in Dallas for work. Except for one "homey" touch—a needlepoint throw pillow on the sofa depicting a rainbow descending from a cloud to a house beside the words HOME, SWEET HOME.

Gee, thanks, Postman. Douche.

Round, half-dome security cameras—like the ones inside I Scream—were mounted to the ceiling, tucked away in every corner. Their red lights flickered to life as Dee entered, just in case she had any illusions of privacy. This house probably had more cameras than a Vegas casino, and as if to remind Dee that her every move would be caught on film, above the mantel a large-screen TV was showing Jeremy's final moments as he flailed around with a dozen shortfin makos in the frothy pink foam of his own gore. The Postman had added a GIF of a shark breaching the water, superimposed on the slo-mo replay of the feeding frenzy, and the hashtag #NiceTryJeremy flashed across the image every time Jeremy thrashed in the water. In the sidebar, the comments scrolled quickly up the screen as the Postmantics continued to voice their approvals and disapprovals of the video—about a sixty-forty split in favor, best she could tell—and Dee wondered what was playing on Jeremy's live dedicated channel at that moment. A feed from his empty house? Or perhaps the channel, like Jeremy, was dead.

Dee turned away, unwilling to watch an endless loop of Jeremy's death, but the sound of his screams was just as disturbing. Was the volume set to maximum? She scanned the coffee table and sofa, looking for a remote control. Shocker: she couldn't find one. Which meant there was no way to turn off the screen or the sound.

So, that was awesome. She'd be surrounded by snuff films every moment of every day. This island kept getting better and better.

An archway at the end of the living room opened into a dining-kitchen combo with a staircase running up one wall. A round four-seater table sat perfectly centered beneath a glass-and-chrome light fixture, and directionals lined the shiny white kitchen. Stove, fridge, microwave, dishwasher, motion-sensitive cameras. All the comforts of home. Tucked beneath the stairs, the utility closet Blair had warned her about. Thankfully, the door stood open, exposing a stacked washer-dryer and, unfortunately, enough empty space to house a weapon-bearing sociopath.

The good news was that if Dee came home to DIYnona hanging out in her laundry cupboard with some razor-sharp knitting needles or a home welding kit, she had a secondary means of escape. The entire back wall of the house was taken up by a sliding glass door. Which was, of course, annoyingly easy to shatter to gain entry, but she wasn't going to think about that right now. Dee tugged on the handle to make sure it was locked, then flipped a nearby light switch. Exterior floods illuminated the backyard. It was a concrete rectangle with a set of wicker lawn chairs that had seen better days, and it was separated from Mara's identical patch by a warped wooden fence.

Dee left the outside light on and turned away from the glass door, surveying the kitchen. She felt helpless, exposed—the red dots from the multitude of cameras were following her every move. Did she already have subscribers to her personal channel? The idea made her skin crawl: creepy dudes cycling through camera feeds from her house until they located her in the kitchen, still wearing her Cinderella gown.

"Screw that," she said out loud.

She dumped Nyles's shopping bag in the fridge and turned to the kitchen drawers. Maybe she could find a knife. Or a mallet. Hell, even a fork—anything she could use as a weapon.

Dee rifled through the drawers, yanking them open with such force that the entire cupboard shook. They were all empty except for one, which held a collection of white plastic cutlery. Sporks. Nothing but sporks, and certainly nothing even remotely resembling a weapon unless her attacker was made of Jell-O.

Still, she slipped a plastic spork from the drawer and tucked it into the front of her dress. It probably wouldn't even break an assailant's skin, but having a weapon, any kind of weapon, made her feel as if she had a chance. Even if she didn't.

Jeremy's screams filled her ears again as the video replay looped back around to his death. His terror was triggering, and Dee felt her heart rate accelerate. Really, a spork against one of The Postman's killers? Was she mental?

Dee rushed into the living room, eyes frantically searching for something else she could use as a weapon. Maybe she could break the leg off the coffee table. She crossed the room, dumped the table on its side, and tried to wrench one of the wooden legs away.

It wouldn't budge, and Dee quickly realized why: the table, the sofa, the chair—each was constructed from one solid piece of wood. Dee would have needed a saw or a sledgehammer to break it apart, and she seriously doubted she'd find either on Alcatraz 2.0.

Well, if she couldn't break the table, maybe she could use the table to break something else? Dee grinned as she heaved the table off the floor and launched it directly at the TV.

She'd expected the TV to short-circuit, silencing it forever, or at the very least for the screen to shatter, splintering the image, like that time she dropped her iPhone and her cracked screen made everything look like a Picasso during his cubism phase. Instead, the table merely bounced off the screen, striking the wall beside the front door before it crash-landed—still in one piece—on the plush brown carpet.

Seriously? Unbreakable glass on a TV screen? Was that even possible?

She tried one of the metal chairs from the kitchen table next. Same result.

Dee turned her attention to the domed cameras. If the furniture and the TV were indestructible, she guessed the cameras would be as well. But maybe she could pry the dome off by using her spork and dismantle the camera within? Worth a shot.

She righted the table, placed it against the wall beneath one of the domes, and climbed on top, picturing the close-up image of her nostrils that the camera must have been capturing. She slipped the spork from her dress and reached out toward the camera with her other hand, but the moment Dee's fingertips touched the domed lid of the camera, a searing pain ripped through her arm.

Dee tore her hand away, clutching it to her body. The cameras were electrified. Just fucking great. She couldn't turn off the TV; she couldn't get near the cameras to cut their feed. The Postman had thought of everything.

Dee's hand still ached as she slowly mounted the stairs to the second floor, where the ever-present noise from the screen below was less noticeable. From the landing, a door opened to the bathroom, which was thankfully camera-free. Or so she thought. When Dee stepped into the room to inspect the shower—a standard bathtub-showerhead combo with a clear plastic curtain—a red dot blipped to life in the middle of the huge mirror above the sink.

At first Dee thought it was a reflection of a camera light from the hallway, but as she peered closer to the mirror, she realized that the camera was embedded in the glass.

What the hell? She couldn't even get privacy in the bathroom? Sure, the toilet was tucked into a nook in the corner, hopefully out of the shot, but the camera's red light directly faced the shower's transparent curtain.

Dee could only imagine how many pervs watched the bathroom feeds from Alcatraz 2.0.

Guess I'll be showering in my underwear.

But at least the see-through curtain nixed the possibility of a *Psycho*-style shower scene—she'd definitely see an attacker coming through the clear curtain.

It was a small victory, but Dee would take it.

Like the drawers in the kitchen, the bathroom yielded no possibilities for a weapon, just a hairbrush, a variety of sparkly makeup accessories, and a dental hygiene kit including toothbrush, toothpaste, and floss.

In the hall beside the bathroom, Dee discovered a linen closet with shelves that fit flush with the door. A dozen light-green bath and hand towels, half as many washcloths, and an extra set of sheets and blankets were stacked inside. Dee grabbed each of the shelves and tugged. If they were removable, she wanted to know. The shelves held firm, which hopefully meant she wouldn't find a masked serial killer curled up with the linens when she got home from work.

Two identical bedrooms flanked each side of the bathroom—one facing the front of the house, one facing the back. Each had a queen-size bed, bureau, nightstand, and closet. The nightstand drawers were empty, except for a pair of neon-orange foam earplugs. An act of kindness to help her sleep despite the ever-present TV noise downstairs? Or a trick to allow serial killers to sneak into her room unnoticed? Dee left the earplugs where they were. She'd take her chances with sleeplessness rather than wake up to find Gassy Al looming over her bed.

Next, Dee opened each of the bedroom closets in turn, spork firmly gripped in her hand, as she half expected the Hardy Girls or Barbaric Barista to jump out at any moment. Luckily, the back bedroom closet was empty, and the accordion doors on the other were already folded open. An olive branch from management. See? Nothing hiding in here . . . yet. Not that she was about to let her guard down. Hell no. That was what The Postman wanted, to lull her into a false sense of security before he pulled the rug out.

And if the wardrobe was any indication, The Postman definitely planned to mess with her.

First off, there were no pants. No jeans, no shorts, no leggings. Which was pretty much all Dee had lived in when she'd been a normal teenager in LA. Jeans, T-shirt, sneakers. Jean shorts, tank top, flip-flops. Jeans, sweater, boots. Rinse, repeat. She liked muted dark colors, the occasional nerd-proud tee, no patterns. This closet was pretty much the complete opposite.

Dresses and skirts, frilly blouses and embellished jackets, all grouped on connected hangers for easy grab-and-go ability. A yellow peasant dress with off-the-shoulder sleeves. An ice-blue A-line dress with a translucent white cardigan. A green pencil skirt with a ruffled purple tank top. A tiered yellow skirt with a royal-blue puff-sleeved tee and a red headband . . .

The last one seemed familiar. The color combination of yellow, blue, and red. Dee glanced down at the ball gown she was still wearing, then back up at the Crayola-inspired closet, and groaned out loud.

Beauty. Rapunzel. The Little Mermaid. Snow White.

Nyles was right. The Postman was turning her into a modern-day fairy-tale princess.

Dee flung Snow White across the room. Bad enough she'd lost her sister, then been wrongly convicted of the murder; now she was going to be humiliated, forced to prance around the island in these stupid clothes while millions of people gawked and laughed and placed bets on how many days she'd survive until her blood was spilled in the name of entertainment.

Screw The Postman, screw the criminal-justice system, screw the government for letting it all happen. She wouldn't play their game, and if that meant she died faster, so be it.

Dee tightened her grip on the spork. She might be a marked girl on Alcatraz 2.0, but she certainly wasn't going down without a fight.

TEN

IT TOOK A COUPLE OF HOURS TO BOOBY-TRAP HER HOUSE, BUT when Dee finally sat down on the sofa, she felt, if not exactly safe, then at least satisfied that she wouldn't be taken by surprise.

After changing into a pair of teal pajamas that consisted of harem pants and an off-the-shoulder tank top, disturbingly like a costume from *Aladdin*, Dee had snatched the dental floss from the bathroom and sporks from the kitchen and constructed her first line of defense. She painstakingly tied a dozen of the plastic utensils to a length of minty green floss, then strung it across the front door, securing it to a curtain rod on one side and the door hinge on the other. She realized that the cameras were capturing her every move, but she didn't care. Even if The Postman's killers knew about her alarm system, they'd still have no way of getting inside without triggering the plastic chimes. If she slept on the sofa, the noise would wake her up and give her a head start to escape through the opposite side of the house.

Next up, the windows in the living room and the two bedrooms, and the sliding glass door. Trickier, since they slid open horizontally instead of vertically. But the dental floss came in handy there, too. She found a stash of cardboard coffee cups in a kitchen cupboard, and after poking two holes in each with a spork prong, she threaded the floss through, then secured its ends to each window handle. Next, Dee filled the cardboard cups with whatever she could find: the rest of the sporks, lip-gloss tubes and eye-shadow palettes from the bathroom drawers, an ugly beaded necklace she found paired with one of the princess dresses. If anyone tried to slide open a window or the glass door, it would pull the attached cup, spilling its contents onto the parquet floor and making enough noise to wake Dee up.

Or at least she hoped. She couldn't have been the first inmate to think of creating their own security system, and The Postman probably had a contingency plan in place for such situations, so Dee couldn't exactly sleep soundly. Instead she sat on the floor of the living room, leaning against the front wall with that ridiculous plastic spork clutched in her hand.

Was Griselda sleeping? Or Ethan? Or Blair? Were they sitting up like Dee, waiting for the danger hours to pass before they caught whatever z's they could before work?

Dee flinched as she heard a noise outside. Crunching, like soft shoes on a gravel path. Was that Cecil B. DeViolent coming for her? Looking to avenge Prince Slycer's death? She held her breath, ears straining against the silence, expecting any moment to hear one of her booby traps triggered as a serial killer entered her house.

Tears welled up in her eyes. This is how it would be. Every night, the same paranoia, the same exhaustion. How long could she keep it up? How long before she didn't care if a Painiac murdered her or not? How long before she gave up trying to find Monica's real killer?

As Dee sat in the darkness, her goal of proving her innocence felt soul-crushingly futile.

Dee wasn't sure exactly when she'd broken Blair's third rule and fallen sound asleep, but she was pretty sure she was dreaming.

It was a nightmare, one she'd had many times before, where she was trapped and fighting for her life. So exactly like her current reality. And this recurring nightmare, just like Alcatraz 2.0, was real.

Or had been. In the dream, Dee was eleven years old again, waking up in a stark white room with smooth metal walls and no door. She screamed for help until her vocal cords were raw. She pounded on the walls until her arms and hands ached. She cried until she was too exhausted to sob.

That was when she heard the voice. A girl, just like her. Nearby, but muffled.

"Hello! Can you hear me? Are you okay?"

The air vent high in the corner near the ceiling.

"H-hello?" Dee said, her voice craggy.

"You can hear me! Oh my God. I've been so scared and alone."

Scared and alone. Where was she? What had happened? She'd been at the library, doing homework after school, like she did every day until her dad picked her up. She'd gone outside to wait for him and someone had approached her from behind. That was all she remembered until she woke up in the room.

"Where are we?" she asked. "What happened?"

"You don't remember?" The girl paused. When she spoke again, her tone changed. She was no longer hopeful, just angry. "You're one of them, aren't you? Do you think I'm *stupid*? I won't trust you. I'll never trust you!" Then the voice fell silent.

Dee didn't remember what exactly she said next, just that she was begging the girl at the other end of the air vent not to disappear, not to go away and leave her alone.

The dream shifted. Dee wasn't sure how long she'd been in the white room—hours or days—and she was so hungry and weak, she could barely stand. But she'd come to trust her new friend: Kimmi, the girl in the air vent.

"Dolores," Kimmi said, her voice like a lilting song. "Are you awake?"

"I'm so scared, Kimmi," Dee repeated for what felt like the millionth time. "Am I going to die?"

"I can help you," Kimmi said.

"Help me?" Dee pushed herself to her feet, tears streaming down her face. This time, she was crying from hope, not from despair.

"Yes," Kimmi said. "Hold on."

There was movement from above, the sound of metal warping out of place. Then fingers appeared through the air vent, pushing it out, twisting it to the side, and pulling it back into the duct.

Dee held her breath as a girl's face appeared in the open vent.

Kimmi's skin was pale, practically white, as if she hadn't been out in the sun for years. Her long blond hair dangled down in perfect ringlets, and her blue eyes were wide with fear.

Dee realized later that the hair should have been her first clue. Kimmi was clean, well-groomed, perfect. Not a captive who hadn't eaten or showered in days.

"I have something for you, Dolores." Kimmi held up a bag. It had a fast-food logo emblazoned across the front.

"I'm so hungry!" Dee cried. "How did you—"

"I ASK THE QUESTIONS!" Kimmi's voice boomed through Dee's cell, pinging off the shiny white walls. She dangled the bag over Dee's head. "And you'll answer them correctly if you want this."

"But—"

"So we'll start with an easy one." Kimmi's voice was syrupy sweet again, her rage vanished. "Do you want to be my sister?"

ELEVEN

DEE OPENED HER EYES. SHE WASN'T IN THE WHITE ROOM ANYmore. Nor was she lying on the cold concrete floor of Slycer's maze, wearing a Cinderella gown. Instead she was dressed in frilly pajamas, curled up on the floor in her strange new home.

She sat up, eyes blinking against the flickering light from the TV. The main feed had stopped replaying Jeremy's death and was cycling through the various Barracks. Dee watched the feed for a moment, registering the different inmates. She didn't recognize any of them except for Ethan, who was doing incline push-ups off his coffee table, and though the sound was still ever-present, Dee had already gotten used to it, like white noise in the background.

Dee yawned, stretching her aching limbs as she teetered to her feet. A dim light permeated the vertical blinds, so diffuse that it left no shadows of the individual slats. It could have been dawn or noon—hard to know through the blanket of fog that had descended over the island the night before—but Dee knew one thing for sure.

"I survived my first night on Alcatraz." She said it out loud, as if hearing the words made them feel like an actual accomplishment instead of dumb luck. She should have been dead by now, and it probably wouldn't be long before The Postman and his band of crazies rectified that situation.

She glanced at a camera in the corner of the living room. Its never-blinking eye must have watched her sleep, along with however many nut jobs had subscribed to her personal feed. Had they heard her boast about surviving? Were the rooms wired for sound as well as video? Safe to assume so.

Fine. Whatever. She already had a target on her back, so flying under the radar wasn't an option. She wasn't going to watch what she said. Freedom of speech was one of the few things still in her power.

A shower and change of clothes further improved her mood, though the camera behind the bathroom mirror was unnerving. She hung a bed-sheet over the curtain rod so her dedicated fans couldn't see her showering, but as she stepped out of the tub, towel already wrapped around her body, she remembered Griselda. Should Dee be playing to her fans, too? Should she let them see . . . everything? Was that a surefire way to stay alive?

Dee stared into the mirror for a moment, then pulled out the bath-room drawer full of sparkly pink cosmetics. *This is what the fans want to see. This is what The Postman wants from me.*

She slammed the drawer closed. The thought made her sick. Dee was not a toy, and Alcatraz 2.0 was not a game. The Postman could try to control her every move, but there were still some things she could do to rebel.

Dee marched into the bedroom and stared at her wardrobe. The "princess casual" daywear, which had thoroughly demoralized her last night, suddenly felt empowering. Instead of pulling a predetermined out-fit from the closet, she paired a lavender Rapunzel top with a pink Sleeping Beauty peasant skirt, then donned a not-so-subtly racist Pocahontas fringed jacket and matching suede ankle boots. Maybe this princess thing wouldn't be so bad after all? They were strong girls who defeated seem-ingly insurmountable evils. #CinderellaSurvivor could do the same.

But her newfound optimism took a bitch slap as she descended back into the living room. The monitor above the fireplace now played a rerun of Slycer's maze, and even though it had been hours since the encounter, the Postmantics were still commenting by the thousands. The stream in the sidebar scrolled so quickly it was hard for Dee to read.

Monica used to be like that, glued to her screen after a kill video, commenting frantically as she tried to keep up with the feed, using her MoBettaStylz screen name. Monica, who'd had aspirations of being a stylist for film and television, had been obsessed with Gucci Hangman and the way he used fashion as an accessory to murder. She never missed one of his videos, praising him for using last season's Prada fad for Pucci-inspired prints in his execution of a former runway model who'd been convicted of murdering a rival in order to obtain her spot in an upcoming fashion-week show, or critiquing Gucci's use of a chain-handle purse to slowly asphyxiate a former YouTube beauty vlogger, while demonstrating the real-time use of highlights and contours on a strangulation victim.

Not that Monica was a blind follower. Every now and then, she had doubts about her Postman devotion. "It's okay because they're murderers . . . right?" she'd ask Dee.

Dee was never sure how to answer. Was subjecting a killer to a taste of his or her own medicine morally acceptable? On paper, sure. That was how the president had sold the country on his outsourcing of the criminal justice system. And though this kind of justice made Dee's skin crawl, she was clearly in the minority. Hundreds of millions of people watched The Postman—they couldn't *all* be wrong, could they?

"It's the law," Dee would respond, in a totally noncommittal way. It was the best she could muster, and it had seemed to satisfy Monica's doubts. At least temporarily.

Secretly, Dee thought it was dangerous to appeal to the most vulgar instincts of humanity, to normalize something as horrific as state-sponsored serial killers. But that's what you got when a former reality TV star was elected president.

Monica had acquired a small fan base for her commentary, and that had come out during Dee's trial as one of her motivations. Dr. Farooq, the court-appointed psychiatrist, testified that Dee was suffering from a deep-seated jealousy of her stepsister. Which wasn't true at all. The last thing Dee wanted was notoriety.

Now, in an ironic twist of fate, #CinderellaSurvivor had gone viral, surpassing any popularity MoBettaStylz had ever gained. Would Monica have been impressed? Excited? Proud of her stepsister? Or would she finally have realized the true and dangerous nature of The Postman?

Hard to say. Monica was sweet and bubbly, the kind of girl everyone loved, but introspection wasn't her strong point. She probably would have been terrified for Dee's safety while simultaneously composing commentary aimed to up her own following.

Of course, Monica was dead. Dee had found her body strangled on the floor of her bedroom. The panic of that moment was still palpable: the immediate realization that something was horribly wrong, the desperation to help Monica, fighting back the wave of nausea as she tried to revive her dead stepsister, the overwhelming ache of pain and anger and loss when she knew it was too late.

Dee could recall the details of that moment as if it had happened an hour ago. The bulging glassy eyes staring straight up at the ceiling fan, open but unseeing. Monica's outfit: a tunic shirt cinched with a wide belt over leggings, the brightly colored pattern ironically vivid and alive. Monica's shirt was torn at the neck, probably in the struggle with her killer, and a heart had been carved into the flesh of Monica's bare shoulder.

The image of that carving was branded in Dee's memory. The broken skin, jagged and torn, a thin line of coagulated blood oozing up from beneath. The lines of the heart were sharp and irregular, as if hastily done, but the shape was still easily recognizable, and wholly disturbing.

The prosecution had intimated that this carving was a sign of Dee's jealousy of her prettier, and more popular, stepsister—a theory that was backed up by the "expert" psychiatrist, Dr. Farooq, who, aside from one hypnosis session, had never asked Dee a single question. Dee and Monica were the same age, in the same class at school, and the prosecution played up the stepsibling rivalry to make it seem like Dee was psychotically envious. And though the police had never found the weapon used to carve the symbol, forensics experts had testified that it was probably a thin, sharp object like a needle or an earring stud.

Or a pair of point-tip tweezers, bright pink with white polka dots, not to be too specific: the exact pair Dee had found stashed in the top drawer of her dresser when she went for her Xanax after calling 911. The blood on the tip wasn't even dry.

Dee didn't know how they'd gotten there—who had put them in her dresser and why—but she instinctively knew she had to get rid of them. Which she did, by flushing them down the toilet. But even without that evidence, a jury had convicted Dee—primarily on the strength of Dr. Farooq's testimony. So, in the end, it hadn't mattered.

Dee was the only one left who believed in her innocence, the only one who could find Monica's real killer. And to do that, she needed to stay alive.

Dee's stomach rumbled, reminding her that in order to stay alive, she was going to need to eat something. She had no idea how long it had been since her last meal, but her body was officially protesting.

She headed for the kitchen, where she could still hear the TV audio from her time in the maze, the clomp of Slycer's footsteps echoing throughout her house, but at least she didn't have to watch herself on an endless loop. After zapping the lasagna, she carefully pulled back the plastic cover, noting with some satisfaction that its seal had remained intact. Just like Blair had told her—make sure the seals on your food haven't been tampered with. She'd gotten lucky meeting Blair and Nyles so soon after her arrival on Alcatraz 2.0. Even bitchy Griselda and airheaded Ethan. Though she would never allow herself to trust them, at least she could use their experience to help her stay alive as long as possible.

There are people who've been surviving here longer than you realize.

It was the way Blair had said it that made the comment stick in Dee's mind. As if she was hinting at a secret. Was there actually a place on the island without cameras?

If so, Dee needed to find it. No cameras meant no murders.

Exploring the island by herself was probably in the Top Three Stupidest Things to Do on Alcatraz 2.0. She would ask Blair about it first, as soon as she arrived at I Scream.

Dee finished the lasagna, then dumped the tray unceremoniously into the trash bin under the sink, and though she was still hungry, she decided to save the apple for later. She could have killed for a cup of coffee—literally, perhaps, if killing other inmates wasn't against the island's rules—but decided some fresh morning air might do the trick instead, so she threw the lock on the sliding glass door and wandered out onto her patio.

The sun was above the horizon now, tingeing the gray fog with a yellow glow, and already Dee could feel its warming presence as the wet blanket slowly began its retreat. Blair was right: things did look brighter when the sun was shining. Literally and figuratively.

Well, except for the lawn furniture. The wicker had a thin layer of moss or mold (or both) growing on its surface. Yeah, Dee wasn't going to be doing any sunbathing on those nasty things. She sighed, turning to go back inside, and came face-to-face with a pair of green eyes staring at her through one of the gaps in the fence.

Like Griselda, Mara appeared to be a few years older than Dee. She wore jeans and a green corduroy blazer buttoned over a plain pin-striped blouse. Her auburn hair was swept back into a low braid, and her green eyes were even more vivid in the daylight. She kind of looked like a prep-school student, and Dee was instantly jealous of her jeans and sensible outerwear.

Instead of darting away the moment she made eye contact like she had last night, Mara just stared. Was Dee supposed to say something? Introduce herself? Blair had said Mara was kind of standoffish, but the silent stare was starting to creep her out.

"I'm Dee," she said. "I just got here yesterday."

Mara cocked her head to the side as if to say *Duh, everyone knows who you are.*

Right. Cinderella Survivor was the new celebrity on Alcatraz 2.0. Great. "And you're Mara." *Who did* you *murder to end up here?*

But instead of acknowledging that it was, in fact, her name, Mara turned on her heel and hurried back inside her house, drawing the sliding door closed behind her.

So her neighbor either wanted nothing at all to do with her or was completely nuts. Maybe both. An antisocial lunatic next door. Just one more fun thing to deal with on Alcatraz 2.0.

Postman Forum * Roster * Prince Slycer * Pretty Pretty Princess

Thread: Pretty Pretty Princess

Nov-8, 8:27 a.m. **#1**
ChoppinChopin2017 Join Date: December 2017
Murdering music one note at a time Posts: 587

PM has totally redeemed himself. Princess wardrobe FTW!

Nov-8, 8:29 a.m. **#2**
MiamiSilenceMachine Join Date: March 2018
The Third Hardy Girl Posts: 112

> <<Originally posted by ChoppinChopin2017>>
> *PM has totally redeemed himself. Princess wardrobe FTW!*

She literally looks like Rainbow Brite orgasmed all over her.

Nov-8, 8:33 a.m. **#3**
321Podcast Join Date: January 2018
This is where I write something funny, right? Posts: 18,555

Stay classy, Miami Silence Machine.

Nov-8, 8:38 a.m. **#4**
MiamiSilenceMachine Join Date: March 2018
The Third Hardy Girl Posts: 113

Please, you were thinking it.

Nov-8, 8:40 a.m. **#5**
Snow Queen in Winter Join Date: August 2017
Yes, I want to build a snowman Posts: 12,576

OMG FINALLY! I've been DYING for an everyday princess wardrobe! OMG OMG OMG OMG I'm so jealous. I want that closet SO BAD. Postman, can you do an auction for her clothes after she bites it? Please please pretty please with sugar on top?

Nov-8, 8:42 a.m. **#6**
ChoppinChopin2017 Join Date: December 2017
Murdering music one note at a time Posts: 588

Jealous? Like you'd have lasted five minutes in Slycer's maze.

Nov-8, 8:43 a.m. **#7**
Snow Queen in Winter Join Date: August 2017
Yes, I want to build a snowman Posts: 12,577

If I knew there was a Snow Queen dress waiting in my closet back home, I'd have taken out ALL the killers.

Nov-8, 8:43 a.m. **#8**
321Podcast Join Date: January 2018
This is where I write something funny, right? Posts: 18,556

Honestly, I think it's degrading to women. Bad enough Slycer only chased young women through his mazes, now The Postman is making #CinderellaSurvivor conform to some kind of puritanical feminine norm?

Nov-8, 8:45 a.m. **#9**
ChoppinChopin2017 Join Date: December 2017
Murdering music one note at a time Posts: 589

> <<Originally posted by Snow Queen in Winter>>
> *OMG FINALLY! I've been DYING for an everyday princess wardrobe! OMG OMG OMG OMG I'm so jealous. I want that closet SO BAD. Postman, can you do an auction for her clothes after she bites it? Please please pretty please with sugar on top?*

YES! And how could #CinderellaSurvivor NOT go immediately for the yellow Beauty dress? Is she BLIND? Fine, the Sleeping Beauty is cool but OMG BEAUTY!!! *swoons*

TWELVE

AS SHIT-TASTIC AS ALCATRAZ 2.0 WAS, DEE FELT EMPOWERED by taking control of her day. Back home, she'd been driven to school, picked up from school, and supervised at activities, rarely getting a moment alone. Not that Dee blamed her dad for his overprotectiveness in the wake of what she'd been through, but despite the fact that she was, technically, in prison, Dee's morning commute to I Scream was the freest she'd felt since before her abduction.

She liked the way the island looked as the fog was slowly beaten away by sunlight and warmth, its wispy tendrils snaking around the duplexes in her neighborhood. Greenery bloomed all around her, flowering grasses and overgrown shrubbery, and the birds—the real ones, not the creepy camera ones—chirping away in the trees were contagiously cheerful. At the end of the Barracks, Dee noticed a sign she'd missed the night before: NINTH STREET. That sounded so normal, so suburban. There were probably Eighth and Tenth Streets as well. Utterly and completely ordinary.

A motor buzzed in the distance, growing louder with each passing second until a drone whizzed overhead, flying off toward the far end of the island. Okay, "normal" except for the ever-present cameras waiting to film her imminent death. That wasn't ordinary at all.

Ninth Street appeared to be the main commuting route between the Barracks and Main Street, and Dee wasn't the only person heading into work. A woman about Blair's age with two-inch-long dark roots growing beneath bleached-blond hair hurried past Dee. She didn't look up, her eyes fixed to the pavement, and her mouth was screwed up to the side as if she was deep in thought.

Dee involuntarily slowed her pace, allowing some distance between herself and the woman. As with Mara, Dee wondered who she had been convicted of killing. Significant other? Total stranger? Coworker? Several other inmates followed—a rail-thin brunette in a tweed pantsuit, a short blond guy who walked with a slight limp, a man with dreadlocks and a heavy parka. They all raced by her, not even acknowledging her presence. Did they know who she was? Did they want to stay as far away from Cinderella Survivor as was humanly possible? That was just fine with Dee.

"Damn, girl," a male voice said from close behind her. "Your booty looks fine in that thing."

Dee glanced over her shoulder. A heavyset man with oily hair trailed behind her, eyeing her backside with a blatant leer. She quickened her pace and said nothing, but instead of taking the hint, he sped up to join her.

"I love that The Postman's been sending us these fine pieces of ass recently," he said. Normally, Dee would have kneed him in the balls and run for her life, but Blair's warning about killing other inmates loomed heavy. Did that apply to *maiming* other inmates as well?

So Dee ignored him, hoping he'd just give up and leave her alone. No such luck.

"What?" he said, his voice indignant. "I don't get a thank-you for the compliment?"

She wanted to point out that being called a fine piece of ass was in no way a compliment, but before she could respond, the guy grabbed her by the wrist.

"Think you're too good for me, huh?" he growled, shoving his face close to hers as he looped his other arm around her back. His breath smelled like dead animal, and his eyes were wild and bloodshot, as if he hadn't slept in weeks.

Dee tried to wrench away, but the arm around her back was like iron, and the hand on her wrist held her so fiercely she was starting to lose circulation.

"You wanna know what I did to the last bitch who thought she could ignore me?" he said. "That's what landed me here. Good story. It might just turn you on."

Panic overwhelmed her. She opened her mouth to scream for help, unsure if anyone would even come to her rescue, when suddenly the guy let her go. Flung her away, in fact, as if he'd discovered that she was toxic to the touch. All the color had drained out of his face, and he glanced nervously at the nearest crow cameras, all five of them pointed directly at Dee and her assailant with their tiny red lights. Without another word, he turned and ran.

Dee stood in the middle of the street, panting, as the guy rounded the corner and disappeared onto Main Street. What in the hell had just happened?

"Penny for your thoughts."

Dee screamed. Her heart leaped up through her throat and she instinctively swung her fist around toward the voice. Nyles managed to dodge in time to avoid a punch to the face, taking the impact of Dee's swing on his shoulder instead.

"Oh my God!" Dee cried when she realized who it was. "I'm so sorry."

"Bloody hell!" Nyles staggered. "That hurt."

"You shouldn't have snuck up on me like that."

"I wasn't exactly stealthy, you know." Nyles rotated his shoulder, easing out the impact of Dee's fist. "Besides, you'd been talking to Rodrigo."

"We were *not* talking," Dee said, her voice still shaky.

"Ah," Nyles said after a pause. "Yes, I've heard the rumors. Did he hurt you?"

"No," Dee lied.

Then he chuckled to himself. "No wonder he was running away from you like the Devil was chasing him. He must have realized that you're Cinderella Survivor. He'll leave you alone from now on."

Right. She was famous, The Postman's newest star and the Painiacs' newest target. None of the other inmates would want that kind of notoriety by association. Except for Nyles, who had diplomatic immunity.

"Are you okay?" Dee asked as Nyles rubbed the spot where she'd punched him.

"Well, I'm still on this island," Nyles said, "so my answer will be relative."

Despite her vow not to let herself get attached to anyone on Alcatraz 2.0, Dee smiled. "I'll assume your snark means that you're not permanently damaged."

"Rather." He grinned. "Not a bad shot, by the way. I bet Ethan could give you some pointers, though."

"Yeah?" It had never occurred to Dee that she could improve her self-defense. But it probably wouldn't be a bad idea. "So weird that Alcatraz two-point-oh has a gym."

"It's more entertaining to watch us attempt to defend ourselves and then fail utterly. Like Jeremy. He was one of Ethan's clients. Spent the last month bulking up, apparently in an attempt to swim for it." Nyles turned to her, eyebrows raised. "Never a good idea, that."

"So I've noticed."

They walked in silence, Nyles still rubbing his shoulder. As they turned onto Main Street, Dee noticed another sign she'd missed last night, affixed to the streetlamp on the corner, with brightly colored letters: WELCOME TO ALCATRAZ 2.0, YOUR HOME AWAY FROM HOME.

Perched on top of the sign was a crow-shaped camera.

Charming sense of humor, Mr. Postman.

"You said yesterday . . ." Dee began, her eyes fixed on the crow as they passed.

"Yes?"

She wasn't sure how much she could trust Nyles, or how much he'd be willing to trust her. But she needed to ask about those cameras. "You said yesterday that nothing happened on this island unless there was a camera around to see it."

"I did," he said cheerfully. "Absolutely true. You saw what happened with Jeremy."

"They left him alone until the drones arrived," Dee replied. But that wasn't what she wanted to know. "And you also said that not every spot on the island was covered by cameras."

Nyles stopped. His eyes darted back and forth as if he was looking for something or someone. "I didn't say that."

"You implied it."

"No," he said sharply. "I didn't."

Why was he being so stubborn? "When we were walking home, you pointed to the softball field and—"

Without warning, Nyles threw his arm around Dee's waist, pulled her body into his, and kissed her.

Dee wasn't sure if it was the pure shock of Nyles's action or the fact that, technically, she'd never kissed a boy before, but instead of pushing him away, she let Nyles kiss her.

When he released her, he was blushing bright crimson.

"What the *hell* was that?" Dee asked, sounding angrier than she felt.

"Uh, I believe I just kissed you."

"Yeah, I know." Her lips still buzzed. "Why?"

Nyles's blush deepened as he shrugged. "No reason."

"No reason? I was asking you a simple question about the cameras on the island and then from out of the blue you just—"

Before she knew what was happening, Nyles had enveloped her again. His kiss was stronger this time, more forceful. She was about to knee him in the crotch and run for it, when she heard his voice in her ear.

"Can't . . . talk . . . here," he whispered in momentary gasps as he broke away from the kiss.

Just as suddenly as he'd seized her, Nyles let her go and stood there, smiling sheepishly. His eyes were apologetic, and Dee realized that the kisses had been a cover, a way to tell her to shut the fuck up without drawing attention to the fact that he was telling her to shut the fuck up. Because, as always, someone was watching. And listening. The kiss was just a fake.

And as the heat rose in her own cheeks, Dee wasn't quite sure if she was relieved by that or horribly disappointed.

THIRTEEN

"YOU'RE LATE," GRISELDA ANNOUNCED THE INSTANT THE SILver bell stopped tinkling. "Blair *won't* be impressed."

"My fault," Nyles said, his chipper mask firmly back in place.

"Yeah, I saw you two sucking face. Princess doesn't waste any time."

Dee was getting tired of being Griselda's punching bag. "I'm sure Ethan would be more than happy to give you a good face sucking."

"Oooh, Princess bites back?" Griselda cooed, feigning fear. "I'm so scared."

"I pack quite a punch," Dee said, narrowing her eyes.

Nyles raised his hand. "I can attest to that."

Griselda rolled her eyes. "What is this Candy Land outfit you've put together today? I thought The Postman had better taste than—"

An electronic doorbell blared through the shop. *Ding-dong! Ding-dong!* The notification for The Postman app: he always rings twice. At that very moment, the sound effect was flooding houses, schools, malls, and movie theaters across the country as millions of cell phones and tablets alerted users that a new murder was about to go live.

Griselda blanched as she turned to the screen above the door. Nyles clenched his jaw, his knuckles white as he gripped the counter with both hands. Dee didn't want to look, didn't want to witness another death even if it was a stranger's, but she couldn't look away.

At first, the screen was dark. In the upper left corner, the word LIVE blinked in a bright yellow block font, letting everyone know that this wasn't a replay or an edited version of events. Then the camera feed switched on, and Dee was staring at an elaborately decorated set.

She knew it was Gucci Hangman even before the silk scarves fluttered across the screen. The set was over-the-top and lush—Gucci's signature. Heavy brocade curtains fringed with gold tassels draped the wall behind a velvet tufted ottoman in deep lavender. Gold-painted Sphinx statues flanked the ottoman, poised on top of a cheetah-print rug. The lighting was muted orange, flickering as if a fire was raging just out of view of the camera, and smoke from burning sticks of incense snaked around four marble-esque columns, one of which stood sentry at each corner of the space. At the top of each column hung a wicker basket.

Through the TV speakers, a muffled cry emanated offscreen, followed by scraping sounds. Moments later, Gucci appeared in the frame.

He'd really outdone himself for the occasion, matching his ornate set with an equally gaudy outfit. He was in drag, just like in all the posters Monica had of him, and today's costume was a rococo masterpiece: a fitted midi dress in a thick, shimmery fabric of burgundy and gold paisley that perfectly complemented his dark brown skin but looked exactly like something Dee's *abuela*, who had died when she was ten, would have picked to upholster a sofa. The dress had ruffled sequined cuffs and a matching collar, and Gucci had paired it with pearl-studded Mary Jane platforms. His face was swathed in an enormous Gucci scarf, bearing the designer's mirror-image *G* logo, that left Dee wondering if the Italian design house had paid for product placement.

Gucci leaned forward as he lumbered into view, and soon Dee

understood the scraping sound: he was pulling a giant burlap sack behind him.

With impressive grace, considering his footwear, Gucci swung the bag up onto the ottoman. Someone inside whimpered as Gucci untied the sack, whisked it upside down, and poured the contents onto the tufted velvet.

And by "contents," Dee meant a person. A person she knew.

"Blair?"

Though it was difficult to see the face of the woman bound and gagged in Gucci's kill room, the blue-streaked hair gave Blair away even before Gucci raised her face to the camera so that the audience could get a good view. Blair's copious blue eye shadow was gone, and it looked as if she was wearing pajamas—a heather-gray tank top and matching ankle-length bottoms—which meant she had probably been taken from her house after she'd gotten ready for bed. Despite her rules, had Blair fallen asleep last night, thinking that since The Postman had already had Dee's encounter with Slycer and Jeremy's failed escape attempt rerun ad nauseam, it might be safe? Or had she been taken in the morning, trying to grab a little rest before she went to I Scream for the afternoon shift?

Gucci arranged her on the ottoman, fussing over her position like a photographer setting up a shot.

Which he is, I guess.

Blair was gagged with another Gucci scarf, this one an iridescent silver, though her ankles and wrists were tightly bound with plastic zip ties. Gucci sat Blair upright, feet planted on the ottoman with her knees bent in front of her and her wrists bound together beneath them.

Blair didn't struggle. She didn't scream or panic or give Gucci any kind of satisfaction that she was afraid. It was a ballsy thing to do, an act of resistance, and Dee deeply admired her for it.

Once he was satisfied with her position, Gucci pranced out of the shot. Music started, some kind of Euro electropop crap, and when Gucci returned moments later, he had a bundle of scarves flung over one shoulder. They were all the same—long and beige with the Gucci diamond pattern and the trademark red and green stripes running down one side. Gucci made a show of them, a magician presenting his props to the audience so that they could be inspected for authenticity. He whisked one off his shoulder, flourishing it around the room like a rhythmic gymnast going for gold, and timed his dance to the beat of the irritating music while he formed a slipknot at one end.

Dee's stomach tightened. "Can't we do something?" She wanted to run out of the shop and down the street toward the warehouse district from which Nyles had escorted her yesterday. That had to be where Blair was being held.

"Like what, Princess?" Griselda said, turning her cold blue eyes on Dee. "*Save* her?"

"Um . . ." *Yeah, kinda.* "Nyles might know—"

"I have no idea where Gucci has her," Nyles said softly, clearly reading Dee's mind. "I was only privy to Slycer's warehouse because it was your first day. Otherwise, the Painiacs' kill locations are a closely guarded secret."

Dee wasn't about to give up. "But we could—"

"There are kill rooms spread across the island," he said, cutting off her thought as if he knew exactly what she was going to say. "Blair could be back in Slycer's warehouse or two dozen other places. By the time we found out which one, she'd be gone."

Gone. The word echoed in Dee's head. She felt the panic welling up inside again, more so than when she'd been a victim in Slycer's maze. The helplessness of watching Blair on a live feed somewhere nearby was even more unbearable. "So, we just do *nothing*?" she asked.

Griselda shook her head. "I told you yesterday, the sooner you get used to the fact that you're going to die, the happier you'll be."

"Happy? *Really?* Is that what we're going for here?"

Griselda didn't answer.

Blair now had four different scarf nooses around her neck, each laced through a metal loop at the top of one of the columns and tied to whatever sat in the baskets tethered to their sides. Gucci was perched on a bedazzled footstool, finishing the last knot of his creation; then he climbed down, placed the stool out of frame, and removed the gag from Blair's mouth.

"Blair Huang," Gucci said in his stiff, deep voice. "You have been found guilty of murdering your elderly neighbor in order to inherit her estate. Do you have any last words?"

Blair glared at him, defiant to the end. "Fuck y—"

"Too late!" Gucci cried. Then he pulled a tasseled cord hanging from the nearest column.

Instantly, the bottom of each wicker basket dropped out, releasing massive kettlebells to which the scarves had been tied. From all four directions, the neckwear went taut, cinching the nooses closed.

Dee wasn't sure if the force of the kettlebells had snapped Blair's neck instantly or what, but she never struggled. Her body twitched once, her eyes wide and dilated, and then went limp as her head was severed at the neck and catapulted through the air like a popped champagne cork.

Dee wanted to scream, but she was afraid that if she opened her mouth, she'd puke all over herself. She couldn't even blink; her eyes were riveted to the screen as Blair's decapitated body pitched to one side, blood oozing from her open neck.

The shot jiggled and then zoomed in on Blair's body, as if Gucci had removed the camera from a tripod and walked across the room with it.

Blair's torso was covered in blood, which soaked into her pajamas, and the skin around her throat was jagged and torn from the force of the strangulation. The white bones of Blair's spine jabbed upward toward the skull that had been ripped away.

Gucci placed an object on the cushion beside the body, and Dee's stomach convulsed again as she realized it was a head. She wanted to look away, but her eyes were locked onto Blair's, which were still open, unseeing, as Gucci's heavily ringed hand rotated it to stare at its own body.

Fucking asshole. How would he *feel if someone ripped his head off, huh?* He *deserved it, not Blair. Even if she'd been guilty of the crime for which she'd been convicted, would she really have deserved* this*?*

But as she watched the screen, Dee saw something that turned her boiling rage to fear. Gucci pushed Blair's body onto its side, then pulled one thin sleeve of her tank top away, exposing the front of the shoulder. In his hand, he held an item that Dee instantly recognized—a pair of tweezers, hot pink with white polka dots—which he used to slowly carve something into Blair's flesh.

A heart.

🕒 4m

Reginald Houseman @reggiedahouseparty
Holy shit, did you see that? Blair's head was like watching an Andre Drummond free throw. #AirBall #TeamGucci #DragQueensDoItRight
← ‖: 301 ₪: 44

🕒 4m

Tamara Gucci @thirdex-mrsgucci
Totally #OBE in @GucciHangman's throne room. That's #OutofBodyExperience, noobs. #TeamGucci
← ‖: 323 ₪: 65

🕒 4m

Naydeen Doyle @NAYDEEEEEEEEEEEN
I give the latest @GucciHangman execution 4/10 stars. The #AirBall was nice, but nothing like the creativity of a @TheRobinsHood scene. #MerryMen #Nottinghamdom
← ‖: 48 ₪: 13

🕒 3m

Jazzy Jayson @doctorfusionbebop
THAT WAS A TOTAL #deCRAPitation! Cuz I'm pretty sure that Asian chick crapped her pants when @GucciHangman squeezed her head off. See what I did there?
← ‖: 86 ₪: 36

🕒 3m

Morris Davis @morrisdavis72195
#TeamGucci weighs in with godlike praise per usual. Do these tasteless cretins not watch other kills? This was bush league compared to @TheMollyMauler. Give me her Colosseum ANY DAY OF THE WEEK AND TWICE ON SUNDAY PLZ!
← ‖: 665 ₪: 240

3m

The Griff @awakewideopen

There's no way that was real, people! A decapitation like that would be unconstitutional under the prohibition of cruel and unusual punishment. WAKE UP AND SMELL THE FAKENESS! #FakeNews #EyesOpen #DontTrustTheFeed

←　　　　　: 87　　　　　: 65

2m

Squirrel WOMAN @boyimnotyourgirl

Not sure who's crazier: The #Postman deniers or the #MerryMen. @TheRobinsHood better than @GucciHangman? Are you on crack? #TeamGucci #AirBall #FTW

←　　　　　: 52　　　　　: 18

2m

Heather Oesterman @heatherfromTampa

Um, will someone explain to me WTF that heart means? Using tweezers to carve a heart into her body seems really out of character for @GucciHangman. Do. Not. Like.

←　　　　　: 177　　　　　: 60

FOURTEEN

DEE CONTINUED TO SEE THE IMAGE OF THE BLOODY HEART long after it had disappeared from the screen. The main video feed was showing a slo-mo replay of Blair's final moments, pausing at key intervals to add pop-up arrows and snarky commentary.

<PAUSE> "This is gonna smart!" with an arrow pointing to one of the kettlebells as it was released from its basket.

<PAUSE> "Another brutal killer bites the dust."

<PAUSE> "Hope you like a tight fit!" as the nooses began to tighten.

<PAUSE> "Air ball!" as Blair's head catapulted through the air.

Millions of people were viewing The Postman's replay, and their comments flooded the sidebar. #AirBall was instantly popular, followed closely by #deCRAPitation and #OBE or #OutofBodyExperience, and the spikes tally rose exponentially. Ninety thousand. Five hundred thousand. One million.

What about Blair's viewership rule? Weren't ratings supposed to be higher in the evening? This was midmorning, and Blair's murder had racked up a million spikes within minutes.

But while a small nugget in the back of her brain was registering these facts, the heart carving was all-consuming. It wasn't a coincidence. Dee rejected that possibility out of hand. Etching a heart in the flesh of a dead woman's shoulder? Okay, not totally out of the realm of possibility for one of the Painiacs, but the needle-point tweezers, pink with white polka dots . . .

Was Gucci trying to send Dee a message? That was her initial reaction, but there was no way Gucci could have known about her finding the tweezers, which left only one option. . . .

Had Gucci Hangman killed Monica?

It made no sense. MoBettaStylz was one of Gucci's biggest fans, probably adding to his merchandise sales through her following. So why would he kill her? Besides, The Postman's killers didn't murder outside Alcatraz 2.0 for fear of winding up as inmates themselves.

Maybe the tweezers were a coincidence, and Gucci was using the heart to tell Dee that she would be the next one to die. The marking on Monica's body was public record, so it was *almost* plausible.

Dee staggered over to a table, knees wobbly and unsure, and sat down. "Shit."

"The first time it's someone you know," Nyles said gently, pulling out the chair beside her, "is always the hardest to watch. At least she didn't suffer."

"Oh yeah," Griselda said, her voice sharp as glass. "I'm sure she didn't feel a fucking thing when her head was ripped out of her spine."

"*Off* her spine," Nyles corrected. "Technically the vertebral column ends at the atlas or C-one vertebra, which forms the joint connecting the skull to the spine, although . . ." He squinted at the screen, taking a closer look at the freeze-frame on the bones protruding from the gory stump that used to be Blair's neck. "Although, it appears that the C-three or the C-four is still attached, which would mean that at least some of the traditional spine was in fact removed with Blair's head, so I suppose in some regard your description was accurate." He turned back to Dee. "I was premed at Stanford."

Griselda stared at him blankly. "Why do I talk to you?"

"The point," Nyles said, resuming his bedside manner, "is that the first one you watch is always the worst. It gets easier."

Easier? Was Dee supposed to find comfort in the fact that eventually she'd get used to watching someone she knew get decapitated in front of a live audience? "It shouldn't."

"I'm so glad you're here to tell us these things," Griselda cried, clasping her hands together in mock excitement. "We really need Princess's moral superiority to point out what horrible bitches we've become."

"Gris," Nyles began, "she didn't mean—"

"Shut up, Nyles," she snapped. "Just because you shoved your tongue down her throat doesn't mean you can make excuses for her. Like somehow I don't care that Blair's dead because I'm not pale and trembling and ready to pass out."

Griselda's words implied that she was truly broken up about Blair's death, and yet she didn't seem to be affected at all. Even Nyles was paler than usual, but Griselda's voice was steady, her breathing normal, and her entire demeanor was calm. It was either the greatest display of self-control Dee had ever seen, or she really wasn't bothered by what she'd just witnessed.

"Besides," Griselda continued, narrowing her eyes, "Princess *should* be upset. She's probably the reason Blair got killed in the first place."

"Gris!" Nyles's voice was sharp, but hardly above a whisper.

Dee caught her breath. "What do you mean?"

"Blair flew under the radar for months," Griselda said with a shrug. "Then you show up, she's nice to you, and boom, dead within twenty-four hours."

"Now, Gris, you're being ridiculous." Nyles stood up, gingerly shifting his body weight back and forth between his feet as if the floor of I Scream were strewn with red-hot coals.

"How?" Griselda countered. "Because I'm picking on your new girlfriend?"

Nyles and Griselda bickered, but their voices faded into the background. Could Dee actually have caused Blair's death? She thought of Mara, who clearly wanted nothing to do with her, of Rodrigo the molester, who'd been ready to get busy until he realized who she was, and the other inmates hurrying by on their way to work, avoiding all contact.

Griselda was right. Sure, Gucci could have carved that heart into anyone's shoulder, but he'd just so happened to choose someone with whom Dee had established a connection. This was Cinderella Survivor's fault. Her and her twenty million spikes.

Blair's death was on Dee's head, just like Monica's.

I'll kill you and everyone you love. . . .

In an instant, Dee was eleven years old again, back in that white doorless room, trying desperately to figure out what the girl in the vent wanted from her, trying to guess what answers would keep her alive. *Why is this happening? Is it something I did? Is it my fault?*

There were secrets Kimmi had shared that Dee had never revealed to anyone. Not even the police. She'd been too terrified. "If you ever tell anyone," Kimmi had said, "I'll kill you and everyone you love. Promise me you won't tell. PROMISE!"

And so Dee had kept her mouth shut about the secrets of the white room. For six years. Until she'd broken down and shared them with someone.

Monica.

Two weeks later, she was dead.

Was the pattern repeating itself? The last time Dee had trusted someone, that someone had ended up dead, strangled on the floor of her bedroom with a heart carved into her shoulder.

Why is this happening? Is it my fault?

Monica wouldn't have been Dee's first choice of stepsister. They were nothing alike. Dee was dark and jaded, and though her dad had kept her in therapy for years after her abduction, it hadn't seemed to do much good. She had shied away from personal relationships, finding it too difficult to trust anyone. Somewhere along the line, Dee had stopped blaming herself for the abduction and starting blaming everyone else: strangers, friends, maybe even her dad. During the three years since her kidnapping, her anger had simmered, waiting to explode, and Dee had isolated herself from her peers, unwilling to let anyone inside.

She'd eat lunch alone in the library, scribbling poems into her notebook just as she had when she was a kid. Back then, her compositions were about the great sadness of her young life—the loneliness of being an only child. She'd even had one of them published in the local paper:

My heart wants a sibling,
A friend to call my own
But I don't know what it means
To have a sister or a clone.

But that was before the white room. After, Dee's poems reflected the darkness and panic that plagued her, which she feared would haunt her forever.

Monica was the exact opposite. Perky and lighthearted, nothing seemed to bother her. They'd been in the same class together since sixth grade, when Dee and her dad had moved to Burbank and assumed new names. When their parents started dating two years later, and then got serious, Dee vowed that she and Monica would never be friends.

Apparently, though, Monica never got that memo. After they'd all moved in together their freshman year of high school, Dee made it clear at every meeting—whether brushing teeth side by side in their Jack-and-Jill bathroom or eating meals across the table from each other—that they were not, and never would be, friends. And every single time, Monica flashed her kind, warm smile and tried again.

It had taken a year, but Dee had finally relented.

They'd bonded over something totally unexpected: a book. Dee read voraciously, an escape from her life and her memories and her decisions. But she'd never seen Monica pick up a book that wasn't required reading for school. Then one day, when Dee was reading *Jane Eyre* for the umpteenth time, Monica walked in and said, "I love Mr. Rochester."

"You've read *Jane Eyre*?" Dee had asked.

Monica had flashed her warm smile. "Of course! I love a good romance about broken people."

Broken people. Dee had never quite understood why she loved that book, but those two words encapsulated it perfectly.

Suddenly it was as if the floodgates had opened. Every human interaction that Dee had avoided since her days in the white room came rushing back tenfold. She wanted Monica's friendship, her approval, her input. And being friends with Monica led to hanging out with Monica's friends. By the end of sophomore year, Dee had a circle, a community, and for the first time in years she participated in activities at school. She even contributed a few of her poems to her high school's literary magazine.

And then, one day, the inevitable: Dee told Monica Kimmi's secret.

They'd been hanging out by the pool in the backyard, enjoying the late Southern California summer, when Monica asked Dee about her kidnapping. Just like that, out of the blue. They'd never talked about it before, and Monica's question caught Dee off guard.

It wasn't the first time she'd told the story. Detectives had heard it. Psychologists had heard it. Her dad. But those hadn't been voluntary. Monica was the first person who heard everything.

Dee told Monica about waking up in the white room, about meeting Kimmi, who she initially thought was a prisoner like herself. Eventually, Dee realized that Kimmi was her abductor, the one holding her there for her own amusement. It had seemed strange to Dee that a teenager could be so vicious, but then Kimmi had talked about her father, and then Dee had understood.

"Her dad," Dee began, her heart pounding in her chest as she related the secret of the white room to Monica. *I'll kill everyone you love. . . .*

"Yeah?"

Dee swallowed down her fear. Kimmi was locked away. It was time to unburden herself. "That room she kept me in. Kimmi said her dad had killed people in there. Many times. She knew because she'd watched a lot of them from the vent. She said he'd made the room white because he liked the way blood looked when it spilled onto the white floor."

It had felt good to tell someone after all those years. The final weight of her trauma removed.

"She was just trying to scare you." Monica had smiled. "I'm sure no one ever died in the white room."

"Yeah," Dee had said. "You're probably right."

At the time of Dee's escape, Kimmi's threat had felt overwhelming, and even though she'd been sent off to a mental hospital for an indeterminate period of confinement, Dee had always felt as though Kimmi would follow through on her threat if Dee ever told anyone about the room.

Still, Dee had never seen Kimmi's dad during her imprisonment, so maybe Monica was right, and Kimmi had made up the story to terrorize her victim.

But what if it was true? What if, by not telling anyone, Dee had ensured that Kimmi's dad was never arrested and more people died in the white room?

The guilt had eaten away at her for years, finally overcoming her fear. And so she'd told someone she trusted.

Then, in the blink of an eye, Monica was dead, and Dee was on trial for her murder.

Dee pushed her childhood fears aside. Kimmi was not responsible for Monica's death. But now Dee was convinced that Gucci Hangman, or whoever he was in the real world, was connected to her stepsister's murder. She just needed a way to prove it.

"Griselda's right," Dee said, cutting into Nyles and Griselda's steady stream of bickering.

"About what?" Griselda asked, eyebrow arched. "That you raided a kindergartner's closet when you got dressed this morning, or that you're the root of all evil?"

Neither? "Blair. It's my fault. I think she was killed because of my—"

Again, from out of nowhere, Nyles swooped in. He cupped her face in his hands and planted his lips on hers.

"Now you're just doing it on purpose," Griselda whispered as Nyles broke away.

Before Dee could answer, Ethan barreled through the door, throwing it open with his beefy arms. "Dude, I'm so sorry about Blair."

Griselda tried to act like nothing bothered her. "Why, did *you* kill her?"

"No." Ethan tilted his head to the side. "But you guys were friends and shit. Right?"

"Friends die," she said plainly. "That's how it is here." Again, not an ounce of real feeling penetrated her mask.

Ethan hoisted himself up on the counter and reached out to take her hand. "I know you're sad on the inside."

"Sad for *you*," she retorted.

Ethan beamed at her, as if Griselda had just given him the loveliest compliment in the world, and for a moment Dee was jealous of his ability to find happiness in just about anything.

Meanwhile, Nyles eyed Dee closely. "Gris," he said at last, holding his debit card out to her. "I'm in the mood for a milk shake. One of your special creations. One for Dee, too. Would you mind?"

"Seriously?" Griselda asked.

He tossed his debit card onto the counter. "I'm afraid so."

She sighed heavily, as if she'd just been asked to do a chore she loathed, then smacked Ethan on the arm. "Get me a bag of ice from the freezer."

While Ethan bounded off to the back room like a puppy excited to be tossed a bone, Griselda snatched Nyles's card, then stomped around behind the counter, slamming cupboard doors and cooler windows as she gathered ingredients. Chocolate syrup, vanilla ice cream, bananas.

Nyles continued to smile, his enormous teeth fully exposed. The grin looked as if it was plastered on his face, held there by an elaborate concoction of duct tape and staples. "You're going to love this," he said, his cheeks twitching with the effort to keep smiling. "I promise."

Dee had no idea why, but clearly Nyles wanted her to play along, to keep her conversation light and generic and absolutely devoid of questions or explanations like the one she'd been about to give when he kissed her. Again.

"I'm sure I will," she said slowly.

Ethan returned, a heavy bag of ice slung over one shoulder. He deposited it in the sink behind the counter, and Griselda proceeded to grab handfuls of cubes and dump them into the industrial-size blender. It was a lot of ice, more than the ratio of ice cream, syrup, and fruit necessitated, and when she slapped on the lid and fired up the blender, the grating of the blades against the ice filled the entire shop with a deafening roar.

Which was, apparently, exactly what Nyles had wanted.

The instant the noise flooded her ears, he leaned forward, his breath hot on her cheek, and whispered just loud enough for her to hear over the din. "Tell me why Blair was killed."

FIFTEEN

DEE OPENED HER MOUTH TO REPLY, BUT THE WORDS STUCK IN her throat. If she told Nyles the truth—that Gucci Hangman was somehow tied to her sister's murder—she'd be trusting him with some portion of her past. And not only was trusting strangers not her forte, but it also didn't end well.

But the alternative—trying to prove her innocence on her own—seemed impossible. She knew almost nothing about the island, and if there really was a way to stay alive on Alcatraz 2.0, she was going to need Nyles's help to find it.

"Blair's death had something to do with my stepsister's murder. I think Gucci Hangman was trying to send me a message."

Nyles stared at her for a moment, eyes unreadable; then he gave an almost imperceptible nod of his head. Instantly, the blender switched off and the room fell silent. Dee wasn't sure if she should say something else and risk a lip plant from Nyles or just sit quietly. She chose the latter.

"Allow me, milady," Ethan said. He grabbed four glasses from the shelf and plopped them on the counter beside Griselda, who poured out the liquefied concoction. Ethan grabbed a glass the instant she was finished, chugged it, then coughed, spraying milk shake all over the counter. "Brain freeze. Holy crap. Dying."

Griselda ignored him. She rounded the counter and set two milk shakes on the table in front of Dee and Nyles, sloshing icy brown gunk all over the place. "Well?"

Dee was pretty sure she was talking to Nyles.

He stared at the table, contemplating his glass. "Ethan," he began slowly, "how many calories would you say are in one of these?"

Ethan scrunched his mouth to the side, and held up his fingers, ticking them off like he was doing math in his head. "A lot."

So much for math.

"That was my thought exactly." He pushed a glass toward Dee, as if he wanted to make sure she had some. "I'm afraid this is going to require an extra-long workout this afternoon. A jog around the island, perhaps?"

"Definitely," Ethan replied.

Nyles leaned in. "You'll join, yes?"

Running wasn't exactly something Dee did voluntarily, but the sharp look in Nyles's eyes practically begged her to say yes.

"Um, sure?"

"Excellent." He polished off the rest of his milk shake, then rose from his chair. "Shall we say four o'clock at the gym?"

Dee's afternoon at I Scream was . . . weird.

On some level, it felt like a normal job at a normal ice-cream parlor that any seventeen-year-old anywhere in the country might have. Griselda directed Dee through cleaning and restocking the cooler, checking inventory for the walk-in freezer in the back, polishing the floors, wiping down tables, washing dishes. It was all pretty mindless, bordering on mundane.

But also totally bizarre. For instance, they had a steady stream of customers—thankfully, no Rodrigo—all of whom Griselda seemed to know. And though the tables were filled, aside from a quick hello before ordering and several clandestine glances in Dee's direction (which she absolutely noticed), no one interacted. Everyone sat alone, avoided eye contact, and refused to strike up a conversation with Dee, Griselda, or any of the other patrons.

Then there was the giant TV screen running nonstop replays of Blair's murder. Dee couldn't avoid the sounds—Gucci's synth-pop sound track, his booming voice, Blair's strangled response, and the repulsive sucking sound Blair's head made when Gucci planted it on the cushion beside her body—but she tried to keep her eyes away from the screen.

Sometimes she'd catch a glimpse of Blair's head catapulting through the air like a diseased pig carcass flung over the walls of a besieged castle by a medieval trebuchet. It was uncanny how Dee always seemed to see the same clip: a super-slo-mo shot of the decapitation. The Postman ran it forward and backward and even had a version where the image toggled between frames as Blair's head was severed. Arrows and diagrams pointed to various tendrils of gore protruding from her neck and her skull, like a fucked-up anatomy lesson in one of Nyles's premed courses, and the fan art and GIFs trending in the comments sidebar were out of control.

There was even one GIF showing Cinderella standing beside Blair's head as it cascaded through the air, staring at its underside as if in disbelief. The implication was clear: Blair's death was in retaliation for Dee's "success" against Slycer.

And then there was this cloud of secrets hanging over her head. About three dozen times during her shift, when the shop was momentarily empty, Dee was about to ask Griselda what the hell was going on. The cloak-and-dagger crap was wigging her out, and she had so many questions, she was about ready to explode.

But she didn't. Explode *or* ask Griselda. Instead she scooped and scrubbed and blended and counted, until her anxiety was too much to bear. Then she attempted small talk while Griselda took inventory during a lull.

"It's pretty quiet in here now."

"If being forced to listen to your boss getting murdered over and over again counts as quiet to you, then yes."

Point to Griselda. Dee tried again. "There are more people on Alcatraz two-point-oh than I realized."

"Only twenty-seven now," Griselda replied, her eyes fixed on her clipboard. "There were forty-eight when I arrived. Over a hundred when Nyles got here."

More than a hundred down to twenty-seven? That seemed weird, but Dee wasn't about to waste a question on it. Griselda's patience with her was already wearing thin.

"What did you do?" Dee asked, not even sure she wanted to know. "To get here."

Griselda snorted. Well, that was something. A reaction other than snark. She tossed her inventory clipboard down on the counter and planted her hands on her hips. "Six months ago, I supposedly murdered my college roommate and my boyfriend after I caught them having sex. It was a crime of passion and jealousy, full of kinky details." She paused, leaning in. "I slit their throats while they were asleep."

"Oh."

She straightened up, grabbed her clipboard, and returned to her task. "Of course I didn't do it. I mean, would I have slit their throats if I'd given a shit that they were banging? Totally. But I'm way hotter than Julie ever was, and besides, Jasper wasn't even my boyfriend, just this dude I did some hacking with once in a while. He was pretty basic—library systems, low-security shit—not in my league at all. But he had a big dick, and sometimes a girl just needs a big dick. I definitely wasn't in love with him like that bitchface shrink said I was during my trial. He wasn't my type."

These were more words than Griselda had spoken to Dee in the almost twenty-four hours they'd known each other, and Dee didn't know if Griselda was fucking with her or if she just really, really enjoyed talking about herself.

Probably both.

"Quarter to four," Griselda said, changing topics abruptly. "Time for your workout, Princess."

Even though it was an hour until closing, Griselda locked up the shop, just as Blair had done the night before. Dee wondered if this was against the rules and whether it would be reflected in their weekly money rations, but at that moment she didn't care. She was pretty sure this whole "go for a long jog" business was a cover, and she was ready to find out what Nyles, Griselda, and Ethan really knew about the island.

The building that housed the gym looked as if it had once been a hardware store, with a raised step for a window display, low ceilings, and only a half dozen pieces of equipment including a set of rusty free weights, a treadmill that would probably fall apart at a slow walking pace, and a rowing machine that might have been made of wood. Not that Dee had been to many workout facilities in her days, but she was pretty sure this one sucked.

Ethan lay on a weight bench doing chest presses. He anchored the bar and sat up as they entered. "Welcome to the party, pal."

"Party?" Dee asked.

Nyles emerged from the back room, dressed in long warm-up pants and a zip-front hoodie. "It's from an action movie," he explained. "Remember? Ethan likes to quote them. Ad nauseam."

"Not ad nauseam," Ethan said cheerfully. "That's from *Die Hard*. My fave."

"Kill me," Griselda muttered.

Ethan beckoned Dee to the back room. "Come on, let's get you suited up."

He managed to find Dee some workout clothes that almost fit. The skintight yoga pants were two sizes too small and hugged her thighs and butt so tightly she must have looked like a lumpy sausage shoved into an undersize casing. Thankfully, Ethan also found her a sweatshirt. An XXL sweatshirt. It required three rolls on each sleeve just to find her hands, and it hung like a tunic, hitting mid-quad. But at least the hideous pants sitch was hidden. The only thing that fit were the beat-up running shoes, sporting mismatched laces and a strip of duct tape along one shoe to keep the seams from splitting.

Meanwhile, Griselda looked gorgeous, of course. She wore leggings and a long-sleeve runner's shirt that fit her like they'd literally been custom-made for her body, highlighting every perfect curve and graceful angle, and the black shirt enhanced the blondness of her hair and the blueness of her eyes. Dee looked frumpy in comparison, but she reminded herself that it didn't matter. Who was she trying to impress, anyway? Not Ethan, and *certainly* not Nyles.

They started out on a slow jog from the gym, heading straight down Main Street toward the north end of the island. The gym was the last of the fake businesses on the strip, nestled beside several boarded-up storefronts: old-fashioned single-story buildings with rock siding and large windows. Beyond that was another open area, though unlike the soccer and baseball facilities near the Barracks, it looked more like an abandoned overgrown lot than a sports field.

The cameras, per usual, were everywhere. Even the deserted storefronts were each adorned with a crow-shaped atrocity that slowly rotated as they passed, and Dee began to despair of ever finding a camera-free oasis on Alcatraz 2.0.

She did her best to keep up with her obviously more athletic colleagues. Ethan jogged like a leashed puppy desperate to be untethered. He kicked his knees high in front of him, as if attempting to get more of a workout than the relatively slow pace would allow, and every few minutes he'd sprint a hundred yards ahead of them, then turn and jog back. If he'd been a different type of guy, Dee would have thought he was showing off, but Ethan was more of a hyperactive child than your average gym-obsessed twenty-something, and Dee really believed he just needed to burn off the energy.

Nyles and Griselda paced each other, running side by side in Stepford-like unison, and Dee was more aware than ever how perfectly suited they were for each other. Tall, good-looking, in shape. They even had matching blond hair. She might have thought they were siblings if she hadn't known better.

Dee lagged behind, struggling with both the exercise and the ill-fitting clothes. The sweatshirt swamped her, the pants constricted, and with every step her legs felt heavier, like she was running through wet cement.

The field gave way to industrial remains. A large pile of dirt rose like a hillock beside a row of cylindrical concrete silos that might once have been a water-treatment plant. The remains of metal trailers and shipping containers, rusted and ripped at the seams from wind and rain, lay scattered across this end of the island, which clearly had not been reclaimed as part of The Postman's plans for Alcatraz 2.0, and Dee wondered if this section, like the warehouses to the east where she'd woken up in a Cinderella dress yesterday afternoon, housed the kill rooms of the Painiacs.

Dee was too busy theorizing about her surroundings to realize that the road in front of her had come to an abrupt end until she plowed directly into Nyles's back.

"Sorry," she said, panting and stumbling to regain her balance.

Nyles looped a wiry but strong arm around her waist to keep her upright. “You’re grand. Might be good to keep your eyes in front of you, though.”

“Right,” she said, steadying herself. “Good idea.” She looked around, and noticed that a twelve-foot-high chain-link fence blocked the road. A rusted and warped warning sign clung stubbornly to it.

BIOHAZARD: QUARANTINE.

AUTHORIZED PERSONNEL ONLY.

“Where are we?” Dee whispered.

“This,” Ethan said, pulling aside a cutaway portion of chain link, “is the end of the world.”

SIXTEEN

GRISELDA PUNCHED HIM IN THE ARM. "STOP BEING STUPID." Then, without waiting for a response, she ducked through the hole in the fence and jogged down the path on the other side.

"After you, milady." Ethan gestured for Dee to follow.

Dee hesitated, remembering the unironic NO SWIMMING sign on the rock wall near the Barracks. "Um, quarantine? Biohazard? Those sound like really good reasons to stay the hell away."

Nyles laughed. "Are you afraid you might get cancer and die? I believe we're in significantly more imminent danger on Alcatraz two-point-oh."

The Brit had a point.

Still, there was the possibility that even if Hannah Ball or Cecil B. DeViolent wasn't waiting for her on the other side of the fence, convicted killers Nyles, Griselda, and Ethan might have just as sinister a plan for her. *Trusting people gets you killed faster.* But without help, she couldn't prove that she had been framed for Monica's death, and convicted killers or not, Nyles, Griselda, and Ethan were her only lifelines.

Dee took a deep breath and scurried through the fence.

If most of Alcatraz 2.0 looked as if no one had inhabited it in twenty years, the northern tip of the island was positively prehistoric. The moment Dee reached the other side of the fence, even the asphalt felt old and crumbly beneath her feet. Tall grasses with white flowers sprouting from their tips had taken root in the cracks of the blacktop, some growing almost as tall as Dee's five feet three inches. They swayed in the wind, obscuring the warped ridges in the road as their roots slowly displaced modern technology.

Bushes spread out of control. Trees flourished, some so overgrown that their branches were sagging beneath their own weight. No power lines or cell-phone towers marred the landscape, and the only signs left that people had once inhabited this part of the island were the decrepit road and the foundational remains of a long-abandoned building, all but reclaimed by Mother Nature.

The sound of waves crashing against the rock wall was louder at this end of the island, which took the full brunt of the current, and the wind felt colder without the barrier of San Francisco high-rises, or even the windbreak of the Barracks.

"This was one of the old navy yards," Nyles said. He stood close behind her, Griselda on one side, Ethan on the other. "Apparently, they sent radioactive ships here to be decontaminated and cocked up the job, so the area was quarantined."

"That sounds safe," Dee said sarcastically.

But Ethan took her comment at face value. "Only safe spot on the island." He sucked in a deep breath, holding the cool air in his lungs for a second before letting it out with a whoosh. "That's why Blair let us in on the secret."

"Blair found this place?" Was this what she'd meant when she said people had been surviving on Alcatraz 2.0 longer than Dee might realize?

"Yes," Nyles said. "Blair and a few others. They're all gone now."

"And why are we here?"

"Look around." Nyles swept his arm in a circle. "What don't you see?"

It took Dee a moment to realize what he meant. "There are no cameras."

"She's not as dumb as she looks," Griselda said.

"Funny," Dee snapped back. "Can't say the same for you."

"Ouch," Ethan said, licking his forefinger. He jabbed it into his thigh and let out a hissing sound. "Burned."

"We shouldn't have brought her here," Griselda said. "I don't trust Princess not to blab about our secrets."

She had no idea how good Dee was at keeping secrets. No idea at all.

"I do," Nyles said softly.

"When this all blows up in your face," Griselda countered, "just remember *I told you so*."

Nyles shot Griselda a look as if to say *Cool it*; then he turned to Dee, his countenance more serious than it had been since they met. "What did you want to tell us about Blair's death?"

"I . . ." Dee paused, scanning the sky. "What about the drones?"

"They do occasional flybys, but nothing regular," Nyles said with a shrug. "Besides, you can hear them coming. Duck under a tree and you're out of sight."

"Okay." No cameras meant no one was watching and listening, so any secret conversations, sharing of information, or plotting of escape attempts could be carried out beyond the prying eyes and ears of both The Postman and the world. If Nyles, Griselda, and Ethan knew about this place, maybe they had other secrets that they'd share too. Anything that kept her alive was a good thing. If she was dead, Monica's real killer would never be brought to justice.

"Gucci's MO is pretty standard, right?" she began. "Elaborate sets, some version of a hanging, lots of Gucci scarves."

Nyles tilted his head. "Gucci fan, I take it?"

"No way." Dee wrinkled her nose, revolted by the thought. "But my stepsister was obsessed with him. Even ran one of Gucci's fan forums."

Griselda wandered away. "She sounds like a charmer."

"Hey!" Outbursts weren't her thing—she mostly internalized her emotions—but Griselda had gone too far. "Back off."

Griselda didn't even flinch. "Fine, so she was sweet and kind and perfect in every way. Is that why you killed her?"

"I didn't kill her!"

"Sure you didn't. You're pure and innocent while the rest of us are assholes for killing our friends and families."

"Not everyone," Dee said. "Just you."

"Sweet!" Ethan said, sitting down on the broken concrete. "Girl fight. Wish I had popcorn."

Griselda ignored him. "You think you're so fucking special, huh?" She shoved her index finger in Dee's face. "You've been here one day, Princess. One. I've been here for eighty-seven. And if you make it that long, you can act like you understand pain and suffering."

Dee clenched her jaw, so angry the world around her seemed to spin. "I've seen suffering you can't even imagine."

Nyles stepped in front of Dee. "Look, it doesn't matter, okay? Guilty or not, we're all stuck here."

"But that's just it," Dee pleaded, pushing aside her anger. "It *does* matter."

"How?" Nyles asked.

Time to explain. "The heart Gucci carved into Blair's shoulder," she said, speaking quickly. "My stepsister's killer did the same thing to her body after she was strangled."

"Post-mortem body modification is hardly unusual around here," Nyles said.

"Yes, but the heart on the shoulder," Dee began. "That's exactly what Monica's killer did after she was dead."

"Dude," Ethan said, eyebrows scrunched together. "Who is Monica?"

Griselda sighed. "Her stepsister."

"The one who died?" Ethan continued.

"How does your body keep on breathing air," Griselda said, "when your brain is *that* stupid?"

Ethan tapped his temple. "Muscle beats import every time. *Fast and Furious*. Words to live by."

Griselda sank her forehead to her knees. "I can't *even* with you."

"Dee," Nyles said, his impatience evident. "I'm sure it seemed dramatic at the time, but I don't see how Gucci's desecration of Blair's body has anything to do with you or your stepsister."

"What if I told you that Gucci used the exact same item to carve that heart as Monica's killer?"

Nyles's eyes arched up toward the sky as he tried to remember. "Which was . . ."

"A pair of needle-nose tweezers," Dee said, filling in the blank. "Hot pink with white polka dots."

"See?" Griselda said, pushing herself back up to her feet. "I told you this was her fault."

"So The Postman wants to tie Blair's death to Cinderella Survivor," Nyles mused, "by using an element from your murder trial. He does that sometimes with new—"

"No," Dee said, cutting him off. "It wasn't a part of my trial. The tweezers were never found."

"Then how do you know they were the item used?"

Dee paused. The answer to his question was not exactly going to strengthen her case for innocence. "Because I found a pair of polka-dot tweezers stashed in my bedroom. Her blood was still on them."

Nyles's brow wrinkled. "And then?"

"And then I flushed them down the toilet."

Griselda threw up her arms. "How convenient!"

"Don't you see?" Dee pleaded. "I never told anyone about those tweezers. I was scared. I thought someone was trying to frame me for her murder. Only two people know about that factoid: me and the real killer. So how did it end up on The Postman?"

Nyles's blue eyes grew wide. "You think Gucci killed your stepsister."

"Or knows who did," Dee said.

"If we can prove it . . ." he began.

"We?" Griselda interjected.

"Then we can prove you're innocent," Nyles finished.

He was getting it. Phew. "And if we can overturn *my* conviction . . ." Dee shifted her gaze from Nyles to the scowling Griselda to the utterly confused Ethan. She wasn't actually convinced that any of them were innocent, but if they felt like they had something to gain from this endeavor, they'd be more likely to help her, right? Right. "If we can prove I didn't do it, then maybe we can prove that none of you are killers either."

SEVENTEEN

"WHERE THE HELL ARE THEY?" THE POSTMAN SAID OUT LOUD, even though there was no one around to hear. That was intentional, of course. The Postman worked alone, assuming total and complete control over Alcatraz 2.0.

It was the only way it would work. There were secrets about the island that only The Postman could know, and so no strangers had been allowed into the inner workings. The Postman controlled it all from a simple computer interface, a monarch ruling the kingdom below, in charge of every aspect of its existence.

The guards at the station? They took orders directly from The Postman via e-mail and messaging. They were notified of incoming prisoners and killers alike, as well as shipments of supplies.

The Postman was even in charge of the electronic security system at the station, only releasing the lock on the weapons cabinet when needed. Like when that idiot tried to make a break for it through the water. It was The Postman who'd been alerted to the escape attempt, The Postman who'd deployed the guards and the drones, and The Postman who'd timed it all perfectly for live coverage of Jeremy's death.

The Postman controlled which of the killers would be on the island at any given time, coordinated their arrivals and departures personally, and even chose the victims. There had been heated debate on the fan forums about whether the victims were picked at random, or if the killers had personal agendas in mind when they went after a prisoner. But no one had ever suspected that The Postman directed who would be executed, and when, and by whom.

It had to be that way. For the ratings. Bad ratings meant bad profits, which meant an unhappy president of the United States. Profit was all he cared about, and as long as The Postman kept delivering, there was carte blanche on Alcatraz 2.0. Which was why certain tweaks had been made in the obtaining of prisoners.

It had been fine at first—the novelty of live-streamed executions ensured an insanely high viewership among all relevant demographics. But after a while, it became clear that watching grizzled criminals meet their bloody ends had become . . . boring.

Nancy Wu had changed all that. The martial-arts expert who'd killed a bouncer after a heated bar fight was young, attractive, exciting. The Postman had played up those aspects by controlling her wardrobe, only allowing her to wear tight leather pants and strapless corsets. Views on her camera feeds had gone through the roof, and after she killed the Caped Capuchin—who was in desperate need of being replaced anyway—Nancy Wu became a cash cow. Merchandise, ad revenue . . . the app hadn't been that profitable since its debut.

And so things had changed on Alcatraz 2.0. Arrest reports throughout the country had been scoured, searching for the young, the attractive, the interesting. A little bit of money went a long way when you already controlled part of the criminal-justice system, and even a flimsy amount of evidence against a defendant could result in a conviction. Once they were on the island, The Postman chose roles for the new arrivals, setting up relationships and dramas that would keep viewers hooked.

Now The Postman was slowly getting rid of the old, the ugly, and the uninteresting, to pave the way for a population of inmates straight out of central casting. The app was going to hit new highs in popularity. Guaranteed.

But at the moment, all of that was secondary. The master plan would have to wait, because The Postman had bigger things to deal with.

Cinderella Survivor had somehow managed to slip off the camera grid. With Blair dead, it should have taken Griselda, Ethan, and the Brit longer to trust the new girl, but clearly they'd already introduced her to the dark end of the island. Of course, The Postman could just send a drone to sweep the area.

No. Let them think they're safe.

That was when people made mistakes. Like Blair. She'd thought she was safe, what with Jeremy's death and the cold-blooded murder of Prince Slycer.

But you were never safe on Alcatraz 2.0.

Never.

EIGHTEEN

"OH, I TOTALLY KILLED SOMEONE." ETHAN LEANED BACK ON his elbows, crossing his legs at the ankles.

"You *did*?" Dee was so used to inmates professing their innocence, she was shocked to hear Ethan easily cop to his crime.

"I snapped that dude's neck." Ethan was utterly nonchalant, like he was describing what he'd eaten for breakfast. "Just twisted it and—" He stuck two fingers in his mouth, jabbing them into the fleshy part of his cheek, then flicked them out, producing a loud popping noise. "Dead."

"Ew?"

"Better him than me," Ethan said with a shrug. "Dude came after me with a freaking switchblade."

Dee couldn't imagine why anyone would want to kill Ethan. "Why?"

"He was one of my training clients at the gym. Kept trying to get me to go out with him, but I don't mix business and pleasure, you know? And then he totally lost it when he saw me on a date with this guy Kristoph."

"So it was self-defense."

"Yep," Ethan said with a grin. "But the judge disallowed the argument, and now, boom, here I am."

Dee wished she could have Ethan's carefree attitude about his current situation. But she didn't. "I shouldn't be here," she began. "And neither should you. Neither should any of you."

"Are you so sure we're all innocent, Princess?" Griselda half smiled. "Are you so sure I didn't slit Julie's and Jasper's throats in cold blood?"

"Your boyfriend's name was Jasper," Ethan said with a snort. "That always cracks my shit up."

Griselda gritted her teeth. "He wasn't my boyfriend." She pointed at Dee. "Are you so sure that Nyles didn't poison his parents with cyanide?"

Dee's eyes grew wide. "They were *poisoned*?"

Nyles nodded. "I found their bodies coiled up on the floor of their hotel room when they came to visit me at Stanford. They must have died in agony."

"I'm so sorry."

"Would you two get a room?" Griselda said.

"Cut it out, Gris," Nyles said. "You told me yourself that you were innocent, and I certainly didn't murder my own parents."

"I'm guessing you all had fast trials like I did?" Dee asked. "Railroaded through without much of a chance?"

"Due process was a bloody joke." Nyles ran his hand through his hair. "This is starting to stink of a conspiracy."

"What kind of conspiracy could there possibly be?" Griselda asked. "There are plenty of capital crimes every year to keep this place packed to the gills."

"Yet it's not, is it?" Nyles said. "The Barracks could easily hold five or six times as many as we have now."

"And isn't it kinda weird," Ethan added, "that so many of us are on the young and hot side?" He winked at Griselda, who rolled her eyes and pushed herself to her feet.

"So what?" she said. "You realize it doesn't fucking matter, right? Even if she's right, there's nothing we can do about it from here."

"You're willing to just give up?" Dee asked. "And die? Don't you want to fight back?"

"Look, Blair showed us this place to give us a chance to survive as long as possible," Griselda said, her pale skin flushed pink. "That does not mean taking on the whole Postman Enterprises system. We'll just die faster."

"You know as well as I do," Nyles said, "that Blair would have been the first one to fight back if she'd had the opportunity."

Ethan nodded. "She told Gucci to fuck off. *So* baller."

"Yeah, and now she's fucking dead." Griselda squared her shoulders, staring Dee right in the eye. "You got Blair killed, and now you want to do the same for us. No thanks."

"Aren't you dead anyway?" Dee asked. She felt enough guilt over Blair's death without Griselda constantly rubbing it in her face. Besides, for all her tough talk, Griselda was showing a cowardly side. "I don't know about you, but I'd rather go out swinging."

"Dude." Ethan patted Dee on the back. "I like your style."

His approval just inflamed Griselda's rage. "You don't know anything about me, Princess."

"I know that you're a bitch."

Nyles threw up his hands. "Will you two cut it out? This isn't getting us anywhere." He pointed at Ethan. "What's our time?"

Ethan glanced at the massive electronic watch on his left wrist. "It's been twelve minutes since we crossed the fence."

Nyles nodded. "We need to wrap this up."

"Why?"

"Cameras tracked us as far as the old water-treatment plant," Nyles explained. "It takes twenty minutes to jog the length of the island and back, so if we're not within camera range by then, someone might notice and send the drones."

"Oh."

"So, let's get down to it. I appreciate the fact that you're innocent, and that you think that by proving your innocence you might be able to get us out of here too, but what, exactly, do you propose to do about it?"

Right. Dee probably should have spent her day at I Scream coming up with a plan instead of trying to make small talk with Griselda.

"I can ask to talk to my dad," she said, sharing the first idea that popped into her head. "Tell him about the tweezers."

"Sure," Griselda said. "I'm sure he'll *totally* believe you."

"I know he'd listen to me." *Do you really?* Dee pictured the look on her dad's face during Dr. Farooq's testimony. Would he even believe her?

Griselda shook her head. "There's no way to get a message off the island, Princess. You can't just request a meeting while you're on Alcatraz two-point-oh. We're completely cut off. No phones, no computer access, nothing."

They had no means whatsoever to contact the outside world? That sounded incredibly dangerous. "What if there's an earthquake or something?"

"We have the guards up at the station," Ethan said. "I guess they're supposed to help in an emergency."

"An emergency," said Griselda. "Good one."

"The guards!" Dee was surprised Nyles hadn't thought of them. "Maybe one of *them* would take a message to my dad."

"Oh, sure," Griselda said. "We'll just waltz up the hill and ring the doorbell."

"It's impossible to get near the station," Nyles explained, "and the sentries won't even talk to us. They have a strict no-fraternization policy."

"They're not allowed to make beer?" Ethan asked.

Nyles tiled his head, confused. "Erm, no."

"Good," Ethan said, letting out a sigh of relief. "That would be weird."

"What about food deliveries?" Dee asked, picturing the tubs of ice cream packed away in the freezer at I Scream. "Who makes those?"

"The guards," Griselda said. "They come at night in an armored personnel carrier, but you can't get close enough to spit at them, let alone talk to them."

Dee wouldn't have been surprised if Griselda knew that from experience.

"Besides," Griselda continued, "they're not on our side, so even if you could get to them, I seriously doubt they'd be willing to take a message to your daddy or your lawyer or anyone else."

"Nyles talks to his lawyers." Ethan was staring off into the tall grass as if contemplating the meaning of life itself.

Dee turned to Nyles. "And you were going to mention that *when*?"

"I'm only allowed access to my solicitors due to my—"

This time Dee joined in with Griselda and Ethan. "Diplomatic immunity."

Nyles pursed his lips. "But only on the second Wednesday of the month."

"Dude!" Ethan said, snapping out of his deep thoughts. "That's in, like, two days."

This was perfect. "You can get a message out," Dee said. "Through your lawyers to my dad."

Nyles bit his lip. "I suppose. It won't be easy, though. My meetings are in one of those prisoner communication rooms through a wall of glass."

"It'll work." Dee wasn't sure how, but she was desperate. Finally there was a beacon of hope on Alcatraz 2.0.

"Now we only have one more challenge," Nyles said as they turned to jog back toward the fence.

"What's that?" asked Dee.

"We have to keep you alive until then."

They returned to the gym to change before beginning the trek back to the Barracks. Dee was happy to have company, as now more than ever she felt the need to be surrounded by people. Which would do her no good when they were all forced to sleep in their own houses at night, but that meant only eight hours out of twenty-four that she had to fend for herself. The rest of the time, she'd have backup.

As they headed up Main Street, they stopped in at the bodega, Alcatraz 2.0's convenience/grocery store, which was essentially a 24/7 automated vending machine, where you dipped your card into a slot and were debited the amount of the door you opened. Like a high-tech version of the old Depression-era cafeterias Dee had seen in black-and-white movies. There were two employees—the bleached blonde Dee had seen walking to work that morning was taking inventory on a clipboard, and a greasy-haired guy sat behind the counter and flipped through an outdated sports magazine.

Dee recognized him right away. It was Rodrigo, the perv who'd tried to assault her that morning.

She froze just inside the door, revulsion washing over her. She remembered the stench of his breath, the fierce grip with which he'd held her wrist, and the disturbing desire she'd seen in his eyes. She didn't want to be anywhere near this creeper, and yet the bodega was the only place to buy prepackaged food for dinner.

"Rodrigo," Nyles said, sweeping up behind Dee. He draped his arm around her shoulders. "You remember Dee, yes? I believe you met her this morning."

Rodrigo glanced up from his newspaper, and his face slowly turned a sickly shade of yellow.

"She's our Cinderella Survivor, you know," Nyles continued, his voice as cheerful as ever. "Quite the rage over on the fan forums, I bet. So glad you two are great chums already."

Rodrigo swallowed as if forcing down a bit of vomit that had crawled up the back of his throat, then mumbled something about deliveries and hurried through a door into the back room.

Nyles glanced down at Dee and smiled. "There. He shouldn't bother you anymore, I dare say."

Nyles had inspired irritation, confusion, and fury since Dee had met him, but at that moment all she felt was gratitude. "Thanks."

"Come on." He guided her toward the refrigerated units. "Let's get you some food."

She pulled her debit card from the pocket of her jacket. "Do you think there's anything on it? I've only been at I Scream for a day."

"There'll be something," Nyles assured her. "Enough to buy dinner and breakfast."

"If you can find anything decent to eat," Ethan added. "What the fuck, Rod?" he shouted toward the back room. "This place is practically empty!"

The bleached-blond woman taking inventory shrugged. "We were supposed to get a shipment today, but it didn't come."

Ethan frowned. "I'm going to complain."

"Right," Griselda said, elbowing past him. "I'm sure The Postman totally gives a shit that you don't care for his selection of frozen meals."

Ethan was right—most of the little doors in the cafeteria were empty—and she wondered how often food supplies ran low on Alcatraz 2.0. Was that just another ploy by The Postman to make their lives more miserable? Were sanctioned murders not getting good enough ratings anymore, so he was manufacturing a real-life *Hunger Games* on the island?

Dee hoped not. She wasn't exactly Katniss, and she doubted she'd survive very long if she had to fight for food. For now she just needed to eat, and since she didn't know how much money was on her card, she decided to start small—a two-pack of frozen bean-and-cheese burritos, which Ethan referred to as a "fart attack," two frozen lasagnas, bottled water, a banana, and a package of instant-coffee granules. Not the double no-foam lattes she loved back home, but it was better than nothing.

Dee noticed that Nyles, Griselda, and Ethan all carefully examined their packaging before leaving. They checked the plastic wrap and trays for puncture marks, and made sure that all safety seals were unbroken. Griselda went so far as to throw out a bottle of orange juice because she thought maybe the plastic notches that held the unopened cap in place had been severed and resealed.

It could never hurt to be extra diligent about food.

It was dark by the time they turned off Ninth Street and into the Barracks. Ethan and Griselda peeled off to their duplex, and Nyles paused in front of Dee's building.

"I'm sorry, by the way," he began, his eyes shifting back and forth as if desperately trying to avoid Dee's face. "About all the snogging earlier."

Dee fought to keep a blush from creeping up her chest to her face. "I know you were just doing it to shut me up."

"Yes," he said flatly. "I mean, no. I mean, it wasn't entirely clinical."

Clinical? "Um, okay."

"That came out wrong."

"Did it?"

Nyles sighed. "I just . . . I'm glad you're here."

Dee arched an eyebrow. "Glad I've been sentenced to death on Alcatraz two-point-oh?"

"Well, yes. Kind of." Now it was Nyles's turn to blush. "I should stop now. Good night."

NINETEEN

DEE WATCHED NYLES DISAPPEAR DOWN THE END OF HER walkway before she opened the door just wide enough to slip inside. It wasn't that she was embarrassed by her plastic utensil warning system, but she wanted Nyles to think that she was tough, and booby-trapping your house with lip-gloss tubes and paper coffee cups wasn't exactly badass.

What the hell was wrong with her? She shouldn't care what Nyles thought, and she certainly shouldn't be flirting with him. "You can't trust these people," she said out loud, as if to remind herself. Nyles, Griselda, and Ethan were a means to an end, a tool she could use to earn her freedom, but they were not and never would be her friends.

She needed to stay focused on her goal: prove her innocence and make sure Monica's real killer got what was coming to him. Toward that, she needed to follow the rules and stay alive. Flirting with the cute British boy with the goofy smile was *not* a priority.

With a heavy sigh, Dee dragged herself into the kitchen, being careful not to let her eyes wander toward the ever-present TV screen, which was still showing Blair's murder. She'd eat some dinner, maybe chug a cup of instant coffee to keep her awake.

Dee had just dropped her grocery bag onto the table when she froze. A half dozen plastic sporks were strewn across the floor by the sliding glass door, and the cardboard cup that had held them was hanging from the handle by its dental-floss tether.

Maybe it just fell by itself. A strong breeze might have rattled the door. Or the balance was off and a shifting spork toppled the whole thing.

Or someone's in the house.

Shit.

Okay, options. She could leave. Run outside, just like Blair and Nyles had suggested. Sixtyish-percent chance of survival, right? She tiptoed backward toward the glass door. It was unlatched, though Dee was sure she'd locked it that morning, and as she slowly slid it open, she heard a noise coming from the utility closet. A slight creak, as if someone had shifted position.

She had a Painiac in her laundry cupboard. What if she could trap him there? That would mean one less killer on the loose. She eyed the dining room chairs. Solid metal. She could wedge one beneath the handle to the closet and prop the legs against the nearby kitchen counter. Whoever was inside would be trapped.

Dee didn't give herself time to debate the idea. As fast as she could move, she lunged at the nearest chair and shoved it into place.

The Painiac inside instantly realized something was wrong. He or she tried to push the door open from the inside, but the chair held firm. Dee backed toward the sliding glass door, just in case the chair gave way.

Her eyes drifted toward the nearest camera in the corner of the kitchen, expecting to see the telltale red light, letting Dee know that her feed was live. Here was Cinderella Survivor facing off against another Painiac, after all.

But the camera was dark.

Dee spun around, seeking out each of the cameras within view. Not a single red light between them. "What the hell?"

"Dee?" The muffled voice came from inside the closet. "Dee, it's me, Mara. F-from next door."

She sounded as if she was choking down a sob, but Dee wasn't totally convinced it wasn't actually Hannah Ball or DIYnona trapped inside.

"Sure it is," Dee said, trying to sound brave.

The intruder didn't plead with her. Instead, Dee heard a wriggling noise from inside the closet; then a white object slid out from beneath the door.

It was an ID card, exactly like Dee's, only the photo on the front was of a girl with long red hair.

"Why are you in my house?" Dee asked, still not totally convinced she wasn't being conned by a Painiac.

Sobs erupted from the closet. "I . . . I . . ."

"Yeah?"

"I was hungry," she wailed.

That didn't make any sense. As long as everyone worked their stupid little jobs, they had money for food. "Why don't you take your card down to the bodega and—"

"There's no money on it."

What had Blair said about Mara? No one had seen her around in a couple of weeks. "Why not?" Dee hadn't meant to do it, but her voice had softened. Immediately, Mara's sobs slowed, then stopped.

"I used to work at the bodega," she said, sniffling. "But my boss, Maximilian, was killed three weeks after I got here. Then it was just me and Rodrigo, and he . . . He tried to . . ."

And then Dee understood exactly why Mara had been in her house. Dee quickly yanked the chair away from the door and threw it open.

Mara had crammed herself into the space between the washer-dryer unit and the wall. Her long hair partially obscured her face, but her green eyes were red and swollen, her cheeks damp with tears.

"Thank you," Mara said, wiping her face with the sleeve of her cable-knit sweater as she slipped out of the closet. "I'm sorry I scared you." Then she darted toward the backyard.

"How do you eat?" Dee asked quickly, before Mara could disappear back into her own house.

Mara paused on the concrete patio. "I had some money saved up. And some food. Maximilian said I could take home the expired stuff, so I had a stockpile."

"Had?"

Mara cast her eyes down, and a flush raced up her chest to her translucent cheeks. "It's been gone for a couple of days."

"So you were looking for food in my kitchen," Dee said. It wasn't even a question. Not that she blamed Mara. Who knew what leftovers and semi-rancid food she'd been existing on since she last worked at the bodega? "And hid in the closet when you heard the front door open."

Mara nodded, eyes still locked on the floor.

Without thinking, Dee reached into the grocery bag and pulled out one of the microwaveable lasagnas and the two-pack of frozen burritos. "Here," she said, holding them out to Mara through the open door. "Take them."

Mara's eyes grew so wide Dee was afraid her eyeballs might pop out of her head. "No, I couldn't. That's your food."

"I can get more." She wasn't entirely sure that was true, but she couldn't eat her own meal knowing that the girl next door was literally starving.

Mara stared at the items in Dee's hands, then tentatively reached out to take them as if expecting at any moment that Dee would snatch them away.

"Thank you." Several heavy tears spilled down Mara's cheeks. "I'll pay you back. I promise."

Then, without another word, Mara was gone.

The next morning, as Dee was slouched over the kitchen counter drinking her second cup of instant coffee after an inadequate three hours of sleep, Mara appeared at her back door. She waved and held up a paper bag.

Is she returning the food? That seemed like a weird gesture. Maybe she didn't want to feel as if she owed Dee anything?

Confused, Dee untied the dental-floss booby trap and opened the door.

"Hey," Mara said, a tiny smile breaking the corners of her mouth.

"Hey."

Mara shoved the crumpled paper bag into Dee's hands. "I brought you something."

It was heavy, much heavier than the lasagna and burritos that she'd given Mara the night before. Unsure of what to expect, Dee opened the bag slowly, hesitantly, and found a collection of metal screws, nuts, and bolts.

"I noticed your booby traps," Mara said. She spoke quickly, as if afraid she might lose her nerve before she got all the words out. "They're actually pretty similar to the ones I rigged up. But I use these instead of plastic sporks. They make more noise."

"Where did you find them?"

"The bodega," Mara said. "Maximilian had stripped down some old vending machines in the back. For parts. I took a bunch of these home my first week and did what you did—made myself an alarm system."

Mara was right—the metal hardware would do a much better job of alerting her to an intruder. It was an incredibly thoughtful gift. "Thank you," Dee said, smiling at Mara. "I mean it."

Mara shrugged, and Dee thought she noticed a faint redness creeping into her cheeks as she turned to leave.

"Hey!" Dee said, stopping her. "Can I ask you something?"

Mara tensed up, immediately on guard. "What?"

"How did you get into my house last night?"

"Oh!" Mara instantly relaxed, as if this was an easier question to answer than whatever she'd thought Dee was going to ask. "Your sliding door was unlocked."

Unlocked? Dee tried to think back to the morning when she'd gone outside and talked to Mara. Had she locked the door behind her? She thought she had, but it felt as if a month had passed since that morning. "Wow. That was stupid of me."

"Not really," Mara said. "It's not like The Postman's killers need a key to get inside."

Good point. "I'm glad you weren't Molly Mauler lurking in my closet."

"Me too," Mara said, deadly serious. "Since she's a forty-three-year-old stay-at-home mom from Marquette, Michigan, who drives a Honda minivan and runs the carpool on Mondays, Wednesdays, and Fridays."

Dee blinked. "Huh?"

"That's her alter ego." Then, before Dee could ask her to elaborate, Mara dashed around the hedge and disappeared into her own house.

TWENTY

AS DEE TREKKED ACROSS THE ISLAND TOWARD I SCREAM, SHE couldn't stop obsessing over Mara's theory about Molly Mauler's true identity.

Dee knew that Painiac fan fiction was a huge thing on The Postman forum. Monica had described some of her favorites that had been written about Gucci.

1. He had been a designer for a major fashion label, and he snapped after he was fired.

2. He and his wife owned an exclusive boutique in Manhattan, and he used to run fashion boot camps for kids during the summer.

3. He was an entertainer in South Beach who had been a contestant on *RuPaul's Drag Race.*

4. He was a long-haul trucker from Mississippi who had turned his rig into a mobile torture chamber.

None of these stories were actual theories about the true identity of Gucci Hangman, only elaborate stories from the minds of his most ardent fans. Mara's "facts" about Molly Mauler could have been the same thing—fiction.

The real-world identities of the Painiacs were closely guarded secrets. The news media and tabloids alike had attempted to seek them out, but not a single shred of evidence had been found that unmasked any of them. Not even after the Caped Capuchin's death, which had ignited a media feeding frenzy. Obituaries had been scoured, screen grabs of the Capuchin analyzed by experts alongside photos of recently deceased males from across the country. There had been dozens of theories, but in the end, nothing had been confirmed and the topic had been dropped.

So Mara's carpool-driving, stay-at-home-mom version of Molly Mauler had to be one more wild speculation. Right? She couldn't *actually* know a Painiac's identity, could she?

It seemed unlikely, but if there was even a snowball's chance in hell that Mara had some inside information about one of the Painiacs, Dee needed to know it. Anything to help her survive for the next twenty-eight hours.

Because, like he'd told her last night, in twenty-eight hours, Nyles would be meeting with his lawyers and asking them to contact Dee's dad with a special message: *Gucci Hangman killed Monica. Your daughter was framed.*

While Dee wasn't 100 percent sure that Gucci was Monica's killer, the situation would take too long to explain. This version was simple, to the point, and hopefully her dad would act on it.

He will. I know he will.

I hope *he will.*

I Scream was a much-needed distraction. Hanging out with Griselda wouldn't have been Dee's first choice for how to spend her day, but the ice-cream shop was crazy busy, as if all twenty-seven inmates on the island wanted ice-cream sundaes to be their last meal, and the hours flew by.

Nyles arrived around noon, and having him there helped. He kept the conversation light, never referencing Alcatraz 2.0 or the Painiacs or his meeting at the guard station the next day. They talked about California, and British poetry, and who made a better Sherlock Holmes—Benedict

Cumberbatch or Robert Downey Jr.—and before Dee knew it, Ethan had shown up for their trek back to the Barracks.

But just when Dee thought she'd make it through a day on Alcatraz 2.0 without a murder, a sound ripped through the shop that sent shivers down her spine.

Ding-dong! Ding-dong!

"Here we go again," Griselda said, seemingly unaffected by the notification.

Did she *never* fear this place?

Meanwhile, Dee's heart raced as she swung around to face the monitor.

The scene was another warehouse, suitably dismal. A brooding light permeated the near darkness, just enough to illuminate the abandoned detritus strewn about the interior: wooden crates stacked haphazardly against the wall, hulks of machinery, and thick chains hanging from the rafters like vines in an industrial jungle. The details were fuzzy and indistinguishable, which allowed Dee's mind to fill in the ominous blanks. Images of torture and brutality were hard to shake.

A spotlight ripped through the warehouse. It panned to the left, glinting off the rusting metal chains, then settled on a giant disc in the middle of the room, painted like an archery target in festive shades of red, yellow, and blue. Tied, spread-eagled, in the middle was a woman.

"That's odd," Nyles said at Dee's side. "I haven't seen her before. I'm always informed when new inmates arrive." He sounded peeved. "That's my *job*."

The woman wore a sparkly gold leotard, appropriate for a magician's assistant, and her black hair had been curled in fat spirals, which covered her face as her head hung forward. But when the woman raised her face to the camera, Dee recognized it right away. Even though the woman's mouth was obscured by a gag, Dee knew her face. It was one she'd never forget.

"Holy shit, it's Dr. Farooq."

Only the words hadn't come from Dee. They'd come from Griselda.

"You know her?" Dee asked.

Griselda's upper lip curled. "She's that bitchface psychiatrist who testified against me at my trial."

Dee's hands began to tremble. "She's the same bitchface psychiatrist who testified against me."

"Me too," Ethan said. "Bitch. Face."

For the first time since Dee had met her, Griselda's calm, cool exterior cracked. "That's impossible," she said, the tremor apparent in her voice. "My trial was in Chicago. Ethan's was in New York. And yours was in LA. They wouldn't have used the same doctor for all three."

"But they did," Dee said. If Dr. Farooq had testified against all three of them, maybe Griselda really was innocent after all?

"Dee's trial ended just days ago," Nyles said. "How did the doctor get here so fast? She'd need to be arrested, tried."

Dee was thinking the exact same thing. *How did Dr. Farooq end up on Alcatraz 2.0?*

A voice crackled from the video screen. "Pray thee, mistress. Dost thou knowest who I am?"

Dr. Farooq nodded meekly. Anyone with half a brain could recognize one of Robin's Hood's setups.

"Dost thou knowest where thou ist?"

Again she nodded.

"And dost thou knowest *why* thou art here?"

This time, Dr. Farooq shook her head violently and tried to speak through the gag, her voice muffled and indistinct.

"Dr. Farooq," Robin said, his voice louder as if he were a town crier about to read a proclamation. "You have been convicted of psychiatric malpractice during your time at the Western Sierra State Mental Hospital, resulting in the negligent death of a patient."

Dee reeled. Western Sierra State Mental Hospital. Where Kimmi had been sent.

"Are you okay?" Nyles asked, his hand on Dee's back. "You look as if you're going to be sick."

"I—I'm fine." Dee pulled a chair away from the nearest table and sat down. The room spun around her. First the connection between Gucci and Monica's death. Now Dr. Farooq, who'd been so instrumental in Dee's conviction, was directly linked to the hospital where Dee's kidnapper had been sent six years ago.

Did this conspiracy go deeper than Dee had realized?

Meanwhile, Dr. Farooq screamed through her gag, less from fear than from indignation. She looked furious as she desperately tried to spit the fabric band out of her mouth, but her cries were quickly drowned out by a creeptastical pipe-organ sound track as slowly the archery target began to spin.

"Let us now bear witness to your demise," Robin said. "May God have mercy on thy eternal soul."

Dr. Farooq's head swiveled from side to side as the rotating target began to pick up speed. She was looking for an escape, just as Dee had done. Dr. Farooq's anger faded and she started to panic. She twisted her body, wrenching her torso back and forth as she pulled frantically at her arms and legs, attempting to free herself from the bonds that restrained her. But the ropes held firm.

"Thou dost squirm too much," Robin cackled. "Dost thou want me to miss?"

With a whoosh and a thwack, an arrow flew through the air and struck the target three inches to the left of her head. Another hiss of air, and a second arrow hit just below her right arm. Then a third, between her legs.

Dr. Farooq was hysterical now, the tear trails arcing across her cheeks as the target continued to spin, and despite the anger she held toward the psychiatrist, Dee felt her fear so tangibly it was as if she was there, strapped to the target in her place. No escape. No reprieve. The end in sight. And she couldn't help but pity the doctor.

Robin chuckled. "Wouldst thou that I use a larger weapon?"

The music stopped, anticipation building in the silence. A crack shattered the quiet as an enormous wooden stake was propelled at Dr. Farooq's body with such force that it impaled her stomach. This time her scream was bloodcurdling, her eyes wide in pain and terror, as the life slowly drained from her body.

The wheel stopped turning. Her head lolled forward.

"Listen to the sound of my voice," Robin said, strangely out of character. "Relax into the past and tell me what you see."

Then the video went black.

TWENTY-ONE

"LISTEN TO THE SOUND OF MY VOICE," DR. FAROOQ SAID. "Relax into the past and tell me what you see."

Dee's eyes were closed, but she could feel Dr. Farooq's breath against her cheek as the psychiatrist leaned in.

"Relax into the past," Dr. Farooq repeated. "There is no present. There is no future. Only you and your memories."

Dee was pretty sure that hypnosis was a load of crap, but since her life was on the line with this trial, she figured she might as well try. If Dr. Farooq could actually regress Dee's memories back a week to the time of Monica's murder, her hypnosis-induced account of what happened that day would prove that she was innocent.

So she relaxed, as Dr. Farooq had told her to do. And listened to the doctor's voice. And allowed herself to fall back into the past.

"You're home after school." Dr. Farooq's voice sounded heavy and far away, as if Dee were hearing it through a pair of earplugs. "In your room. Your sister Monica is next door. Is that correct?"

"Hm-mm," Dee said. She felt dreamy, like she was floating in a pool of warm water, every inch of her body submerged but her face.

"How do you know Monica is in her room?"

"We walked home from school. Together."

"Yes, but how do you *know*?" There was a sharpness in Dr. Farooq's voice that unnerved Dee. Like she was being reprimanded for not knowing the correct answer to a math problem.

"I—"

"Can you hear her?"

"No. She's doing homework."

"But surely you can hear her. Your rooms are so close."

Dee felt as if something were holding her down, binding her arms and legs, and she struggled to remain free. "No," she said, almost shouting the word.

"Relax." The word was instantly soothing, and Dee felt free again, the panic abating. "Relax. Now, you're lying on your bed, and you can hear your sister, Monica, in her room."

No. Dee said it in her mind, then heard a different word spoken in her own voice. "Yes."

"You hear Monica on the phone. With one of her friends."

No. Monica never talked on the phone. Just texted and posted on social media. "Yes."

"They're talking about you, Dee. Talking about how they don't like you. How they don't want to be your friend anymore."

"NO!" The word burst from Dee's lips. She had to fight to get it out—every muscle in her body felt as if it was being controlled by someone else—but Dee couldn't agree to what Dr. Farooq was saying it. It wasn't right. It wasn't true.

Was it?

"Relax, Dee. Relax. There is no present. There is no future. Relax into the past."

"Relax," Dee repeated.

"You thought Monica was your friend." Dr. Farooq's voice was silky smooth. So easy on the ears. "You thought she cared about you. But you realize she only wants to humiliate you."

"Yes."

"And you hate her. You want her to feel the same kind of pain she's made you feel."

"Yes."

"You go to her room, silently open the door. She doesn't hear you as she's turning off her phone."

No.

"Your hands are around Monica's neck. Squeezing. You hate her. You want her dead. You've been waiting a long time to let out your rage."

The bonds were back, thick ropes around Dee's arms and legs. They cut into her flesh, pulling her body down below the surface of the water. She fought against them, flailing as she tried to kick for the surface. *No! No! No!* She didn't do this. She didn't kill Monica.

"Monica's eyes bulge from their sockets. Her face turns red, then purple. Her strength is failing, and you can feel the cartilage in her throat snap as you crush her windpipe."

No!

"Now she's still. Her chest doesn't move. Her heart doesn't beat. And you let her dead body fall to the floor. Don't you, Dee?"

Yes. She's had this rage burning inside her ever since her days in the white room. Six years. The anger had to burst, didn't it? That's what Dr. Farooq is saying. And she knows. She knows everything.

"Yes."

Dee heard a soft click in the background, like a finger on a keyboard. "Now, Dee, tell me in your own words what happened that day in your house."

Dee sat motionless beside her lawyer, listening to the sound of her own voice on the recording: "I go to her room, silently opening the door. My hands are around Monica's neck. Squeezing. I hate her. I want her dead. I've been waiting a long time to let out my rage."

"No," Dee said. "That's a lie. That never happened."

"The defendant will remain silent," the judge ordered. "You will have your chance to testify."

Dee rocketed to her feet and pointed her finger at Dr. Farooq. "But she's *lying*! She *made* me say those things!"

Dr. Farooq turned to the judge. "Sometimes during a hypnotic regression, the subject transposes their guilt onto the guide. In this case, Dee's subconscious has blocked out her participation in Monica's murder, instead shifting the blame to me." Then she smiled at the jury. "All too common in my line of work, I assure you."

The jury smiled back. They were on her side.

"I didn't do this," Dee said, desperate that someone would believe her.

"Miss Guerrera," the judge said. "Sit down or I will find you in contempt."

But Dee didn't care. She spun around, searching for her father in the packed courthouse. He sat two rows behind her, his face gaunt. Tears streamed down his cheeks.

"She's lying," Dee said, pleading with him. "I didn't do this."

The judge banged his gavel while Dee's attorney pulled her arm, trying to get her to sit back down.

"I didn't do it!" Dee screamed. "I didn't! I didn't! I didn't!"

"I didn't kill her," Dee said.

"Yeah, Princess," Griselda said. The words were still flippant, but there was something softer about her tone. "You've told us about a billion times."

"What's wrong, Dee?" Nyles knelt by her side, his hand on top of hers.

"Dr. Farooq tried to make me believe that I killed Monica," Dee explained. The vision of Monica's death was so real, so visceral. But it was fake—it had to be.

"She's gone now," Nyles said. "Perhaps justice really has been served on Alcatraz?"

Dee turned to meet his gaze. "But don't you see? She was killed for a reason."

"Yeah," Griselda said. "For landing all of us in here."

"I thought Robin said it was a malpractice thing," Ethan said. "Or am I making that up?"

"She never had a trial," Dee said, choosing not to explain to Ethan that malpractice was not a capital crime. "I bet everything Robin said was a lie. The Postman wanted to get her out of the way so she could never testify against *him* for my sister's death."

"Against The Postman?" Nyles asked. "I thought you said that Gucci Hangman killed your sister."

Dee shook her head. First Gucci Hangman, then Robin's Hood. Both giving her clues. The Painiacs probably had no idea what they meant—they'd been given information from above and they were just following orders. Monica's death wasn't the action of a lone, unhinged Painiac. It was connected to something bigger—to Kimmi and the white room and The Postman.

"One thing's for sure," Ethan said, scratching his chin. "Someone really doesn't want our trials to be reopened."

Postman Forum * Roster * Robin's Hood * Dr. Farooq?

Thread: Dr. Farooq?

Nov-9, 4:46 p.m. **#1**
Mr. Hef Join Date: February 2018
All the ladies love me Posts: 34

Who the hell was that woman? I mean, no announcement of a new inmate, no footage from her trial. What's going on?

Nov-9, 4:46 p.m. **#2**
Domino Joe Join Date: October 2017
Black, white, and awesome all over Posts: 3,422

Not every trial is televised. Just the juicy ones.

Nov-9, 4:48 p.m. **#3**
Mr. Hef Join Date: February 2018
All the ladies love me Posts: 35

I guess. But it still seems strange. First #CinderellaSurvivor is thrown into Slycer's maze on the very first day, now this Dr. Farooq? The Postman used to give all the inmates a week or two before one of the executioners was let loose on them. Why the change?

Nov-9, 4:49 p.m. **#4**
Mary Mary Most Contrary Join Date: July 2017
How does my garden grow? Posts: 850

Maybe this doctor chick was too boring to keep around? Spikes on this video have been way down. Even the #MerryMen aren't posting about it.

Nov-9, 4:50 p.m. **#5**
The Griff Join Date: July 2017
Wide Awake Eyes Open Posts: 37,138

OPEN YOUR EYES, PEOPLE! Don't you remember who Dr. Farooq is? She testified against #CinderellaSurvivor just last week. See? IT'S A CONSPIRACY!!!!!

Nov-9, 4:52 p.m. **#6**
Dr. Mendez Join Date: February 2018
They call me Mister Doctor Posts: 1,163

Um, what kind of conspiracy could this possibly be? A conspiracy to punish convicted criminals? A conspiracy to lower crime rates through tougher sentencing laws? I'll take that kind of conspiracy in a heartbeat. Have you seen the latest statistics from the Justice Department? Violent crimes are down 25% since last summer. Coincidence? I think not.

Nov-9, 4:55 p.m. **#7**
The Griff Join Date: July 2017
Wide Awake Eyes Open Posts: 37,139

> <<Originally posted by Dr. Mendez>>
> *Violent crimes are down 25% since last summer. Coincidence? I think not.*

And yet, if violent crimes are down, why did The Postman announce just last week that there would be a large new shipment of inmates arriving on Alcatraz 2.0? And have you noticed how all the recent arrivals are young and attractive? OPEN YOUR EYES! This is Ratings Manipulation 101! I'd bet you a million dollars that this new "batch" of inmates all look like supermodels.

Nov-9, 4:56 p.m. **#8**
Domino Joe Join Date: October 2017
Black, white, and awesome all over Posts: 3,423

Yeah, like you have a million dollars. Just keep wearing your tinfoil hat and living in your mom's basement, dude!

Nov-9, 4:59 p.m. **#9**
Mr. Hef Join Date: February 2018
All the ladies love me Posts: 36

I have to admit that The Griff has a point. This does seem weird. And potentially illegal. I thought the attorney general was supposed to be overseeing Alcatraz 2.0 personally, but did you hear his latest press conference? Said that Alcatraz 2.0 was totally under the control of The Postman. Except nobody knows who The Postman is! Is he really a Hollywood producer like the rumors say? Or maybe just a DOJ figurehead? Or is he POTUS himself?

TWENTY-TWO

FOR THE FIRST TIME SINCE DEE HAD ARRIVED ON THE ISLAND, the fog didn't creep across the bay toward Alcatraz 2.0 as the sun disappeared behind the horizon. The night was clear and moonless, but even though the moisture was gone from the air, Dee felt chilled to the bone.

She'd been in a daze since Dr. Farooq's murder. Locking up I Scream, buying dinner at the bodega, walking back to the Barracks—all of it seemed removed and far away, as if the fog that usually surrounded the island had instead enveloped Dee's mind.

Kimmi. Dr. Farooq. Western Sierra State Mental Hospital.

Dr. Farooq had worked there. Kimmi was a patient there. They were both connected to Dee. Could they both also be connected to The Postman?

I'll kill everyone you love.

Could Kimmi's *dad* be The Postman?

Do you want to be my sister?

Over and over, hour after hour, Kimmi had asked Dee the same question from the air vent. At first, Dee would answer with her own questions: *Who are you? Do you go to my school? Where am I?* And the most important of all, *Why me?*

The "why me" part haunted Dee in the periods between Kimmi's visits. She'd sit in the blaring silence, trying to figure it out. Had she done something wrong? Was that why she was in the white room? Was Kimmi angry at her? Punishing her?

Do you want to be my sister?

Dee wasn't sure how to answer. She'd always wanted a sister. She'd even written a poem about it, just a few months before, which had been published in the local paper. Being an only child could be lonely, especially with a single parent who worked long hours. Dee spent a lot of time with babysitters and in after-school programs, and while friends were fun, they weren't the same as having a built-in playmate and companion.

But now Dee wished she'd never written that poem, never hoped for a sister. Because Kimmi scared the crap out of her.

"Do you want to be my sister?"

"Why me?" Dee sobbed. "Why are you doing this to me?"

Kimmi tilted her head to the side, confused that Dee didn't know the answer already. "Because we're so much alike."

That had stuck with Dee, the idea that she was as ruthless and as twisted as her kidnapper. Therapists had tried to convince her otherwise, using big concepts like "Stockholm syndrome" and "psychological imprinting," but Dee had always felt, deep down, that maybe Kimmi was right.

And Dr. Farooq's recording seemed to prove it.

Stop.

Dee wasn't Kimmi. Would never be Kimmi. She wasn't selfish, and she cared about people. Like Mara.

The lights were on in Mara's house, every window brightly illuminated. It felt almost warm and inviting against the chill of the night, and though Dee knew instinctively that no place on Alcatraz 2.0 was ever safe, having a next-door neighbor was a nice illusion.

She knocked lightly at the door. "Mara? It's Dee."

Silence. She didn't hear a sound from inside. No creak of floorboards, no patter of footfalls. Immediately Dee's heart began to pound in her chest. Something was wrong. Mara knew the sound of her voice, and Dee was pretty sure that she'd open up if she could.

"Mara?" Dee pounded on the door, feeling the same panic as when she'd found Monica's body on the floor of her room, unnatural, unmoving. "Mara, are you all—"

The door flew open while Dee was mid-knock. Mara leaned against it, her eyes heavy with sleep. "Sorry," she said, stifling a yawn. "I must have dozed off."

Dee wasn't sure why she did it, but without thinking, she grabbed Mara by each shoulder and hugged her. It only lasted a second, but it was enough time for Dee to feel herself choking up.

She knew it was completely ridiculous. She hardly knew this girl. Mara wasn't Monica: Dee needed to remember that.

"Sorry," she said, releasing Mara quickly. The awkwardness of that hug hung between them. "I brought you some dinner."

Mara shook herself, throwing off whatever images were running through her mind. "Really?"

Dee handed the bag to her. "It's lasagna again. The bodega was kind of empty."

"I don't mind." Mara stared into the bag thoughtfully. "That's weird, though. They should have had a food delivery yesterday."

"Maybe Nyles can ask—" Dee paused. She was about to say that Nyles could ask about the food delivery tomorrow when he met with his attorney, but she caught a movement out of the corner of her eye. Across the street, one of the crow-shaped cameras had just swiveled to face them.

Someone was always watching, always listening, and the last thing Dee wanted to do was to tip off The Postman that Nyles's visitation tomorrow would be anything other than 100 percent routine and normal.

"Nothing," Dee said quickly. "Hey, if you want to come over in the morning, I have some coffee and bananas. For breakfast."

Mara bit her lip, debating the offer. Dee knew what she was thinking: *You shouldn't trust anyone on Alcatraz 2.0.* And yet Dee really hoped Mara would say yes.

"Okay," Mara said. "See you then."

Mara shut her front door, and Dee waited until she heard the bolt click into place before she returned to her own house and began her nightly search for intruders.

The downstairs was empty; then Dee swept the upstairs: bathroom, shower stall, both bedroom closets. And though the red dots indicated that all the cameras in Dee's house were live, evoking a creeping sensation across her skin as if something horrible was about to happen, no masked serial killers lurked anywhere.

Back in the kitchen, Dee looked at the other lasagna at the bottom of her bag, but though she hadn't eaten much that day, she wasn't the least bit hungry. Just exhausted.

She desperately wanted to sleep, but that might be a fatal mistake. She needed to stay alive until Nyles's attorneys could get a message to her dad, and if that meant she didn't sleep again until she was off Alcatraz 2.0, then so be it.

But that resolve didn't make her any less tired. Maybe a shower would wake her up?

Dee had seen enough horror movies to know that getting in the shower was a bad idea in the best of circumstances, which these were not.

A washcloth soaked in cold water might be just the trick to revive her.

She headed upstairs, yawned as she yanked open the linen-closet door, and froze.

Written on the inside of the door, in the bright pink lipstick from her cosmetics drawer, was a message:

YOU'LL ALWAYS BE MY SISTER, DOLORES. ALWAYS.

TWENTY-THREE

DEE SAT UP ALL NIGHT ON THE STAIRS. SHE THOUGHT IT WAS the most strategic location in the house. If someone came in through the upstairs windows, then she could make a run for it downstairs. Plus, she'd tied the sheets from her bed together and anchored them to the dresser in the front bedroom, so if someone smashed through the sliding glass door downstairs or kicked in the front entrance, she could escape from the second floor. Like a true fairy-tale princess shinnying down from her tower. It might even score points on fan forums for being a Rapunzelesque maneuver.

Of course, if the Hardy Girls split up and entered her house on both levels at the same time, she was pretty much screwed.

She had been exhausted when she'd gone upstairs to wash her face, but the message on the inside of the closet door had sobered her up immediately. If she'd had any doubts about the connection between Kimmi and The Postman, they evaporated in an instant.

Because nobody else knew her real name.

The trial had been on total lockdown, since both Dee and her kidnapper were minors. Pseudonyms were used for both of them, and no press was allowed in the courtroom. Kimmi was only fourteen at the time, and since she hadn't physically harmed Dee by keeping her locked in the family's safe room for almost a week—except for the lack of food and sanitation, Dee's lawyer had pointed out, but whatever—the juvenile court accepted a plea deal. Kimmi was sentenced to the Western Sierra State Mental Hospital for a period no less than ten years. Which meant that she should still be there.

Should.

After the sentencing, Dee and her dad had tried to return to normal lives. Dee went back to school, her dad went back to work at the production company, and despite her insomnia, her constant fear of being alone, and the twice-weekly visits to a therapist, life had settled down.

Then, suddenly, a couple of months after the trial had ended, Dee's dad sold their condo in Manhattan Beach and moved himself and his daughter to Burbank.

The move was swift, and her dad had given her no warning. He picked her up from school on a Friday afternoon, and when they got home, the movers had already packed up the entire condo. They left that day, and on the drive out to Burbank in Friday rush-hour traffic, Dee's dad had told her that from now on, her name wasn't Dolores Hernandez, but Dee Guerrera. She was never to tell anyone who she really was and she could never contact her old friends. He took her cell phone, replaced it with a new one, and erased all her contacts from the cloud. Her dad had never been particularly strict when it came to rules, but on this point he was adamant—they had to leave their old lives behind.

They were starting over.

And from that day on, the name Dolores was never spoken.

So who else knew about it? Kimmi, of course. Kimmi's dad. Dee's dad. The police detectives who had taken Dee's initial testimony, Dr. Farooq, and the therapist Dee had seen right after her abduction. It was a short list.

Could The Postman have gotten his hands on the details of Dee's trial? Possibly. He seemed all-powerful. But the simpler solution was that he was intimately acquainted with both Kimmi and Dee.

Was it really possible that Kimmi's dad was The Postman? Dee didn't see why not. No one seemed to know anything about The Postman other than that he was a Hollywood producer who had come up with the perfect solution for America's rising tide of violent crime. Even though most of the news reports that Dee had seen swore that violent crime in America was at an all-time low. But apparently, facts didn't matter under this presidency. The government cut a deal with The Postman and turned over a portion of the prison system to him, and once The Postman app was launched, introducing 250 million Americans to televised capital punishment, no one cared about the rationale anymore. You couldn't argue with ratings.

But why would a Hollywood producer want to run a glorified death row? Sure, the ultimate reality show was ridiculously popular, but this whole setup must have been ridiculously expensive, too. Was it really worth the expenditure? What could The Postman hope to gain: Power? Fame? The sick thrill of having so many lives in his hands?

The white room. Kimmi had said that her dad killed people there. What if it was true? What if the entire rationale behind Alcatraz 2.0 was to satisfy The Postman's own bloodlust?

She needed to talk to Nyles. He'd be walking up to the guard station in a few hours for his noon meeting with his attorneys. She'd have to trust him with the secret of her past, the thought of which made her head ache. But there was no helping it. If she was right, the world needed to know.

It was half past seven when Dee slowly rose from her vigil on the stairs. She didn't bother to get changed, just splashed some water on her face as usual, ignoring the sparkly cosmetics provided for her intended use, and headed downstairs. Coffee and a banana, then she'd wait for Nyles out front. She didn't want to miss him.

Dee was nuking her coffee, when Mara appeared at the back door.

She clearly wasn't expecting Dee to follow through on her offer of breakfast. Mara knocked on the sliding glass door but kept her arms wrapped tightly around her body, as if she thought Dee might tell her to fuck off.

Sadly, there was a part of Dee that wanted to, not because she didn't like her neighbor, but because she was concerned for Mara's safety.

People connected to Dee ended up dead, plain and simple. Monica. Blair. Even Dr. Farooq. It was bad enough that Nyles, Ethan, and even that pain in the ass Griselda might be in the firing line. Did she really want to add another name to the list?

Still, she didn't have the heart to ignore her neighbor. Just a quick cup of coffee wouldn't hurt.

"Hey," Dee said, lifting the booby-trap cardboard cup from the counter as she slid open the door. "Hungry?"

Mara didn't step inside. "Are you sure? I have some burrito left over. I can just eat—"

Dee shoved a banana into Mara's hand. "I'm sure."

They ate bananas and sipped black, watery coffee outside on the moldy wicker furniture and made small talk. Dee learned that Mara was from Orange County, just an hour and a half away from where Dee lived in Burbank, and had been about to start college when she was arrested over the summer.

"Mr. Carpenter was a teacher at my high school," Mara said. "He taught Safety Ed and remedial math. They said I shot him dead in his classroom after summer school one day. A premeditated fit of jealousy."

She bowed her head, her face pinched with embarrassment. "Supposedly, I was in love with him and he rejected me."

"Were you?"

"Ew, no! I didn't even know who he was."

"What happened at the trial?"

"All these horrible girls from school testified that I used to hang around Mr. Carpenter's classroom." Mara clenched her jaw, her fingers wrapped so tightly around her coffee cup that Dee was afraid it might crumple. "They supposedly found my fingerprints on the murder weapon, but I'd never even seen a gun in my life, let alone fired one. I wouldn't know how. The whole thing felt like the Salem witch trials, you know? Guilty no matter what."

Dee smiled wryly. "I know how you feel."

"Well," Mara said, standing up. "Thanks for breakfast. I should let you go to work."

"Can I ask you something?" Dee asked, before her neighbor dashed back into her own house.

Mara glanced at her apprehensively. "Okay."

"Did you write fan fiction on The Postman forum?"

Mara's green eyes grew wide. "I would never." She sounded mortally offended.

"Oh, sorry," Dee said quickly. "I just thought that stuff about Molly you mentioned—"

"It's *not* fiction."

Something about Mara's tone—sharp and serious, like a child who tells a fanciful tale but insists it really happened—gave Dee pause.

"You mean Molly Mauler is actually a forty-three-year-old stay-at-home mom from Michigan?"

Mara gave an emphatic nod, then dropped her voice. "Her name is Ruth Martinello and she lives at one-fifty-seven Hillcrest Avenue."

"That can't be true."

"It *is.*" Mara's voice was hardly above a whisper. "And I can do better than that. I know *all* of the killers' secret identities. Where they live, what they do, and most importantly, *where they kill.*" She leaned forward. "That's the reason I'm still alive."

TWENTY-FOUR

DEE STARED AT MARA, HER HEART RACING. COULD IT BE TRUE? Was there really a secret to staying alive on Alcatraz 2.0 after all? Dee slid the glass door closed and glanced around the backyard. The nearest crow camera was perched on the fence about twenty feet away. Maybe if they kept their voices down, it wouldn't pick up their audio.

"How do you know all that?" she whispered.

"Logic."

Logic was figuring out who was in the CONFIDENTIAL envelope during a game of Clue, not unmasking the well-kept secret identities of The Postman's killers.

"Every serial killer has a unique style," Mara said quickly. "Like a fingerprint of their murders. The way they dress, the way they talk, the way they kill, and where they do it. They like order and routine. If you piece together enough of them, a picture starts to form."

Dee thought of Kimmi's white room, and what she'd said her dad had done there. Routine. Order. But Dee had difficulty believing that watching a dozen videos of Molly Mauler tossing victims to hungry lions like Caligula in the Colosseum would reveal enough hints about her alter ego for Mara to narrow it down to one person in the Upper Midwest.

"You did all this research here?" Dee asked. "From Alcatraz two-point-oh?"

"Of course not. I've been studying The Postman's killers for over a year." She seemed totally unembarrassed about the fact that she was some kind of Postmantic superfan. Dee didn't want to judge—after all, Monica with her MoBettaStylz alter ego had been one of Gucci Hangman's biggest fans—but the idea of analyzing the Painiacs and their kills seemed incredibly disturbing.

"You don't believe me," Mara said, misinterpreting Dee's silence.

"No, I just . . ." Dee wasn't sure what to say. *I think it's weird? It creeps me out?*

Mara pursed her lips, took a deep breath, and sat back down on the moss-covered wicker chair.

"My first clue was the accent. Molly may not sound like she has one, but if you slow the video down and run a static filter to remove microphone interference and background noise, you'll notice first and foremost the 'th' stopping. Molly says 'the' like 'da.' Just slightly. That narrowed her area of origin down to the Great Lakes region. Secondly, she speaks with a northern-cities vowel shift, also indicative of the inland north. Lastly, when Molly unleashed a hormonally enraged congress of male chimpanzees on former Michigan congressman Daniel Yssap after he was convicted of killing that intern he'd been having an affair with, she referred to him as a 'dumb Yooper,' which is really only used in the Upper Peninsula. From there, tracking her down was a relatively simple process of Facebook stalking, travel records, and Instagram posts."

Dee stared at her blankly. "Wow."

Mara smiled. "And once I knew where she was from, I understood the joke of her moniker."

"How so?"

"Molly Mauler from Marquette, Michigan? It's like she was dropping a clue."

Mara's excitement over her deductions was familiar to Dee—it reminded her of how Monica used to talk about Gucci.

"Why are you being so nice to me?" Mara blurted out, her voice no longer a whisper.

It was a good question, a smart one, considering where they were. Dee didn't know Mara at all, and she realized that she'd broken Blair's first rule of Alcatraz 2.0: Never volunteer to help anyone.

But she couldn't help herself, and she knew exactly why.

"Because you remind me of my sister."

"I do?"

Dee nodded. "She died."

Mara stared at her with unblinking eyes. Did she know that Dee had been convicted of killing Monica? Probably. It would have been all over The Postman's feed. But Mara never alluded to it.

"I'm sorry," Mara said. "There's too much death in the world."

"Tell me about—"

And then, as if on cue, the double doorbell notification rang out from the living room.

Ding-dong! Ding-dong!

Dee and Mara sat frozen in their chairs. Dee didn't want to look, but she knew she must. What if it was someone else connected to her trial? The judge? One of the detectives? Her attorney?

She took a deep breath and marched through the kitchen and into the living room, Mara following close behind. And though she was prepared to see something horrible on the screen, what she saw drained all the warmth from her body.

Nyles and Griselda hung side by side by their wrists from the rafters twenty-five feet above a concrete floor. The interior of the room had the height of one of the old warehouses, but instead of corrugated metal and moldering wood, this space was painted a cheerful yellow, with exposed metal support beams flooded with natural light. Nyles and Griselda were gagged, their ankles cuffed and their wrists bound with a heavy cord that was looped through metal hooks attached to thick, rusty chains. Nyles wore a pair of plaid pajama bottoms and a long-sleeve thermal shirt, but Griselda was still in her club-girl getup from yesterday. They must have been nabbed from the Barracks either late last night or this morning, and Griselda, like Dee, probably hadn't gone to bed last night.

Griselda glared at the camera, her teeth bared over the black fabric of her gag. She was desperately trying to show resistance to the end, just as Blair had done, and despite their differences, Dee had to admire her courage.

Nyles, meanwhile, looked utterly confused. His eyebrows were drawn together, and he kept trying to speak through his gag, and though the words were incomprehensible, Dee knew exactly what he was saying.

"Diplomatic immunity," she said out loud.

"Huh?" Mara asked.

Dee pressed her palm to her forehead. It was damp with sweat from her growing panic. "This doesn't make sense. Nyles's case is in appeal. He has diplomatic immunity. He was supposed to meet his lawyer today and . . ." She let her voice trail off. Did she really want to get Mara involved in the plan? She'd managed to stay alive on Alcatraz 2.0, keeping out of sight and out of mind. And everyone involved with Dee had a tendency to end up dead. Would Mara be next?

"And what?" Mara asked.

"I . . ." She was saved an explanation by a voice on the live feed. It was electronically manipulated to sound like a metallic, robotic tone, and it was like nothing Dee had ever heard on The Postman before.

"Cinderella Survivor," it crackled. "We have your friends."

Oh God. It was happening again. Just like Blair, Nyles and Griselda were going to die, and it was all her fault.

"My girls are dying to play with them."

The Hardy Girls skipped into the frame, holding hands. The sisters, who usually dressed up as famous duos from history, wore matching powder-blue dresses with puff sleeves, and lacy white knee socks in black patent-leather Mary Janes. Their light brown hair was combed to one side and secured with barrettes that allowed it to swoop gently over the white bandit masks that covered their eyes.

The girls stopped directly beneath Nyles and Griselda, whose feet dangled above the girls' heads, and curtsied.

"The girls have been taking swimming lessons," the voice continued, harsh and soulless. "And they'd like some new friends to take to the pool."

The Hardy Girls skipped back out of view. They returned moments later, pushing a large glass tank on wheels. It had a thick black hose attached to a hole in one side. Dee was pretty sure she recognized the tank from Molly Mauler's piranha kill a few weeks ago, and as the Hardy Girls positioned the tank directly beneath her friends, she remembered Molly's victim, locked in that tank filled with flesh-eating superfish, the clear water slowly turning a foamy, rusty red as it filled with blood and chunks of flesh.

Once they had the tank perfectly aligned, the sisters disappeared to different corners of the room. Dee heard the squeak of a wheel turning, then a whoosh, and seconds later, water began pouring through the hose into the tank.

Immediately the hooks holding Nyles's and Griselda's wrists separated, dropping them into the tank, where they collapsed into a heap.

As Griselda and Nyles struggled with their bonds, the water sloshed around them, already an inch deep. Meanwhile, the Hardy Girls skipped back up to the tank with twin rolling ladders, which they positioned on either side. They climbed up and flipped a transparent panel from the back side of the tank over the top, creating a lid, which they then padlocked into place at the two front corners.

The plan was clear. The water would eventually fill the tank, and even if Nyles and Griselda could free themselves from the ropes, they'd still be unable to escape from the tank and would drown.

"It should be completely full in twenty minutes." A red digital timer appeared in the corner of the screen. "Can you save them, Cinderella Survivor? Their fate is in your hands."

TWENTY-FIVE

DEE STARED AT THE CLOCK AS IT COUNTED DOWN. NINETEEN minutes and fifty-five seconds. Fifty-four seconds. Fifty-three.

Their fate is in my hands.

"Wow," Mara said, letting out a breath. "The Postman must really hate you."

You have no idea.

"I feel bad for Nyles. He was really nice to me my first day."

"I have to save them," Dee blurted out.

Mara laughed. "Save them? Why?"

Because they're my friends.

Dee stopped herself before she said the words. No one had friends on Alcatraz 2.0, and yet her instinct showed where her heart was. Nyles and even Griselda were her friends. They'd risked their own safety to help her. She wasn't going to let them die.

"Because they're my—"

Dee's answer was cut off by a quick series of raps at her front door before it flew open, ripping the spearmint dental floss and spork contraption away from the wall. Ethan bounded into the living room. Mara screamed and fled for the backyard.

"Mara!" Dee cried. "It's okay! He's a friend."

"Dude!" Ethan said, oblivious to Mara's presence. "What are you going to do?" Then he paused and turned around. "And why was your door unlocked?" He sniffed the air. "And why does your living room smell minty fresh?"

"I want to save them," Dee said, feeling utterly helpless. "But with all those warehouses on the island, it'll be a miracle if we find Griselda and Nyles in time."

"Th-the old navy brig," Mara said tentatively, peeking out from behind the dining room wall, as if ready to bolt out the back again at the smallest sign of danger.

Dee caught her breath. "What?"

Mara's voice sounded small, but she spoke with total conviction. "When the Hardy Girls dressed up as Merricat and Constance Blackwood and killed Nikolai Ivankov by force-feeding him sugar-covered blackberries until his stomach exploded, I compared screen grabs of their kill room to photos of the old naval prison on the island. Part of it was turned into a wine-tasting room twenty years ago, but there is a ninety-five-percent chance that it's the same place."

"Duuuuude," Ethan said slowly. "She's so badass. Wait." He cocked his head to the side. "Who the hell are you?"

"This is Mara. She lives next door."

Ethan nodded. "You used to work at the bodega. I remember the red hair. Any idea why there's, like, no food in there right now?"

That was *so* not important at the moment. "Ethan, do you know where the navy brig is?"

"Not really. But we could probably find it."

She appreciated his use of the pronoun "we," but without knowing exactly where the prison was, they had no chance of reaching Nyles and Griselda in time. They needed a guide.

"Mara," Dee began gently, "can you take us there?"

Mara recoiled. Her shoulders pinched toward her ears and rolled forward, as if she were trying to wrap herself into a cocoon. "Go to a kill room? Voluntarily?"

Eighteen minutes and forty-nine seconds. "We don't have time to find it ourselves. Please, Mara."

"I—"

"You won't even have to go in. Just point it out and go home."

Mara's eyes shifted from Dee's face to the TV screen. Nyles had managed to wiggle his wrists free of the ropes and was working to untie Griselda. The water had risen past their ankles. Would they even have the full twenty minutes? Dee wouldn't have put it past The Postman to lie to them.

"Mara, please!"

She swallowed. "Okay."

"Sweet!" Ethan cried. Then he turned and sprinted outside. "I'll meet you at the corner."

"Where are you going?"

"I need to suit up!" he shouted over his shoulder.

Suit up? Dee looked down at her own outfit. A yellow fit-and-flare dress with ruffled sleeves and patent-leather flats. Running across the island in that getup would make quite a spectacle for The Postman's cameras, but she didn't have time to change. She grabbed her key ring from the kitchen counter and followed Ethan out the door.

Mara didn't say a word, just chewed on her bottom lip as Dee locked up.

"It'll be okay," Dee said, catching one last look at the countdown screen through the living room window. Eighteen minutes, four seconds.

"I know."

Both of them were full of crap, but who was going to call it out? It was easier to believe the lie.

They were almost at the corner when Ethan barreled out of his house. He wore camouflage cargo pants with his cross-trainers, a matching bandanna around his shaved head, and that was it. He was shirtless, his sharply cut muscles and menagerie of tattoos flexing with every stride, and as he joined them, Dee realized that he'd smeared some black stuff in diagonal lines across his face.

"You've *got* to be kidding me," she said.

"What?" Ethan flexed, bouncing his pectorals as he alternated sides. "I'm Arnold Schwarzenegger in *Commando*." He cleared his throat and attempted an Austrian accent. "Let off some steam, Bennett."

Perfect. Ethan thought that he was in an eighties action movie, Dee was dressed like a princess cosplayer, and they were about to go up against two grown-women serial killers posing as little girls. Worst day ever?

Ethan set his stopwatch. "Sixteen minutes. Let's get this show on the road."

Dee sighed. They had no plan, only half an idea where they were going, and everyone's life was on the line. "Lead the way, Mara."

"Down Ninth Street," she said, pointing.

Ethan ran ahead, sprinting down Ninth so fast Dee and Mara could barely keep up. "She's your baggage," he called back, still in his Arnold voice. "You fall behind, and you're on your own."

"Isn't that from *Predator*?" Mara asked.

"Just go with it," Dee said, impressed that Mara could identify one of Ethan's quotes.

Dee tried to keep a mental clock in her head while they ran, but it was difficult to judge the seconds from the pace of their steps and the pounding in her ears as her heart accelerated into the red zone. They raced by the sports fields and Bizarro Main Street, a briny wind lashing at them from the north. Ethan had already jogged ahead when Mara stopped in front of what appeared to be an abandoned school.

"Hey!" Dee called to Ethan. "It's this way, Magellan."

"Sweet!" He sprinted back. "What movie is that from?"

Dee was starting to understand Griselda's exasperation. "History?"

He shook his head. "Haven't seen it."

They followed Mara down an unfamiliar street. Near the end she slowed, then stopped near a shiny, light-stone building set back from the street behind a large, overgrown parking lot.

A huge fence ringed the property, making it more reminiscent of its original penal purpose than a remodeled wine-tasting room. There was wire mesh instead of chain link, and about ten feet up, it curved inward toward the building at a forty-five-degree angle, ensuring that it was impossible for anyone inside its confines to climb out. Instead of the usual crow-shape cameras, the fence was dotted with old-fashioned security cams, which looked like large metallic mailboxes perched on rotating arms. They slowly panned the interior of the old prison courtyard, back and forth, each at its own pace, probably the same way they'd operated fifty years ago when the navy still used the brig.

Well, at least The Postman was into recycling.

Beyond the fence, a large three-story building faced with beige slate loomed in the morning sunshine. It looked less foreboding than its barrier, with lots of large windows of blue-tinted glass, but as Dee approached, she realized that metal doors had been installed on the inside of the windows, sealing off the building from whatever sunlight they might have provided.

"Twelve minutes, three seconds," Ethan said. He didn't even sound out of breath. "I'll check the perimeter."

"We should stick together," Dee said, panting. Too late. He dashed around the corner of the fence into what looked like an old driveway, and disappeared. "Damn it, Ethan."

"I think there's a door at the end of the driveway," Mara said. She stood in the middle of the street, refusing to approach the property.

"Okay." Dee smiled. "Thank you."

"Be careful."

Dee nodded, then spun around to follow Ethan. She could see his camouflage weaving down the driveway, pausing to crouch behind low bushes like the leader of some Navy SEAL team raiding an enemy stronghold. Dee wasn't entirely sure why he bothered, since he was clearly in view of half a dozen cameras at once, but whatever. Ethan was playing out his own action movie in his head, and the cameras just added to the fantasy.

When he reached the front door, Ethan pressed his body against it, looking left and right as if scanning for the surveillance he already knew existed, then somersaulted away and crouched in a crevice near a window.

At least he was having fun.

Ethan was power-squatting in front of the window when Dee arrived, hands cupped around his eyes as he tried to peer inside through a thin vertical pane.

"See anything?" Dee asked.

He let out a high-pitched shriek and jumped away. "Shit, dude," he said, panting. "You scared me."

Seriously? "Do you see anything?" she repeated.

"Looks empty."

Dee glanced at his watch. Eleven minutes. "Let's hope not." She and Ethan were probably about to walk into their deaths, but the option was to turn around, go home, and watch Nyles and Griselda drown on an eternal loop from every TV screen on the island.

So, really, there wasn't an option at all.

Dee took a deep breath and approached the door.

"I might be able to break it down," Ethan said. He stood up and bent his right knee, catching his foot in his hand so he could stretch out his quad. "One good ninja kick might do it."

Dee had no idea what a ninja kick might be, but she decided to try the door before Ethan started breaking things. She was utterly surprised when it swung open.

"Or we could just open it," Ethan said, bounding up behind her. "Good job."

Stepping into the lobby of the old navy brig was like stepping back in time. A low counter sat to their right, a thick blanket of dust covering its surface, with a NO FIREARMS BEYOND THIS POINT sign affixed to the wall. A row of small lockers faced them, all of which were open, empty, and rusting, and a hallway snaked off to the right. Everything looked decrepit and abandoned, except for the shiny new domed security cameras—identical to the ones that filled Dee's house and I Scream—that had been installed on the ceiling, their red lights ablaze.

Someone was watching, which meant they were in the right place.

Dee tapped Ethan on the shoulder, then silently pointed to the nearest lens. "It's a trap."

"Oh, totally," he said, sounding excited. "That's why I came. Boo-yah!"

Great. She had Rambo as a partner. This couldn't possibly go wrong.

Ethan spun around, scanning the lobby, then paused at a spot by the counter, where a fire extinguisher was bolted to the wall. "Aha!" He planted one hand on the counter and vaulted over it, kicking up a frenzy of clumpy dust particles, then ripped the extinguisher off its mount. He tucked the canister under one arm and held the hose in his hand like a gun. "You've got to ask yourself one question."

"Huh?"

"'Do I feel lucky?'" Ethan continued. "Well, do ya, punk?"

"Is that another movie thing?" she asked wearily, half wishing that she had Mara there to interpret.

Ethan frowned. "It's freaking *Dirty Harry*. Were you raised under a rock?"

You have no idea. "Anything back there *I* can use?"

"Um . . ." He peered under the counter lips pressed together. Suddenly his face lit up. "Here you go." He tossed a rusty stapler to her.

"This will be perfect if I want to do minor skin damage."

"Better than nothing," Ethan said. "Let's do this."

Ethan leaped back over the counter just as easily with the large extinguisher as when he was without it, and Dee, stapler in hand, followed him around the corner.

TRAZBET.COM

(an affiliate of Postman Enterprises, Inc.)

INMATE: Dee Guerrera (#CinderellaSurvivor)
DAYS ALIVE: 2
INMATE: Ethan Robinson (#EthanTheBuff)
DAYS ALIVE: 27
PERIOD: 9 November 12:00 a.m. – 9 November 11:59 p.m.
CONDITIONS: Interior, Well-Lit

TIME TILL DEATH (rounded)	**ODDS**	**$2 PAYOUT**
5 minutes	10-1	$22.00
10 minutes	9-2	$11.00
15 minutes	9-5	$5.60
20 minutes	1-1	$4.00
25 minutes	3-5	$3.20
30 minutes	11-1	$24.00
NO SHOW	16-1	$34.00

TWENTY-SIX

DEE WASN'T SURE WHAT SHE'D BEEN EXPECTING. A WALL OF total darkness. A giant hulk of a prison with iron bars and walkways. Or a corridor lined with giant chain saws.

Any of those things would have been expected on Alcatraz 2.0. Instead, Dee saw just a hallway. Normal. Old-fashioned. Homey.

It was well lit with bell-shaped overhead fixtures, and doors peeled off in opposite directions every ten to twelve feet. The floor was blanketed with blue-and-gray industrial carpet and, weirdest of all, the walls were papered. White with lavender flowers.

Lilacs, maybe? Hyacinth? Dee was shitty at botany.

"Looks like my grandma's house in Jersey." Ethan sniffed the air. "Smells like it too. Wet newspaper and BO."

"This seems familiar," Dee said as she gazed down the hallway. "Like from a dream or something."

"Your dreams suck."

"Thanks?"

A red light flickered to life inside a domed lens at the far end of the hall, and immediately two figures stepped into view beneath it. They wore matching powder-blue dresses with white knee socks and bandit masks, and they were holding hands. The Hardy Girls.

Suddenly the weird hallway made sense. The sociopathic sister act was dressed as the ghostly Grady Girls, and they were standing in a re-creation of the Overlook Hotel from *The Shining.*

"We are so screwed," Dee breathed.

"Play with us, DeeDee," they said in singsong unison. "Forever and ever and ever."

"Come at me, bro!" Ethan yelled, extinguisher hose in hand.

But the Hardy Girls didn't move. Instead, Dee heard what sounded like a small engine revving in the distance. The sound got louder, closer, and two objects rounded the corner, followed immediately by two more. They looked like old-fashioned Big Wheel trikes, each with a blue plastic seat, a red body, metal handlebars, two fat wheels in the back, and a single larger one in the front. They were toys, built for a child, but no five-year-old sat in the driver's seat. Instead, each trike seemed to pedal of its own accord by remote control as they raced down the hall toward Dee and Ethan.

"That's it?" Ethan laughed, letting his guard down. "That's all you've got?"

Dee had to admit, it did seem rather ludicrous that the Hardy Girls were sending a legion of remote-controlled kiddie toys their way, but she also knew that underestimating one of the Painiacs was the fastest way to dead. And since every single one of the cameras in the hallway had shifted its focus to the oncoming trikes, the toys had to be more dangerous than they looked.

"Stay away from them!" Dee cried, backing away.

"Why?" The big wheels were halfway down the hall, closing in fast. "They can't hurt—"

Without warning, one of the Big Wheels veered sharply to the left and crashed headlong into the wall. At the instant of impact, the toy bike exploded. It was so violent, the hallway shook, and Dee could feel the reverberations in the air.

"Holy shit!" Ethan scampered down the hall, right on Dee's heels. They rounded the corner and jumped up onto the counter just as a second Big Wheel misjudged the turn and crashed into the wall of lockers. Twisted metal ricocheted toward them, and Dee and Ethan had to roll onto the floor behind the counter to keep from getting skewered.

"This counter won't protect us from those explosives," Dee said. They *so* didn't have time for this. Somewhere in this building, Nyles and Griselda were about to drown while she was playing hide-and-seek with a couple of highly explosive kiddie toys.

The remote-control engines revved again. The last two trikes were coming for them.

"I didn't think I'd go out like this," Ethan mused. "Hiding from a Big Wheel."

Dee spotted the camera directly overhead. The dome had been shattered, hit by shrapnel from the exploding lockers. Which meant, for the time being at least, no one could see them. "You're not going to die here."

Her focus shifted to the door leading out from behind the counter. It probably opened back into the hallway, but at least it would give them the element of surprise. It was a chance they'd have to take.

"Come on!" She grabbed Ethan by the arm and yanked open the door.

Instead of the creepy re-creation of the Overlook Hotel, the door opened onto a tight, dark passageway. Dee shoved Ethan through and had just squeezed in beside him when one of the trikes careened into the lobby counter. The force of the explosion slammed the door closed behind her, throwing them into total darkness.

Three down, one to go.

Dee and Ethan were pressed between a smooth metal wall of the old brig, and wood beams that supported some kind of structure on the other side. "That must be the hallway," Dee whispered, her eyes adjusting to the lack of light. "We're behind the set."

"Cool."

Dee kept her hand on Ethan's arm as he edged forward. She held her breath, listening for the last Big Wheel engine, but it was eerily quiet. Had The Postman, or whoever was directing this scene, lost track of them?

The set ended before a towering metal door, which swung open easily at Ethan's touch. They stepped through, and Dee thought they must have taken a wrong turn.

"Is this the same hallway?" Ethan asked.

This set was identical to the last one. Same wallpaper, same carpeting, same ceiling lights, same camera placement. Except there was no sign of the explosion the first trike had made when it had blown away a section of the wall, just smooth, unblemished lilac-and-white wallpaper. "I don't think so."

"But those are the same chicks, right?"

Dee spun around. The Hardy Girls were back, standing side by side at the end of the hallway, just as before. Only this time they each wielded a red-handled ax.

"PLAY WITH US, DEEDEE!"

In the distance Dee could hear the high-pitched hum of a toy engine. The last remote-controlled trike was coming up behind them. They were trapped.

"Screw this." Ethan opened the valve on the fire extinguisher. "I ain't got time to bleed!"

He bolted forward, spraying the Hardy Girls with foam. It squirted from the hose in a fine stream, but seemed to expand on contact, coating the carpet with a sticky mess as Ethan waved the hose around.

"Aim for the cameras!" Dee cried, hoping the foam would obscure the shot.

Ethan obeyed, spraying the ceiling haphazardly.

The Hardy Girls looked momentarily stunned, and Ethan was practically on top of them when they finally jolted into action. The taller sister gripped her ax with both hands, held it up over her head, and charged.

But Ethan was faster and more agile.

As she swung the ax down at his head, he flipped the canister from beneath his arm, catching the blade with it. The ax dug into the metal and stuck there as the pressure from inside the canister raced out through the gap. The extinguisher and ax, now a symbiotic being, flew from Ethan's hands and crashed into the wall. Ethan lunged for the ax handle as the canister spun around on the floor like a wheel of fireworks, the hose lashing out in all directions as it slowly lost pressure. But the carpet was slick with foam. Ethan lost his balance and went sprawling, sliding into the wall.

The shorter Hardy Girl lost no time. Like her sister, she swung the ax over her head, letting out a bloodcurdling scream as she attacked.

Dee didn't even have time to think. The slippery floor reminded her of a childhood toy, the old Slip 'N Slide her dad would set up on the lawn. She could cover more ground sliding headfirst down the grass than running across it. Dee took several running strides toward Ethan's assailant, then dove forward on her stomach.

She slid ten feet, barreling into the Hardy Girl's legs like a bowling ball taking out the last pin for a spare. The Hardy Girl face-planted onto the floor, breaking her fall with the razor-sharp ax, which embedded itself in the plywood below the carpet. Dee rolled on her side, stopping her momentum in time to see the other sister lunge at her. But Ethan was on his feet. He grabbed Dee's assailant around the waist and hurled her down the hallway.

Dee had known Ethan was strong, but she wasn't sure she'd realized *how* strong. He tossed that serial killer like she was a rag doll. She seemed to hang suspended, arms and legs spread-eagled, mouth snarled up with pure hatred, just as the final Big Wheel rounded the corner and accelerated toward them.

There was no way Ethan could have known that the explosives-laden toy would arrive at that moment. Even the airborne Hardy Girl didn't seem to process her situation immediately. She hit the floor with a thud, and just had time to sit up and see the trike pedaling toward her before impact.

Smoke filled the fake hallway as the force of the explosion rocked its foundations, knocking Ethan to his knees. Which was a good thing, because bits and pieces of the detonated Hardy Girl went flying in every direction. One of her hands grazed Ethan's cheek before smacking into the wall—a final assault, even in death. All that was left of her was a bloody charred blob on the floor, a few severed-limb fragments, and a splatter of tissue on the lilac-covered walls.

Dee blinked, her eyes watering in the smoke-filled air, and rolled on her side, fully expecting to see the glint of an ax blade as the other sister dove at her. But as the smoke cleared, all Dee could see in the devastation of extinguisher foam and body parts was Ethan, slowly climbing to his feet.

The other sister, and her weapon, had vanished.

TWENTY-SEVEN

"HOW MUCH TIME DO WE HAVE LEFT?" DEE ASKED, SCRAMbling to her feet.

Ethan glanced at his watch. "Two and a half minutes."

"Shit." Dee stepped over a severed foot, still in its black Mary Jane, and peeked around the edge of the wall, fully expecting the missing sister to leap out at her from the shadows. Instead she saw that the hotel hallway abruptly ended at two double doors that opened into the next room. "We have to hurry."

"On it." Ethan put one foot on the inert fire extinguisher and wrenched the ax out of the canister. "Now I have a machine gun. Ho-ho-ho."

"That's not a machine gun."

Ethan rolled his eyes. "It's from *Die Hard*."

His favorite. "Of course it is."

The doors opened onto a massive space spanning the full three stories that Dee had seen from the outside. The walls were pale yellow, the fluorescents so bright they stung her eyes, but even as she blinked against the painful light, she saw the tank in the middle of the room.

They'd made it.

The water was near the top, less than a foot from the lid that the Hardy Girls had padlocked into place. Nyles and Griselda had kicked off their shoes and managed to free themselves from the ropes. They were treading water, their faces just barely visible above the waterline.

The camera, a massive hooded creature like the kind used on movie and television shoots, stood on a tripod across the room, but as much as Dee wanted to watch Ethan take his ax to the wretched thing, they didn't have time.

"Ethan!" she cried, pointing to the tank. "Break the glass!"

"On it." He raced forward, ax raised above his head, and brought the head down against the side of the tank with all his strength.

A teeny-tiny dent appeared in the glass.

"Shit!" Ethan said.

"Keep at it," Dee instructed. "I'll try to kill the water."

Ethan whaled away on the side of the tank while Dee crouched beside the thick fireman's hose. It looked as if it should unscrew easily, but the metric shit-ton of water surging through its thick fibers made the hose impossibly heavy. Dee tried to twist the end, but the water pressure kept the docking mechanism firmly in place.

Maybe Ethan could get it to budge? He'd managed to open the dent into a large crack, but hadn't broken through the tank just yet. Dee started to call him over, but the words never made it out of her mouth.

As she looked up, she found Nyles's face in front of hers. He was submerged, his dirty-blond hair swirly around his narrow features, and he was pointing furiously at something behind Dee.

Dee was still processing Nyles's warning when she saw a reflection in the glass. Just a momentary flash of shiny metal against the thick tank wall as the surviving Hardy Girl brought down her ax, aiming straight for Dee's head.

Dee had a split second to react. She dove forward, over the hose, and felt the rush of air as the blade missed her by inches.

But it didn't miss the hose. The momentum of the Hardy Girl's swing severed it clean in half.

The massive canvas hose flopped onto the floor like a snake whose head had been cut off. It slithered away, gushing water onto the concrete. More importantly, without its fuel source the tank began to drain.

Which was awesome for Nyles and Griselda, who were only inches away from being completely submerged. Not as awesome for Dee, who was cornered by the Hardy Girl.

"You killed my sister," she said, the singsong voice from the Grady Girls impression totally abandoned.

Dee slid back, arms and legs slipping in the thin layer of water that coated the floor. "Ethan!" she screamed, but he was still swinging away against the tank wall and didn't seem to hear her over the rush of water and the cracking of safety glass.

"No one's going to help you now, Cinderella Survivor." She raised the ax over her head. "A hundred million spikes coming my way."

Dee raised her arm in front of her face, expecting to feel the blade slice into her skin. Instead she heard a thud, and then the Hardy Girl staggered sideways. Her ax clattered to the floor, and she collapsed into a pile, eyes open, her head at an unnatural angle.

Behind her, fire extinguisher in hand, was Mara.

It took some work to get Nyles and Griselda out of the tank. Ethan finally managed to break through the thick double-paned glass, but it didn't shatter; instead, a spiderweb of cracks spread outward from the epicenter of Ethan's blows, like it was a car windshield in an accident. Then he used the ax blade to wrench bits of the pane away until there was a space large enough for Nyles and Griselda. He hooked the ax through a belt loop on his pants and lifted Griselda to safety.

"Don't I get a thank-you kiss?" he asked.

"If by *kiss* you mean *punch* . . ." She nailed him in the shoulder. "Then yes."

"Damn, girl." Ethan dropped her and rubbed his shoulder. "That's the last time I save *your* life."

Nyles tossed their shoes out of the tank, then tried to haul himself through the hole. He had to contort his long, thin body in order to fit, rotating his hips to the point where he was flopped on his back, stuck. "A little help here?"

Ethan looped his arms around Nyles's torso and dragged him to safety, breaking off a giant chunk of the double pane in the process. He then spun Nyles around in a circle, his legs flailing like a kite's tail while water droplets sprayed the room, before placing him back on his feet.

"Er, do you want a thank-you kiss from me as well?" Nyles asked.

Ethan held up his hand. "Nah, I only like hot dudes."

Nyles wrinkled his upper lip while he wiped bits of crumbled glass from his soaking-wet pajama bottoms. "Can someone tell me what in the bloody hell just happened?"

"You, me, death averted," Griselda replied.

But Nyles wasn't listening. "The ambassador will hear about this. I have diplomatic immunity!"

"Wait!" Ethan cried, holding up both of his hands.

Nyles looked confused. "Huh?"

Ethan crouched in front of him, his right hand forming a gun aimed right at Nyles. "Say it again."

"Say what?"

"The same thing you say, like, twenty times a day."

Nyles tilted his head to the side. "That I have diplomatic immunity?"

"BAM!" Ethan pretended to fire the gun. "It's just been revoked."

Nyles turned to Dee. "Any idea what he's talking about?"

Dee couldn't help but laugh. "It's one of his action movies, I think."

Ethan blew on his finger gun like he was putting out a candle. "*Lethal Weapon Two.* I've been waiting months for someone to try and kill you so I could use that line."

"You realize how disturbed you sound right now," Nyles said. "Yes?"

Ethan sighed, bliss radiating from every pore. "That was better than a kiss. Thank you, dude."

"Can we get out of here?"

Dee turned around and the laughter died on her lips. Mara still stood over the Hardy Girl she'd killed, staring down at her with unblinking eyes. She looked shaky, as if she was about to vomit or pass out, or both.

"What the hell is *she* doing here?" Griselda asked as she wrung water from the hem of her skirt. Though the words had Griselda's usual hard edge, her face was paler than usual. It was the closest thing Dee had seen to fear from her coworker.

"This is Mara," Dee said quickly, rushing to her side. "My neighbor."

"She used to work at the bodega," Ethan added.

"I know who she is," Griselda snapped. "But why is she here? Now?"

Dee smiled. "She's the one who knew where to find you guys."

Nyles was immediately interested. "How?"

Mara blinked, pulling her eyes away from the Hardy Girl. Her pale skin was drained of all color. "The Hardy Girls always use the same location," she began. "I compared old photos of structures on the island—"

"Until you found one that was similar in size," Nyles interjected, finishing her thought. He spoke quickly, obviously excited. "And then cross-referenced that with historical records until you found a perfect match?"

"Um, yeah," Mara said. "I used to study The Postman's killers all the time. You know, before."

"Not weird at all," Griselda said sarcastically.

But instead of being intimidated, Mara appraised Griselda like a doctor examining a patient. "I thought it might come in handy if I ever ended up in here."

"And since that information just saved our lives," Nyles exclaimed, "I say well done!" He grabbed Mara's hand and pumped it up and down vigorously. "An absolutely brilliant execution of the scientific method."

"We helped too," Ethan said.

"Yes, of course." He shook Ethan's hand, then grabbed Dee and hugged her tightly. "I really do appreciate it."

Dee felt the heat rising to her cheeks as Nyles released her. "You'd have done the same for me."

"You sure about that, Princess?"

If she was honest with herself, she probably wasn't sure that Nyles or Ethan or Griselda would have come to her aid. She wasn't sure if her actions made her a better person, or just incredibly stupid.

"Yes," she said, meeting Griselda's cool gaze. "Yes, I am."

7m

BozzieJ @RedSnow1RedSnow2

Um, can someone explain to me how Andrew, Claire, Brian, Bender, and Allison just took out BOTH of the Hardy Girls? #HuntingTheHunters #NotMyPostman

← | : 1,361 ₪: 470

7m

Nikola Testicla @NikolaTesticla

I feel like the @TheHardyGirls were the victims of sticking to theme. While I appreciate the trikes and axes (though the double drowning was MEH), taking some creative license might have ended differently. #NotSpikeWorthy #EvenInDeath #NotMyPostman

← | : 244 ₪: 63

6m

Benny Nda Jetts @EltonJohnForevzz

I'm surprised the conspiracy theory nut jobs haven't weighed in on this one yet. #DontTrustThoseWhoDontTrustTheFeed #ComePlayWithUs

← | : 52 ₪: 98

6m

Ellen Enchanted @EllenMEnchanted2

@RedSnow1RedSnow2 WHO?

← | : 38 ₪: 5

6m

Extreme Giants Fan @bleedorangeandblack

Where's the edited replay? @ThePostman_PEI usually has them up by now.

← | : 380 ₪: 221

⏲ 6m

BozzieJ @RedSnow1RedSnow2

The Breakfast Club.

⏲ 6m

> **Ella Enchanted** @EllenMEnchanted2
> @RedSnow1RedSnow2 WHO?

← | : 171 ₪: 20

⏲ 5m

The Griff @awakewideopen

EMERGENCY!! Sources tell me something is wrong over at @ThePostman_PEI. Have you noticed how the bodega has been empty? NO deliveries. And there's no edited footage of @TheHardyGirls up yet. #FakeNews #EyesOpen #DontTrustTheFeed

← | : 590 ₪: 402

⏲ 5m

Benny Nda Jetts @EltonJohnForevzz

I stand corrected.

⏲ 5m

> **The Griff** @awakewideopen
> EMERGENCY!! Sources tell me something is wrong over at @ThePostman_PEI. Have you noticed how the bodega has been empty? NO deliveries. And there's no edited footage of @TheHardyGirls up yet. #FakeNews #EyesOpen #DontTrustTheFeed

← | : 52 ₪: 18

⏲ 5m

Capuchin's Ghost @CapedCapuchinGhost

@RedSnow1RedSnow2 @BozzieJ More like the Death Row Breakfast Club. Did I win the Internet? #DeathRowBreakfastClub #DRBC

← | : 12,553 ₪: 7,800

TWENTY-EIGHT

SUNNY SKIES MET DEE AND HER BEDRAGGLED FRIENDS AS they emerged from the brig and made their way back to Main Street. Ethan spent the trip relating his adventures during the rescue attempt, adding elements from his favorite action flicks.

"And then there was this massive explosion," he said, trotting backward to face Griselda. "Shit was flying everywhere. I threw myself in front of Dee to protect her."

"It's a shame you weren't killed," Griselda said.

"Right?" Ethan said, totally oblivious to her sarcasm. "I mean, I should have died like five times. Maybe ten." He patted the ax dangling at his side. "But it takes more than a couple of chicks with axes to take me out."

Dee didn't correct him on the details. Not worth it. She couldn't have saved Nyles and Griselda on her own, and she figured that by risking his life to help, Ethan had earned the right to tell the story in whatever way he chose.

"I can't wait to see how I look on film," he added.

"Yes," Nyles said absently. "I'm sure you can't."

While Ethan was basking in the glory of his very own action movie, Nyles was oddly silent, his mood growing more somber every minute. He lagged behind, and once or twice Dee caught him glancing up at her from beneath lowered brows. His face was troubled, matching his thoughts, and Dee was pretty sure she knew exactly what he was thinking.

He'd almost died. And it was all Dee's fault.

"I'm sorry," she said to him quietly, dropping into step beside him.

"For what?"

"I think that Hardy Girls thing was because of me."

His lips curved into a tight smile. "I suppose it was bound to happen eventually."

Dee was pretty sure he was trying to alleviate her guilt, but she wasn't sure either of them believed it.

"I shouldn't have fallen asleep," he said, shaking off the brooding mood that had fallen over him, evincing some of his signature charm. "That's when they get you."

First Blair was taken at night; now Griselda and Nyles. Dee was pretty sure she would never sleep again.

They headed to the gym, where Ethan washed the camo paint off his face while Nyles and Griselda changed into dry clothes. Mara sat quietly on a weight bench, her calm pose in direct conflict with her jittery, fidgeting hands.

"Why didn't you return to the Barracks?" Dee asked. She'd never wanted to get Mara involved.

A tiny smile crept up the sides of Mara's face. "I meant to. But, I don't know. I realized you might need help."

"Thank you." The words seemed totally inadequate. "For saving my life."

"You're welcome."

"One hundred million spikes?" Ethan gaped at the TV screen as he emerged from the men's room, wiping his face with a towel. "Dude, that's got to be a record."

The video played on a loop, straight through from the moment Dee and Ethan entered the old prison. Usually by now The Postman would have chopped up the video, adding slo-mo edits and commentary, breaking the feed into different camera angles showing in different windows on the screen, but not this time. Just the facts, from beginning to end, and the only embellishments came from the fan commentary scrolling up the side.

It had been twenty minutes since the rescue, but already the Postmantics had come up with a special name for Dee and her friends.

Death Row Breakfast Club—and the #DRBC hashtag—was trending hard.

Someone had even photoshopped an image of the movie poster for *The Breakfast Club* with the faces of Dee, Mara, Griselda, Ethan, and Nyles superimposed onto the actors and actresses.

Dee scowled as she realized that she'd been cast as the prissy princess Claire, though she had to admit it was accurate, based on her wardrobe. Ethan was every bit the jock. Mara was kind of a basket case. Gender aside, if ever there was a grating smartass like Bender, it was certainly Griselda. And Nyles was perfect as—

"The *nerd*?" Nyles leaned against the wall, shaking the excess water from his damp hair as he gazed dejectedly at the screen. "You can't be serious."

Griselda arched an eyebrow. "Who did you expect to be? The jock?"

"No, not exactly."

"The hot one?" she pressed.

Nyles wrinkled his upper lip. "If by 'hot one' you mean the tall, masculine bloke wearing too many layers of clothes, then yes, I suppose I fit that mold more closely than you do."

"Why?" Mara asked. "Because she has a vagina?"

"'S okay, dude." Ethan held his fist out to Nyles for a bump. "That actor turned out to be smokin' hot. There's still hope for you."

Nyles exhaled slowly, far from mollified. "This might be the most depressing conversation of my life."

The room fell silent and heavy with unspoken words. No one wanted to start a substantive conversation in front of the cameras, but Dee didn't need her friends to say anything to know what they were thinking. Now it wasn't just Dee with a target on her back. The Death Row Breakfast Club had thwarted The Postman's plans and killed two more of his Painiacs. There was no way he'd let that slide.

"I'm surprised he's showing the video all the way through," Mara said, her eyes glued to the footage of Ethan spraying the hallway with extinguisher foam. "Does he really want the world to watch us kill two of his executioners?"

"One hundred million views is why," Nyles said. He eyed the nearest camera. "That's the most spikes I've ever seen."

"I'm hungry," Ethan said, standing up.

"Shocking," Griselda replied.

Ethan grabbed a clean T-shirt and pulled it over his head. "Let's go to the bodega."

"I didn't exactly remember to bring my card with me when I was kidnapped," Nyles said.

"'S okay, dude. My treat."

Without a better plan in mind, they followed Ethan out of the gym.

"I'm gonna get two beefy rice bowls," Ethan continued, bouncing on his toes like a child as they approached the market. He gripped the door handle with his meaty hand. "And a protein bar. And—"

He tugged on the door, but it wouldn't budge. The bodega was locked.

"What the fuck?" Ethan said, rattling the locked doors back and forth. Dee was half surprised the lock didn't give. "It's feeding time, Rodrigo. Open up!"

Nyles peered through the window. "The lights are off. I don't think anyone's been here today."

Dee didn't like this. First the missing deliveries, and now the store was closed altogether. "Is there a back door?"

Mara nodded. "Usually locked, but you never know."

They had to loop back down to the gym in order to access the alley that ran behind the businesses on Main Street. It was littered with cardboard boxes, strewn about after the last delivery, most likely, and dusty milk crates.

"What's today?" Mara asked as Ethan pounded on the back door.

"Wednesday."

"There should have been a delivery yesterday."

Griselda nodded. "Same at I Scream." She gazed down the alley at the back of the ice-cream shop. "I don't see anything."

"Dudes, I'm starving to death," Ethan whined. "What are we going to do?"

"Aren't there bananas and stuff at the shop?" Dee asked.

"We'll have to go back to the Barracks to get the key," Griselda said.

"Fuck that," Ethan said. He raced down the alley to the back door of I Scream, and without slowing down, barreled into it.

Dee half expected the metal door to implode due to the force of Ethan's impact, but it held firm, and Ethan bounced like a tennis ball smacked with an inside-out backhand.

"Damn it!" He rubbed his forearm. "That fucking hurt."

Griselda snorted. "Try it with your head next time."

"Or your ax?" Mara suggested, pointing to the weapon dangling from Ethan's belt.

Ethan stared at the door ruefully. "Schwarzenegger would have used his shoulder."

"Or . . ." Nyles grabbed the handle. "He might have tried the doorknob."

"I locked it," Griselda said. "Last night."

But when Nyles tugged, the back door swung open easily.

"What the fuck is going on?" Griselda's voice was sharp, on edge.

Mara sucked in a breath. "It's a trap. One of the killers is inside."

"Who cares?" Ethan whipped out his ax and barreled through the open door. "I've got a fucking ax now."

They tentatively followed him inside as Ethan swept through I Scream with his ax raised, expecting to find a Painiac lurking in the freezer unit or under one of the tables, but there was clearly no one hiding in the shop. Though visibly disappointed, Ethan found solace in making a child's dream breakfast of banana splits. He dropped the ax on the counter and proceeded to scoop massive balls of strawberry ice cream into a bowl.

Six-year-old Dee's head would have exploded from joy at the prospect of eating dessert in the morning, but today she wasn't hungry. On the monitor, the rescue video had just reset, showing Dee, Mara, and Ethan running down Ninth Street toward the old brig. The spikes had doubled since they had been in the gym. *Two hundred million?* That was like two-thirds of the entire United States. What kind of a messed-up world were they living in where everyone watched in rapt attention while some sicko serial killers attempted to murder teenagers?

The comments scrolled nonstop, a steady stream of critique and observation. But as Dee watched with unseeing eyes, her brain began to pick out words that didn't usually show up from the Postmantics. Things like "unfair" and "I thought there were rules" and "diplomatic immunity."

She smiled at the last one and was about to point it out to Nyles, when the comment beneath it sent chills down her spine.

🕒 5m

Tamara Gucci @thirdex-mrsgucci
WTF is going on with the feeds? Half the channels have gone dead. I can't see #SilverFoxLibrarian's house AT ALL. Seriously, WTF @ThePostman_PEI???

← | : 26,434 ₪: 7,110

🕒 5m

Viktor Heinz @ViktorViktorViktor
@thirdex-mrsgucci Huh. UR right. Can't see anything but Main St. And 9th. And I Scream. And that room with the dead @TheHardyGirls girl. And . . .

← | : 35 ₪: 12

🕒 4m

Blake the Flake @blakeflakesseven
Why is nobody talking about the fact that #CinderellaSurvivor has now killed THREE of @ThePostman_PEI's executioners? How is that EVEN POSSIBLE?!

← | : 4,531 ₪: 222

🕒 4m

Tiny Striker @musicboxdancer11
You'd think @ThePostman_PEI would have had better odds for #CinderellaSurvivor up on @Trazbet.

← | : 78 ₪: 40

🕒 4m

Alfred E. Mnemonics @alfredemnemonics
Hey @TimeWarner! I think there's an Internet outage around #Alcatraz2. Can you fix pleez?

← | : 11,845 ₪: 536

The Griff @awakewideopen — 3m

@alfredemnemonics There's no Internet outage. @ThePostman_PEI doesn't want you to see what's going on! The rest of the island is dark? How convenient! So, you can't see what's really happening! I'm sure the rest of the inmates are just on a lunch break. #DontTrustTheFeed #EyesOpen

← | : 3,430 ₪: 474

Johnson Tyne @johnsons_johnso — 2m

At least we can still see the hotties. Did anyone else catch #EthanR telling #NylesTheBrit that he wasn't his type? I thought he was into #Skankselda?

← | : 318 ₪: 72

Justice 4Me @justice4mebutnotall — 2m

Hey! I thought #NylesTheBrit had diplomatic immunity? Isn't he off-limits?

← | : 76 ₪: 30

Monica MoBetta @MoBettaStylz — 1m

Kimmi released three weeks ago. Stay alive. I'm working on it. —p

← | : 4 ₪: 0

TWENTY-NINE

"DO YOU WANT TO BE MY SISTER?"

Dee's eyes flew open. The question was so familiar by now, but this time it sounded different. Kimmi's voice was closer. Not drifting down from the air vent, but right behind her.

Kimmi was in the white room.

She must have come in while Dee was sleeping, though Dee had no idea how. She'd felt every inch of the walls, looking for a door, but had never found so much as a crack in the tiles, let alone the seam of a door. Had Kimmi come down from the vent? Was that the only way out?

"Do you want to be my sister?" she repeated. Dee heard the faint exhale of Kimmi's breath, the soft swoosh of fabric as she shifted position.

Dee didn't move. Maybe if Kimmi thought she was still asleep, she'd leave.

"I know you're not sleeping, Dolores. Do you *not* want to be my sister?" There was a nastiness in her tone that made Dee's breath catch in her chest. "Do you want me to think you don't like me?"

"No!" Dee said. She pushed herself into a sitting position and spun around to face Kimmi.

Dee's tormentor sat cross-legged on the smooth, glossy floor. She wore jeans and a gray long-sleeve shirt, and her blond hair hung on either side of her face, which was sharp and hawkish.

"So?" Kimmi prompted.

Dee swallowed. Her tongue was parched and swollen from lack of water, and her stomach ached with hunger. What did Kimmi want her to say? What was the right answer?

"I . . . I want to be your sister," Dee said, stumbling over the words.

"More than *anything*?"

Dee nodded, choking down a sob.

"Play with me."

Dee glanced around the room, empty except for the two of them and a couple of crumpled fast-food bags.

"Play?"

Kimmi rolled her eyes dramatically, and the blue irises all but disappeared into the top of her skull. "*Pretend*, silly. Tell me what we'll play."

Dee couldn't even remember what kind of toys she'd played with when she was younger. It was as if nothing else existed—no memories, no past—beyond the walls of the white room. "Dolls?"

"No!"

"Video games?"

Kimmi had clicked her tongue. "I can do that with my brother."

"You have a brother?"

"*I* ASK THE QUESTIONS!"

Dee's heart raced. If she didn't come up with an acceptable answer, Kimmi might get violent. Okay, okay. *Think*. What did teenage girls like to do?

"We can go shopping."

Kimmi sucked in a breath. "Oooooh!"

"And . . . and try on clothes."

"And?"

"And you can pick stuff out for me."

Kimmi squealed. "Oh my God, we'll have so much fun. Do you really want to be my sister?"

"Yes."

A sly smile crept up the left side of Kimmi's face. "Do you want to braid my hair?"

Dee was light-headed, exhausted, and beginning to lose hope that she'd ever escape, but she braided Kimmi's long tresses with trembling hands. The plaits were wonky and uneven, but Kimmi either couldn't tell or didn't care. When Dee finished, Kimmi spun her around so that they could trade places.

Kimmi's technique was brutal. She pulled Dee's hair mercilessly, creating braids so tight Dee's entire scalp ached. When she finished, Kimmi roughly unwound the braids, causing Dee's eyes to well up with tears from the pain.

"Again," Kimmi said, and started another twist.

Dee never said a word. Never yelped out in pain or asked a question. She sat and endured while Kimmi prattled on and on about all the fun they were going to have together. Games and shopping, jump rope and classroom gossip, adventures and secrets. Forever and ever and ever.

Just when Dee was sure all of her hair must have been ripped out by the roots, Kimmi suddenly stood up.

"That was a fun game," she said. Then her tone shifted. "Go stand in the corner. Face the wall."

Dee's knees were wobbly as she pushed herself to her feet and stumbled to the far corner of the room. She couldn't see what Kimmi was doing, but she heard a soft beep followed by a click.

"We'll play games together forever, Dolores." Kimmi sighed as if sorry to leave the white room. "Sisters and best friends. I'll never let you go."

Dee continued to face the wall until she heard a second click. When she turned around, Kimmi had vanished.

"Thank you, user Justice 4Me," Nyles said, slapping his hand on the table. "I *do* have diplomatic immunity." He turned to Dee. "I mean, really. There are supposed to be rules about this thing, and . . ." His voice trailed off. "Dee, are you okay?"

Dee shook herself, emerging from a nightmare.

Ethan pulled out the chair beside her. "Seriously, dude. You look like you saw a ghost."

I did.

"What is it?" Mara's voice sounded anxious. "What did you see?"

"My sister . . ." It was all Dee could muster. A sob took her voice.

Her dad was trying to warn her. Trying to help her. Dee had wished rather than believed that he thought she was innocent, but now here was proof. She wasn't alone. Somewhere back in the real world, someone still cared.

Nyles slipped his arm around Dee's shoulders. "Gris," he began, "I rather feel like—"

"Yeah, yeah," she said. "Milk shake. On it."

Nyles waited until the blender started crunching ice cubes before he spoke again. By that time, Dee had managed to calm down.

"It's okay." His rounded British vowels were strangely soothing. "We know you didn't kill her, and we're going to find out who did, okay?"

Dee pressed the palms of her hands against her eyes. "Her screen name was in the comments."

Ethan's eyes widened. "I saw that shirtless tattooed magician guy text from inside a coffin buried beneath twenty feet of concrete. Do you think maybe she's alive in her grave?"

Dee pictured the cold, lifeless body, a mass of stiff limbs and pale skin that had once been Monica, and seriously doubted it.

"Someone's using her account," Mara suggested. "Trying to get a message to you."

"My dad. He said . . ." Shit. The last thing Dee wanted to do was tell them about Kimmi. Not only were they on camera, but also would learning about Dee's traumatic past really make them any more likely to believe her? No. The opposite.

"He said they're trying to appeal my case," she lied. None of them had seen the comment as it scrolled by on the screen, so no one could contradict her. "He thinks he knows who actually killed Monica."

"Ah!" Nyles smiled. "Now two of us will have immunity."

Mara shook her head. "What if it's really The Postman pretending to be your dad?"

"No." Dee was positive that the message had came from her dad. He'd even signed it with a *p* for Papa, the same way he'd signed the little notes he used to leave in her lunch box when she was a kid.

"Even if it is your dad," Mara pressed, "how are you going to stay alive long enough for him to get you out of here?"

Dee let out a long breath. Mara had a point. She was the number-one target on Alcatraz 2.0, now more than ever. Would she even survive the night, let alone a week or more, until her dad could facilitate her release? If that was even a possibility?

Gris switched the blender off, and the room fell silent.

"More ice, Gris," Nyles called over his shoulder. "Nice and slushy."

"There *isn't* any more ice." Griselda returned to the table with a pitcher of slush. "No delivery, remember?"

“I don’t like this,” Mara said, staring at the pitcher.

Ethan took a spoonful of icy chunks. “What do you mean?”

“Doesn’t it feel kind of empty around here?”

Dee gazed through the front window. Mara was right. Usually there were people moving about, going to and from their jobs, but today Main Street felt deserted.

“It’s early,” Nyles said, dismissing her fears. “The shop doesn’t get busy until the afternoon.”

“But it’s almost eleven,” Dee countered. “Yesterday we’d served half the island by then.”

“Dude,” Ethan said, dipping his spoon into the pitcher. “When you say ‘shop,’ do you spell it in your head like ‘shopp-ie’? Isn’t that a Brit thing?”

“No.” Nyles turned his back on Ethan. “I do not.”

“Maybe they assumed we wouldn’t open today,” Griselda said, backtracking. “Since I almost died and shit.”

“The library looks closed.” Dee craned her neck to see down the street. “And the hair salon.”

Ethan’s face lit up. “Alcatroliday! Like Christmas. Or Arnold Schwarzenegger’s birthday.”

But Dee wasn’t as excited by the prospect of a prison holiday. Mara was right: something weird was happening. “That’s not normal, is it? For Main Street to be closed?”

“Decidedly not,” Nyles said.

The hair stood up on Dee’s arms. “Where is everyone?”

“Maybe they’re hiding,” Mara suggested.

“Staycations aren’t really part of The Postman’s model,” Griselda countered.

"We need to search the Barracks," Dee said. "Go door to door and find out what's going on."

Griselda threw her arms up. "Why bother? If they're home, yay. If they're not, yay. If they're dead, yay."

"Dead?" Mara squeaked. "Who said anything about everyone being dead?"

"And what if he sends the guards in, huh?" Griselda continued. "What if they decide to just liquidate us and start over with new inventory?"

"Gris has a point," Nyles said.

"I'd rather be shot while I'm fighting," Dee said, "than drowned like a rat."

"Losers always whine about their best," Ethan said, nodding sagely. "Winners go home and fuck the prom queen. That's from *The Rock*, which is like totally appropriate to our sitch because it's set on the original Alcatraz."

"Oh my God!" Griselda cried. "Enough with the action-movie bullshit. This is not a movie. There's no script."

Arguing wasn't going to get them anywhere. "There's only one way to find out where everybody is," Dee said, "and that's to search the island. Agreed?"

Ethan punched his fist into the air. "Agreed!"

"Fine!" Griselda said, turning toward Ninth Street. "Let's get this over with."

THIRTY

THE TRIP ACROSS THE ISLAND TO THE BARRACKS REMINDED Dee of her first night, when the fear and isolation of Alcatraz 2.0 had been overwhelming. That night, Dee had followed Blair and the others, dogged by cameras that seemed to follow her every move.

But today, as they hurried down Ninth Street past the sports fields, Dee noticed that the crow cameras were oddly stationary. Instead of shadowing them, they just stared straight ahead, only picking up what crossed directly in front of their lenses.

When they reached the Barracks, Dee took the initiative and marched straight up to the first set of houses. It wasn't so much bravery as martyrdom: her friends had suffered enough because of her.

Dee took a deep breath and rang the doorbell.

All she got in response was silence.

Although that was to be expected. It wasn't as if the Avon lady did her rounds on Alcatraz 2.0. A ringing doorbell might mean a visit from one of The Postman's killers, and if it had been Dee, there was no way in hell she'd have answered.

"Anyone know who lives here?" she asked.

"Dude at the library," Ethan replied. "Tall, silver fox. I think his name's Steve? Steven? Steve-O?"

"Because Steve-O is such a common name," Griselda said. She stood back on the sidewalk, arms folded across her chest, refusing to participate.

Dee tried again, knocking this time. "Hello, Steve?" She tried to sound neighborly. "This is Dee from down the street. Are you home?"

Griselda sighed. "I'm *sure* that'll work."

"I'll do recon," Ethan said. He leaped off the edge of the porch like he was launching himself off the side of a cliff, hit the grass in a crouch, and immediately somersaulted around the side of the house.

"Try the handle?" Nyles suggested. He stood at Dee's shoulder with Mara tucked in behind him, peeking out around his narrow shoulders. "Maybe it's unlocked?"

Dee glanced at him out of the corner of her eyes. "In your seven months, one week, and six days on Alcatraz two-point-oh, have you known anyone to leave their front door unlocked?"

Nyles pursed his lips. "No, but everything else seems to be unlocked today. Why not the Barracks?"

"Good point." Dee gripped the handle and twisted.

It turned, and the door swung inward.

"Blinds are drawn," Ethan said, jogging back to the porch. "Can't see shit. Want me to bust down the—" He saw that Dee had already opened it, and his face fell. "Aw, man! I never get to have any fun."

"You can go first," Dee suggested. "Won't that be a blast?"

He winked at her. "You know me so well."

"Yes, yes," Nyles said, irritably. "You two are soul mates. Let's just get on with this, shall we?" Then he pushed past Ethan straight into the living room.

"My name is Nyles," he called out in a strong, steady voice. "Just checking to see if you're all right."

As with the doorbell, there was no response.

"This is a bad idea," Mara said, tiptoeing behind Dee as she stepped inside.

Dee agreed. The emptiness of the island, the silence of the house, had her on edge. "It'll be fine," she lied.

The house smelled musty. Like a crypt that had been closed for centuries. She inched her way in, scanning the living room as she went. It was dark inside, lit only by the bluish glow from the ever-present TV screen, which filled the living room with the Hardy Girls' screams as it replayed their battle in the foam-filled hallway.

"I look good," Ethan said from behind Dee. "I should go with that look more often."

"You look like a 'roided-up dickwad," Griselda said. She clearly hadn't wanted to stay outside by herself, despite her dislike of Dee's plan. "So yeah, run with it."

Nyles led them through the dining room to the kitchen. He opened the fridge, jumping aside in the process as if there might be someone hiding inside. Ethan whipped open the utility closet, striking a martial-arts pose. But instead of discovering a masked Gassy Al with a canister of sarin gas, they discovered that the closet, like everything else on the ground floor, was empty.

"That leaves upstairs," Dee said, staring up the darkened staircase.

Griselda swept her hand across her body, gesturing for Dee to go first. "After you."

Dee knew the moment she set foot on the stairs that she was in the presence of death. She couldn't have explained exactly how, though. Was it a smell? A heaviness? A premonition? Authors frequently used phrases such as "death hung in the air" to describe the discovery of a murder scene, and Dee had always thumbed her nose at those clichés. Right up until she'd experienced it for herself.

Dee had known there was something wrong in Monica's room. When you cohabitate with a person long enough, you internalize the sounds and rhythms of their everyday life, and that afternoon had been off. Weird. Different. Dee hadn't realized when she knocked at her sister's door, quietly calling her name, that what she'd find on the inside were lips that couldn't speak and ears that couldn't hear. Hell, she'd seen the body on the floor and hadn't immediately comprehended that Monica was dead.

Afterward, Dee understood what those authors had been talking about. There was a scent Dee couldn't shake. It clung to her clothes, to her hair, to the inside of her nostrils, and no number of showers, no amount of scented body wash or perfume, could get rid of it. It was nondescript, neither sweet nor spicy nor sour. Just heavy. Dark.

The smell of death.

And Dee caught its whiff at the top of the stairs.

"Steve's dead."

"What?" Mara cried.

Nyles grabbed Dee by the shoulders, pulling her away. "Where is he? What happened? Don't look, okay?"

Dee fought the urge to laugh. She'd probably seen more death up close than Nyles had, even with his premed classes.

They found Steve in bed, on his left side facing the door, the covers pulled up over his shoulders. His body was curled into a loose fetal position as if he were sleeping, but his skin was tinged purplish gray, his chest was unmoving, and his eyes were open but unseeing.

Dee knew he wasn't going to wake up. Ever.

It only took half an hour to check all the Barracks on Alcatraz 2.0. At first Dee and her friends went as a group, but after three or four houses they split up, searching two duplexes at a time.

The story was the same at each house, with very little variation: corpse in bed, corpse on the sofa, corpse slumped over the dining room table. All without marks on their bodies, or any clue as to how they had died. It was as if death had taken them by surprise. One guy had been in the middle of playing solitaire, another reading a library book in the easy chair by the bricked-up fireplace. Rodrigo looked as if he'd collapsed on the bathroom floor, his pants around his ankles.

"Twenty bucks says he was spanking it," Ethan suggested.

Mara gasped. "That's so gross."

"Love isn't gross, baby." He flashed a smile. "It's all natural."

Dee backed out of the bathroom and closed the door behind her, the same way they'd found it. "Not like you can ask him."

"True." Ethan clicked his tongue as he followed Dee and Mara downstairs. "And it's not like I have twenty bucks anyway."

Nyles and Griselda were waiting outside. "Same?" Nyles asked.

Dee nodded. "You?"

"One dead body," Griselda said. "Everything's normal."

"That makes twenty-two in all," Mara said.

Twenty-two lives lost in the blink of an eye. Dee could hardly believe it. She'd seen plenty of death in the last few weeks, but this much all at once?

"I don't understand," she said, sitting down on the curb, forehead in her hands. "Why are they all dead?"

Mara sat beside her. "And why wasn't any of it on camera?"

Dee's head popped up. "That's right. The cameras inside the Barracks—they were all dark. And The Postman feed is still showing the Death Row Breakfast Club."

Nyles cleared his throat. "Can we stop calling us that?"

"Don't worry, Nerdigan," Griselda said with a sly half smile. "You're still gonna be Anthony Michael Hall, whether they use the hashtag or not."

He scowled. "I hate you."

"Seriously, guys," Dee said. "If the whole point of this island is to film our deaths for maximum public amusement, then why the hell would The Postman kill off three-fourths—"

"More like four-fifths," Nyles corrected her.

He always had to be so precise. No wonder he was premed. "Why would The Postman kill off most of the people on the island and not capitalize on it?" She looked around, scanning the bright blue sky for signs of the drones. "Even now, you'd think he'd have those things right on top of us as we found all the bodies."

"Affirmative," Ethan said, lapsing back into his action-hero, faux-militaristic persona. "Skies are negative for bogeys, alpha delta."

Griselda shook her head. "I literally don't even understand what you're saying."

"Maybe he's got a new crop of prisoners arriving," Mara suggested, "and he needs to make room?"

"Rodrigo did mention a rumor about new inmates," Nyles mused. "But I can't imagine we'd get a shipment large enough to fill the entire Barracks. There were one hundred and fourteen of us when I arrived, and the island can hold almost double that amount."

Shipment. Like they were a commodity.

"Even if that's true," Dee said, "why pass up the opportunity to film it?"

"Duh. Because there was something better to film," Griselda said. "Us."

"Like he can't film more than one thing at a time?" Dee was frustrated.

None of it made sense. "Besides, he orchestrated this. You and Nyles, the Hardy Girls, taunting me to come rescue you. It was all a distraction while he killed off everyone else on the island."

"These poor bastards certainly didn't see it coming," Nyles mused.

"Maybe they all got raptured?" Ethan suggested.

No one responded.

"Poison?" Mara suggested after a pause.

"They didn't look like they were in pain when they died," Griselda said. "I'm pretty sure poison is painful."

Dee had to admit she was right. "Sleeping pills, maybe?"

"No," Nyles said. He was staring at the last house, rubbing his chin in thought. "It would be nearly impossible to get everyone to imbibe them voluntarily, and if water or drinks had been spiked, the atrocious taste would be a dead giveaway." He paused, cringing at his own use of the word "dead."

Ethan gripped his throat with both hands. "Do you think it was in the food?"

Griselda shook her head. "We'd be dead already, moron."

"The purplish hue of the skin denotes a cyanotic reaction," Nyles mused. "And the petechiae across the face suggest asphyxiation. My guess is that they were gassed. The houses must be wired for it." He pointed to a vent on the outside of the nearest house. "The Postman could have installed a valve to cut off the fresh air and replace it with a quick and lethal asphyxiant. It probably happened very quickly."

Dee's booby-trapped living room seemed like even more of a joke. No spork was going to save her from a gas attack.

"So the only reason we're alive is because we went to save your asses?" Ethan asked. "Selflessness for the win."

But Nyles shook his head. "No, these people have been dead for at least twelve hours."

"What?" Dee cried.

"Oh yes," Nyles said. "We were all in our own apartments when the rest of the inmates were exterminated. Which means we have another problem altogether."

As much as Dee didn't want to admit it, Nyles was right. "The Postman wants us alive."

THIRTY-ONE

"I'M NOT SURE THE CHINESE-WATER-TORTURE SITCH COUNTS as 'wanting us alive,'" Griselda said.

"He didn't gas us for a reason," Nyles said. "Whether or not that reason is to kill us later is entirely up to him."

"I am so fucking confused," Ethan said.

"Shocking," Griselda muttered.

Nyles crossed his arms over his chest, one hand cradling his chin. "I don't understand why none of this was on camera. I've never seen a death on Alcatraz two-point-oh go unpublicized. Or unmonetized."

Dee was right there with him. "And did you notice the crow cameras as we headed back to the Barracks? They didn't even move."

Mara turned, searching for the nearest camera mounted on a streetlamp. "You're right. It's not facing us."

"And I haven't seen any drones flying around today either," Dee said. "It's as if The Postman doesn't want anyone to know what's happening."

"We need to talk to someone!" Mara cried, her breaths coming in short gasps. "Everyone needs to know what he's done."

Griselda snorted. "Right, we'll just dial up our local prison liaison and let them know that we're dissatisfied with our Alcatraz two-point-oh experience."

"Talk to someone," Dee repeated. "That's it!" She grabbed Ethan's wrist, twisting it so she could see the face of his watch. "Ten minutes to twelve." They still had time to make Nyles's appointment with his attorneys.

"My God!" Nyles exclaimed. "I'd totally forgotten."

Usually when Nyles seemed to be inside Dee's head, it was unsettling, but suddenly she didn't mind so much. "Can we make it?"

"Make what?" Ethan said. "Lunch? I'm hungry."

"Absolutely," Nyles said, grabbing Dee's hand. She felt a shock of electricity race up her arm. "This way!"

Dee and Nyles speed-walked through the Barracks without actually breaking into a run, Griselda, Ethan, and Mara following close behind. Everyone seemed to feel the urgency of the situation. Nyles's lawyers represented their only connection to the outside world. Maybe their only chance at survival.

Nyles had held Dee's hand for a few steps before he let go, and even though it should have been the last thing on her mind, Dee found herself obsessing over it. Had he merely taken her hand in excitement, a thoughtless gesture in the heat of the moment? Had he just wanted to get everyone up to the guard station as quickly as possible, and Dee was the closest person to grab?

And why the hell are you even worrying about this right now?

Dee shook herself, forcing her brain to focus on the life-and-death battle being waged on the island. Twenty-two lives had been snuffed out in the blink of an eye. The Postman had violated his own rules, and if Nyles's lawyers could tell the world, Dee and her friends might have a chance.

They skirted the water, past the spot where Jeremy had met his bloody end just a few nights ago, and headed toward the southern end of Alcatraz 2.0. The road ascended sharply as the island narrowed into an isthmus. Looming above them, hewn into the rocks, was the Alcatraz 2.0 guard station.

While the rest of Alcatraz 2.0 had been intentionally left to feel like a fake suburban town from twenty years ago, the guard station was 100 percent modern, 100 percent industrial, 100 percent intimidating. The concrete structure was elevated by the island, surrounded by a twenty-foot steel wall topped with an aggressive amount of barbed wire. Balustrades and turrets faced both the water and the land, jutting out at sharp angles so that every inch of Alcatraz 2.0 was in view. A helipad had been built on stilts to one side of the main building, and on the other, a short pier thrust twenty feet into the water. Two speedboats were moored there, and Dee realized that this was the entry and exit for all the Painiacs. How many of them were still on the island? Maybe secured inside the guard station at that very moment? The idea made her shudder.

Dee half expected the searchlights to be fired up the instant they started the ascent toward the main gate, and for dozens of guards to appear on the catwalk, automatic weapons loaded and ready. But instead they were met with an eerie stillness.

Nyles slowed his pace as they approached the main gate. A human-size door had been cut into the massive steel wall, and it stood open, exposing a sliver of the courtyard inside the compound. A small hut, surrounded by two-ton traffic barriers, stood sentry out front, and beside it, an enormous American flag hung limply from its pole.

"That's odd," Nyles said. "The door's never open."

"Then how do you get in?" Ethan asked.

"The sentry calls up to the control center. Then someone comes and opens the door from the inside."

"So if the inmates decide to revolt," Mara said, instantly grasping the rationale, "they can't get inside. Even if they overpower the sentry."

Nyles approached the sentry's hut, craning his head to see inside the narrow window. "Hello? It's Nyles Harding. I'm here to meet with my solicitors."

A breeze gusted past them, rippling the Stars and Stripes, but other than that, there was no movement.

Nyles glanced down at Dee. "This isn't normal."

"Has anything about today been normal?"

"Good point." Then he grabbed her hand, more gently than before, and together they entered the hut.

It was abandoned. A clipboard was perched on the high-backed stool, as if it had been left there by the guard when he was called away from his post. A red phone receiver sat in its cradle, the only means of communication inside the station, but the rest of the hut was empty.

It must have been an incredibly boring job, sitting there by yourself with nothing but the view of the San Francisco skyline and the flat grid of Alcatraz 2.0 to look at, Boring yet dangerous. It seemed pretty clear that the sentry was meant to be a sacrificial lamb if the inmates of Alcatraz 2.0 ever decided to rise up against their captors.

Maybe that was why the hut was abandoned? With only five prisoners left alive on the island, maybe the guards weren't worried so much about their safety anymore?

Keeping Dee's hand firmly in his own, Nyles picked up the security phone. Dee didn't hear a dial tone or a voice on the other end.

"Hello?" Nyles said, tentatively. "Is anyone there?" He waited a few seconds before repeating himself, then finally replaced the receiver back into its cradle. "Nothing."

"Fuck this," Ethan said. "I'm going in."

"Wait!" Nyles cried. But it was too late. Ethan sprinted through the open door into the courtyard like a commando on a suicide mission.

Without a second thought, Dee followed, dragging Nyles with her. Ethan had been there when she'd needed to rescue Nyles and Griselda, and she wasn't going to let him face the guard station alone. She ducked through the narrow doorway to where Ethan stood frozen.

"Dude," he breathed. But he wasn't talking to Dee. His eyes were fixed on something across the courtyard.

Dee stepped out from behind Ethan's mass and saw exactly what had stopped him in his tracks. A dozen bodies, all in the gray-and-black uniforms of the Alcatraz 2.0 prison guards, were sprawled across the ground. Some were clasping their throats, others appeared to be in the act of crawling across the asphalt, and all had the familiar purplish hue to their skin.

All of them were dead.

Ethan sat on the black asphalt, legs tucked up in front of him, as he leaned back against the wall of the guard station. "I'm starving."

Griselda titled her head to the side. "We're trapped an on island full of bloating corpses, and you're worried about *lunch*?"

"I only had bananas and ice cream for breakfast," he complained. "No protein. And besides, we should all be worried about where our next meal is coming from."

"We should all be worried," Nyles said, "about how we're going to get out of here."

Nyles was right. If the scene at the Barracks had been unnerving, what they'd found inside the guard station was positively horrifying. The dozen dead guards in the courtyard had represented the tip of the iceberg. It appeared as if they had all fled the building through the same exit: one guard had collapsed mid-escape, his corpse propping the door open. After Nyles had established that the guards had died at approximately the same time as the rest of Alcatraz 2.0's inmates, and that the lethal gas had most likely dissipated as it had in the Barracks, Dee led them inside to search for survivors.

Ethan was game to explore the interior, of course. Nyles and Mara weren't so sure, but it was Griselda, weirdly enough, who had tipped the vote in Dee's favor. Her argument was persuasive.

"Find me a computer," Griselda had said, "and in five minutes I'll make sure the whole world knows what's going on in here."

Unfortunately, neither she nor Dee had found what they were looking for. No computers, and no survivors.

After stepping over the dead guard, they'd entered a large meeting room. It looked as if the entire garrison had been gathered together last-minute. A few folding chairs had been set up, haphazardly clustered around the room, but most of the guards must have been standing, facing the enormous screen mounted at the far end of the room.

All of this was speculation, of course, because there was no one left standing in the meeting room. The guards lay where they'd fallen, bodies on top of bodies, probably unaware of what was happening until it was too late.

Except for the bodies in the courtyard. Judging by the distribution of victims, that dozen must have been at the back of the meeting room by the door, perhaps farthest from the vents that delivered the fatal asphyxiant, and so they'd had a few extra seconds to react. Not enough, however. Even the ones who'd made it out into the fresh air had done so too late.

Nyles estimated sixty bodies between the meeting room and the courtyard. He and Ethan had tried opening the two interior doors that led out of the room, but both had security locks and wouldn't budge. They'd searched a few nearby bodies for anything that could help—keys, cell phones, weapons. But each guard had the same single possession on him: an ID badge. Nothing else.

And so the Death Row Breakfast Club had gone back outside to figure out what the hell to do next.

"I wish there was a helicopter on that pad." Ethan gazed at the empty helipad. "I'd fly us out of here so fast. Get to the chopper!" he cried in his Schwarzenegger voice, then sighed dreamily.

"You know how to fly a helicopter?" Nyles asked.

"Nope," Ethan replied. "But it would be so awesome to try."

Griselda shook her head. "Yes, because dying in a fireball is so awesome."

"Maybe one of the boats?" Mara suggested.

Nyles ran a hand through is hair. "Only if we can find the keys. Unless the Terminator here knows how to hot-wire a speedboat?"

Ethan gave him a thumbs-down. "No can do."

"We can probably break into the bodega," Dee said. "For food."

Mara's eyes grew wide. "But that's against the rules."

"Who's going to enforce them?" Griselda said. "Look around—everyone's dead."

"There's hardly anything left in the bodega," Ethan said, dismissing the idea. "Maybe enough for a day."

Mara paused for a moment, staring at the building behind them. "The guard station must have a kitchen."

Ethan jumped to his feet. "Dude, yes! Nyles, my man, do you know where the mess hall is?"

Nyles sighed. "I've only been in a holding cell. They didn't exactly set a place for me at supper."

"Bummer." He glanced around the courtyard, surveying the scene of dead guards. Then he marched up to the nearest body and patted him down.

"What are you doing?" Dee asked, less grossed out than confused.

By way of an answer, Ethan held up the guard's ID badge. "Just finding us a way inside."

Postman Forum * Alcatraz 2.0 * Logistics * Camera Feeds

Thread: Camera Feeds

Nov-10, 12:02 p.m. **#52,101**
The Griff Join Date: July 2017
Wide Awake Eyes Open Posts: 37,302

IT'S HAPPENING, PEOPLE! Looks like all hell has broken loose on Alcatraz 2.0. Camera feeds are out or frozen all over the island—no tracking capabilities, no motion sensor activations. Why? Is this just a FLUKE? A power outage? A GLITCH? Of course not. The cameras are frozen so that we can't see what's happening. "PAY NO ATTENTION TO THE MAN BEHIND THE CURTAIN!" The Postman says. Not this time, buddy. This is the smoking gun—Alcatraz 2.0 is fake, and the world is about to discover it!

Nov-10, 12:04 p.m. **#52,102**
Haru Tanaka Join Date: May 2018
Eternal Treasure Posts: 251

Can anyone see the #DRBC? They walked back to the Barracks, but then all those cameras seem to be down. Do they think they were able to take the cameras out like they took out the Hardy Girls?

Nov-10, 12:05 p.m. **#52,103**
Theo Kojak Join Date: March 2018
Who loves ya, baby? Posts: 1,145

I work in makeup special effects in Atlanta, and I can tell you this for sure: that decapitation a couple of days ago was no effect. 100% real, I'd bet my reputation on it.

Nov-10, 12:10 p.m. **#52,104**
Peggy Flynn Join Date: February 2018
May the road rise up to meet you Posts: 2,027

The issue isn't whether or not Alcatraz 2.0 is real, Griff. It's what's happened to The Postman. Have you noticed his feed? No posts since yesterday. Do you think he's on vacation?

Nov-10, 12:10 p.m. **#52,105**
Whitey Kahn Join Date: November 2017
And you got a letter and you got a letter Posts: 8,873

I took a screen grab from channel 327 about a half hour ago. You can clearly see the #DRBC walking up the coastal road toward the guard station, but after that, I couldn't find them anywhere. Auto tracking is off on all camera banks, even the ones that are working. And other than those five, I haven't been able to catch a single person on the island. WTF is going on?

Nov-10, 12:11 p.m. **#52,106**
Postman Op 5 (Moderator) Join Date: June 2017
I've banned a man for less Posts: 25,696

We mods don't like to delete posts, but The Griff, you have been warned in the past about making outlandish claims without evidence to back them up. This forum was intended as a safe place for constructive conversations about all aspects of The Postman and Alcatraz 2.0. It is not a sounding board for antigovernment conspiracy theories. Either initiate actual CONVERSATIONS, or keep your posts to yourself.

Nov-10, 12:17 p.m. **#52,107**
Tim Timmerson Join Date: May 2018
I like money Posts: 82

I don't know why the cameras are out but I can tell you for sure that what happens on Alcatraz 2.0 isn't fake. My sister's ex-fiancé has a sailboat in Sausalito and one night when he was heading north past Alcatraz 2.0 he could actually HEAR the screams of someone being killed. Said he could never watch the app after that. Felt too real.

Nov-10, 12:18 p.m. **#52,108**
Hannibal the Cannibal Join Date: January 2018
I love it when a plan comes together Posts: 560

I know he's a bit of a joke around here, but what if The Griff's right? I mean, something is clearly wrong on Alcatraz 2.0. Maybe it's bigger than anyone thought? Maybe the reason we can't see anyone else is because they're all dead?

Nov-10, 12:22 p.m.
The Griff
Wide Awake Eyes Open

#52,109
Join Date: July 2017
Posts: 37,303

[CONTENT DELETED BY MODERATOR]

THIRTY-TWO

"WHAT IF THERE'S SOMEONE STILL ALIVE IN HERE?" MARA asked as they crept down the first hallway.

Griselda shrugged. "They'll probably shoot us." But her cavalier delivery was in direct contrast to the fact that she walked so closely behind Ethan she was practically riding piggyback.

"None of the guards in the meeting room had weapons," Dee said, trying to sound soothing. "And if there is anyone left alive, they're on our side now."

Mara wasn't convinced. "This is a bad idea."

As they pressed deeper into the facility, Dee wasn't sure Mara was wrong. The guard station was unnerving. Gray tile floors, matching walls, rows of overhead fluorescents evenly spaced between security doors. And everything smelled crisply sterile, generically institutional. They could have been in a hospital or a government office building or a prison.

Ethan's pilfered ID badge did the trick, mostly. Every main set of doors opened easily with just a swipe of the card, but while he tried to do the same at the various offices they passed—Captain So-and-So, HR, Intake—none of them opened. The owner clearly hadn't had top clearance.

But even a top-clearance badge wouldn't have helped them get their hands on a gun. They passed two weapons lockers tucked into recesses of the wall in each hallway. Locked, of course. And with no discernible means of opening them: no padlocks, no card readers.

It was as if The Postman wanted to make sure that no one had the means to protect themselves unless he allowed it. Not the inmates, not even the guards.

Finally, after two identical lengths of industrial corridors, they entered the residential wing of the facility. Instead of offices and gray hallways, they found an activity room painted a cheerful shade of peach. Ping-Pong, pool table, a video-game system set up on a giant TV. Sofas, lounge chairs, magazines. All the comforts of home.

Including a computer.

Griselda sprinted across the room as soon as she saw it. A rotating skull screen saver bounced around the monitor, which paused the instant Griselda touched the mouse, waking the desktop from sleep mode. As the screen saver vanished, Griselda yanked the chair away from the table and sat, frantically tapping the keyboard.

Dee was right behind her. She leaned over Griselda's shoulder, eyes glued to the monitor. If they could access the Internet, they could get a message off the island. "Is it working?"

Griselda placed a hand on the side of the monitor-CPU combo. "It's purring."

"Awesome!" Ethan said. "I think the mess hall is through here. I'll find us some snacks."

"And I'll do something helpful," Nyles said. "Like find a phone."

Dee considered going with him, but he disappeared around the corner just as the computer screen blipped to life, displaying the corporate symbol of Postman Enterprises, Inc. Below the logo was a field labeled PASSWORD.

"Shit," Dee said. They'd never be able to guess the security password.

But Griselda was unperturbed. "Gimme a sec." A series of strokes brought up an MS-DOS-style window in the corner of the screen. Griselda keyed in a command, then another, and then the screen went bonkers, pixelating into a massive blur before it cleared itself.

Instead of The Postman Enterprises, Inc. logo, Dee and Griselda were staring at an e-mail window. The last person who had used the computer must have been checking his inbox when he'd been called away to that fatal meeting. He had worked for the intake department, judging by his e-mail, but it was the sender's address that sent Dee's heart thundering in her chest. "It's from Postman Enterprises, Inc."

"I bet it's from the big guy himself," Griselda said. "I heard he doesn't trust his staff with anything."

"'Arrival schedule,'" Dee said, reading the subject line. "'November ninth.'"

"Yesterday," Griselda said. Then she read the beginning of the e-mail out loud. "'Boat A, arriving eight p.m. Contents: HG.' That must have been the Hardy Girls." She laughed drily. "Good to know."

"'Boat B, arriving ten p.m.,'" Dee read.

"That's just two hours before everyone else on the island was gassed."

Dee continued out loud. "'GA, BB, HB, DIY, CDV, MM.'" The meaning was clear—Gassy Al, Barbaric Barista, Hannah Ball, DIYnona, Cecil B. DeViolent, and Molly Mauler. "If Robin's Hood and Gucci Hangman never left, that means all of the remaining Painiacs have been on the island since last night."

"We need to get the *fuck* out of here." Griselda glided the mouse over to the refresh button for the guard's e-mail server, but Dee grabbed her hand. "Wait."

She spun the scroll wheel, moving the screen down so she could see the rest of the e-mail. "'Be advised: new executioners en route. Cancel current roster credentials, effective immediately. No exit.'" Dee glanced up at Griselda. "What does that mean?"

"I think The Postman is replacing the Painiacs."

Dee's brain whirled. If The Postman was planning to get rid of his current Painiacs, could his stunt with the Hardy Girls have been part of that plan? What if he'd never intended for Dee to be the victim—what if he'd wanted to liquidate his sister-act killers all along?

Griselda whipped the cursor back to the reload button and clicked it. "All the more reason to get off this island."

Dee held her breath. This nightmare might be over in a matter of seconds if only they could get Internet access. A wheel spun in the middle of the screen, distorting the e-mail text, then stopped. Instead of a refreshed page, an error message popped up on the screen.

NO INTERNET CONNECTION FOUND

"Shit!" Dee smacked her palm against the table. She should have known it wouldn't be that easy. The Postman had been a step ahead of them all along. Why would he slip up now?

But Griselda appeared unfazed. She had minimized the browser window and opened another command window. "Could be a firewall," she explained while she typed frantically. "Which I can bypass."

Dee waited while she attempted several work-arounds, all of which were totally above Dee's computer-savvy pay grade, but after a few minutes, Griselda pushed the keyboard away in disgust. "The whole network is down."

"Any way to fix it?"

Griselda peered over the top of the monitor. "Network cable connected," she said. "Through the wall. I'm going to see where it leads." She jumped to her feet and disappeared around the corner.

Dee scanned the activities room. Mara must have gone with Nyles or Ethan, neither of whom had returned. They'd promised to stick together when they entered the station, and now here they were, separated and alone. *That's when they get you.*

"There's a phone in an open office next door," Nyles said, returning slightly out of breath. "Plus two more down the hall in another common space. All dead like the one in the sentry hut."

"Of course they are."

"Where did everyone go?"

"Griselda's looking for the Internet router. No connection," she said, before Nyles could ask.

"Figures."

"And Mara went with Ethan to find the kitchen."

Nyles frowned. "They should be back by now. This wing isn't that large."

Griselda rounded the corner to the activity room, shaking her head. "Found the router. It's on, but no dice. Also found this cell phone in one of the desks, but *something* is blocking the network signal." She held up a newer-model Android phone, the lack of network bars apparent on the home screen.

"Something?" Nyles asked.

"Military-grade network scrambling device, is my guess."

Nyles pursed his lips. "Can we switch it off?"

Griselda shrugged. "Sure, if we could find it. But it could be anywhere in the building."

"No phones, no Internet," Dee said. "We're completely cut off."

Nyles dropped onto the sofa. "Well, this is a bloody nightmare. Why did The Postman kill everyone else but not us? It doesn't make any sense!"

"Yeah," Dee said. "I know." Except she was lying. It *did* make sense.

Perfect sense. She thought of the message scrawled on the inside of her linen closet, of her dad's desperate attempt to tell her about Kimmi, of Kimmi's probable connection to The Postman.

Kimmi had been released from the Western Sierra State Mental Hospital and was exacting revenge on Dee.

Kimmi had wanted Dee all to herself. A plaything. A toy. A devoted companion. Now she was playing out the rest of their scenario. *I'll kill everyone you love.*

As with Monica and Blair, the deaths of her friends would be on her head. Didn't they deserve to know why?

"I . . ." she began, but stopped. She'd told Monica about Kimmi, and just days later, Monica was dead. Would she be helping Nyles and Griselda by telling them the truth, or signing their death warrants? And at this point, did it even matter?

"Yes?"

But before Dee could finish, Mara burst into the room.

"Ethan!" she said, panting heavily. "Have you seen him?"

Dee shook her head. "Not since he left to find food."

"Shit!"

Dee had never heard Mara swear before, and the panic in both her face and her voice was apparent. A prickly sensation slowly made its way up the back of Dee's neck. "What's wrong?"

Mara's eyes shifted from Dee to Griselda. "Ethan's disappeared."

THIRTY-THREE

GRISELDA SEIZED MARA BY THE SHOULDERS. "WHERE DID YOU see him last?"

"We'd found the cafeteria," Mara said, her voice shaky. "But the ID badge wouldn't open the kitchen door, so he was going to try and find another way in. I waited, but he never came back."

"Show me."

They raced out of the activities room, down a short hallway, and finally emerged into the cafeteria. It looked remarkably like the one in Dee's high school—cavernous ceilings and lively acoustics, with a dozen round tables flanked by plastic chairs. An enormous video screen was embedded in the wall at one end, still showing the rescue of Nyles and Griselda, the acoustics of the battle in the *Shining* hallway pinging throughout the room. And at the back there was a cafeteria-style window, closed and locked with metal blinds, where the food was served. Somewhere, on the other side, was Ethan.

"Ethan!" Griselda cried. "Where are you?"

As if in answer, the sickening double-doorbell sound effect pinged through the cafeteria.

Ding-dong! Ding-dong!

"No," Dee breathed. "Please, no."

They all turned toward the TV screen, and there, in the middle of the shot, was Ethan.

He was in a room made of glass. Floor-to-ceiling windows on all sides, penning him in like it was a prison cell. But he wasn't tied up or restrained in any way, and instead of standing calmly in the middle of the room, he pounded on the glass, trying to break free.

"You won't take me without a fight, asshole!" Ethan yelled. Then he punched the glass with his bare fist. It gave slightly but didn't break.

"Can anyone hear where it's coming from?" Dee asked desperately.

They stood still, ears straining to catch the reverberations of Ethan's pounding fists coming from somewhere outside the cafeteria, but it was impossible to hear anything other than what came through the speakers.

"We have to find him." Griselda ran headlong at the locked cafeteria window, leaping up on the counter with the grace of an Olympic hurdler. She pulled at the metal blinds, hopelessly trying to break the lock that held them in place. Mara climbed up to help.

"Goddamn it!" Griselda screamed in frustration. "Why did we leave the ax at the shop?"

Meanwhile, Nyles and Dee tried the doors. The one on the far wall opened easily, and sunlight streamed into the cafeteria. Beyond, Dee could see the main courtyard of the guard station.

"He wouldn't have gone outside," Dee said, letting it close.

"Agreed." There was only one other option—the door beside the cafeteria window.

Nyles rammed his shoulder against the metal exterior, but it didn't budge.

"Guys!" Ethan's voice. It almost sounded as if it was coming from inside the cafeteria instead of through speakers, and Nyles, Dee, Griselda, and Mara all stopped and stared at the video.

"This is it for me," Ethan said, staring straight at the camera. His face was strangely calm. "Gris . . ." He smiled. "You know I know."

Griselda pressed her lips together so hard they practically disappeared, and the bulging muscles in her jaw belied the fierce clenching beneath. She must have felt more for Ethan than Dee had realized.

"Stay alive for me, okay? You have to tell the world about . . ." Ethan's voice trailed off as a figure moved into the frame. He was in shadow, but he carried an old-fashioned megaphone, like the kind they used in black-and-white movies. Which could only mean one thing.

"Cecil B. DeViolent," Griselda said. "That *son of a bitch*."

Cecil held the megaphone up to his mouth, turning to the side so that the camera caught his full silhouette. "Lights!"

Immediately, dozens of open-faced tungsten lights ignited, flooding the darkness around the glass room with a warm glow.

With the lights on, Dee could see that the set was some kind of office. There were several desks—off-white metal with a row of drawers alongside and computer monitors on top—flanked by wheeled chairs, and a half dozen large pieces of furniture: file cabinets, printer stations, massive outdated computer servers. Definitely an office environment, but not the least bit modern. Even the desktop computers looked like the old Apples she'd seen in a technology museum: big and heavy with black screens and unwieldy keyboards.

And to make the whole thing even weirder, the office was decorated for Christmas. Each desk had a tiny fake Christmas tree, complete with lights, and garlands had been strung along the wall behind the glass cell.

Cecil held up the megaphone again. "Actors to their places!"

He disappeared out of frame. When he returned, he carried a mannequin.

With his back to the camera, Cecil lugged the human-size doll across the set and arranged it on the floor beside one of the desks. It was dressed in black pants and a black button-down shirt, open to the sternum. Or what would have been the sternum if it weren't made of plastic. It had what looked like a toy machine gun slung around one arm, and on its head a long blond wig.

Somewhere in the depths of Dee's brain, a memory stirred. This scene was familiar. Something she'd seen before. But what was it?

Once satisfied with the placement of the dummy, Cecil moved across the room and crouched behind one of the servers. Finally, in the light, Dee saw that he was dressed for the location. He wore a dark business suit, light blue shirt, burgundy tie. A full beard, probably fake, shrouded his face, along with a pair of large sunglasses. By his side was a handgun.

Ethan stopped pounding on the glass and watched intently as Cecil set the scene. Slowly, a smile spread across Ethan's face. "Oh my fucking God, are you serious here? *Die Hard*? This is awesome!"

Only Ethan would be excited that his imminent death would mimic a scene from his favorite movie.

"But I need a machine gun, Cecil," he said, immediately serious. "John McClane has one, remember? You're not following the script."

Cecil paused, as if thinking. Was he really going to give Ethan a machine gun? A working one? That would give him a chance. Dee's heart raced. All Ethan needed was a chance.

But Dee's momentary hope was immediately dashed. Cecil shook his head, then cupped his hand to his face.

"Roll film. Aaaaaand action!"

"Dude, you suck!" Ethan said.

But Cecil wasn't listening. He turned to the blond dummy. *"Karl,"* he said, *"schiess auf das Fenster."*

"Cut!" Ethan yelled, his face more irate than fearful. "Hey, douche! Hans says, *'Schiess dem Fenster!'* Did you even watch the movie?"

Cecil's shoulders drooped; his head tilted to the side in irritation. He stared at Ethan for a moment, as if he was going to argue the point, then muttered, "Fine."

"Seriously," Ethan said, folding his arms across his chest. "I expected a little bit more professionalism from you."

Cecil took a long, deep breath through pursed lips, then let it out with a slow hiss. "Resetting. Aaaaaaand action!" He snapped back into character and began the scene over. *"Karl, schiess dem Fenster."*

Ethan nodded appreciatively. "Thank you."

Karl, the dummy, didn't respond. So Cecil, a.k.a. Hans, clarified his statement. "Shoot the glass."

Ethan braced himself. "Yippee-ki-yay, motherfucker."

A wall of gunfire erupted. The glass room in which Ethan was imprisoned seemed to explode from the impact, glass and bullets flying in from all directions.

Ethan didn't even flinch. He stood firm in the middle of the room while his body was simultaneously riddled with bullets and impaled by thousands of razor-sharp shards of glass.

As suddenly as it began, the gunfire stopped. Ethan, bloodied almost beyond recognition, a smile still plastered across his face, collapsed to the floor.

Postman Forum * Roster * Cecil B. DeViolent * Die Hard

Thread: Die Hard

Nov-10, 1:17 p.m. **#1**
Ahmed Sulari Join Date: January 2018
Trainwreck Posts: 1,487

Look, I love a good John McClane riff as much as the next guy, especially if the "next guy" is the vic, but where did that come from? All hell's breaking loose over on the **camera feed threads** because apparently the #DRBC hasn't been seen since they headed up the hill toward the guard station. Almost all of the live feeds are dead, and now this happens? Where was Ethan when he got captured? Where is the rest of the #DRBC?

Nov-10, 1:20 p.m. **#2**
Squirrel Woman Join Date: May 2018
I'm nobody's "girl" Posts: 215

Yeah, and what about that message that Ethan sent out before he was killed? They have to tell the world about what? Was that code or something? #SoConfused

---

Nov-10, 1:23 PM **#3**
Skullcrusher Chic Join Date: July 2017
"Chaos is a ladder" Posts: 26,213

Technically, Cecil's *"Schiess auf das Fenster"* is correct, I believe. So aside from the fact that Hans is speaking horrific German, why is it that Karl, his countryman, doesn't understand what he means until he says it in English?

Nov-10, 1:24 p.m. **#4**
The Griff Join Date: July 2017
Wide Awake Eyes Open Posts: 37,317

Have to tell the world about the conspiracy! It's all coming together. This Death Row Breakfast Club uncovered a dark secret about Alcatraz 2.0 that The Postman does not want anyone to know about. That's why all the cameras are dark.

Nov-10, 1:27 p.m. **#5**
Ji-Woo S. Join Date: April 2018
Shake off the haters Posts: 339

I think The Postman has lost control of the island. Did you see the press release from the DOJ this morning? Sounded like they were purposefully attempting to distance themselves from The Postman and Alcatraz 2.0, admitting that they have no oversight of the island prison. Quite a change of tune since they've been taking credit for the prison's high ratings since the beginning!

Nov-10, 1:30 p.m. **#6**
Chol K'Golmad Join Date: January 2018
tlhIngan Hol Dajatlh'a? Posts: 840

Personally, I think this is all part of the game. The Postman is upping the ante. I bet the rest of the inmates are all in quarantine or on lockdown or house arrest until he's done dealing with these assholes. He let them think they could win by faking the Hardy Girls' deaths and now he's going to pick them off one by one. BRILLIANT.

Nov-10, 1:34 p.m. **#7**
Nehir Asuman Join Date: December 2017
Class Struggler Posts: 559

And how did The Postman fake that Hardy Girl's broken neck? The redhead clocked her something fierce with that extinguisher. For your theory to work, she'd either have to be really weak or in on the whole thing!

Nov-10, 1:35 p.m. **#8**
Randy Lahey Join Date: September 2017
Assistant Trailer Park Supervisor Posts: 2,712

A traitorous inmate, secretly planted there by The Postman? Now THAT would be the greatest ratings coup EVER! Hey, Postman—are you listening????

THIRTY-FOUR

"NO!"

It was more howl than cry, the sound of Griselda's soul ripping apart as she dropped to her knees.

There was no love lost between the two of them, but Dee raced over and threw her arms around Griselda's neck. "I'm so sorry." There wasn't much else to say. Nothing would bring Ethan back.

"I think," Nyles began, his voice shaky, "if Ethan could have scripted his own death, that would have been it."

It was true. Reenacting a scene from *Die Hard* was practically a dream come true for Ethan, though probably without the bloody, gruesome death part at the end, and even though Dee had never been shot, as with Blair she found comfort in believing that Ethan's death had been instantaneous and painless.

"Yeah," Griselda said, her voice craggy. "He would have . . ." She didn't finish the sentence. Her body went rigid.

Dee pulled away. "What's wrong?"

"He would have wanted it that way." She was watching the screen, which was rerunning Ethan's death.

"Actors to their places!" Cecil yelled on the video replay.

"Yeah," Dee agreed. "He would have."

Griselda's face hardened; her eyes flashed with anger. "It's the kind of death that Ethan would have wanted. *Ethan.*"

"What are you going on about?" Nyles said.

Griselda swung around. "The set, the dummy—Cecil must have planned it all in advance."

"All of The Postman's killers plan their murders well in advance," Mara said.

"Exactly. And there were, what, like ten minutes between when Ethan was taken and the live feed started?"

"That's weird," Mara said. "Cecil *always* uses warehouse two-fourteen-B. It used to be a soundstage for a company that produced dungeon pornography." She shook her head. "But that's on the far side of the island. There's no way Cecil could have gotten over there between the time Ethan disappeared and when that video began."

"Which means Cecil set up the *Die Hard* scene here, in the guard station."

"And if that's true," Dee said, realizing what Griselda meant, "how did The Postman know that Ethan would be here today?"

Ethan hadn't been jogging around the island when he'd been captured. He hadn't been taken from the Barracks or the gym, places one would expect to find Ethan if he was going to be the next victim. It was true that Nyles was supposed to be at the guard station today, but not the rest of them. They'd gone there on a whim.

"He's been leading us around like calves to the slaughter," Dee said, her stomach sinking. "He knew that the guards were all dead, and that if Nyles survived the Hardy Girls, he'd discover what had happened up here."

"But not that Ethan would be with him," Griselda countered.

"Maybe not," Mara said, "but, Nyles, what's the first thing you would have done if you'd come up here alone and found everyone dead?"

Nyles's eyes sought out Dee's face. "I'd have raced back to find you."

Dee smiled. "And we all would have returned here. Not much of a stretch to assume Ethan would be with us."

"Seems like a lot of what-ifs," Griselda said, unconvinced.

"Can you think of a better explanation?" Dee asked.

"No." Griselda's eyes shifted from Dee to Mara and back again. "Unless one of us is a traitor."

And by "one of us," Griselda meant Mara.

Mara took an involuntary step backward. "Me? You think I work for The P-Postman?"

"She helped save your life," Dee said, instantly defensive.

"Gris," Nyles started. "I don't think we should be turning on each—"

Griselda cut him off. "But she's not really one of us, is she? And she knows an awful lot about all the Painiacs. Too much."

"If she's been working for The Postman," Dee said, at Mara's side, "then why did she kill the last Hardy Girl to save my life?"

"You saw the manifest," Griselda said. "The Postman is cycling out his killers."

"WHAT?" Nyles and Mara exclaimed in unison.

"Oh yes," Griselda replied, eyes wide. "We found an e-mail open on the desktop. He sent all the old Painiacs to Alcatraz two-point-oh yesterday, and he's planning on bringing in a whole new crop. The Painiacs won't be allowed to leave this island. Get it? Princess even suggested that The Postman wanted us to take out the Hardy Girls to save him the trouble."

Dee thought of how reluctant Mara had been to get involved in the first place, how Dee had had to beg for her help. She wasn't going to let Griselda pin all of this on her. "But it was my idea for all of us to come up here. Not Mara's."

Griselda planted her hands on her hips. "Fine. Then maybe *you're* the traitor. All of our problems started when you arrived anyway."

"Now you're being ridiculous," Nyles said. "Our heads were all on the chopping block already. It has nothing to do with Dee."

Griselda paused for a moment, her conviction about Dee's guilt wavering. She released a slow breath, and her body seemed to cave. "Well, even if she's not one of them, it doesn't change the fact that we've got an island full of dead bodies and a small army of government-sanctioned serial killers who could literally be anywhere." Griselda threw her hands up. "You got a plan to save us from that, Princess?"

Serial killers who could be anywhere . . .

But not really anywhere.

Dee turned to Mara. "Where does DIYnona do her kills?"

"The old chapel," she said. "Judging by the windows and what's left of the altar. She's done a lot of redecorating."

"And the Barbaric Barista?"

"Coffee Unlimited," she replied without hesitation. "It was an espresso import company with a small café not far from Main Street."

Mara knew about all the Painiacs: where they killed, and how. So far, The Postman had been a step ahead of them—dictating their actions, manipulating their thoughts. He'd had the advantage because he had complete control of the island.

But what if they could change that?

"We have to tell someone what's happening here," Dee said, her jaw tightening as she realized what she was going to have to do.

"Wow, brilliant," Griselda said. "Do we also need air to breathe and food to eat?"

But Nyles noticed the change in Dee's demeanor. "What are you thinking?"

"There's only one guaranteed way to get airtime on Alcatraz two-point-oh," Dee said. Ethan had been onto something without even realizing it, right before Cecil cut him off. No deaths happened on Alcatraz 2.0 without a camera watching, and right now what Dee needed most of all was a live camera feed. And Mara was the key to finding it.

"Dee," Mara began, "no."

But her mind was made up.

Without another word, Dee turned and marched out of the cafeteria.

THIRTY-FIVE

IT WAS DARK WHEN DEE, NYLES, GRISELDA, AND MARA emerged from Dee's house. A slivered moon hung above the horizon, and though the sparkling lights of the Embarcadero twinkled across the water, on Alcatraz 2.0 only the muted streetlights fought off the all-consuming darkness.

The fog had hung back, thankfully. Though it would have shrouded the island in a suitably atmospheric haze, conjuring up images of Jack the Ripper stalking prostitutes through murky London streets, it also affected the cameras, obscuring their ever-present gaze.

Since Dee's arrival, she'd loathed those cameras. They brought fear and pain and death. But tonight she eyed the nearest crow-cam with a rueful smile, relieved to see it rotate toward them. The Postman might have shut the cameras down earlier for his own purposes, but the motion-sensing crows were operating once again. Which was a good thing. It was more important than ever that her image be captured clearly for the world to see.

They'd stopped at each of their houses to change and gather food; then they'd shared a silent meal in Dee's kitchen. While Nyles, Griselda, and Mara were dressed for a chilly fall night—in long pants and warm layers—Dee had decided to play the part of dutiful victim. Instead of mixing and matching her princess garb, she'd chosen a pre-matched outfit that fit her fan-given nickname. A powder-blue knee-length dress in textured damask, corseted in the back, with a light crinoline underneath. She doused her cheekbones with a heavy coating of the shimmery highlighter from The Postman's preselected makeup array, and lacquered her lips with sticky pink gloss. Hell, Dee even donned the black choker she'd worn her first day on the island, and the clear Lucite kitten heels that evoked Cinderella's glass slippers.

"You look like my four-year-old niece on dress-up day at preschool." Griselda walked behind Dee as they made their way down to Ninth Street.

"If The Postman wants Cinderella Survivor," Dee said with a shrug, "then I'm going to give her to him."

"You're braver than I am," Griselda replied. It was the closest thing to a compliment Dee had ever heard from her mouth.

The plan was simple: they had to get themselves captured. *Viewership goes up between eight at night and two in the morning,* Blair had said. Well, Dee and her friends were about to give The Postman his largest ratings spike yet. They were going to walk straight into the lion's den, visiting every single kill room on the island until they stumbled upon one of the Painiacs. Then, game on.

"Where to first?" Dee asked as they passed the soccer field.

"Molly Mauler always uses the auditorium at the old elementary school," Mara began. At least her Sherlockian deductions would ensure they'd be well prepared for whatever nightmare might await. "I recognized the art deco stage and balcony where Molly watches the slaughter."

"Is that the one up the street from the old brig?" Dee asked.

"Yep."

"If Molly has her arsenal of man-eating animals within," Nyles said, "we should be able to hear them from outside."

"Oh, good," Griselda said. "So we'll be able to identify which species is going to tear us limb from limb. Yay."

"We'll be able," Nyles said, lifting his chin haughtily, "to have some warning."

Dee really hoped so. Of all the ways to die on Alcatraz 2.0, getting eaten alive by an endangered species seemed like the worst.

"After Molly," Mara explained, speaking quickly as if she wanted to make sure she got all the information out, "we'll try Robin's Hood at the old dry dock."

Dee nodded. "Check."

"More so than the other Painiacs, Robin has a tendency to heavily restrain his victims," Mara continued, "so we have to be careful."

Right. Because offering yourself up as a victim to a serial killer was such a careful thing to do.

Mara kept her voice low as they ran down the list, still dogged by cameras. Gucci Hangman's warehouse was conveniently located next to Robin's dry dock, and Dee half hoped that Gucci would be there. She owed him one for Blair.

After Gucci they'd try Barbaric Barista, whose kills didn't take as much prep time as some of the other Painiacs. BB maintained a torture chamber of hipster delights, from a life-size artisanal coffee grinder to an old-timey barber's chair where victims got more than a little taken off the top. If they were ambushed by the lumberjack-bearded, man-bun-sporting BB, Dee hoped her knowledge of obscure Los Angeles indie bands might keep him talking long enough for their plan to work.

Mara's intel on cannibalistic chef Hannah Ball was slightly less reliable, mainly because Hannah was the newest of The Postman's killers, with only a half dozen murders under her belt, so there wasn't as much to go on. Still, Mara was pretty sure that Brews 'N' Brats—the last decent dining establishment to exist on Treasure Island—was the only place that would have the necessary culinary infrastructure to accommodate Hannah's cannibalistic cooking supplies: a human-size stockpot, an enormous sausage stuffer, and a two-story deep fryer.

Cecil B. DeViolent was a long shot. Ethan had only been murdered eight hours ago, and the idea that Cecil would be set up for another "shoot" in the old porn soundstage was slim.

But according to Mara, it had been weeks since DIYnona's last kill, and since the chapel was always set up the same way—with a crafter's dream array of supplies for macramé, glass blowing, origami, silk-screening, and a dozen other decorative arts—DIYnona might be ready to go at a moment's notice.

And then there was Gassy Al. His signature gas chamber was airtight, with glass doors and high ceilings through which both Al and The Postman's viewers got a 360-degree view of the victim's torment, and Mara had deduced that it could only be located at one place on the island.

"If I was putting money on it," Mara said, her countenance more pensive than before, "I'd say that we're most likely to find Gassy Al, wearing his black executioner's cowl at the old Treasure Island Pavilion near the pier."

"I'd always wondered where that gas chamber might be," Nyles said. "Nicely done."

"It was a little tricky to find." Mara dropped her eyes, clearly not used to praise. "The original structure's been surrounded by an outer wall since the last time Google Maps footage was shot on the island." She sounded proud, as if her esoteric knowledge of the Painiacs was finally appreciated. Which was true. Mara's debriefing might literally save their lives, so even though Dee found her neighbor's obsession with The Postman app to be a little unsettling, it was about to come in handy.

"But Al doesn't wear the cowl," Griselda said after a pause. "That's Robin."

Mara flushed, mortified by her mistake. "Right. Sorry. But look, I'm positive about the pavilion."

Griselda shook her head. "You'd better be."

"I'm sure Mara's right," Dee said. "We'll hit Al last."

Although there was still Prince Slycer.

Yes, he was dead. Of that, Nyles was 100 percent sure. He'd felt Slycer's jugular and there had been no pulse. Couldn't exactly fake that kind of symptom. And yet, if they didn't encounter any of the Painiacs on their tour, Dee would suggest Slycer's warehouse maze as their last stop.

If The Postman really wanted to make a statement, that was where he'd do it.

Nine locations. Eventually Dee and her friends would run into a Painiac, and then they'd have The Postman's undivided attention.

She figured they'd get ten seconds max before The Postman realized what they were doing and cut the feed. Or the sound. Or both. Either way, it didn't matter. They only needed a few seconds to tell the world what was really happening on Alcatraz 2.0.

Of course, then they'd have another problem entirely. Surviving.

But there were four of them. And as with the Hardy Girls, Dee and her friends had proven that if they worked together and trusted one another, they could win.

Are you sure *you can trust them?*

That nagging voice in the back of her brain refused to go away. Dee had allowed herself to trust these people, just as she'd allowed herself to trust Kimmi.

How had that worked out?

THIRTY-SIX

DEE LAY ON THE FLOOR, PRETENDING TO SLEEP. TWICE NOW, Kimmi had shown up in the white room, emerging through the hidden door while Dee was sound asleep. Last time, she'd woken Dee with a fierce kick to her lower back, the pain from the blow almost as terrifying as the unpredictability of her captor's mood, but Kimmi's state of mind seemed to swing violently back and forth, and as soon as Dee sat up, Kimmi was all smiles.

"Sing me a song," she'd said sweetly. "A song about your pretty new sister and how much you love her. You have to earn nice things."

Dee had played along, inventing lyrics on the spot about how pretty Kimmi was, and how lucky Dee was to have her as a big sister. Dee had been made to beg for food. To braid hair and paint toenails and "play" other "games," Kimmi's code word for torture. But somehow that stupid little song about the wonderful and beautiful Kimmi had been the last straw.

So while she'd continued to sing, inwardly she'd been plotting.

The door. She'd searched for it, tried to trigger it, but without success. The only one who could open that door was Kimmi, and so Dee would have to be ready the next time her kidnapper entered the white room.

After Kimmi had left that day, dropping a greasy bag of cold french fries on the floor as she retreated through the hidden door, Dee had tried to act as normal as possible. She'd opened her eyes as she spun around from her place in the corner, then pounced on the bag, scarfed down its contents. All exactly as Kimmi would expect. When she was done, Dee had sat down on the floor and waited.

It was hard to know how much time had passed, since the lights were always on and Dee had no sense as to the passing of day and night, but she tried to mimic her daily "routine" as closely as possible. After staring at the walls for a while, she executed a perimeter search of the room for at least the dozenth time, feeling her way down the smooth walls as she sought an escape. She pretended to be excited in one corner, as if she thought she'd found something, but after a thorough examination of the area, Dee pretended to give up, breaking down into fake tears. Then she curled up into a ball and, making sure her hair was artfully covering her face, she acted as if she was asleep.

Only, Dee was wide awake and on alert. She regulated her breathing and lay utterly still for what felt like an eternity. Her muscles ached, desperate for a change of position. The cold, hard floor felt as if it was stabbing her body in a million different places, but she didn't move. She was sure that Kimmi was watching her somehow. Waiting. And Dee had to be ready to act the instant she heard . . .

Click.

The door release. Dee had memorized the sound, which meant that Kimmi was about to creep into the white room. Through her tangled hair, Dee saw a section of the far wall crack open.

Now!

Dee jumped to her feet and rushed the door. She arrived just as Kimmi stepped through. The older girl was shocked to find Dee barreling toward her, and it dulled her reaction. Even though Dee was smaller, she had momentum on her side. She shoved Kimmi so hard, she stumbled, falling back against a steep flight of stairs.

Dee ran for her life. She pumped her weakened legs as fast as she could, racing up the stairs. She heard a shriek of rage from behind her, then pounding footsteps.

Kimmi was in pursuit.

"Help me!" Dee screamed. Maybe there was someone home. But was that a good thing? Kimmi had told Dee that her dad used the white room to kill people. Would Dee be next?

She had to take the chance.

"Somebody, help!"

The door at the top of the stairs was closed, but as Dee wrenched the knob, it turned easily.

"Stop it!" Kimmi cried. "You're mine!"

Dee tumbled through the door and into a hallway. Bright sunshine flooded the space. It was the middle of the day, which meant even if nobody else was in the house, there had to be people outside: gardeners, stay-at-home parents, deliverymen. Her sneakers squeaked against the shiny hardwood floors as she bolted down the hall, searching for the front door. "Help me! Someone help me!"

A knock in the distance. "Hello? Is everyone okay in there?"

Someone was at the front door. Someone *heard* her.

Dee ran in the direction of the voice, through what looked like an expansive kitchen into an arched foyer. "I've been kidnapped!" she cried. She saw the front door, saw the body of someone outlined in the beveled glass window beside it. "My name is Dolores Hernandez and I've been—"

Dee's hand was on the door handle when someone grabbed her from behind.

"No!" Kimmi hissed. "I won't let you go. I'll never let you go!"

Kimmi dragged Dee away from the front door, away from freedom, back toward the white room. Dee struggled against her but was too weak to fight her off. "Call nine-one-one!" she cried, tears streaming down her face. "Don't let her take me back. Please!"

There was a sound of splintering wood. A flood of sunlight. A man raced across the foyer toward her, his body outlined by the sun. His hands were around her, pulling her free of Kimmi.

"I've got you," he said, racing out of the house. He had a van parked out front, and Dee was just able to recognize the US Postal Service logo on the side before he deposited her in the driver's seat.

"Hello?" he said into his cell phone. "Is this nine-one-one? I'd like to report an emergency."

Nyles isn't Kimmi, Dee said to herself. *Neither is Mara or Griselda. You can trust them.*

Dee's skin was icy cold as she walked down the middle of Ninth Street, her toes partially numb from the ridiculous shoes, and though she'd intentionally left the house without a jacket so as not to cover up her thematic outfit, she silently cursed that decision, wrapping her arms around her waist to stave off the shivers.

"Would you like my jacket?" Nyles offered, peeling the black corduroy off his shoulders. Which was totally and adorably sweet of him.

"No, thanks," she said. "This outfit is clickbait, remember?"

"More like bait for pedos," Griselda said.

Ahead of them, Mara stopped. "Here it is."

The abandoned elementary-school auditorium was oddly out of place. In a compound that appeared to be cobbled together from portables, corrugated metal storage units, and a few other single-story structures, the auditorium soared above everything, a hulking mass in the darkness.

And not only was it taller than the rest of the school, but its art deco style was completely anachronistic. Heavily adorned with sculptural flourishes and ornate geometric lines, it must have been a remnant of the world's fair that had prompted the building of the island in the first place.

Nyles took Dee's hand and led her up a short set of steps, their crumbling masonry precarious beneath Dee's unstable footwear. They stopped at metal double doors, more modern than the rest of the building and in significantly better shape. Even in the subdued light, Dee could see that the material was sound, rust free, and most likely impenetrable.

"Are they meant to keep strangers out," Nyles mused, "or victims in?"

Dee sighed. "Only one way to find out." She swung open the door.

The smell hit her first, a mix of wet dog and manure that instantly reminded her of field trips to the Los Angeles Zoo, and as Dee stood on the threshold, she half expected to hear the deafening roar of a lion or a howling hyena cackle echoing from inside.

But the auditorium was blessedly quiet.

The moonlight streaming through the front door illuminated a small patch of the lobby, just enough for Dee to discern the threadbare carpeting, stained and ripped from years of neglect. She followed Nyles inside, ears straining against the oppressive silence, and as her eyes adjusted to the darkness, she saw that the doors leading from the lobby into the main body of the auditorium stood wide open.

The interior glowed a dull blue from a dozen tall, thin windows that stretched nearly to the vaulted roof, giving the old auditorium the appearance of a small cathedral. The bottom floor of the multipurpose room had been cleared of the chairs and tables that would have filled it during school lunches or holiday performances, leaving a vast empty space.

Well, mostly empty. There were notable exceptions: two large animal pens stood down center on the auditorium's stage.

"I'll give you this one," Griselda said, at Mara's side. "This is definitely Molly's setup."

"Thanks," Mara said. In the pale light, her skin looked positively transparent. "But where's Molly?"

Nyles and Dee crossed the auditorium, her kitten heels clacking against the tile floor. The cages loomed before them. They were identical: rectangular, about ten feet high, with thick iron bars pitted and marred with use and age. One side of each cage was missing entirely.

"Weird." Dee climbed up onto the stage for a closer look. "The hinges on this side are gone."

Nyles joined her. "Looks as if the doors have been removed."

"Why would Molly dismantle her cages?" Griselda asked, mounting the stairs beside the proscenium. "That's her thing. It'd be like Robin's Hood burning his bow and arrows."

"The doors must be around here somewhere." Dee searched the darkened area upstage.

"Look!" Nyles pointed at a set of deep grooves in the splintered floorboards where something had been dragged on or off the stage recently.

Griselda folded her arms. "I've got a bad feeling about this."

Dee's eyes drifted from the scratch marks to a dark patch beside them, as if the old wooden stage had been stained by something.

Blood.

Dee could easily picture the scene that had played out. An inmate, probably drugged during the kidnapping, wakes to the deafening roar of Bengal tigers, famished and ready for mealtime, pacing menacingly in the cages. A moment of panic, the desperate search for an escape, Molly's taunting. Then, the inevitable. Screams of agony, a body torn limb from limb, gore spilling from the victim's remains, the coppery metallic tang of blood filling the air as . . .

A thud broke Dee from her thoughts. She froze, visions of mangled bodies and ravenous beasts forgotten. What was that? Footsteps? A door closing? Was Molly here after all?

She spun around toward the open auditorium. "Did anyone hear . . ." But the rest of the sentence faded on her lips. The floor of the auditorium was empty.

Mara was gone.

THIRTY-SEVEN

"MARA!" DEE CRIED. SHE RACED DOWN THE STEPS TO THE auditorium floor. "Mara, where are you?"

Nyles was beside her. "Outside," he said, grabbing her hand. "I thought I heard a door close."

Dee ran as fast as her stupid kitten heels would allow, with Griselda following close behind. They burst through the metal doors onto the crisp, dark night, but the street was abandoned.

"MARA!" Dee listened, desperate to hear Mara's reply rippling through the still air, but the only response was the gentle swoosh of the evening wind.

Someone had taken her. Dee knew it. They'd been on the stage, backs to the auditorium, examining the cages. One of the Painiacs could have slipped into the school behind them and grabbed Mara while no one was looking.

How long had it been—two minutes? Five? Luckily, whoever had Mara didn't have much of a head start.

Dee spun around, grabbing Nyles by both arms. "We have to go after Monica."

Nyles tilted his head to the side. "Mara."

"Yes, of course," said Dee. Had Nyles lost his mind?

"You said Monica."

"I did?"

Nyles nodded.

Whatever. The name didn't matter. "We still have time to save her."

Griselda's lips hardened into thin lines. "Like we still had time to save Ethan?"

"Like we still had time to save *you*," Dee said, lashing out. She was tired of Griselda's shitty attitude.

Griselda arched an eyebrow. "There are seven other locations on the island. We'll never find her in time."

She was right. Searching them one at a time, Mara might be dead before they reached her. "Then we split up."

"Are you out of your freaking mind, Princess?"

But Dee wasn't listening. "I'll take Gassy Al's pavilion," she said, hurrying down the broken steps, "then make my way back across the island and meet you in the middle."

"Dee, wait!" Nyles called.

"Go to the dry dock first and the coffeehouse!" she cried over her shoulder. "Please!"

Nyles opened his mouth to protest, then paused and gave her a curt nod.

Dee turned on her heels and sprinted across the island.

Dee's feet were sore and blistered as she ran, but she didn't slow down until she reached the pavilion. Her decision to try Gassy Al's kill room first wasn't random. Mara seemed to think that he was the one they'd be most likely to encounter, and Dee prayed that she was right.

But as Dee approached the pavilion, her heart sank.

Everything was dark and silent.

Dee limped around the perimeter, hoping for signs of life. A rectangular outer structure of cinder blocks and mortar had been built around the glass-walled pavilion, and though the metal door—which opened onto a grassy hillock on the north side—looked formidable, it swung noiselessly open with the slightest pull. Inside, the wall formed a courtyard around the tented structure, which was ringed with cameras for a full view of the "fun." Furnished with wood-framed lawn chairs embellished with brightly hued cushions, this spot was where Gassy Al toyed with his victims.

It was the perfect setup, too. Once used for weddings, luncheons, and special events of all flavors, the pavilion had see-through glass walls and a vaulted tentlike ceiling, which must have presented quite a spectacle back in its heyday. Without the surrounding wall, it would have faced the water, offering visitors a panoramic view of the San Francisco skyline, and as Dee slowly circled the inner building, she could picture the lavish scenes it must have hosted once upon a time.

But now the lights were off inside the tent, leaving its contents dark and mysterious. Al, like Gucci, liked to dress up his set in a variety of outlandish themes, ranging from historical re-creations like the Tokyo subway sarin gas attack and a Depression-era death row to postapocalyptic fantasies reminiscent of *Mad Max*.

But not tonight, and as Dee turned to leave, she could only hope that Nyles and Griselda had already found Mara and saved her.

CRASH!

Just as she reached it, the metal door swung closed, locking her inside the courtyard.

"Mara!" she cried, hope reignited. *Come on. Please!*

Suddenly the lights inside the pavilion came on, flooding the courtyard with piercing whiteness.

Dee squinted against it, her eyeballs screaming out in agony as they raced to constrict, but as they adjusted, she found herself staring at a familiar scene.

It was a girl's bedroom, complete with false walls on three sides. A twin bed stood in the middle of the space. The frame was white wrought iron, its paint chipped in places, with princessy flourishes. Probably meant for a child. But this was clearly a teen's room, judging by the posters that adorned the false walls: separate shrines to the Hemsworth brothers and Michael B. Jordan, plus a wall entirely devoted to outfits worn by a certain Gucci Hangman, including fabric samples, runway dupes, and sketches.

More importantly, it was a room Dee recognized. The Hemsworths and Michael B. Jordan were Monica's celebrity crushes; Gucci Hangman, Monica's obsession. The crocheted afghan on the bed. The cube-shaped mood-light alarm clock on the nightstand, glowing purplish blue. The half-empty bottle of lime sparkling water beside it. Every detail was exact.

Dee was staring at Monica's bedroom.

Only instead of Monica on the floor, her face purple and her bulging eyes lifeless, Mara lay facedown on the bed.

THIRTY-EIGHT

"WAKE UP!" DEE POUNDED ON THE GLASS WITH HER FISTS. IT felt as solid as the cinder-block wall that surrounded her. "Mara! Get up! You have to get up!"

The figure on the bed didn't stir.

"Do you want her to wake up?" a voice asked. It was robotic and devoid of inflection, as if computer generated. She spun around, ready to find Gassy Al standing beside her, but there was no one. Just a speaker mounted on the wall. "I can make that happen."

The sound of rushing wind filled Dee's ears. Mara began to stir. Al must have drugged her and then woken her up with a blast of oxygen, like when Dee had woken in the white room, or on a dusty warehouse floor on Alcatraz 2.0.

It took Mara a few seconds to fully regain consciousness. She sat up, eyes heavy, and glanced around the "room." Instantly she registered the danger.

Mara jumped to her feet, and Dee got a full look at her. Not only had she been imprisoned in a replica of Monica's bedroom, but Mara had been dressed up in a similar outfit to the one Dee's stepsister had been wearing the day she was murdered: dark leggings, a tunic cinched with a wide silver belt, and flip-flops.

Gassy Al or The Postman or whoever the hell was in charge knew *way* too much about Monica's murder.

Mara was in full panic mode when she spotted Dee. She raced over and slapped her palms against the glass. "Help me!" she screamed, her voice muted by the thick wall of glass between them. "Dee, get me out of here!"

"Look familiar?" the voice asked.

"Let her go!" Dee cried out. "It's me you want."

The voice ignored her, as if it hadn't heard a word she said. "You have to earn nice things."

Dee froze. That was exactly what Kimmi used to say when she was taunting Dee.

"What does that mean?" Mara said, her eyes wide in terror.

Before Dee could explain, a sickening hiss filled the speaker. The pavilion was starting to fill with gas.

"Concentrated Uragan D-two," the voice on the speaker announced. "Frequently used as a pesticide. Incredibly effective."

All thoughts of exposing The Postman and the atrocities on Alcatraz 2.0 fled from Dee's brain. All she could think about was saving Mara. "Cover your mouth!" she yelled, and held the hem of her dress up to her face, to mimic the action. She must have flashed half of America, but she didn't care. Keeping Mara alive was all that mattered.

Mara nodded, understanding. She ripped off the belt and, without hesitating, pulled the tunic over her head, exposing a lace bralette underneath. She wadded the tunic into a tight ball and held it to her mouth and nose; then, spotting the sparkling water on the nightstand, she doused the tunic with it.

She stood there, frozen, and for an instant Dee thought it was all over. The effects of the gas were already kicking in, and soon Mara would be convulsing on the floor. But instead of dropping like a rock, Mara spun around and jumped onto the bed, leaping gracefully from it to the dresser to the top of the fake bedroom wall.

Dee didn't remember shit from chemistry class, other than the fact that some gases were lighter than air, others heavier. She could only hope that Mara had guessed correctly, and that the Uragan D2 would sink before it mixed fully with the breathable air in the chamber, giving Mara extra time.

Which Dee was going to need. The glass felt sturdy and thick when she was pounding on it with her fists, just like the Hardy Girls' tank. She didn't have Ethan's ax, so there was no way she'd be able to break through the walls, and there was no door leading into the pavilion. At least none that she could see. Which left one option.

The tensile roof.

Dee kicked off her shoes and stashed one down the front of her dress. The tentlike structure looked like it might be made of fabric, and Dee was hoping she could rip through it. Barefoot, she dragged one of the wooden chairs over to another, tossed the cushions onto the ground, and lifted it on top, repeating the action until she'd built a rickety lawn chair tower reaching two-thirds of the way to the edge of the roof. Without hesitating, she scaled the side of her makeshift ladder, until she was balancing precariously on the uppermost chair. Dee could just reach the roof with her fingertips, its smooth fabric tantalizingly close. But there was nothing to grab onto, no ledge or bar she could use to hoist herself up. She could, however, easily reach the top of the cinder-block wall behind her. She leaned back, the furniture tower swaying beneath her, looped her arm over the top of the wall, and heaved herself onto it.

The gap between the top of the wall and the vaulted roof of the pavilion looked to be about ten feet, and if Dee had been James Bond or

Natasha Romanova, she could easily have leaped across it, landing effortlessly on the edge of the roof before scaling the sloping, white peak as easily as a Himalayan Sherpa scaling a shallow hillside. But she wasn't a superspy or a superhero. She was a relatively unathletic high school senior, barefoot in a corset-laced prom dress. Odds of her missing the roof and landing in a broken heap on the ground were at least fifty-fifty.

Mara still held the wet tunic to her nose and mouth. She balanced atop the false wall on her hand and knees, her face obscured by her hair, shoulders convulsing as she coughed.

Dee was running out of time. She took a deep breath, crouched as low as she could, and launched herself across the gap.

She landed stomach first, the angle between the tensile roof and the window catching her just below her rib cage. It knocked the wind out of her, and it wasn't until she began to slide backward that Dee even realized she'd made the jump. Gasping for air, she clawed at the dew-slicked material, desperate to get a grip. She'd expected the tentlike structure to bow under her weight, but it was tauter than she'd realized, and barely gave way. She managed to haul her right leg up onto the hard edge of the glass wall, planting her foot to maintain balance, and stared up at the peaked roof.

Mara was in the middle of the pavilion. Dee would have to scale the side of the tent between the two peaks in order to reach her. It was going to be like rock-climbing a glacier.

But at least she had an ice pick.

She fished the shoe out from the bust of her dress and turned it upside down to use the heel as a hammer.

The first whack left an indentation in the plastic fabric, but it didn't break the surface. Dee swung harder and the heel went straight through, poking a neat little hole. Finally, a practical purpose for her stupid shoes.

Using the hole as a toehold, she heaved herself up the side of the tent. One puncture hole at a time. At least she was allowing fresh air into the pavilion.

"Dee! What are you doing?"

Dee glanced down over her shoulder and saw Nyles outside the courtyard wall with Griselda by his side.

"Mara's in there," she explained quickly.

Nyles nodded. "Hang on. We'll get the door open."

Yeah, like she was just going to hang out there while Mara suffocated inside. Not a chance. With one more heave of her Lucite heel, Dee hauled herself over the peak in the tensile roof, then allowed her body to slide down the other side.

She must have been right above Mara now. Or at least she hoped she was as she whaled away at the roof fabric with her trusty shoe. When she had half a dozen holes, she could see down to the pavilion below.

Mara was almost directly beneath her on top of the wall, hunched over with the tunic still pressed to her face.

Dee wasted no time. She threaded her fingers into the holes she'd made and, leaning back, used gravity to tear a gap in the roof. She took a deep breath of fresh air, then thrust her head through the hole into the gas-filled pavilion.

"Mara! Grab my hand!"

Hopefully, the tautness of the roof would hold their combined weight.

Mara glanced up. Her eyes were red and puffy, which meant the gas had reached her hiding place on top of the wall. But she was still conscious, still had fight left in her. Mara balanced precariously on top of the fake bedroom wall as she pushed herself to her feet.

"Don't look down," Dee said. She stretched her arm as far as she could, wedging her shoulder against the fabric roof. She could feel the structure sagging beneath her. If it collapsed, she and Mara would both be dead.

"Dee, be careful." Nyles's voice was closer now.

Dee craned her neck around and saw his head pop up over the peak of the roof. *Great.* He was coming to "rescue" her. The last thing she needed right now.

Mara let the tunic fall to the ground and stood on her tiptoes, reaching up to Dee.

Their fingertips grazed, but Mara wasn't tall enough to reach Dee's hand.

"Your time is running out," the electronic voice chimed in.

As if Dee needed reminding.

"Jump!" Dee cried. "You'll have to jump for my hand!" She squeezed more of her body through the widening hold in the tensile roof, feeling it droop farther into the pavilion. They were so close. Dee could almost reach her.

But not close enough. Mara suddenly began to convulse, her body shaking violently from head to toe. Her jaw slackened, and white foam oozed from the corner of her mouth. As Dee watched in horror, Mara reeled, lost her balance, and fell off the wall.

"No!"

Mara tumbled onto the bed, landing smack in the middle of the mattress. The convulsions were more violent now, her body clenched up into a ball as the poisonous gas took effect. Mara flopped onto her side, head raised toward the roof, and Dee could see the terror and pain in her eyes.

Then Mara collapsed facedown onto the bed.

◷ 4m

Zingelbert Bembledack @zingelbertnotgerry
Can someone please explain to me what the freaking bloody fuckity hell is going on?
← | : 13,522 ₪: 6,212

◷ 4m

Gluon Fusion @HBthelastparticle
I have so many questions. Why did they go to that auditorium? How did they not realize the redhead was gone? What the hell possessed @TheGassyAl to kill her in someone's bedroom?
← | : 5,960 ₪: 1,201

◷ 4m

Eureka Samantha @eureka_sammy150
There literally isn't a GIF yet made to express my level of what-the-fuckery. #ThePostmanJumpedTheShark #WhereIsEveryone #WTFHemsworths
← | : 5,003 ₪: 1,558

◷ 3m

Gluon Fusion @HBthelastparticle
I mean, is that Red's bedroom? Or from a TV show? Is it a set we're supposed to recognize?
← | : 2,597 ₪: 1,163

◷ 3m

Dennis Purgatory @denizenofpurgatory
I still say @awakewideopen has the right idea. Something is rotten in the state of @Alcatraz2. #EyesOpen #FakeNews #DontTrustTheFeed
← | : 712 ₪: 207

◷ 2m

Janeisha Barrett @janeishaEbeforeI
I kinda don't even care what's going on as long as the kill videos keep coming. Has anyone checked out @Trazbet yet? There's a fortune to be made.
← | : 991 ₪: 569

⏱ 2m

Hamilton Ramilton @iambearnation3712

I feel robbed. Didn't get to see @TheGassyAl at all! #Gassolites #BearNation #BigAndHandsome

← | : 142 ₪: 57

⏱2m

The Griff @awakewideopen

THANK YOU @denizenofpurgatory!!!!

⏱3m

> **Dennis Purgatory** @denizenofpurgatory
>
> I still say @awakewideopen has the right idea. Something is rotten in the state of @Alcatraz2. #EyesOpen #FakeNews #DontTrustTheFeed

← | : 1,000 ₪: 624

⏱1m

Benny Nda Jetts @EltonJohnForevzz

Noticed that @ThePostman_PEI has gone silent for over 24 hours. NEVER HAPPENED BEFORE.

← | : 287 ₪: 199

⏱ 1m

Bradley Fornow @ForeverForFourYears

Maybe @ThePostman_PEI has gone to #Alcatraz2 himself? That would explain why the cameras have been "selectively" down. Trying to protect his identity?

← | : 17 ₪: 3

THIRTY-NINE

DEE GAZED DOWN AT MARA'S BODY. DRESSED LIKE MONICA, IN Monica's bedroom.

Rage ignited inside her. A burning, fiery anger like she'd never felt in her entire life. Fuck crying. What good would that do?

She turned away from the bedroom scene below and let go of her grip on the tented roof. She slid down to the edge, stopping her momentum on the hard corner of glass.

"Careful!" Nyles cried for the millionth time. He stood on top of the lawn-chair tower about twenty feet away. "Edge your way over to me and I'll help you down."

Like a crab skirting the side of a cliff, Dee inched across the bottom of the roof, bare heels digging into the sharp corners of the glass wall beneath. But the pain didn't bother her. It only stoked the angry fire within.

"I've got you," Nyles said, taking her hand in his own. "Slowly now. Take my hand and I'll—"

But Dee wasn't doing anything slowly ever again. She dropped right on top of Nyles. The lawn chairs toppled over, and they collapsed onto the pile of chair cushions that Dee had discarded earlier. Griselda leaped out of the way just in time.

Nyles grunted beneath Dee's weight, but she didn't even stop to ask if he was okay. She bolted to her feet and spun around to face the camera.

"I know it's you, Kimmi!" she yelled, pointing her finger at the camera.

"Who's Kimmi?" Griselda asked, helping Nyles to his feet.

Dee ignored her. "But you and The Postman won't win, do you hear me? We're going to shut you down." The tears had started, hot and angry, pouring down her cheeks. But Dee didn't even pause to wipe them away. "Listen up, America: The Postman's killed everyone else on the island. Guards. Inmates. None of it was on camera."

"It's a conspiracy," Nyles added. He stood at her shoulder, facing the camera. "All of us were falsely convicted."

Griselda joined. "Robin's Hood's last victim? She was the expert witness that testified against us. The Postman is knocking off anyone who can prove the trials were rigged."

"And if we could end up sentenced here," Dee added, "so could you. So could *any* of you."

The Postman needed to be exposed, and Alcatraz 2.0 had to be shut down so no more innocent people would die. None of the deaths would be in vain.

"Alcatraz two-point-oh is a sham," Dee said. "There's no justice here, no eye for an eye. The only one guilty of murder is The Postman."

Then, as they stared up at the camera, the red light blipped out.

The Postman had cut the feed.

"We did it," Nyles breathed. "I can't believe it." He grabbed Dee around the waist and hugged her tightly.

She let her body relax into his. It felt as if a huge weight had been lifted. "We did it."

"Do you think it worked?" Griselda asked.

Nyles released Dee. "We have to get to a monitor."

He was right. They just needed to confirm that their message had gotten out. The comments feed would be flooded with people calling for an investigation. She followed Nyles and Griselda out of the courtyard, but before she passed beyond the metal door, she turned and took one last look at Mara, at her stiff dead body sprawled on Monica's bed.

"I'm so sorry," Dee whispered, rounding the back side of the pavilion, trying to get a look at Mara's face. "I should never have gotten you involved."

That's when she saw it. Something she wouldn't have noticed standing directly in front of the bedroom scene. Behind the fake walls of Monica's room, there was a hand.

Dee blinked. Was she seeing things? She approached slowly, and discovered that the hand was attached to an arm, the arm to a body. A massive, overweight body.

It was clad all in black, including a hood that covered the entire head, with two rounds cut out for the eyes. An executioner's cowl. But not professionally made. The eyeholes were jagged and looked as if they'd been hand cut with a pair of scissors, and the fabric was flimsy and worn.

He lay on his side, head resting on his arm, as if he'd just curled up for a disco nap, but the massive blade protruding from his sternum suggested that this nap would be slightly more permanent.

She stared at the body. The front of the executioner's robe didn't appear shiny in the overhead light. It wasn't wet. The blood had long dried.

And just like that, a cloud lifted.

Kimmi, Monica, the weirdness on Alcatraz 2.0—it all made sense. Dee couldn't believe it—how had she not realized this earlier? It was all so simple, and as Dee stared into the pavilion, she started to laugh.

"Dee?" There was panic in Nyles's voice. "Where are you? What's wrong?"

"Nothing." Dee calmed herself. She needed a plan, something that would end this nightmare once and for all. She needed time to think.

"You see something funny in there?" Griselda asked, eyebrow arched, as Dee emerged through the metal doorway.

You have no idea. "I'm fine."

There was a question on Nyles's face, but he didn't ask it. "We should get back to the Barracks."

"Totally." As she led them into the dark night, her mind raced. *Not the Barracks. I have to get back to the shop.* "Um, let's go to I Scream instead."

"The Barracks are closer," Griselda said. "Why go all the way back to Main Street?"

Dee's eyes darted to the nearest camera mounted atop a dim streetlamp. "I'm starving."

Griselda arched an eyebrow. "Seriously?"

Nyles glanced at the camera, then back to Dee. "You're starving," he said slowly, understanding her code. "Right." Then he cleared his throat and spoke quickly. "I'm sure we could all use something to eat."

They entered I Scream through the back door, which was still unlocked, just as they had found it that morning. The lights flooded the pink-and-white shop with an unnervingly cheerful glow as Dee's eyes darted around the interior, searching. She found what she was looking for almost immediately. On the counter beside the blenders. A red ax.

"Okay, Postmantics," Nyles said, rubbing his hands together as he took a seat in front of the TV monitor. "Tell us what's being done to get us out of here."

Griselda stood beside him, her hand on the back of his chair. They both read the scrolling comments in silence as Dee slipped behind the counter and silently lifted the ax off the Formica surface, tucking it behind her back.

"What in bloody hell is going on?" Nyles asked after a few moments. His eyes were fixed on the screen, which showed Mara falling onto the bed in the pavilion, convulsing. "'Death Row Breakfast Club is played out,'" he read. "'Can't The Postman give us something else?'"

Griselda also read posts out loud. "'I loved the way Ally Sheedy foamed at the mouth while she bit it.' 'I'm betting the house that hashtag-CinderellaSurvivor dies last.'" She turned back to Dee. "Didn't they listen to anything we said?"

Dee shook her head calmly. "No. Because they never heard a word."

Nyles rocketed to his feet. "What?"

"Look," Dee said, pointing at the screen with her free hand. It showed the three of them shoulder to shoulder shouting at the camera, but without any sound. Beneath it, a caption read #DRBC THREATENS THE POSTMAN.

"That son of a bitch!" Griselda yelled.

"He was never going to let us expose him," Dee said. "He's been a step ahead of us all along, remember?"

Griselda tilted her head. "Sounds like you knew this was going to happen."

Dee edged her way around the counter, heading for the back door. "I had an idea."

"Are you going to share it with us?"

Dee gripped the ax tightly behind her. She was about to put all her cards on the table, and she really, really hoped she was right.

"I need to tell you a story . . ." Dee began.

FORTY

THE POSTMAN STARED AT THE SCREEN. *I CAN'T BELIEVE SHE told them about Kimmi.*

Nyles and Griselda gaped. They were totally stunned. Unsurprisingly, it was Griselda who came to her senses first, storming up to Dee.

"Are you fucking *kidding* me? How could you keep something like this from us?"

"I was trying to protect you," Dee said.

"Bullshit!"

"Everyone I tell turns up dead." Dee was calm. Too calm. The Postman smiled. Maybe she'd finally gone over the edge? The Postman had hoped that losing Mara would be like losing Monica all over again. *Looks like it worked.*

"But you endangered us anyway," Nyles said.

Instead of answering, Dee burst out laughing. "You were never in danger."

Nyles and Griselda exchanged a glance. "Um," he said, slowly, "there was a tank. Some water. We practically drowned."

Dee shook her head slowly. "The Postman would never let his own children die."

"Pardon?"

"She's lost her fucking mind," Griselda said.

Dee took a deep breath, centering herself. "I am *not* crazy. Kimmi was fourteen when she kidnapped me, and since I'm seventeen now, that would make her twenty. Same age as you, Griselda. She was also blond, with blue eyes."

"She kept you in a fucking room for a week," Griselda said, rolling her eyes. "If I *was* her, I'm pretty sure you'd have known the minute you met me."

"Maybe." Dee smiled wickedly. "Plastic surgery? That nose is too perfect to be real."

"As if," Griselda said.

"Or maybe the trauma affected my memory. PTSD can do that."

Griselda pointed at her chest. "*I* am not Kimmi."

"Plus," Dee continued without acknowledging her, "Kimmi had a brother."

Now it was Nyles's turn to laugh. "You think Gris and I—"

"Ever since I got here, I thought you two looked like brother and sister." Dee spoke faster, her crazy meter rising. "How convenient that you had diplomatic immunity, and that Gris, despite being on the island for months, had never been kidnapped."

"But—" Nyles began.

"The Postman *wanted* Ethan and Mara and me to kill the Hardy Girls. He's replacing his Painiacs, so why not let us kill a couple off and increase his ratings? I'm sure if we hadn't gotten there in time, one of the Hardy Girls would have released you."

"I wish it had been you in that tank," Griselda scowled, "instead of us."

The Postman smiled.

"You tried to throw me off your trail," Dee said, whirling on her. "Up at the guard station, by suggesting that Mara was a traitor. You just didn't want me to realize it was one of you."

The soft lines of Griselda's face hardened. "You think I killed Ethan."

"I think you handed him over to Cecil," Dee said. "When you went to go check on the network cable." She turned to Nyles. "Or your brother could have done it when he was searching for a phone."

Griselda looked as if she wanted to rip Dee's face off, her brow lowered, her eyes smoldering with rage. "I fucking hate you."

This is working out even better than I'd planned. They turned on each other faster than I thought they would.

"I should have realized it sooner, that Kimmi's dad and The Postman were the same person. You two have been feeding information to him all along." She glared at Griselda. "Trying to finish what you started, Kimmi."

Nyles looked distraught. "Dee, surely you don't believe this."

"Slycer spoke," Dee said, eyeing him closely. "Right before I killed him. And he had a British accent. Just like yours."

"But, Dee," Nyles pleaded, "you and I . . . we . . ."

"You had me going." Dee swallowed. "I thought you really liked me."

Nyles took a deep breath. "I think you need to calm down. I know Mara's death was quite a shock, but right now we have to stick together and figure out a way off this island." He stepped toward her, then stopped cold as Dee whipped her hand out from behind her back, revealing the ax.

"Stay away from me!" Dee screamed. Her face was red, her eyes wild.

"Whoa." Griselda held up her hands before her. "Crazy goes to eleven."

"Always a joke," Dee said. "Never any emotion. Just like a sociopath. Just like Kimmi."

Nyles remained calm, approaching Dee like he was attempting to dissuade a lion in the savanna from pouncing. "Dee, put down the ax."

"I think The Postman is on the island," Dee said.

"That's insane." Griselda laughed. "Why would he be *here*?"

"That's the only way you two have been able to communicate with him. In person. So I'm going to find him, I'm going to kill him, and I'm going to shut this island down."

"Okay . . ." Nyles said slowly. "How?"

"The Postman must have an Internet connection to post the videos. If I can get to it, I can expose all of you."

"We've already been to the guard station," Nyles said. "No Internet. Where could he possibly be hiding it?"

Dee narrowed her eyes. "The only place I'd never think to visit."

"Fine." Griselda shrugged as if she didn't give a shit. "Your funeral."

For a moment, Dee's confidence faltered. The Postman could see the confusion in her eyes. *She's wondering why they aren't trying to stop her.* Dee glanced at the door, her only means of escape.

The instant she broke eye contact, Nyles sprang into action. He flew across the room, his movements nimbler than expected, and threw his arms around Dee's body.

It's as if I scripted this myself.

"Let go of me!" she screamed, trying to lift the ax. But Nyles held her firm, pinning her arms to her side. She kicked. Her bare feet planted against the wall, and she was able to push off, sending them both careening across the shop. They crashed into a table—Nyles, Dee, and the ax—and all sprawled across the slick tile floor in opposite directions. Griselda stopped the ax with her foot, stomping on it with her combat boot, then bent down and picked it up.

"Look who's got the ax now," she said, smiling at Dee.

But Dee was back on her feet. "You can't have me, Kimmi. I'll die first."

Before Griselda or Nyles could answer, Dee fled the shop.

Perfect.

The Postman checked the feed, cycling through the camera banks that covered the alley behind Main Street. Dee, barefoot and still in that ridiculous Cinderella outfit, sprinted down the dark gravelly path, stumbling occasionally on the chewed-up asphalt. When she reached Ninth Street, she didn't even hesitate. She turned left and headed east.

Toward me.

The Postman leaned back. Dee had taken the bait, but was she smart enough to know what awaited her?

I really, really hope so.

FORTY-ONE

DEE WASN'T BLUFFING WHEN SHE SAID SHE KNEW EXACTLY where The Postman was hiding. The place where it all began: Slycer's maze.

And if she'd had any doubts, they vanished as she approached the hulking warehouse. The crows that lined the roofs of every building on the block—the ones that Dee had so naively assumed were just birds that first afternoon on the island—were alive. The cameras rotated in synchronized motion as she trudged down the street, each tracking her with a single red dot of light. The Postman was live, and Dee was the main attraction.

The exterior of the warehouse looked strange. Perhaps it was the darkness of the night, the slivered moon long since disappeared below the horizon, or perhaps it was because she was coming instead of going this time, standing before its weathered wooden door instead of fleeing through it.

She didn't know for sure what she'd find in the maze, but she could guess. The Postman would be waiting, of that she was absolutely positive. Would he have the remaining Painiacs there as well? Odds were pretty good. But at least Dee was prepared for them, thanks to Mara's encyclopedic knowledge of the Painiacs, their tactics and weaknesses. And after finding Gassy Al's corpse tucked away inside the pavilion, Dee had understood what The Postman wanted her to do.

Now if she could just find a pair of shoes. The only thing worse than the Lucite kitten heels? Entering Slycer's warehouse barefoot.

Oh well, no helping that now. Dee marched up to the main entrance of the warehouse, grabbed the metal handle firmly, and slid the door open.

An area of Slycer's imposing maze walls had been cleared away, revealing a large rectangular space, carpeted with the plastic green blades of an Astroturf rug crisscrossed with lines of white paint. It looked like a small football field, complete with end zones. A large floodlight hung above the field, centered on the fifty-yard line, and black security cameras, like the kind found in a bank, were perched on top of the maze walls, all aimed directly at the field.

The plastic grass felt strangely agreeable against her feet, warmer than the unrelenting chill of the concrete floor, and the crinkly blades had a massaging affect against her sore, blistered skin. Maybe this wouldn't be so bad after all?

Then the music started.

Speakers mounted to the interior warehouse walls erupted with a folk-rock-meets-techno-yodeling soundtrack, and even before she saw the man bun, Dee knew that her first obstacle would be Barbaric Barista.

She stood motionless at the edge of the field, her body tense, her ears straining to hear anything above the Alpine techno music, when suddenly a tinkling bell cut through the noise.

Rrrrrring!

It was a familiar sound, old-fashioned but easily recognizable. One of those lever-operated bells attached to a bicycle.

The instant her brain registered the origin of the bell, it sounded again, and Barbaric Barista sailed around the corner on a powder-blue beach cruiser.

If he hadn't been a known sociopath, Dee would have laughed out loud at BB's appearance. In addition to the man bun wound loosely on the top of his head, BB wore a red-and-black-plaid flannel shirt, carefully tailored to fit tightly to his lithe, almost skeletal body, and a pair of lavender cuffed skinny chinos. On his feet, leather flip-flops curved around the bicycle pedals with each rotation, and across his back he'd slung a leather messenger bag, stuffed to bursting.

And then there was the beard.

The video screen in her prison cell really hadn't done Barbaric Barista's massive, grizzled facial hair justice. Carefully groomed to appear carefree and overgrown, BB's brown beard was eight inches long *at least*, climbing up both cheeks until it disappeared into his sideburns, and it was capped with a waxed mustache, twirled up at the ends, which gave his face the appearance of a permanent smile.

Mara had dropped a little nugget about that beard. BB was incredibly vain about his facial hair. It was his pride and joy. And perhaps his Achilles' heel.

BB piloted his rickety bike around the outer perimeter of the field, his eyes shielded from view by an oversize pair of horn-rimmed sunglasses. Mara had suggested that BB lived in the hipster mecca of Williamsburg, Brooklyn, and if it was anything like Silver Lake in Los Angeles, Dee could easily see how BB would have blended in.

Just like a serial killer.

Barbaric Barista executed a lazy figure eight on his bike before he spoke. "Do you like games, Cinderella?" His voice had a smarmy, ironic lilt.

Games. Just like Kimmi used to play. "Not especially."

He ignored her. "I like games."

"I'm sure you do."

"My favorite," he continued, as if reading from a script, "is Ultimate Frisbee. Ever played?"

At least I know what's in his bag. Dee was on full alert now. Razor-sharp Frisbees that might cut off her hands? Frisbees that shot laser beams? Rabid dogs that chased said Frisbees?

He backpedaled, applying the brakes with a strangled squeak. When his bike came to a full stop, he dismounted, threw down the kickstand, and swung his bag so that it was in front of him. "It's usually played in teams, but since it's just you and me today, I thought I'd make up my own rules."

"Shocking."

He pulled a Frisbee from his bag—plastic and red, it looked like the kind you'd pick up at any toy store, but Dee notice that he handled it gingerly, reverently, as if he was afraid it might break apart in his hands.

"I throw this to you, and you try to catch it," BB said. "Easy, right?"

"Right." She had to be on her guard. No telling what BB's game of Ultimate Frisbee might actually entail.

"Awesome!" he cried. "Last one standing wins." Then he torqued his body and let the Frisbee fly.

He was a good shot. The disc started low and rose gracefully as it crossed the field. It flew in a straight line with hardly any arc, and if Dee had stayed put, she could easily have caught it in her hands. But there was no way in hell she was actually going to play by BB's rules. So she held firm until the toy was a few feet away, then darted aside.

It glided by her, slowly losing altitude until it hit the front wall of the warehouse. The instant the rim of the red plastic disc made contact with the corrugated metal, it exploded, leaving a two-foot-wide hole.

"Shit." *Exploding Frisbees? Really? How the hell is that even possible?*

Dee had no time to ponder physics and aerodynamics—BB had already unleashed another projectile. It approached even faster than the first, and Dee barely had time to dive to her right as it soared by. This one exploded in the Astroturf, the shock waves temporarily knocking away Dee's breath as chunks of fake plastic grass rained down around her. The smell was acid and toxic, and Dee wondered how many carcinogens were invading her lungs as she climbed to her feet.

BB launched his barrage furiously, and Dee had to keep her eye on two or three discs at once as she bobbed and weaved her way around the Ultimate Frisbee course.

"I can do this all night, Cinderella," the Barbaric Barista sneered. Dee noticed an edge of irritation in his voice. Good. She liked the idea that she was pissing him off.

"You're going to run out of Frisbees eventually," Dee panted.

"You won't last that long," he replied.

She had to hit the ground to avoid a low-flying saucer; then she immediately rolled aside to miss another. Both exploded instantly. How did BB keep from blowing himself up as he handled the precariously explosive-laden lawn toys? Or while he'd been riding his stupid bike around the field?

She crouched, just missing another one, and this time she noticed a flashing red light coming from a small black box on the underside of the Frisbee.

So that's how he can carry these things around in his messenger bag.

The box probably had a switch, and BB was arming the Frisbees just before he launched them. The impact caused the explosion. Maybe if she could get to his bag and turn a few of them on, he'd blow himself to pieces?

It was worth a try. Now she just needed to distract him.

"Oh my God!" Dee said, climbing to her feet. She widened her eyes and pointed at BB. "What happened to your beard?"

"What?" Barbaric Barista gasped in horror, as if someone had just killed his firstborn. He let the unarmed Frisbee in his hand fall to the ground and dropped his eyes to his prized facial hair, grasping at it with both hands. His beard was his weakness, just as Mara had predicted.

He was only preoccupied for a second.

But that was all Dee needed.

She sprinted right at him, tackling him by the legs. They both went sprawling across the Astroturf. In the confusion, Dee thrust her hand into BB's bag, fumbling blindly with her fingertips for a switch on the underside of one of the Frisbees. She found something that felt like hard plastic, and sensed the satisfactory click as she pushed the lever into place, activating the explosive. Then she yanked her hand out of the bag and scrambled away.

As she fled, her feet slipped on the plastic grass, rolling her ankle. She yelped in pain, toppling forward onto all fours, and when she flopped onto her back she half expected to find Barbaric Barista bearing down.

But BB must have realized that she'd activated one of the discs, because he lay frozen at the edge of the fake grass. Slowly, his hand inching toward his head, he tried to lift the messenger bag's strap off his shoulder while he slid away from it. But his hip was caught beneath the bag, and the moment he shifted, it began to slide toward the ground.

Barbaric Barista's eyes met Dee's just before impact. "You bitch."

Or at least that's what he would have said.

The explosion blew him apart before he could finish.

FORTY-TWO

THE ONLY THING WORSE THAN THE SMELL OF BURNING PLASTIC grass was the smell of burning man bun *mixed* with burning plastic grass.

Dee limped across the field, carefully stepping over bits of smoldering appendages. Her rolled ankle throbbed, but it could still bear her weight, though tenderly. Not sprained, not broken. She'd just have to deal. If only she had a pair of . . .

Near the edge of the field, Dee stopped. Lying side by side, as if placed there by magic, were BB's flip-flops.

They must have been blown off his gross hairy man-feet by the force of the explosion, and though Dee was relatively sure she'd just tiptoed around one of his legs that was severed at the ankle, the brown leather mandals looked blood-free and pristine.

What was worse, going barefoot or wearing the hipster shoes of a dead serial killer?

With a shrug, Dee slipped her feet into the flip-flops. They were about a size too large, but nothing she couldn't manage.

Well, that was one problem solved. Only about a million left.

But she'd start with the most immediate one: What she was supposed to do next?

Barbaric Barista had been waiting for her. The football field, the exploding Frisbees—those had been planned in advance. Dee's eyes traveled to the nearest camera, the red dot of light squarely facing her. The Postman was filming every moment as she took out yet another of his Painiacs.

So Dee's hunch had been right: The Postman wanted his killers dead. There was a new batch of them arriving soon, and it was time to liquidate the old ones. Dee was pretty sure the Painiacs had no idea they were being set up. Maybe she could use that information to her advantage? There was only one way to find out.

Dee poked her head tentatively into the corridor where BB had emerged on his bike, half expecting someone to jump out at her with a machete or a poisonous snake, but all she found was another messenger bag.

It was the identical twin to the one BB had been carrying, and as Dee carefully lifted the flap with her toe, she could see a dozen or more red Frisbees packed inside. BB must have brought another round of ammo and stashed it back there in case he needed it. Weird place to leave them, but whatever.

Dee was pretty sure she couldn't hit the broad side of a barn with one of those Frisbees, but now that she knew how they worked, she at least had a weapon.

Ho-ho-ho, Dee said to herself as she looped the bag over her shoulder. *Now I have exploding Frisbees.*

She smiled. Ethan would have been so proud.

The corridor was narrow, hardly wide enough for a person to squeeze through, and it twisted and turned at sharp ninety-degree angles until Dee was hopelessly confused as to which direction she'd come from and which way she was going. It was dark in this coiled interior of Slycer's old maze, and at each corner, she expected to encounter some life-threatening booby trap, or worse, another Painiac. But all she saw were the cameras. Cameras everywhere.

She limped her way through the maze for what felt like an eternity before a ball of flame flew past her face, impaling the wall beside her. An arrow with a flaming tip.

Behind her, a crash as if something heavy and metallic had fallen to the ground. She spun around to find an iron gate impeding her retreat. Well, now she knew where one of the gates from Molly's cages had ended up. Dee was trapped with Robin's Hood.

But she quickly realized that he was only half the challenge. Robin was there, of course—poised beside a large, bubbling hot tub with a bow in one hand, an open Zippo lighter in the other—but he wasn't alone. Standing on a scaffold behind him was Hannah Ball.

Robin was dressed in what appeared to be a makeshift outfit. His black tights were opaque, but not completely, showing lighter patches around the knees and a hint of the control-top panel peeking out mid-thigh from beneath a heather-gray long-sleeve shirt, which he wore as a tunic. Black boots laced up past the ankle, but they were scruffy and well worn, the leather creased near the toes, as if he'd hiked halfway across the country in them. Only the executioner's cowl—his signature look—appeared professionally designed and not thrown together at the last minute.

This manifestation of Robin's Hood certainly didn't match the dapper-dandy highwayman persona that graced all his merch, which seemed highly suspicious until Dee remembered that Robin hadn't actually appeared on the video during Dr. Farooq's murder. Had that been a last-minute assignment? Had Robin been given insufficient time to plan an elaborate costume? Possibly. But it was pretty clear that Robin hadn't left the island after Dr. Farooq's death, so his current outfit had been cobbled together from whatever he could find.

Hannah Ball, on the other hand, had come prepared. Of course, her costume wasn't nearly as complicated. The chef with a penchant for human flesh dressed as . . . a chef. She wore a white double-breasted coat with black buttons running in parallel rows down the front, and sleeves cuffed just above the wrist, paired with matching white pants and black kitchen clogs. Her dark, wiry hair fell in two tight braids in front of her shoulders, peeking out from beneath her quintessential chef's hat, which was tall and poufy, inflated like a balloon. But instead of sitting on her brow, the brim of the hat extended downward to the bridge of her nose, covering her forehead and eyes, with two oval holes cut into it so that she could see.

"Greetings, dear Cinderella!" Robin cried, his voice loud and booming with an affected pomposity that made him sound like an actor at a Medieval Times restaurant. "We are honored to be the first to welcome thee to this maze of delights."

The first? So Robin and Hannah didn't know that Dee had already disposed of Barbaric Barista? Interesting. Dee wondered what, exactly, The Postman had told his Painiacs to get them into the maze.

There was an awkward pause, as if both Hannah and Robin were waiting for the other to speak. As far as Dee knew, there had never been a Painiac collaboration, so these two clearly weren't used to working together.

After a few seconds, Robin cleared his throat and nodded his head in Hannah's direction, prompting her to say something.

"Right, sorry," Hannah muttered, then jutted out her chin. "You've arrived just in time for dinner." Her voice, also in character, was high and snooty, like a bad impersonation of Julia Child. "I'm planning one of my specialties."

"Let me guess," Dee said, channeling some of Griselda's snark. "Filet of

Cinderella? Cinderella fricassee? Princess soufflé with a side of Cinderella sauce?"

"Er . . ." Robin exchanged a confused glance with Hannah. "No?"

"No!" Hannah repeated, stomping her foot for emphasis. The scaffolding rocked back and forth. "Tonight I shall demonstrate my sous-vide technique with kabob of Cinderella."

Dee had no idea what sous-vide technique might be, but she guessed that it had something to do with the bubbling hot tub. She eyed Robin's quiver of arrows. The kabob part was self-explanatory.

"This hot tub," Hannah explained obligingly, "has been heated to exactly two hundred and twelve degrees Fahrenheit, the exact temperature at which water boils."

Great.

"The meat," she continued, "once impaled upon the kabob, is sealed in an airtight plastic container before it is submerged in the water bath, thus providing an even cooking time—"

Robin interrupted her. "While *you*, dear princess, suffocate and bleed to death while you're being boiled alive."

Yeah, because she totally hadn't put those pieces together already.

Hannah was clearly annoyed at being cut off during her soliloquy. "Even. Cooking. Time," she said, emphasizing each syllable.

Robin bowed at the waist. "A thousand pardons, good lady."

"Hmph." Hannah drew herself up, puffing out her chest before continuing. "And ensuring that the inside of Cinderella is properly cooked without charring the delicate flesh on the outside, while . . ."

Dee had heard enough. She wasn't going to become sous-vide anything. She slipped her hand into the messenger bag, and pulled out a Frisbee.

She'd only get one shot, maybe two, before Robin realized what was going on and peppered her with flaming arrows. Unlike the Frisbee field, where she'd had plenty of room to maneuver around Barbaric Barista's slow-moving projectiles, this tight space had little room for Dee to navigate in, and Robin, who was an excellent marksman, had weapons that moved a hell of a lot faster than flying plastic discs.

Meanwhile, Dee hadn't thrown a Frisbee since she was a kid, and as she carefully hid the bright red toy behind her body, she hoped her crappy throwing technique didn't produce some kind of boomerang effect and send the explosive directly back to her.

There was only one way to find out. With a flick of her thumb, she threw the switch arming the Frisbee, then twisted her body and uncorked her weapon.

It was a thing of beauty watching that red plastic disc soar through the air, and Dee could have sworn that time slowed down as she, Hannah, and Robin all stared fixedly at the lawn toy, which slowly glided down to the floor to rest peacefully at Robin's feet.

"Fuck!" Dee said. *Seriously?* She'd gotten the one dud in BB's arsenal. Could her luck be any worse?

Robin crouched down and picked up the toy. "What confounded contraption of the Devil is this?" he exclaimed, as if he'd never seen a Frisbee before. He turned it over and stared at the underbelly, and Dee noticed that the red light that indicated the armed status of the device wasn't flashing.

"She's trying to distract you," Hannah said. "Hurry up and shoot her."

"Madam," Robin said, his voice haughty, "I do not 'hurry up' and do anything." Then he let the Frisbee fall from his hand, picked an arrow from his quiver, and flicked the Zippo to life.

Screw this. Dee dropped the messenger bag to the floor and shoved both hands inside, arming as many devices as she could. Then she grabbed the bag by the handle and spun around, swinging it like a hammer throw, and launched it at Robin's head.

The heavy bag landed at Robin's feet beside the discarded Frisbee, and for a moment, Dee thought she was screwed and the entire contents of the bag was faulty. But before she could even register the fear, the bag detonated.

The hand holding the Zippo went flying in one direction, Robin's arm and head went flying in another, and the force of the explosion rocked the support beams of the scaffolding. Hannah staggered as the wooden structure swayed from side to side, grabbing one of the beams for support. Before she could get a firm hold, the edifice buckled, and the platform on which she stood tilted downward toward the hot tub.

Hannah lost her balance, arms flailing as she desperately tried to grab hold of anything to prevent her fall. But it was too late. With a heavy splash, the chef plummeted into the boiling water, where bits of Robin bobbed like veggies in a broth.

There was a hiss, followed by a sickening gurgled scream as Hannah frantically splashed around in 212-degree water. Her cries were so horrifying that Dee's stomach clenched involuntarily, and if she'd eaten anything in the last twelve hours, she probably would have puked it up on her pilfered leather flip-flops.

An arm emerged from the water, clinging desperately to the side of the hot tub. The skin was bubbling, blistered, and red. Hannah's fingers had swollen up, now looking more like raw, overstuffed sausages than human digits, and as they gripped the edge of the glossy acrylic shell, Hannah was able to raise her head out of the water.

At least Dee thought it was her head. The chef's hat was gone, as well as the dark brown wig she'd worn. Most of Hannah's actual blond hair had been boiled away from her scalp, leaving small, frizzled clumps protruding from her scalded skin. Her eyes were wide despite heavy swelling around her brow bone, and her skin was beginning to peel away, exposing puffy pink fatty tissue beneath.

Dee's instinct was to run to the hot tub and try to save Hannah, even though she was a psychopathic serial killer who would just as soon drag Dee down with her as escape a horrifying death. But the point was moot. Hannah's strength gave way, and she slipped back into the boiling depths. There was a momentary splash as some water sloshed over the side, and then Hannah was gone.

FORTY-THREE

DEE WAITED A FEW MOMENTS BEFORE SHE APPROACHED THE hot tub, half-afraid that Hannah might rise up from the steaming depths, skin and gore hanging loosely from her body like rotting clothes on a corpse, and attack. But as the smell of boiling flesh wafted across the warehouse toward her, she realized that Hannah Ball, like Robin's Hood and Barbaric Barista, was not to be feared any longer.

Three down, four to go. Dee was second-guessing her tactic of having used all the explosive Frisbees. Now she was left without a weapon. Robin's bow and his quiver of arrows had been obliterated in the explosion, Hannah hadn't brought any knives with her that Dee could see, and the only things left in the room were the hot tub and Robin's Zippo lighter.

With a shrug of resignation, Dee picked up the lighter, cringing as she slipped it from the severed hand that still gripped it, and dropped it into the bodice of her dress. Then she skirted the edge of the hot tub—stepping over chunks of Robin's Hood—and continued into the maze.

After her long, twisty journey from the Ultimate Frisbee field, Dee was surprised to take barely a handful of turns before the smell of burning candle wax filled her nostrils.

She paused, inhaling deeply. The smell was pleasant, significantly more so than the smoldering man bun or boiling human flesh that had nauseated her in the last twenty minutes, and it reminded her of going to church with her dad every Sunday and lighting a candle in memory of the mother she'd never known.

Gucci, Cecil, Molly, and DIYnona were left. Gucci had been known to use candles to set his extravagant scenes, like the one he'd designed for his murder of Blair, and the idea of getting back at her friend's killer caused a dark smile to curl the edges of Dee's mouth. It would be justice served.

Dee paused; her smile vanished. How many Painiacs had died by her hand? Sure, they were deranged serial killers and the world was better off without them, but did that absolve Dee of their deaths? Because that was the whole pretext of Alcatraz 2.0—justice served. Had Dee, in some way, *become* a Painiac?

The idea made her breath catch in her chest. *No!* She wasn't like them, would never be like them. She was fighting for survival. It was different.

She took a deep breath and pushed the doubt from her mind. Doubt caused hesitation, and hesitation might get her killed. Right now she had to focus on Gucci. She set her jaw, steeling herself against what he might have in store for her, and peeked around the edge of the maze wall.

The room was long and narrow, more like a double hallway than the large Astroturf field, and instead of garish rococo furnishings and lush upholstery, it looked like the art classroom at Dee's high school. White laminate tables lined one wall, each arranged with a different set of items: skeins of yarn, magazine clippings with vats of glue, mason jars, a wood-turning lathe, and, on the nearest table, a massive jar full of brightly colored beads. Seated at the far end of the room on a wheeled office chair was DIYnona.

The handicrafter was dressed simply in jeans and a T-shirt. Her wiry gray hair was swept up into a jaunty ponytail, and she wore a leathery apron to protect her clothing from the variety of art supplies she used in her do-it-yourself crafts. At first glance, Ynona could easily have been mistaken for a middle-aged employee at the local big-box craft supply store, complete with sunny eyes, crinkled up at the corners, which suggested a bright, cheerful smile beneath. But you never saw DIYnona's smile, cheerful or otherwise. She wore a tankless portable respirator—the kind painters used when they spray-gunned interiors—which covered her nose and mouth.

The rest of The Postman's lineup appeared to be on the young and fit side—even the portly Gassy Al had cut an imposing figure with his height—so Dee was struck by how frail Ynona looked in contrast. Her hands were delicate, the skin almost tissue-thin, exposing the deep blue veins beneath. Her body was slight and bony, and as she rolled her chair forward she was half-afraid that Ynona would keel over from the sheer weight of the respirator.

But she also knew better than to underestimate this Painiac. Mara had warned her of knitting-needle impalements, stained-glass embalming, human book bindings, and death by pottery wheel. Ynona loved her DIY crafts, and she would get incensed when her victims made fun of them. Well, at least Dee knew how to throw Ynona off her game.

"Oh, hello, my dear," Ynona said, her voice muffled by the mask. "What a lovely surprise."

As if she'd had no idea Dee was coming and just happened to have half of a Michaels store inventory set up in the middle of a warehouse maze on Murder Island. *Lady, please.*

Ynona tilted her head to the side. "I take it you've disposed of my rivals? Good. That means more fun for us!"

Rivals? She must be referring to the other Painiacs. So if Ynona knew that she wasn't Dee's first encounter, and that Dee had "disposed" of the others, why was she sitting there cheerfully waiting for Dee's arrival?

"I've prepared such an exciting assortment of activities for us today," Ynona continued. "Beadwork, knitting, wood turning, decoupage, candle making." She paused, sweeping her arm toward the line of tables. "Won't you choose one you like?"

Dee examined the assembled craft supplies. Yarn for knitting, jars of beads, the lathe, glue, and magazines for the decoupage, and the mason jars must be for the candles. She sniffed. The smell of candle wax was stronger than ever, but where was it coming from?

Dee didn't look up—she didn't want to clue Ynona in to what she was thinking—but that was the only logical place the wax could be: suspended above her in some kind of giant superheated vat. She shuddered at the thought of being encased in it: embalmed alive. It made Hannah's hot tub seem like a fun dip in the pool.

"Beadwork, knitting, wood turning, decoupage, or candle making," Ynona repeated, the cheerfulness ebbing from her tone. "Which one?"

Right. She wanted Dee to pick a craft. Dee noticed that Ynona remained at the far end of the long, thin room, as if the crafty killer wanted to stay far away from a potential molten wax bath. How was it triggered? Remote control? Maybe, but then Ynona would have to time it perfectly.

"Come forward," Ynona prodded. "Choose one."

She wanted Dee to move farther into the room. . . .

Trip wire. That had to be it. As soon as Dee crossed to a craft table, *swoosh.* Human candle.

"Hmmm," Dee said, pretending to think. "I don't know how to knit, but I've always wanted to learn." She held her chin in her hand as if contemplating her options, then let her eyes drop to the floor. About five steps in front of her, Dee could just make out a thin black cord stretched knee-high across the room. "Do you think you could show me?"

Ynona sighed, sounding very much like Darth Vader through her respirator. "Of course, dearie. Just take a seat first. . . ."

"Or maybe decoupage?" Dee suggested. *If I could just get her to come over here.* "Is that like scrapbooking?"

"No!" Ynona snapped. "It is not like scrapbooking." She muttered something under her breath that sounded very much like "stupid kids" before she regained her poise. "Decoupage," she said calmly, "is an ancient decorative practice dating back to Eastern Siberian tomb art in the Middle Ages."

Dee rolled her eyes. Normally, she would have stopped herself, not wanting to hurt anyone's feelings. But pissing Ynona off was her number-one goal. If she could get the handicrafter to lose her focus, maybe she could lure Ynona into her own trap.

"Sounds lame," Dee said. "In fact, all of these sound lame. What kind of person wastes their life with meaningless crafts?"

"Why, you snooty little brat." Ynona stood up, hands balled into fists at her side, and moved forward.

Even angry, she wouldn't be so stupid as to trip the wire herself. And though Dee thought she might be strong enough to take the old lady if it came down to a fight, the odds were good that they might trigger the wire together and both get the ultimate wax job.

Then Dee's eyes landed on the jar of beads.

"Come here!" Ynona commanded as she approached.

Dee acted as if she was going to comply. "Fine!" she said with a heavy sigh. She took a couple of steps, expertly slipping out of her flip-flops in the process; then, just as she was about to hit the trip wire, she leaped in the air, grunting as her lame ankle pushed off the concrete. Dee cleared the trip wire and landed chest first on the nearest table, and, with a sweep of her arm, she knocked the jar of beads onto the floor.

A thousand round bits of plastic scattered across the concrete. Ynona, unable to stop her forward momentum in time, brought her foot down on top of them and immediately lost her balance, arms flailing as she tried to right herself. She looked like a giraffe on roller skates as she careened across the concrete, sliding on the round beads.

Dee jumped from table to table, heading away from the trip wire. She turned in time to see Ynona hit the floor, knocking the respirator askew.

She must have felt the wire as she landed on top of it and desperately tried to crawl away from the target zone. Dangling directly above her, an enormous oil-drum Bunsen-burner contraption began to tip on its side.

On the bead-covered concrete floor, Ynona couldn't get any traction. She flung the respirator aside, exposing an ugly, snarling face. But Dee only saw the real DIYnona for an instant before the woman was swamped in a downpour of liquid wax.

Ynona tried to scream, but the viscous fluid flowed into her mouth, choking her. She contorted in pain, but the motions were dreamlike, choreographed. The wax began to harden immediately, and Dee watched in fixated horror as Ynona's movements slowed, her limbs locked into their death throes. She looked like the plaster molds of the Pompeii victims Dee had seen in a museum once: humanlike, but not.

Dee could only contemplate Ynona's embalming for an instant before she faced her own life-or-death situation. The enormous cauldron that had drenched Ynona in molten wax had swung down like a pendulum, but the weight of its contents must have been too much for the metal arms that suspended it from the ceiling. As the cauldron reached the highest point of its swing, it ripped away from one tether, and as gravity began to reverse the motion, the remaining beam gave way.

The hot metal cauldron careened through the air, directly at Dee. She dove off the table and barely avoided getting crushed.

Dee slammed into the floor. Her left arm broke her fall, and she immediately felt something snap.

She cried out in pain, rolling onto her side and cradling the injured arm against her stomach as the cauldron smashed into the table where Dee had been standing moments before. She heard a sickening crack of wood as the cauldron demolished a portion of the maze wall, but the pain in her arm was all-consuming. Her vision blurred as white-hot bolts of agony rocketed from her elbow to her wrist, and Dee's brain only barely recognized that a huge portion of the wall teetered above her. The entire section had buckled from the force of the impact, and the cauldron itself lay on the table, slowly rolling toward her.

Her broken body was slow to respond as she tried to claw her way toward the doorway. And just as Dee had given up any idea of escape and was bracing for impact, she felt an arm around her waist. Someone lifted her off the floor and half dragged, half flung her through the doorway to safety as Ynona's section of the maze imploded.

TRAZBET.COM

(an affiliate of Postman Enterprises, Inc.)

INMATE: Dee Guerrera (#CinderellaSurvivor)
DAYS ALIVE: 3
PERIOD: 10 November 12:00 a.m. – 10 November 11:59 p.m.
CONDITIONS: Hard and Dark

EXECUTIONER	**ML**	**ODDS**	**$2 PAYOUT**
Barbaric Barista	SUSPENDED		
Cecil B. DeViolent	7-2	9-2	$11.00
DIYnona	SUSPENDED		
Gassy Al	17-1	16-1	$34.00
Gucci Hangman	7-2	9-2	$11.00
Hannah Ball	SUSPENDED		
Hardy Girls	SUSPENDED		
Molly Mauler	1-2	2-5	$2.80
Prince Slycer	SUSPENDED		
Robin's Hood	SUSPENDED		

FORTY-FOUR

THE BACK OF DEE'S HEAD SLAMMED ONTO THE CONCRETE floor, adding a new mind-numbing pain to her growing collection. She took a deep breath, eyes closed, and her chest felt heavy, as if someone or something was on top of her.

Dee blinked open her eyes. Dust and debris fluttered down around her, but she distinctly recognized a head of shaggy blond hair hovering over her.

"You all right?" Nyles asked.

Dee smiled. "Auntie Em?"

"Unlike Ethan's action films," Nyles said, pushing himself back onto his knees, "I actually recognize that reference." He put a hand behind Dee's neck and eased her into a sitting position. "Slowly," he said. "You took quite a spill."

It was a spill, all right.

Dee winced as she sat up, her left arm pulsating with pain. "Ynona was tougher than she looked."

Nyles pursed his lips. "This is my fault. I should have gotten here earlier."

"Everything taken care of?" she asked.

He nodded, glancing at the camera directly over their heads. "You don't have to worry about Griselda anymore," he said slowly.

Dee nodded, understanding him perfectly. Their subterfuge hadn't been easy—the cameras were always on, and Dee had had to trust that Nyles had understood what she wanted him to do.

"I'm glad you're here," she said, then immediately felt like an asshole. Now they were both caught in Slycer's maze. She should be apologizing to Nyles for putting his life in danger again, instead of being selfishly grateful that she didn't have to face the rest of the Painiacs alone.

Nyles laughed. "I'm glad I'm here too. Shall we have a look at that arm of yours?"

Tenderly, Nyles ran his palm up and down the skin of her left forearm, pausing near the wrist. "A fracture, I believe. It's already beginning to swell." He whipped off his jacket, then pulled his long-sleeve shirt over his head.

Nyles's skin was pale, indicating a mere passing acquaintance with the sun, but his muscles were defined, his body lean. He might not have had Ethan's bulk, but now Dee understood why Nyles was stronger than she'd assumed based on his gaunt frame.

He grabbed a piece of wood from the shattered wall, gently placed it under her arm, then bound it to her with his shirt, tying it off at her shoulder to create a makeshift sling.

"It won't stop the pain," Nyles said, his eyes full of concern, "but it will immobilize the break somewhat. Until we can get you to a doctor."

Or until I'm dead.

Nyles pulled his jacket back on and helped Dee to her feet. "Shall we?"

Dee nodded. "Let's see what's next."

Dee and Nyles didn't need to go very far before they stumbled upon the next trial. After they rounded the very first corner, the wall slid closed behind them, locking them into a wide-open room. It ran parallel to the narrow corridor that now served as the final resting place of DIYnona, but while it was just as long, this space looked significantly wider, though that might have been an optical illusion. The wall through which they'd entered was mirrored like a dance rehearsal room.

Illusion or not, it was wide enough to hold an elevated stage that ran about two-thirds the length of the room plus a haphazard assortment of metal scaffolding and stacked wooden crates, set up as bleacher-style seating opposite the mirrors.

Dee had spent enough time with her stepsister to recognize a fashion runway when she saw one, even if it was embedded in some kind of industrial-waste storeroom.

"Actors to their places!" a voice called from the distance.

Dee's heart rate accelerated as Cecil B. DeViolent stepped out from behind the stacked crates.

He wore a simple black blazer over a white collared shirt, fastened at the throat with a shiny black button. Cecil still had the dark shades, but he'd ditched the facial hair and sandy brown wig from his *Die Hard* reenactment and replaced it with floppy blond hair that almost reached his chin. The look was familiar, but also generic, and Dee had no idea what film scene he was going to re-create.

What she *did* know was that that son of a bitch had just murdered Ethan, and even though it had been the kind of death that Ethan had always wanted, it took all of Dee's self-control not to sprint past the runway, tackle Cecil, and throttle him with her bare hands.

It was tempting. She'd have the element of surprise, and Cecil, though eight inches taller than Dee, wasn't a particularly large man. She could probably take him.

But moments later, Dee was glad she'd kept her emotions in check. A second figure stepped out from behind Cecil. He wore a futuristic pant-suit of red lamé and Lycra, and matching patent-leather platform boots with five-inch stiletto heels. But the shaved head and signature red-and-green scarf tied around his nose and mouth like a Wild West bandit gave Gucci Hangman away.

Gucci and Cecil, a match made in hell.

"What the actual fuck?" Gucci stood at Cecil's side, staring at Nyles and Dee with a hand on his hip. "There weren't supposed to be *two* of them."

Cecil tilted his head, as if just registering that fact for the first time. "Huh."

"That reward isn't big enough to take them both out." Gucci whipped his head around to face Cecil. "Especially since I have to share it with you."

There was a reward on the table for finishing Dee off. That was how The Postman had ensured that his Painiacs would all be in the maze. Money.

Cecil nudged him with his elbow. "Perhaps you'd rather forfeit," he said through gritted teeth, "and take the punishment?"

Gucci shuddered, the first sign of emotion Dee had ever seen from a Painiac. "Fine. Let's finish them off already."

So money was the prize, but what was the punishment? Dee could guess. With a new wave of killers en route, losing this battle meant elimination. Just like Dee and Nyles, Gucci and Cecil were fighting for their lives.

"That's what I thought." Cecil cleared his throat. "Actors to their places!"

Gucci turned to the mirror and straightened his red leather outfit.

"What's happening?" Nyles whispered in Dee's ear.

"I don't . . ." Dee made a sweep of the set, taking in all the details of the runway. Suddenly she knew exactly where she was, who Gucci and Cecil were supposed to be, and she burst out laughing.

"Are you okay?" Nyles asked.

"*Zoolander*!" she said.

It made perfect sense, of course. A blockbuster movie about male models in the fashion industry, it was the appropriate melding of Gucci and Cecil. And though Dee had been a baby when it was in theaters, it happened to have been one of Monica's favorite movies, so luckily, Dee knew this scene pretty well. *The walk-off challenge between Zoolander and Hansel.*

"That's another one of your American movies, isn't it?"

"Come on," Dee whispered, "you haven't seen *Zoolander*? Ben Stiller? Owen Wilson? Male models?"

"No," he said. "But I feel as if I'm going to hate it."

"I *said*," Cecil repeated, turning to Gucci, who was re-spiking his hair, "actors to their places."

With a haughty shake of his head, Gucci pranced by Cecil and stepped up onto the stage.

"This will be a straight walk-off," Cecil began, with a hint of a British accent as he tried, somewhat unsuccessfully, to mimic David Bowie's voice. "Old-school rules. First model walks; second model duplicates, then elaborates."

Gucci tilted his head back and forth as if limbering up his neck muscles, then nodded.

"Loser," Cecil added, "has a gasoline fight."

Gasoline fight? That wasn't part of the scene. Dee was pretty sure that she and Gucci were supposed to take turns walking down the runway until Bowie declared Gucci-as-Zoolander disqualified, and boom, scene over. Not the kind of re-creation Cecil normally directed, which ended in an explosion, a fire, a man-eating shark, giant lasers, or a barrage of bullets. What did these two have planned?

"I don't understand," Nyles said helplessly.

Dee pulled him aside. "You're going to have to do this one." She glanced down at her bound arm and twisted ankle. "I can't."

"Right." Nyles nodded. "What am I supposed to do?"

"It's a model walk-off," she explained quickly. "Gucci is going to walk down the runway and back. You have to mimic exactly what he does, and then add your own embellishment."

Nyles's eyes grew wide. "Embellishment?"

Dee glanced back at Cecil, who had climbed up into the makeshift rafters to judge the competition. "Just keep the competition going as long as you can. I'll try to find a way out."

"Two terms premed at Stanford," Nyles said with a sigh, "and I'm doing a model walk-off."

"Age before beauty," Gucci said. He towered over them at the end of the runway, then executed a near-perfect pirouette on the toe of one shiny red boot and pranced back to the beginning of the runway.

Cecil crossed one lean leg over the other and reclined against the metal scaffolds atop a stack of wooden crates, like a king taking his throne. "Aaaaaaand, action!"

As soon as the words left Cecil's lips, music erupted from speakers mounted on all four walls. Michael Jackson's "Beat It," just like in the film. At least Cecil had the details right this time.

From the far end of the runway, Gucci planted his hands against the maze wall and bent forward at the waist, jutting out his sculpted rump as he wiggled it from side to side

"You'll be great," Dee said, guiding Nyles toward the raised runway. Then, before she could even process what she was doing, she kissed him lightly on the lips. "Good luck."

FORTY-FIVE

DEE PICKED HER WAY UP INTO THE BLEACHERS, TRYING NOT TO put any weight on either her twisted ankle or her broken arm, as Gucci began the competition. He strutted down the runway, hands planted on hips that swung side to side like the pendulum on a grandfather clock. At the end he shifted his weight to his right leg, then his left, and finally flicked his head around and headed back the way he came.

When he returned to his starting place, he swept his arm across his body, beckoning his opponent to the stage.

For a moment, Dee wasn't sure if Nyles was going to be able to do it. He stood at the back of the runway, glancing sidelong at his opponent as if searching for inspiration. Gucci gave Nyles the once-over, then rolled his eyes.

Which seemed to spur Nyles into action.

He stuck his hands on his hips, his jacket parted to reveal his bare torso, and with his elbows jutted outward exactly as Gucci had done, Nyles began his walk.

Duplicate, then elaborate. Dee prayed that Nyles had been paying attention. If he couldn't duplicate a walk, then he'd be disqualified. And then what had Cecil said? Gasoline fight?

That could *not* be good.

But Dee's worries proved to be unfounded. Nyles did an excellent Gucci impression. When he got to the end of the runway, he posed perfectly to the right and then the left, just as Gucci had done, and for his "elaboration," Nyles slipped off his jacket and tossed it over his shoulder as he retreated.

Dee let out a slow breath. Nyles had this under control. Now she just had to figure out what Cecil and Gucci had planned. She stole a look at Cecil sitting nearby. His attention was wholly focused on Gucci's next walk, so hopefully he wouldn't notice if Dee did a little reconnaissance.

She shifted her body on the wooden crate so she could get a full view of the bleachers, cobbled together from the leftover industrial infrastructure of the warehouse. Everything looked dingy, old, rusted, or moldy, but more importantly, none of it looked dangerous.

Movement from Dee's left caught her eye. Down below her, beneath the bleachers. She was positive she'd seen a shadow, as if someone had darted behind a stack of crates, and as she bent down to get a better view, she caught a flash of color in the darkness.

If it had been painted gray or brown like everything else in Cecil's set design, Dee might have missed it all together, but the three-foot-tall, bright red gasoline tank was easy to spot. It was mounted to a wheeled caddy, complete with hose and pump, and looked as if it could hold several gallons of fuel.

A chill ran down Dee's spine. Cecil and Gucci were planning to douse her and Nyles with fuel and burn them alive.

Unless Dee got to the tank first.

Back on the runway, Gucci was midway through another walk. He took a step, then swung his leg up in a high kick that would have impressed the Rockettes. Nyles looked at Dee and shook his head, indicating that there was no way he could duplicate Gucci's high kick. But he had to. Not only that, but Dee needed him to keep Gucci and Cecil occupied for as long as possible.

Stretch, Dee mouthed, hoping Nyles would be able to figure out what she meant.

He cocked his head to the side in confusion.

Dee lifted her injured arm, grimacing as a razor-sharp pain ripped through her entire left side, and brought the fingers of both hands together, then dragged them apart as if she were pulling taffy. *Stretch,* she mouthed again.

Nyles paused for a moment, then nodded slowly. If ever there was a time for Nyles to read her mind, this was it.

His high kick wasn't nearly as high or as straight or as impressive as Gucci's, but he managed to get through it, then busted out with a series of dance moves that would have made Beyoncé proud.

His prolonged choreography was exactly what Dee was hoping for. Gucci and Cecil were mesmerized by the display, which gave Dee the opportunity to creep down the wall of crates. By the time Nyles ended with some kind of Macarena–Funky Chicken hybrid that should probably have been banned from dance floors across the world, she'd reached the tank.

Gucci glared as Nyles retreated to the top of the runway. "Seriously?" he said, the scarf pulling with each syllable.

"Duplicate," Nyles said, throwing the rules back at him, "and elaborate. Unless you can't?"

"You wish."

Cecil's attention was fixed on Gucci's next walk, his hand held before him as if he were taking notes on it with an invisible pen.

Dee would only get one shot at this, so her plan had to work. It took her a few seconds to unscrew the hose from the base of the tank, and though it was dark, Dee could see the shiny liquid flowing across the floor as the acrid stench dissipated into the air. The fuel spread, flowing along the lines of the wooden crates, and by the time Dee emerged from behind the bleachers, she could see the highly flammable liquid pooling around the base of the runway.

Gucci had just finished copying the last of Nyles's improvised moves, when he added one of his own, descending into a perfect split.

While he held the pose, Dee pulled Robin's Zippo lighter from the bodice of her dress, flashed it at Nyles, then nodded her head toward the corner of the room.

Nyles pulled on his jacket and raced down the runway, ignoring all choreography.

"Hey!" Gucci cried. "He's not duplicating! He's not duplicating!"

Nyles jumped off the end of the stage to Dee's side as Gucci gave chase, pointing and complaining like a spoiled child.

Cecil slowly rose to his feet. "I believe we have a winner," he proclaimed.

Dee wasn't sure how neither of them smelled the commercial unleaded spreading through the warehouse, but it didn't matter now.

"This is for Blair and Ethan," Dee said. She held up the Zippo and flicked it to life. "Disqualified!"

Dee tossed the lighter into the pool of gasoline at the base of the runway; then she and Nyles ran like hell.

🕒 3m

Tonya Bologna @Tonya_in_Bologna
Was anyone watching channels 432 & 433? There's someone else in the maze. Under the bleachers. #CinderellaSurvivor is getting help!
← | : 137 ₪: 43

🕒 3m

Staci McCandeless @StaciMcCintheSLC
#CinderellaSurvivor's got help? No wonder! That's the ONLY way she's been able to beat @ThePostman_PEI so far. Inside job? I feel cheated. What's this #RadioSilence bullshit, @ThePostman_PEI? #WeWantAnswers
← | : 250 ₪: 141

🕒 3m

Judy Kline @PTrnFTmom_808
Wait, I thought #CinderellaSurvivor hated the dorky Brit? There wasn't any sound on the scene, but I'm pretty sure she threatened him with an ax like an hour ago. Now they're making out? #LoveIsWeird #AKissWithAnAxIsBetterThanNone
← | : 38 ₪: 12

🕒 2m

Phoebe Temptressta @realphoebetemptressta
Dear @GucciHangman—while your high kicks were flawless #JealousOfMyBoogie #TeamRaven, WHAT were you thinking with that red lamé monstrosity? Yes, Zoolander, I get it. But have some pride! #PRIDE
← | : 388 ₪: 202

🕒 2m

Mitchell M. David @SDsNumber1DivorceLaw
No replays happening, but right before @BarbaricBarista ate it, I could have sworn I saw someone moving behind the maze walls. Then miraculously a new bag of Frisbees appeared? It's as if @ThePostman_PEI WANTS all of his killers dead. #YouveGotAnswers
← | : 17 ₪: 65

1m

The Griff @awakewideopen
Ya think? #DontTrustTheFeed #EyesOpen #Alcatraz2Conspiracy #DOJInvestigate #WeWantAnswers

2m

> **Mitchell M. David** @SDsNumber1DivorceLaw
> No replays happening, but right before @BarbaricBarista ate it, I could have sworn I saw someone moving behind the maze walls. Then miraculously a new bag of Frisbees appeared? It's as if @ThePostman_PEI WANTS all of his killers dead. #YouveGotAnswers

← | : 47 ₪: 72

1m

Blake the Flake @blakeflakesseven
@awakewideopen @SDsNumber1DivorceLaw As much as it pains me to say it, you might be right. Where's @TheJusticeDept in all this? And @attorneygeneral? OR @POTUS??? He's the one who sold the prison system off to @ThePostman_PEI in the first place. #Accountability #WeWantAnswers

← | : 56 ₪: 31

FORTY-SIX

THERE WAS NO VISIBLE EXIT FROM THE *ZOOLANDER* SET, SO Nyles and Dee crouched in the far corner as fire erupted from the lighter, racing away in several directions at once, down the edge of the runway and back to the makeshift bleachers. Within seconds, the entire wooden construction seemed to be engulfed in flames, killing the Michael Jackson background music. Dee had only seen fire spread like that in the movies, and she wondered if Cecil B. DeViolent appreciated the irony.

Probably not. It had taken Cecil a few seconds to recognize the danger, watching with bemused interest as the flames swept toward Gucci Hangman, but then his head followed the trail of fire as it raced beneath his seat. Dee couldn't see his eyes, but she could practically pinpoint the moment he realized he was sitting on top of a gasoline tank. He twisted around, searching for an escape, and quickly realized that he was surrounded.

Gucci wasn't faring much better. Flames licked the sides of the runway, essentially encircling him in a wall of fire. There was only one way out.

Holding his arms in front of his face, and with as much of a running start as his five-inch stilettos would allow, Gucci leaped through the mounting fire. His feet slid out from under him as he hit the concrete and he went sprawling across the floor. He smashed into one of the mirrors and lay motionless.

An ear-shattering explosion ripped through the warehouse. Whatever fuel remained in the gas tank had just ignited. The detonation shattered the bleachers, which collapsed into the seething fire beneath, taking Cecil B. DeViolent with them. Dee curled herself into Nyles as the wall of mirrors exploded behind her. Shards of knifelike glass blew upward, mixing with bits of metal and smoking embers, then rained down around them.

So much for Cecil, but just when Dee thought they were home free, Gucci Hangman raised his head.

For a moment, she thought that Gucci had come through the inferno unscathed. Then she saw the flames spreading up his back.

Apparently, red lamé was highly flammable.

Gucci let out a scream even more horrifying than Hannah Ball's had been, his eyes fixed on Dee. He crawled toward her, dragging his body with his well-manicured fingers. Dee could smell his burning flesh as the flames raced across his body.

Nyles leaped to his feet. "Come on!" He hauled Dee up by her good arm and dragged her away.

But they'd forgotten about the minefield of broken glass.

Dee cried out in pain as shards pierced the soft soles of her feet, and she collapsed, dragging Nyles to the floor with her. He scrambled to push himself upright, slicing his hands in the process. As they struggled to escape, Dee could feel the heat radiating from Gucci's body. He clawed toward her, and her bloodied feet slipped against the concrete as she tried to back away.

Nyles threw himself on top of Dee in an effort to protect her, but as Gucci's arm reached out to grab her ankle, his strength gave way.

"Oh my God," Dee gasped. Together she and Nyles watched in horror as the fire engulfed Gucci Hangman. His face seemed to melt away as the flames disintegrated his signature scarf, and Dee felt as if she were staring into the face of the Devil himself—a mask of fire with two gaping black holes for eyes.

Just then, an overhead sprinkler system kicked in, dousing the warehouse in water.

The deluge seemed to go on forever. Nyles tried to keep Dee dry, but she didn't mind the water. The coolness felt good against her skin, and though the wounds in her feet stung, the fiery ache in her fractured wrist was somewhat dulled by the cold. Finally the water pressure waned, slowing to a trickle before stopping completely. Dee lay on her back, soaked to the bone, blinking through wet eyelashes at Nyles, who lay on top of her. Behind him, the ruins of the *Zoolander* set smoldered, and the blood from her feet and Nyles's hands streaked through the pooled water, dissipating from red to pink.

"Hey," Nyles said, smiling. Water dripped from his hair onto her face. "Still alive?"

"Barely."

"Good enough."

He rolled off her and cradled his hands in his lap. A dozen or more shards of glass protruded from his palms, the skin ragged beneath. He tried to pull one out, but his hands were shaking from pain and shock.

"Let me." Dee laid his hands on top of her wounded arm, and with her good hand yanked the largest piece from the fleshy area near Nyles's right thumb. He winced but didn't cry out, clenching his jaw fiercely against the agony.

"I hope you weren't planning on being a surgeon, Doctor Strange," Dee said, trying to distract him as she continued to tear bits of glass from his palms.

"Ah yes, I get that reference," Nyles said through gritted teeth. "Perhaps I shall resort to magic as well."

"You should grow a beard, too. Complete the look."

"Barbaric Barista wore off on you, did he?" Nyles grinned. "I just might, you know. Grow a long snarled thing."

Dee rolled her eyes. "Don't you dare."

"You wouldn't like to kiss me if I had overgrown whiskers, eh?"

Dee removed the last piece of glass, then glanced up at Nyles. "No, I'd still kiss you."

Nyles winked at her before shifting his attention to her lacerated feet. "Your turn."

As Nyles worked, Dee stared up at the warehouse rafters and tried to think about anything other than the searing torture.

With a surgeon's precision, Nyles wrenched the jagged fragments from the soles of her feet.

It felt like a movie scene, something she'd seen before but hardly remembered. An action flick, maybe? Ethan would have known.

Dee was exhausted. She just wanted to close her eyes and go to sleep. It would be so easy to just stay here with Nyles and the water and the smell of charred flesh and wet dog. . . .

"Wet dog?"

Nyles didn't look up. "Huh?"

Dee sniffed the air again. The stench was unmistakable. "I smell wet dog. That means Molly Mauler and her wild animals."

"It'll be a trap," Nyles said. He finished with Dee's feet and removed the sling from her arm. He tied the sleeves around her neck, cradling her broken arm in the rest of the fabric; then Nyles used his teeth to tear what remained of his wet shirt into strips. "Even if we can find the way out of here, we'd probably round a corner, a door would slide closed, and *boom*: lion appetizer."

"We can't have that," Dee said. She bit her lower lip as Nyles bound her feet tightly with pieces of his shirt. They throbbed as he tied a constricting knot; then immediately the pain began to ebb.

"No."

Nyles wrapped his hands in a similar fashion, tightening each knot with his teeth. "She wouldn't be in the kill room with us, though. Which means she must be up high somewhere. Watching."

Dee's eyes drifted up to the metal scaffolding. It hadn't burned in the fire, and it reached all the way to the top of the wall.

Nyles followed her gaze, immediately grasping her idea. "Stay here."

He touched one of the metal poles with the back of his hand, as if expecting it to be blisteringly hot. Then, content that it didn't sear the skin off his body, Nyles hoisted one foot up onto the nearest bar and began to climb.

Nyles reached the top of the wall with relative ease and flattened his body against it. He stared out across the maze for several minutes before easing his way back down.

"There's a way out of here behind the scaffolding," Nyles explained. "The maze continues for about fifty feet, then opens into a large penned-in area near the corner of the warehouse."

"Did you see Molly?"

"She's perched on top of the wall, dressed like some kind of deranged circus clown." He shuddered. "We could get to her by crossing the tops of the maze walls, but she'd see us coming."

A plan was forming in Dee's mind. "Do you think you can memorize the maze path between here and there?"

"Absolutely."

Dee held out her hands. "Then help me up. I think I know a way to get Molly off that wall."

TRAZBET.COM

(an affiliate of Postman Enterprises, Inc.)

INMATE:	Dee Guerrera (#CinderellaSurvivor) *INJURY ALERT!*
DAYS ALIVE:	3
INMATE:	Nyles Harding (#DiplomaticImmunity)
DAYS ALIVE:	223
PERIOD:	10 November 12:00 a.m. – 10 November 11:59 p.m.
CONDITIONS:	Hard and Dark

EXECUTIONER	**ML**	**ODDS**	**$2 PAYOUT**
Barbaric Barista	SUSPENDED		
Cecil B. DeViolent	SUSPENDED		
DIYnona	SUSPENDED		
Gassy Al	17-1	3-5	$3.20
Gucci Hangman	SUSPENDED		
Hannah Ball	SUSPENDED		
Hardy Girls	SUSPENDED		
Molly Mauler	1-2	1-5	$2.40
Prince Slycer	SUSPENDED		
Robin's Hood	SUSPENDED		

FORTY-SEVEN

IN A DAY FILLED WITH DISGUSTING THINGS, EXTRACTING Ynona from her waxy tomb was the worst. Even grosser than fishing Hannah's braided wig out of the still-boiling hot tub and shaking off bits of fatty skin that had adhered to it during its soak.

Okay, maybe that was the grossest, but wrestling Ynona's wax-crusted corpse into her wheelie chair was a close second.

It wasn't so much that she was handling a dead body—sadly, that wasn't a new experience for Dee—but that the wax coating on Ynona was still warm and slippery from the sprinkler bath, which made it feel as if Ynona weren't actually dead at all.

"She looks surreal," Nyles said, staring at the ceraceous corpse as Dee arranged Hannah's wig on Ynona's head. "Like a Dada painting. Or an Ernst."

"Do you think it'll fool Molly?"

"Up close, not a chance. But from above? In bad lighting? It might work."

Dee wiggled the wheeled chair back and forth to make sure that the colored yarn kept the body secured. Waxy Ynona in Hannah's gore-splattered dark brown wig would at least make Molly curious.

I hope.

Nyles crouched down and smeared the wax away from Ynona's feet, exposing a pair of green rubber Crocs. It took some doing, but he managed to pull them from Ynona's stiffened limbs. Then, kneeling before Dee, he offered to put them on her. "They're not glass slippers, Cinderella, but they might help."

"Thanks, Prince Charming."

The rubber Crocs stretched around Dee's bandages, and though walking was still painful, Nyles was right—the ache was lessened.

"Shall we?" Nyles asked, straightening up.

Dee nodded. "Cinderella Survivor two-point-oh is ready to roll."

Dee carefully climbed the scaffolding in the *Zoolander* room, slowly placing her weight on each foot and making sure her hold was secure. If she made too much noise, it might draw Molly's attention, and then they'd be screwed.

When she reached the top of the wall, she flattened herself against it, just as Nyles had done, and scanned the maze.

Molly Mauler sat on top of the wall at a corner, using the two converging edges as her seat. As Nyles had described, she wore some kind of circus getup—striped red-and-white tights, a full black skirt with a massive crinoline petticoat beneath, and a black-and-white corset top. Her face was painted with demonic clown makeup, complete with "evil" eyebrows, drawn at a steep angle from her forehead down to the inner corners of her eyes, and the requisite red foam nose.

Molly bounced her legs against the wall like a bored child whose patience had worn thin, and she was entertaining herself with a white plastic object in her hand. She'd press a button and a door on a cage would start to open. There must have been wolves inside it, because they would howl with excitement as the door crept up a few inches, but then Molly would click the button again, sealing the cage tight. She'd whipped the wolves into a frenzy, but even that was starting to bore her. She glanced at her watch, clearly antsy.

You won't have to wait much longer, Molly.

Dee's eyes drifted to the right, where Nyles hurried through the twists and turns of the maze, pushing Ynona's chair as fast as its wax-clogged wheels would go. As he approached Molly's lair, he slowed, counting his path turn by turn. Left, right, left, right, right, right, left. He stopped cold right before the entrance, and then he gave the chair a massive shove.

Molly was instantly alert. "It's about time, Cinderella Survivor," she said, her voice cackling with delight. "I was worried the sprinklers might have drowned you."

She waited, expecting a response.

But Waxy Ynona wasn't going to give her one.

"Cat got your tongue?" Molly said. "Or should I say, *wolves* got your tongue?"

Nice one.

Again, Molly waited for a response, but this time she seemed more suspicious, leaning forward to peer at the body in the chair.

"Is she gone yet?" Nyles panted, his head peeking over the edge of the wall. He'd made it back to her in record time.

"Shh!" Dee held her breath.

"Seriously?" Molly said at last. She placed the white rectangular object beside her, then reached down behind the far side of the wall and flipped something over the top. The wolves began to howl again, sensing new activity, and as Molly turned to climb down, Dee realized she had a rope ladder.

As soon as Molly's head disappeared, Dee pressed herself up into a standing position. The wooden beams of the maze walls were less than a foot wide, and not particularly sturdy, which made the journey a little bit like running the length of a wobbly balance beam high up in the air on feet that had been numbed up with Novocain. She just gritted her teeth against the stupefying pain and kept her eyes locked on Nyles straight ahead of her.

Below, Molly was examining the body that was strapped to the chair. She lifted a braid of the wig and gave it a tug. The fake hair slid easily from Ynona's wax-crusted head.

"What the fuck?" Molly said, dropping the wig. Then she turned, looked up, and spotted Dee.

They locked eyes, holding each other's gaze for what felt like an eternity. Dee saw Molly's confusion morph into rage and, just for an instant, fear. Then her eyes dropped to the ladder.

At the same moment that Molly broke into a sprint, Nyles lunged for the ladder and started to pull it up. Molly launched her body at it like an NBA forward attacking the net, and managed to catch hold of the bottom rung.

Dee tried to help, but with the advantage of gravity, Molly yanked the rope ladder from their hands. The smooth nylon burned as it whipped through Dee's palms, and Nyles grunted, his bandages little help against friction. The wolves growled, their guttural rumbles reverberating through the walls, as Molly began to climb.

But Dee wasn't about to give up. The ladder was attached to two of the stud beams by carabiner clips fastened to metal rings that had been drilled into the wood.

"Nyles, the clips!" she shouted. If they could unlatch the carabiners, the ladder would drop to the floor with Molly on it. They each reached for one, straining against the weight of the grown woman climbing up the other side. Luckily, the nylon rope had some give to it, and by planting one leg against the beam for leverage, Nyles was able to pull the first carabiner far enough to slip the rope out.

Its stabilization gone, the free end of the ladder whipped through the air. The wall rocked back and forth as the ladder twisted around, slamming Molly against the cage. The wolves went ballistic, throwing their bodies against the metal bars in an attempt to get a piece of her, and Molly had to kick her feet against the bars to push herself away.

Dee swung a leg off the side of the wall, straddling it for balance against its unsteady motion, but Nyles wasn't quick enough. Dee watched in horror as he teetered forward toward the wolf pen.

He flailed his arm, shifting his balance just as the wall wobbled in the opposite direction, and instead of falling forward, Nyles stumbled off the other side, plummeting into the darkness below.

"Nyles!" Dee cried. She could barely discern the outline of his body on the concrete beneath her as tears blurred her vision. Was he dead? Had another person she cared about died because of her?

A scream from the wolf pen reminded Dee that she wasn't out of danger yet. The wolves had caught strands of Molly's hair in their snapping jaws. She yelped out in pain as the wolf pack pulled chunks from her scalp. Molly pawed at the next rung of the ladder, desperate to escape.

But as the wolves pulled her toward the cage, Dee saw the rope ladder slacken. She reached for the second carabiner and quickly unlatched it. Then, with one final heave, she pulled the nylon loop from the shackle and let the entire weight collapse to the floor.

As she slowly stood up, Molly looked even more demonic: makeup smeared, tights torn, hair a rat's nest dotted with bald spots. But Dee had to give her credit—she didn't panic for an instant.

"When I get my hands on you," Molly began, her voice disturbingly calm, "I won't need one of my animals to dismantle you limb from limb."

It wasn't a threat Dee took lightly. "The Postman wants you dead." She thought of Nyles, his body splayed out on the ground beneath her. "He wants us all dead."

"No," Molly snarled. "Just *you*."

"I know about the reward," Dee said. She wanted Molly to understand what was happening, to surrender to Dee before she had to do something unspeakable to protect herself. "And I know that there's a new lineup of killers set to arrive on Alcatraz two-point-oh next week."

Molly's rage faltered. "You do?"

Dee nodded. "I know he promised to keep you around if you killed me, but trust me, he's not. He's going to kill all of us. Your only chance is to let me go."

Dee watched Molly contemplate this new information. She glanced back at DIYnona dressed in Hannah's wig. Would she believe the truth? Or would distrust and bloodlust win out?

Molly picked up one end of the ladder. With a loud grunt, she tossed it up toward the top of the wolf cage.

Well, there was Dee's answer.

The ladder crashed back to the floor, but Dee saw what Molly was trying to do: the top edge of the cage door had a lip on it. If she could get the ladder to catch, she could scale the side of the cage and from there jump onto the top of the wall.

There was only one way to stop her: Dee had to open the cage.

She'd been hoping to avoid that scenario. She'd had no choice with the others, killing them to save herself. But she would have been content to leave Molly trapped in her animal pen where she couldn't do any harm. The idea of allowing someone to be eaten alive—even someone as loathsome as Molly Mauler a.k.a. Ruth Martinello of 157 Hillcrest Avenue in

Marquette, Michigan—made Dee's heart ache. But she couldn't let Molly escape and potentially kill her.

Dee picked up the white remote control, closed her eyes, and pressed the button.

The screams were unbearable, and though Dee pressed her fingers into her ears, she couldn't block out the spine-chilling sound.

It was over quickly, though Dee wasn't about to look down. She didn't need to see the carnage to know that Molly Mauler had gotten a taste of her own medicine. And that the wolves had gotten a taste of Molly.

Suddenly the wall shook violently, and Dee had to grip it with both hands to keep from falling. The wolves were still hungry. They threw themselves at the maze wall, bloody paws and snouts splattering the wood with Molly's remains as they tried to claw up to Dee. They were frenzied, and Dee was afraid they might bring the wall down as they repeatedly launched themselves against it.

Time to leave. Without the benefit of the rope ladder, it wasn't going to be pretty. She lowered herself down on the far side of Molly's pen, dangling as far as she could by the fingertips of her good arm, then let herself fall.

The pain of impact rocketed up through her numbed feet to her shins. If her ankle hadn't been sprained before, it certainly was now, but her left leg appeared to be unbroken, and she was able to crawl to Nyles's side, urgently seeking signs of life.

"Nyles?" A sob caught in her throat. "Nyles, say something." His shoulder lay at an unnatural angle beneath his body, but she didn't see any blood from a head wound, and as she reached a tentative hand toward his throat, she practically shrieked with happiness. His pulse was strong. Nyles was still alive.

She was so ecstatic, she almost didn't hear the voice behind her.

"Hello, Cinderella."

Dee's sobs stopped instantly. The voice was familiar, and Dee knew what she was going to see even before she rolled over to face it.

"Prince Slycer."

Part of her had always known that this was what she'd find at the end of the maze.

Slycer looked exactly the same as when they'd last met. Well, almost. There wasn't any blood nor any trace of a stab wound on his stark white Prince Charming coat. But other than that, the costume was identical, as well as the night-vision goggles and the ugly, twisting blade.

Except this Slycer was noticeably shorter.

It was time to end the charade once and for all.

"Take off the mask," Dee said, her voice remarkably steady as she struggled to her feet using her good leg. "Kimmi."

Slycer stood utterly still for a moment, then slowly raised a hand to the night-vision goggles and slid them off.

Mara dropped the mask to the floor and smiled.

FORTY-EIGHT

"YOU DON'T LOOK SURPRISED," KIMMI SAID. SHE SOUNDED DISappointed.

Dee limped forward, wedging herself between Kimmi and Nyles. "I had my suspicions."

"Bullshit," Kimmi said. "You totally thought Mara was dead."

The fall from the ceiling—Mara had landed perfectly in the middle of the bed, her face turned away so that Dee couldn't see her. "You did a pretty good job of faking it."

"Right? I just had some foam pellets for my mouth, but you totally made that video spikeworthy by climbing up on the freaking roof. The mattress was hard as hell when I landed on it." She rubbed her lower back. "I might have a bruise."

You're going to have more than that when I'm done with you. "Who was she? The real Mara?"

Kimmi shrugged. "Some chick who was scared shitless. Daddy thought it would boost ratings to bring in a crop of young, attractive inmates, but some of them just gave up the moment they arrived on Alcatraz two-point-oh. Mara kept her head down, didn't interact with people. Can you believe she only had two subscribers to her personal feed? *Two!* I think a dead cat could get more than that. She was so boring. I did her a favor, to be honest. The day before you arrived, I killed her, dyed my hair, added colored contacts, and presto! You had a new best friend."

Her callousness at murdering the real Mara was disgusting, but after all that Dee had suffered at Kimmi's hands, it wasn't surprising.

"You never even recognized me," Kimmi preened. "I've always been one step ahead of you."

Not always.

"I searched for you while I was in the hospital," Kimmi continued, her eyes narrow, her voice sharp. "Daddy helped. But you'd changed your name."

"Your dad is The Postman," Dee said slowly, as if she wanted to make sure that Kimmi understood every word.

Kimmi's blue eyes, now free of the colored contacts, grew wide. "Yes! I'm impressed."

"Don't be."

"Daddy went to talk to your dad a few months after my trial ended. He wanted to buy the rights to our story and turn it into a reality show. Wouldn't that have been awesome?"

Dee hadn't understood her dad's reasoning at the time. She'd wanted to be Dolores Hernandez, not Dee Guerrera. She'd wanted to stay at her school with her friends, not move to an entirely new city. But her dad, as with all things, had been right.

"But it's a good thing he didn't, because Alcatraz two-point-oh is a much better idea for a reality show. I really wanted you to see it. We scanned every school in the country, looking for you. Smart of your dad to keep you in LA. We never even thought to look there."

"We're smarter than you give us credit for," Dee said.

Kimmi glanced down at her knife. "Maybe. But that idiot sister of yours wasn't. She led me right to you. Can you believe she tried to e-mail me?"

This time, Dee was genuinely surprised. How had Monica been able to track Kimmi down? "What?"

"Oh, yeah. She pretended to be writing an article on teens and mental health for her school newspaper." Kimmi gave Dee a thumbs-up. "Ooooh, good one, Monica."

SHUT UP! Dee screamed the words in her head but remained silent. She needed to keep Kimmi talking at all costs.

"Imagine my reaction," Kimmi laughed, "when I found that you'd replaced me with another sister!" She clicked her tongue. "How could you?"

"You do realize that's not how it works, right? My dad and stepmom found each other. I had nothing to do with it."

"You could have shut Monica out!" Kimmi cried. "But no, you had to let her in, let her get close, tell her your secrets. Like a sister. Do you have any idea how much that *hurt* me?"

Dee clenched her jaw. "You're not my sister."

Kimmi exploded. "BUT I SHOULD HAVE BEEN! Not her. Not some stupid girl who only cared about fashion and boys and Gucci Hangman."

"So you killed her."

"No, *I* didn't kill her," Kimmi said, pointing the knife at Dee's sternum. "Daddy did." She sighed. "He loved that sort of thing."

Loved? Past tense?

"Murderer."

Kimmi rolled her eyes. "Don't be so dramatic. She, like, barely felt anything. Daddy didn't even torture her first. He wanted to, but I told him no. Daddy always did what I told him to."

"So you and your psychopath dad killed my stepsister, then framed me for her murder?"

Kimmi spread her hands, as if to proclaim her helplessness. "How else was I supposed to get you here?"

"Here on this island. To kill me. Think about what you're saying."

"But it was just a game!" Kimmi cried. "One of our little games. Don't you remember how much fun we used to have?"

"No," Dee said, remembering the torture of hair braiding in the white room. "I don't."

"He wasn't going to kill you," Kimmi protested. "The day you arrived, I was waiting for you in this maze. My plan was that 'Mara' would help you escape the Slycer, and then you would have realized how much you needed me and we could have lived here on Alcatraz two-point-oh together. Best friends. Sisters. Forever."

She was even more insane than Dee had realized.

"Never," Dee said.

"Oh, come on! Look at how much fun we've had in the last few days. It could have been like that all the time."

Over my dead body.

"But you had to go and ruin it," Kimmi said, with a sad shake of her head. She advanced toward Dee. "And now here we are."

Dee eyed a camera mounted to the wall of the warehouse. She needed to keep Kimmi talking.

"Why did you have innocent people sent to Alcatraz two-point-oh?" Dee blurted out, hoping that Kimmi would take the bait. Her ankle throbbed, she was having difficulty staying focused, and it took every ounce of strength she had left to stay on her feet.

"Daddy," Kimmi began, then paused, shaking her head. "Daddy knew about ratings. He was a genius with them. He saw that spikes were dropping and realized he needed to spice things up around here. Who wants to see a gross old man get murdered? Nobody. But a hot chick? Or a buff young guy? Instant ratings hike."

Keep talking. "And Dr. Farooq was part of it?"

"That bitch." Kimmi practically spat out the words. "Can you believe she told Daddy I was dangerously psychotic? I mean, is that even a diagnosis? What kind of doctor *was* she?"

"The kind who would take bribes to testify against innocent people," Dee prompted.

"Greed was her downfall," Kimmi said cheerfully. "But that was Daddy's deal. And once Daddy died, I got my revenge. Who's dangerously psychotic now, Dr. Farooq? Oh, we'll never know, because you're dead."

But Dee hardly even registered Kimmi's confessing to Dr. Farooq's murder. All she heard was that Kimmi's dad was dead. *The Postman is dead. . . .*

"Prince Slycer was The Postman," Dee said slowly, as the last piece of the puzzle clicked into place. *Keep her talking.* "Which means you've been running the island ever since I killed him." The lack of food deliveries, the failing infrastructure. Even the momentary lapses in camera movement. Kimmi couldn't control them when she was running around the island with Dee and her friends.

"I controlled most of it from my smartphone," Kimmi bragged. "Even while I was on the bed and you thought I'd died. Isn't that the best game ever?"

"You killed all the guards, who might have noticed that things were different," Dee continued, staying on track. "And the rest of the inmates, knowing your dad already had a new wave coming. So your only problem was the Painiacs. They'd eventually realize that someone else was running the show."

"True," Kimmi said, eyeing her sidelong as if surprised that Dee had figured it out. "Which is why I'm replacing them."

"And why you were helping me kill them off."

Kimmi gasped. "You saw that?"

"The Frisbees, the gas tank. You took care of the last Hardy Girl and Gassy Al yourself, and with the guards already dead, you wanted me to deal with the rest of the Painiacs in the maze. Then there'd be no one left who knew The Postman was your dad and not you."

"Maybe."

Dee nodded at a camera overhead. "But now everyone knows. It's all over, Kimmi."

Kimmi turned to look at the camera, then burst out laughing. "Are you kidding me? Do you really think I'd have a camera running while I admitted all of this? Am I an idiot or something?"

Dee didn't answer. She'd heard everything she needed: the truth about Monica's murder, the sham trials, the innocence of her friends, and the deep conspiracy of corruption that fueled Alcatraz 2.0. But there was something else she needed to know. Something personal.

"Why me? Why did you pick me?"

Kimmi tilted her head to the side, her eyebrows bunched in confusion, and suddenly Dee was eleven years old again, staring up at Kimmi's face in the air vent. "You don't know?"

"Why?" Dee repeated.

Then Kimmi laughed—not an evil-villain-mastermind laugh or a psychotic-serial-killer laugh, but a laugh of pure, delighted surprise.

"'My heart wants a sibling,'" she quoted, still snickering. "'A friend to call my own. But I don't know what it means / To have a sister or a clone.'"

Dee sucked in a breath. "My poem."

"'To My Unknown Sister,'" Kimmi said. "I saw an article about it online when I was thirteen—and it was like you'd taken the words right from my own brain."

That stupid poem. She'd seen the ad for a local poetry competition and so desperately wanted to submit something, so she wrote about the one thing that had obsessed her as a ten-year-old: a sibling. Those ridiculous verses had literally ruined her life.

"I wanted a sister," Dee said, her voice razor-sharp. "More than anything in the world. But I never, ever wanted you."

Kimmi stopped laughing. Her eyes narrowed as she dropped her chin. "We could have stayed here forever. You and me. Sisters. I would have hired new Painiacs, and we could have gone on as before. But you ruined it, and now all that the world will find is your dead, mangled body, and those of your friends. While I will have miraculously survived Gassy Al's chamber. I'll be a hero, and then someone else will get to be my sister."

She started toward Dee, knife raised.

There was nowhere for Dee to go, but she had one more surprise for Kimmi. "Did you get all of that?" she shouted.

Kimmi stopped dead, waiting. Dee looked around, panic spreading out from the pit of her stomach at the silence. "I said," she repeated, "did you get all of that?"

"Got it!" Griselda rounded the corner of the maze, laptop balanced on her forearm and the Hardy Girls' ax tucked into the waistband of her skirt. "Sorry I missed my cue. I was, like, so totally obsessed with the comments feed." She looked up from the screen, her eyes trailing to Nyles. "Is he okay?"

"I'm fine," Nyles said. He raised himself on his good arm, the other hanging limply at his side. "Dislocated shoulder and possible concussion, but I'll survive."

"I was so worried," Griselda said drily, sounding anything but. She typed on the keyboard with her free hand. "Live feed is broadcasting. We got all of it."

Kimmi swung back and forth between Dee and Griselda. "But . . . the fight. You thought Griselda was me."

Dee sighed. It was petty to feel so satisfied, but after all that Kimmi had done, Dee was practically giddy to know she finally had the upper hand.

"We faked it," Dee said simply. "I realized when I saw Gassy Al's body in the pavilion that something was wrong. Griselda was right, Robin's Hood always wore the executioner's cowl, but you knew Al had made his own because you'd already seen him. When you killed him and hid his body in the pavilion."

"This isn't possible." Kimmi turned around, spotting camera after camera in the warehouse. Each one had its red light on, recording everything. "I was a step ahead of you the whole time."

"Almost," Nyles said, "but not quite. Dee figured it out at the last second."

"She explained it as we walked back to I Scream," Griselda added. "Said we had to fake a big fight so you'd think Dee was on her own." She smiled. "Not like fighting with Dee was that much of a stretch."

"While you were focused on me," Dee continued, keeping her eyes locked onto Kimmi, "Griselda found the laptop you had stashed in your house."

"And the body of the real Mara." Griselda wrinkled her nose. "Chopped up. In the fridge. Totally disgusting, FYI."

"It was a guess," Dee said, "that you'd have a laptop and Internet access." She smiled at Griselda.

"I had to break through a locked door with the ax to find them, but

I did," Griselda said, beaming back at Dee. "And now the whole world knows about your bullshit. So we should be getting out of here ASAP."

"No." Kimmi's face turned red, and her fingers clenched the knife so tightly her knuckles turned stark white. "You ruined everything!"

Then she pulled back the knife and rushed at Griselda.

Images of Blair's decapitated head and Ethan's bullet-riddled body flashed through Dee's mind. Then Monica's body dead on the floor of her bedroom. Kimmi had taken so much from her. She wouldn't let Griselda be added to that list.

Her twisted ankle screaming out in pain, Dee launched herself forward, collaring the back of Kimmi's Prince Slycer costume with her good arm. With all the strength she had left, she wrenched Kimmi around and threw her onto the floor.

Kimmi sprawled onto the concrete, but unlike her father, who'd conveniently fallen on his sword, Kimmi lost her grip on the knife from the force of impact. It slid across the concrete, spinning to a stop at Dee's feet.

"Dee!" Nyles cried. "Look out!"

Kimmi leaped back up and charged. Dee had no time to think. She reached for the knife, her fingers closing around the handle just as Kimmi was upon her. Dee wanted to stop Kimmi, restrain her so she could be tried and punished for her crimes, but she never got the chance.

Kimmi lunged just as Dee angled the knife toward her.

They hung there, Kimmi's hands around Dee's throat, their bodies pressed together as if in an embrace, faces inches apart. Dee still held the handle of the twelve-inch-long knife, her hand pressed up against Kimmi's abdomen. The blade had impaled her.

Kimmi's features tensed up, her eyes wild with pain and rage. Then it all drained away. Her mouth relaxed, her eyes found Dee's, and she smiled.

"We would," she began, struggling with each word, "have been good. As sisters."

But Dee felt no compassion toward her tormentor. Kimmi didn't deserve any.

"No," she said. She let go of the knife and stepped back. Kimmi dropped to her knees. "No, we wouldn't."

A wave of terror passed over Kimmi's face, her arm outstretched toward Dee. Then she toppled forward, thrusting the blade farther into her body.

7m

Bradley Fornow @ForeverForFourYears
This just in: @spkerofthehouse has called an emergency session of Congress. Do we hear "impeachment," anyone?
← | : 87,381 ₪: 71,226

7m

Naydeen Doyle @NAYDEEEEEEEEEEEN
Holy shit. #LockThemUp

8m

> CNN **@BreakingNews**
> Multiple sources report that the FBI has swarmed DOJ offices in the wake of the Alcatraz 2.0 scandal. CNN has obtained leaked e-mails from DOJ staff members showing that the attorney general knew about the sham trials.

← | : 13,559 ₪: 7,671

7m

321_Podcast @321_podcast_live
The floodgates are open. Everyone at the White House and the DOJ will be desperately trying to save their own skin. I expect the smoking gun leading directly to POTUS's involvement to appear in 3 . . . 2 . . . 1 . . . #LockThemUp
← | : 2,245 ₪: 830

7m

Benny Nda Jetts @EltonJohnForevzz
I no joke live down the street from the VP's residence at Observatory Circle and about a million black cars just raced up the drive and there's a military helicopter circling overhead.
← | : 4,254 ₪: 3,918

⏲ 6m

BozzieJ @RedSnow1RedSnow2

Where's the Trazbet line on that? #LockThemUp

> ⏲ 7m
>
> **321_Podcast** @321_podcast_live
>
> The floodgates are open. Everyone at the White House and the DOJ will be desperately trying to save their own skin. I expect the smoking gun leading directly to POTUS's involvement to appear in 3 . . . 2 . . . 1 . . . #LockThemUp

← | : 2,403 ₪: 857

⏲ 6m

Mr. Hef @ImHefLadiesLoveMe

Who else will be complicit in this horror show? POTUS, Attorney Gen, obvs. How about the VP? House Speaker? Senate Majority Leader? They all let this happen to us and should all be held accountable. #VoteThemOut #LockThemUp

← | : 7,540 ₪: 4,007

⏲ 5m

The Griff @awakewideopen

Hearing that ACLU is filing suits against multiple members of the current administration as well as members of Congress, citing negligence under the Federal Tort Claims Act. #EyesOpen #VoteThemOut #LockThemUp

← | : 11,312 ₪: 7,977

FORTY-NINE

THE CRISP NIGHT AIR REVIVED DEE. SHE'D BEEN DOZING A little, nodding in and out of consciousness as she rode piggyback on Griselda down Ninth Street.

"The authorities will be here soon," Nyles said, shuffling along beside her. He held his dislocated arm close to his body and lurched slightly as he walked. "And they'll get you fixed up."

Dee's leg and wrist throbbed, blood pounding through them with each beat of her heart, but all she thought about was Nyles. "What about your arm?"

"Easy," he replied cheerfully. "They'll just pop it back in and I'll be good as new."

"In other words," Griselda said, "they'll have to amputate."

Dee snorted. It was good to know that she was the same old Griselda.

It took them forever to reach the western end of the island, but Griselda finally deposited Dee on the rocks by the water as Nyles eased himself down beside her. From there they could monitor the helipad at the guard station as well as the pier. Whichever way help was arriving, they'd see it.

Griselda flipped open Kimmi's laptop. "The FBI has issued arrest warrants for the attorney general—that douche—and The Postman. Guess they want to make sure he's actually dead. And it looks like Congress is going to start impeachment proceedings against the president."

"Good riddance," Nyles said. "Bloody lot of criminals, all of them."

"Yeah, but our government will be in shambles," Griselda said. "Who knows what mess comes next?"

Nyles draped his good arm around Dee's shoulders. "Then we'll all just have to move back to the UK."

Dee was hardly listening. She gazed out across the water at the twinkling lights of San Francisco, their reflection rippling in the calm waters of the predawn bay. "They'll come for us, right? They won't just leave us here?"

Nyles smiled. "Do you really think your father would forget about you?"

"Good point."

"Well, if the authorities forget about us," Griselda added, still combing through the feeds, "the Postmantics sure as hell won't. Half of them want to make out with us, the other half are threatening our lives."

"So life after Alcatraz two-point-oh might be a bit like life on Alcatraz two-point-oh," Nyles mused. "Now I'm *definitely* going back to the UK."

"Really?" Dee said quickly, realizing in that moment how disappointed she'd be if he did.

Nyles's eyes found hers. "No. No, I don't think I could go back now."

Griselda groaned. "You two are going to make me barf."

Nyles put his hand on Griselda's arm. "The first thing we're going to do is get Ethan out of that guard station. He deserves a hero's memorial."

"Yeah," Griselda said, turning to face the station. Dee saw the glint of tears in her eyes. "He does."

"And you," Nyles said, smiling at Dee. "You're about to be the most famous girl in the world."

Dee laughed drily. "You told me that in the maze," she said. "After I killed Slycer."

"I did?"

"You're repeating yourself, Romeo," Griselda said.

"Ah, well, this time it's real. You just upended the entire American penal system." His eyes flitted away from Dee's face. "Everyone will want to talk to you, interview you. You, eh, probably won't have time for anything else."

Dee didn't want to be famous. She didn't want to be interviewed or celebrated or even congratulated. She wanted to put Kimmi and The Postman and everything that had happened on Alcatraz 2.0 behind her.

All but one thing.

"I'll have time for you," she said, placing her hand on top of Nyles's.

"Yeah?"

She smiled. "Always."

He leaned forward to kiss her. Slowly this time, not the panicked rush to keep her from saying something he didn't want the cameras to pick up. And Dee angled her head to meet him.

But the instant Nyles's lips met hers, a movement from behind caught Dee's eyes as one of the crow cameras mounted on a streetlamp slowly turned to face them.

THE END?

ACKNOWLEDGMENTS

IT TAKES A VILLAGE TO PRODUCE A BOOK. HERE IS WHERE I get to thank mine.

To Kieran Viola and Eric Geron, éditeurs extraordinaires, whose invaluable vision and guidance shaped this novel in countless ways. I am eternally grateful for your faith and trust.

To Ginger Clark, my partner in literary crime over these many years. So much of this book is due to your vision for my career, your unwavering belief in my writing, and your business savvy.

To the amazing team at Freeform Books, including Emily Meehan, Mary Mudd, Guy Cunningham, Marci Senders, Sara Liebling, Cassie McGinty, and Holly Nagel. I'm in awe of your talents and dedication, and thankful that I get to work with you.

To the rest of my Curtis Brown family, who have toiled so tirelessly on my behalf for going on eight books: Holly Frederick, Madeline Tavis, Tess Callero, Jonathan Lyons, and Sarah Perillo. You're the only people that could make this Irishwoman wear orange with pride.

To the Wolfpack, the world's best-looking critique group, for forcing me to work harder, shoot higher, and cook . . . more often: Julia Shahin Collard, B. T. Gottfred, Nadine Nettmann, James Raney, and Jennifer Wolfe.

And lastly, but never leastly, to my husband, John Griffin. You literally make everything better, from my writing to my editing to my life. I am truly the luckiest of women.

Turn the page for a peek inside the next installment in the thrilling #MURDERTRENDING series!

645,982 likes

tristan_mckee Hey, The Postman fans—are you missing your number one app? Does your day feel incomplete without updates from your favorite Painiac? If so, then this is your lucky day!

Merchant-Bronson Productions and FundMyFun.com announce the newest television sensation: Who Wants to Be a Painiac?, a game show version of The Postman set to air on the Reality Network. Go to www.FundMyFun.com/whowantstobeapainiac to show your Postmanticity!!!! If we raise $250,000 by December 15, open call auditions will take place on the 17th, 9 a.m., at Stu-Stu-Studio in Burbank, California. MAKE YOUR DREAMS COME TRUE! Donate now! #Painiacs #WhoWantsToBeAPainiac #Auditions #RealityTV #MerchantBronson #RealityNetwork #ThePostman #Postmantics

1 HOUR AGO

RECENT ACTIVITY

capedcapuchinghost *immediately checks flights to LA* SO THERE! Excited AF!!!!!!
#ThePostmanForever

wolfgang_collins Is this a Postman Enterprises, Inc. affiliated show? Cuz I thought the FBI shut the whole company down. #izConfused

ellen_enchanted2 Hold up. Good taste aside, how is this legal?

mcdonnelson @ellen_enchanted2 Who cares! The Painiacs are coming back! I've been in withdrawal.

phoebe_temptressta Putting together my costume as I type. With one hand. #SoundsDirtyButIsnt

ihate_snailmail @ellen_enchanted2 I'm reporting this to the authorities ASAP and I suggest you do the same. With the manhunt for The Postman under way and PEI under federal indictment, there is absolutely no way this should be allowed to happen. ESPECIALLY considering the actions of these morally corrupt Postman "fans" in recent weeks trying to hunt down #CinderellaSuvivor...

eltonjohn4evzz @ihate_snailmail Oh, like the Postmantics are the only ones to blame? You anti-Postman activists are just as bad. Those witch hunts for the former Painiacs' families? Not exactly legal, asshole.

splendour420 #FundMyFun just hit $35,000 in less than an hour. #PostmanticPower

judy_kline @ihate_snailmail A certain SECRET message board is already organizing a protest at Stu-Stu-Studio for December 17. Message me if you want an invitation to join the group.

snowqueenwinter Painiac auditions? This is my dream!!!! I need a costume, right? We should all come in costume? Like with a persona and everything? Right, of course we should. HAHAHAHAHA. I'm such a spaz. Just so juiced!

wicked_josh Do you think my Gucci Hangman cosplay would be okay to audition in? Or should I do something original?

skullcrusherchic @judy_kline Oh yeah? Well there's another SECRET message board (you're not the only ones, dickhead) and we'll be at auditions to protect the auditioners. Postmantics? Feel free to DM me to get an invite. Freedom of speech, bitches.

eureka_sammy150 @judy_kline Messaged you

squirrelwoman @skullcrusherchic ME ME ME

pqe_bachmann @skullcrusherchic DM sent

ihate_snailmail @skullcrusherchic You're disgusting. Reported you to Instagram for violation of its policies.
#FreedomOfSpeechBitches

maiv_moms @judy_kline DM'd you

jiwoo_s @wicked_josh Def something original.

thegriff If ever there was evidence that The Postman was a multi-conglomerate conspiracy aimed at controlling the masses through coordinated entertainment ventures, THIS WOULD BE IT!
#DontTrustTheFeed #WideAwakeEyesOpen #FakeNews #ThePostmanAlive

skullcrusherchic @ihate_snailmail Yeah, and we're coming for you next.
#WitchHunt #FedxersMustDie

darkness_falls @judy_kline There's a special place in Hell reserved for harassing supposed Painiac family members. I heard you people are showing up at funerals across the country, accusing every old lady in a closed coffin of being D.I.Ynona. With no proof, no evidence. Do you realize how fucked up that is?

fedx_delivery @skullcrusherchic Not if we get you first...

ADD A COMMENT

BELTWAY BULLETIN

POLITICS - US Edition

November 23rd, 08:32 am ET

The Battle for the Presidency

by Adrienne Quiñones

In case you've been living in a cave for the last two weeks, let me get you up to speed.

It has been thirteen days since the House of Representatives passed H.Res.1334, adopting six articles of impeachment against the president of the United States on grounds of high crimes and misdemeanors, as well as the highly controversial charge of treason, in accordance with Article II of the United States Constitution.

Despite the urging of his closest advisers, the president has not resigned from office a la Richard Nixon to avoid trial and probable conviction by a two-thirds Senate vote, which could, in the estimation of several hundred legal pundits, lead to criminal charges. Instead, sequestering himself inside the West Wing like a child who refuses to accept punishment, the president stubbornly clings to what little power he retains.

While there is little doubt that the current presidency won't survive the impeachment trial, several key facts in the Alcatraz 2.0 investigation remain nebulous. Authorities still have not released the identity of The Postman, Alcatraz 2.0's mastermind, ringleader, and presiding warden, fueling speculation that no one—not even the NSA—knows who he really is. Or was. Because no one can confirm whether The Postman is actually dead or alive.

Internet theories on The Postman's identity are as vast and numerous as the stars in the cosmos. Every media billionaire who hasn't been seen in the last two weeks has been tapped as the potential mass murderer. As of yet, no credible evidence has been produced in favor of any one individual.

Who might know The Postman's real name? The president, for sure, but he's probably not spilling the beans any time soon. The former attorney general refuses to name names until his demand for immunity has been accepted, but most insiders think the ex-AG is bluffing. But the House managers who will be prosecuting the impeachment trial seem pretty confident in their case, as evidenced by the inclusion of the treason charge. Could it be they have a couple of surprise witnesses up their congressional sleeves?

And then there's Dee Guerrera, along with fellow "Death Row Breakfast Club" survivors, Nyles Harding and Griselda Sinclair. Could the Alcatraz 2.0 whistle-blowers know the identity of The Postman? The trio *did* have access to sensitive information during their final hours on the prison island, but far from being forthcoming with the media, the Alcatraz 2.0 survivors have gone into hiding as legions of The Postman's rabid fans, self-dubbed the "Postmantics," attempt to hunt them down.

To complicate matters, another group of anti-Postman activists are gaining in number, and while the Postmantics' goal is to make the Death Row Breakfast Club pay for their supposed crimes, the Fed-Xers (get it?) are stalking funerals across the country, searching for the real identities of the deceased Painiacs.

One thing is sure: between the impeachment, the Postmantics, and the Fed-Xers, the American people are going to learn more about Alcatraz 2.0 than they ever wanted to know.

Set your DVRs and stock up on salty snacks. This doozy of an impeachment trial is set to begin December 17.

Please send feedback to the author at aquinones@beltbull.com or on Twitter at @aquinonesBB.

ONE

BECCA WINCED, SQUINTING AGAINST THE BRIGHT FLASH of midmorning sunlight as it reflected off the impossibly shiny surface of her mom's coffin.

There should be some kind of law against sunny days and funerals.

Ten feet away, Reverend Hamlin's understated monotone droned on and on about God and servants and souls, and though Becca should have been grieving or mourning or at the very least recalling all the cherished memories of her dead mom as the polished brown casket was lowered into the ground, all she could think about was how stupid it was.

Why bother polishing the casket? That thing was literally getting buried in the ground where no one would ever see it. And the plush interior? Did the bloody, mangled remains of her mom's body give even half a shit that they'd splurged for the tufted velour lining over the base-model crepe?

"Earth to earth," Reverend Hamlin recited. "Ashes to ashes, dust to dust."

To her left, Becca's younger brother, Rafa, sniffled and swallowed while he gazed woefully at the giant hole in the ground, attempting to conceal his sorrow behind a mask of self-imposed manliness, which was probably what he thought dudes were supposed to do at their mom's funeral, even though he was only ten. Becca reached down and grabbed his hand, giving it a squeeze. She wished she could shield him from this misery.

Behind them, Becca could feel Rita's convulsive yet silent sobs as she watched her partner of almost twenty years laid to rest, her hand gripping Ruth's sapphire-and-white-gold wedding ring, which now hung around Rita's neck on a chain.

Her mom and brother were mourning. Because that's what normal people did at funerals. They cried.

Meanwhile Becca was trying not to stare at Reverend Hamlin's nose hairs as they fluttered in and out of his nostrils with every breath.

What the hell was wrong with her?

It wasn't that Becca didn't love her mom or miss her mom or desperately wish the car crash that took her mom's life hadn't happened. She had no idea why she was unable to cry, which only added to her guilt. Because Becca had looked forward to her mom's semi-regular trips to Arizona, which meant three days indulging in the things Ruth didn't approve of, namely plaid miniskirts and ripped tees, nacho cheese sauce eaten straight from the jar, and uninterrupted access to The Postman app. Her mom's number one pet peeve.

Can.

Not.

Hang.

Ruth loved to lecture Becca on the dangers of violence and young minds and yada yada yada. Becca would smile and pretend to listen . . . and keep watching. In secret.

Which is exactly what she'd been doing—alone in her bedroom, obsessing over the fallout of the Alcatraz 2.0 shutdown—when the phone had rung with the news of her mom's accident.

Guilt burrito, anyone?

"When our earthly journey is ended . . ." Reverend Hamlin's nose hairs quivered dramatically as he brought home the final prayer. "Lead us rejoicing into your kingdom, where you live and reign forever and ever. Amen."

Amen, Becca mouthed.

The mourners began to disperse, voices low and mumbling as they offered final condolences to Rita, then picked their way around the granite slabs that marked the uniform rows of graves. Becca's best friends Jackie and Mateo, arms wrapped around each other for comfort, flashed Becca a tight smile before disappearing hand in hand down the hillside. Becca recognized other faces in the crowd—people from church, people from her school, parents who had known Ruth from the PTA. It looked as if most of Marquette, Michigan, had turned out for the funeral.

"Your mom loved you both very much," Rita said, her voice steady.

Rafa heaved. "I miss her."

"I miss her too," Rita said, pulling Rafa to her side and squeezing his shoulders tightly. "But she'll always be with us. I promise."

Becca reached out and tousled Rafa's wavy black hair. She may have been crappy at this mourning thing, but she was good at being a big sister. And Rafa needed her right now.

Rita smiled as she watched her children. Her warm brown eyes, though red-rimmed from crying, lit up her face. Her dark skin was luminous, her curly hair bounced around her ears, and Becca was struck by how beautiful her mom was, even in the face of tragedy.

"You look so much like her," Rita said, eyes fixed on Becca's face.

Becca fought the urge to cringe. Secretly, Becca had always wished she'd gotten Rita's genes like Rafa, instead of the pasty white skin and plethora of freckles she'd inherited from Ruth. No such luck.

"Believe it or not," Rita continued, reading Becca's mind, "you're more like her than you realize."

Don't call your mom crazy. Don't call your mom crazy. "Really?"

Rita nodded. Her eyes drifted to the open grave, glassy and unseeing, and when she spoke again, her voice sounded far away. "There was more to Ruth Martinello than you knew."

Becca wasn't about to contradict her mom five minutes after she'd buried her wife—even her penchant for deflective sarcasm had its limit—but she couldn't bring herself to agree. *There was more to Ruth Martinello than you knew.* For reals? If there was one person on this planet who was exactly what you'd expect her to be, it was Ruth Martinello. From her warm, ever-present smile to her sensible L.L.Bean cropped chinos and buttoned-up pastel cardigans, Ruth was the epitome of the friendly, supportive stay-at-home mom. She was the kind of person who helped everyone—neighbors, strangers, even her high school best friend in Arizona, who was dealing with chemo treatments for breast cancer. Ruth was always the first one to reach out with selfless altruism, which made Becca embarrassed of her own snarky edge and self-serving attitude.

While Becca was pondering Rita's comment, she caught movement out of the corner of her eye Just a quick flash, like sunlight glinting off the side of a coffin. She turned as her mom lead Rafa to the car, and saw a figure standing near a sprawling oak tree about fifty yards from the grave site.

It was a girl, Becca could tell by the outline of her body against the bright blue sky, even though she was wearing pants and a boxy black jacket. Her dark hair was cut into an asymmetrical bob—the left side shorter than the right, which hung loosely in front of her face, and she was holding a video camera in her hand.

Why was this pervy chick filming at a cemetery? Who gave her permission to document Ruth's funeral? And who still used a video camera? What was this, 2009?

Before she could even speculate as to the answers to these questions, the girl slipped behind the tree and hurried off down the hill.

"What the hell?" Becca said out loud. She took a few steps toward the rapidly departing girl and shouted, "Hey! Stop! What are you doing?"

"Becca?" Rita called from the car. "Come on. We need to get home. People will be arriving for the reception."

Becca paused. She desperately wanted to sprint across the lawn toward the weird chick with the lopsided hair and demand to know why she'd been filming Ruth's funeral, but as she stood indecisively, a car rounded the cemetery drive. Becca saw the long side of the girl's hair flick toward her as she turned her head from the driver's seat. Their eyes met for a split second; then the girl made a hard left at a fork in the path and disappeared down the hill.

TWO

GOING BACK TO SCHOOL AFTER YOUR MOM DIED WAS THE fucking worst.

"Hey, Becca. Sorry for your loss."

"Becca, I am *so* sorry about your mom."

"It's Becca, right? Hey, tough break."

Can.

Not.

Hang.

Becca hardly knew these people, didn't believe the sincerity of their comments for half a freaking second, and it took literally every ounce of self-control not to answer with "Fuck off!" each time. Like the true asshole she was.

The only things that would get her through this day from Hell were her friends.

"Hey," Jackie said the moment she saw Becca in the hall. Her bright smile contradicted the concern in her eyes. "How are you?"

Becca shrugged. "Fine, I guess."

Mateo, always by his girlfriend's side, folded his arms across his chest. "You guess?"

"That's less 'typical teenage avoidance strategy' and more 'I honestly don't know,'" Becca replied. "Emotions are hard." She appreciated that her friends were worried about her, but they should know her well enough by now to realize that a main course of genuine emotion with a heaping side of sincerity was not on the Becca menu.

Jackie's smile relaxed. "Hard for *you.*"

Becca rolled her eyes as she dialed in her locker combination. Jackie had been studying psych books ever since her parents' divorce and loved nothing more than "helping" her friends with nonprofessional diagnoses. "Yeah, yeah. I'm stunted. We know."

Mateo gave his girlfriend a look that said *Maybe not right now, Jackie?* "You don't have to talk about any of it. We're just here to support you."

"Of course." Jackie nodded in agreement. "You know we love you."

Becca was grateful for her friends. Grateful that they'd offered to come over the second she'd told them about her mom's accident, even though it was the night Jackie's mom worked the late shift at the hospital, which meant she and Mateo had most definitely been in some stage of sexy times when Becca had texted. She was grateful that they'd both been at the funeral, and she was grateful that they hadn't made her talk about any of it. Until now.

"Okay, Dr. Phil," Becca said with a sly grin. She needed to nip all this sincerity in the bud. "I'll let you know if I feel anything less than one hundred percent supported. Or maybe ninety percent? I think I could probably handle only feeling ninety percent supported by you guys. But if we drop to eighty-five, I'm fucking out of here."

Jackie shook her head, her long blond ponytail swinging across her back like a pendulum. “Smart-ass.”

“Always.” Becca clicked her locker door closed. “Come on, tell me something fun on the way to Bio.”

Jackie slipped her hand into Mateo’s as they threaded a path through the horde of students. “Apparently, Kasie McInerney’s boyfriend brought a new girlfriend home with him from college for Thanksgiving break.”

“Ouch.”

“Yeah,” Jackie said. “He never even broke up with Kasie. They were together three years and he’s only been down in Madison for three months.”

Becca tried not to glance at her friends. Would their relationship survive the trip to college next fall? Becca doubted it. And then what, would she be forced to choose between them a year from now when Jackie brought a new boyfriend home from college? *This is why I don’t date.*

But Jackie clearly didn’t see the potential parallel as she barreled on with the post-Thanksgiving-break gossip. “And Darlene Ahlberg has been telling anyone who’ll listen she’s visiting her aunt in LA for winter break again.”

Becca arched an eyebrow. “What agent supposedly wants to sign her this time?”

“Worse than that,” Jackie said. “She wants to audition for that new game show. *Who Wants to Be a Painiac?*”

“Becca!” some rando sophomore boy in an oversize flannel shouted as he passed her in the hall. “I feel you, girl!”

“I could have you arrested for that,” Becca called out in response, then turned back to her friends. “What’s this about Painiacs?” she said, feigning ignorance.

"I forgot you've been unplugged," Mateo said. "Some production company is crowdsourcing a game show based on the Painiacs from Alcatraz two-point-oh."

"Oooh," Becca said. Only she didn't need Mateo to explain *Who Wants to Be a Painiac?* to her. She knew exactly what it was. The members of her Postmantics Facebook group had been discussing it nonstop since the Instagram post went live Saturday morning.

The day of your mom's funeral.

She really didn't want to explain to her friends that she'd been obsessing over her Facebook group feed instead of processing her grief, so it was easier to just pretend she had no idea what they were talking about. "Interesting."

"Disguting is more like it," Jackie said, sounding as if she was about to vomit. "I can't believe someone thinks that's a good idea."

"Thankfully, we'll be up the mountain over winter break when it airs," Mateo said, then smiled expectantly at Becca. "You're still coming with us, right?"

Becca hesitated. A couple of weeks ago, she'd jumped at the chance to spend a week with Jackie, Mateo, and his family at their cabin near the ski resort at Keyes Peak, but now she wasn't sure if she should leave her mom and Rafa alone so close to Christmas.

"It'll be good for you," Jackie said, sensing her uncertainty. "You need to do something fun. What's the point of having two weeks off from school if all you do is stay home?"

"I don't know," Becca said. "Sleeping for two straight weeks seems kinda exciting right now."

"You're coming," Jackie said. "That's final."

"Fine," Becca said with a grin as she ducked into the Bio lab. "But I won't like it."

The rest of the day was a blur. Bio to Calculus. English to Humanities. Government to Art History to study hall. Becca was on autopilot for most of it, moving from classroom to cafeteria to hallway like she'd done for days and months and years. For the most part, everything was the same: the same people, the same lessons, the same hallway chatter, though the daily conversations had shifted from The Postman's most recent kills to the latest police reports about vigilantes hunting down the Painiacs' families or reports on the whereabouts of the Death Row Breakfast Club. Still, the same fevered pitch of pop culture enthusiasm infected the halls of Marquette Senior High School, and yet somehow, today felt different.

It wasn't just the stream of "Sorry, Becca" or her friends' attempts to keep their conversations buoyant and substance-free that was weird. An out-of-body sensation haunted her. For a few moments, here and there, Becca almost forgot that her mom had died. She'd be laughing at one of Mateo's jokes or internal-monologue-ing about how boring Mr. Cartwright's lectures were, and in that instant, her life was exactly the same as it had been two weeks ago. It was as if she was floating above the tragedy that was her life, gazing down upon it with an objective eye. Then a memory would come flooding back, punching Becca in the gut and momentarily knocking the breath from her. She'd be graveside again, her mom and brother weeping, while Becca did nothing.

By the time the final bell rang, Becca had a throbbing headache. All she wanted to do was go home and collapse into bed.

Usually—which meant every single day—she went to Jackie's after school, but today Becca couldn't handle two hours of good-natured gossip and animal memes on YouTube. She dashed off a quick text of explanation to her best friend, then headed for the parking lot.

Becca stomped across the asphalt toward Rita's old Ford Explorer, a beat-up hulk of non-ecologically-friendly SUV, and practically ripped the door off the hinges as she opened it, angry that school hadn't offered her a complete escape from reality. She tossed her backpack across to the passenger's seat, then climbed behind the wheel. But she didn't start the car. She just sat there, panting, waiting for the tears to stream down her face.

They never came.

What the hell was wrong with her? Why couldn't she cry?

The lot began to empty out. The furor of post-school chaos crescendoed, then dissipated, leaving Becca alone in her car. But as stillness settled around her, Becca became keenly aware of someone standing in the trees, watching her.

There was a sharp sound, a foot snapping a dried twig in half that Becca could barely hear through the cracked car window, but it was enough for Becca to look up into the trees. Standing much as she had at the cemetery, half-obscured by the thin trunk of a white pine, was the girl with the camera.